WE NEVER STOOD ALONE

BOB DEGRAY

WW2 Christian Fiction
ww2christianfiction.com

Published by:
WW2 Christian Fiction
15922 Camp Fire Road
Friendswood, TX 77546 USA

ISBN-13: 978-0-9965938-2-3

Dedication

And I will walk among you and will be your God,
and you shall be my people.
Leviticus 26:12 (ESV)

We Never Stood Alone is dedicated to the families of Trinity Fellowship in Friendswood, Texas. These are not their stories, but without their stories I could not have told this one.

Acknowledgements

This is a work of historical fiction. The main characters are all fictional and any resemblance to actual people living or dead is purely coincidental. However the main historical stories, from the details of daily life to the great events of 1939 and 1940 are as true to fact as I could make them. In addition, the setting, as can be readily deduced, is a fictionalized version of the towns of Goring and Streatley on the Thames River, and the church is a very fictionalized version of the Goring Free Church. I'm grateful to Nigel Gordon-Potts, the minister of Goring Free for the information and tour he gave me in 2014. Differences between Goring/Streatley and Stokely are mostly intentional, and all for the sake of the fiction.

I'd like to acknowledge the essential contribution that the authors of so many books, articles and websites made to the accuracy of this fiction. Thanks especially to the BBC, whose online World War 2 resources seem endless, and to the Imperial War Museum, which has an image for almost every rabbit trail of curiosity. I'd like to thank the British Library for granting me research access (because that is way cool), but I do wish they would make it easier to copy material. I'd also like to thank the Goring Library for their help and willingness to let me photograph their unique resources.

I'm thankful too for the people in London, Oxfordshire, and Berkshire who spent hours telling my wife and me of their experiences during the war and after.

I'm also grateful for my editor, Catherine A. Fitzsimmons of Coventry, U.K., who helped immensely both with the 'Britishism' of my American speech patterns and the detection of anachronisms, not to mention grammar and wording. My friend Sherry Early also did an awesome final read. Any errors that remain in the manuscript are mine. Kristine Cottermann of Exodus Design did a great job of turning my mental images and penciled drawings into compelling graphics.

On a more personal level, I'm grateful to the people of Trinity Fellowship, the church which has allowed me to be their pastor for 23 years. Their lives have shown me what it looks like for Jesus to be real even in difficult circumstances.

I want to thank my family for their support of my writing, which is yet another reason why Daddy sits in the chair with the computer. I'm grateful for your kindness and understanding.

Gail, I can't thank you enough for all that you have meant to me and done for me over the past 36 years. You are God's gift to me and your love and support have made possible any good work I have done. Thanks too for reading the manuscript early and often.

Jesus, thank you for your constant presence, forgiveness, and love. Thank you for your Word which so perfectly reveals to me what I so imperfectly follow.

Soli Deo Gloria

Contents

The People of Stokely

Here, roughly in order of appearance and with as few spoilers as possible, are the key families and individuals in *We Never Stood Alone*. A more detailed listing, including minor characters can be found on ww2christianfiction.com

Reverend Lloyd and Annie Robins – Lloyd has been the minister at Stokely Free since 1931. He became a believer during World War 1 through the witness of a Canadian Lieutenant named Pete Miller. Lloyd later went to Canada to attend Toronto Bible College, and returned to begin ministry first in Birmingham and then in Stokely. Annie grew up near Bristol and met Lloyd at Swindon Chapel. They have three children, Lizzie (11), Georgie (5), and Maggie (2). Norah Applewaithe, a divorcee, helps Annie with the cooking and housework at the manse.

Bert and Meg Butler – Bert was paralyzed from the waist down in an accident at the Miles Aircraft factory. Meg is helping make ends meet by bringing in laundry. They have three children of their own (Freddy, Harry and little Emma).

Meg and Bert are also caring for Meg's niece and nephew (Nellie and Billy) who came out as evacuees. Meg's brother, Tom Timms died of consumption and their mum, Muriel was having trouble juggling the care of the children, care for her parents, Mildred and Alf Cotton and her job at a London department store.

Ned and Alice Powell – Ned was Lloyd's platoon sergeant during the Great War. His family has farmed just outside Stokely for generations. He and Alice are childless, so he has always had to hire hands to work at the farm. He also relies on his old Fordson tractor and his two Shire horses, Buster and Bluster. Ned's nephew and his wife,

Charlie and Dot Simmonds also live in Stokely. Their son is named after his uncle.

Arthur and Rosey Cripps – Arthur is a former Royal Navy captain who is now the lockkeeper at the Stokely lock (on the Thames River). His wife Rosey is not in the greatest of health, but is still an avid student of Biblical prophecy. They have taken in their nephew, Stanley Payne whose father disappeared after evacuating 14 year old Stanley to his sister in Stokely.

Eleanor Blount – Lady of Blount Manor. Her late husband, Cyril, was descended through many generations of Lords and Ladies at the Manor and at one time own all the land north of Stokely (on the Oxfordshire side). Lady Blount has tried hard to preserve the estate in difficult times.

Rachel Busby – Rachel is also a widow. She has lived in Stokely since the first war. Rachel's husband, a doctor, and her three children all died in the Spanish Flu of 1919. Her mum, Virginia Townend, lived with her in Rosewood cottage, near Blount Manor until her death in 1934.

Percy Wilkins – Percy was the groom at Blount Manor until Lady Blount had to sell off all the livestock. Now he lives in a little shack down by the river. He tells awful jokes.

Alan and Susan Ward – Alan is a senior clerk for the Great Western Railroad and the Junior Warden of Stokely Free Church. He was unable to serve in the Great War, but he named his sons Nelson and Wellington.

James Grierson – James is the principal of the Royal Veterinary College (London) and has come to Stokely to look for an estate where the College might be housed if war breaks out. He and Lloyd Robins have a mutual friend, Pete Miller.

Harold Mills – Harold is a broker's agent in Stokely and a new member of Stokely Free

Henry Padbury – Henry is a math professor at the University of Reading. He is Cambridge educated and was offered positions at both Oxford and Cambridge, but chose to teach closer to his home (and his church) in Stokely, where he cared for his parents, who have now both passed on. Mrs. Waverly is Henry's cook and housekeeper.

Phillip and Marjorie Clarke – Philip is the only solicitor (lawyer) in Stokely. He and his wife have four children. Lenny, the oldest, is an Oxford grad and is working in London. Holly is married to Robert Allen and lives in Coventry with their two little ones, Ivy and Rose. Edwin has just joined the Royal Air Force as a radio operator. The youngest, Violet, is still a teen-ager at home.

Ernest and Evelyn Cooper – Ernest work for the General Post Office in telephone systems. He and Evelyn have two daughters, Phyllis (16) and Lily (11).

Map of Stokely

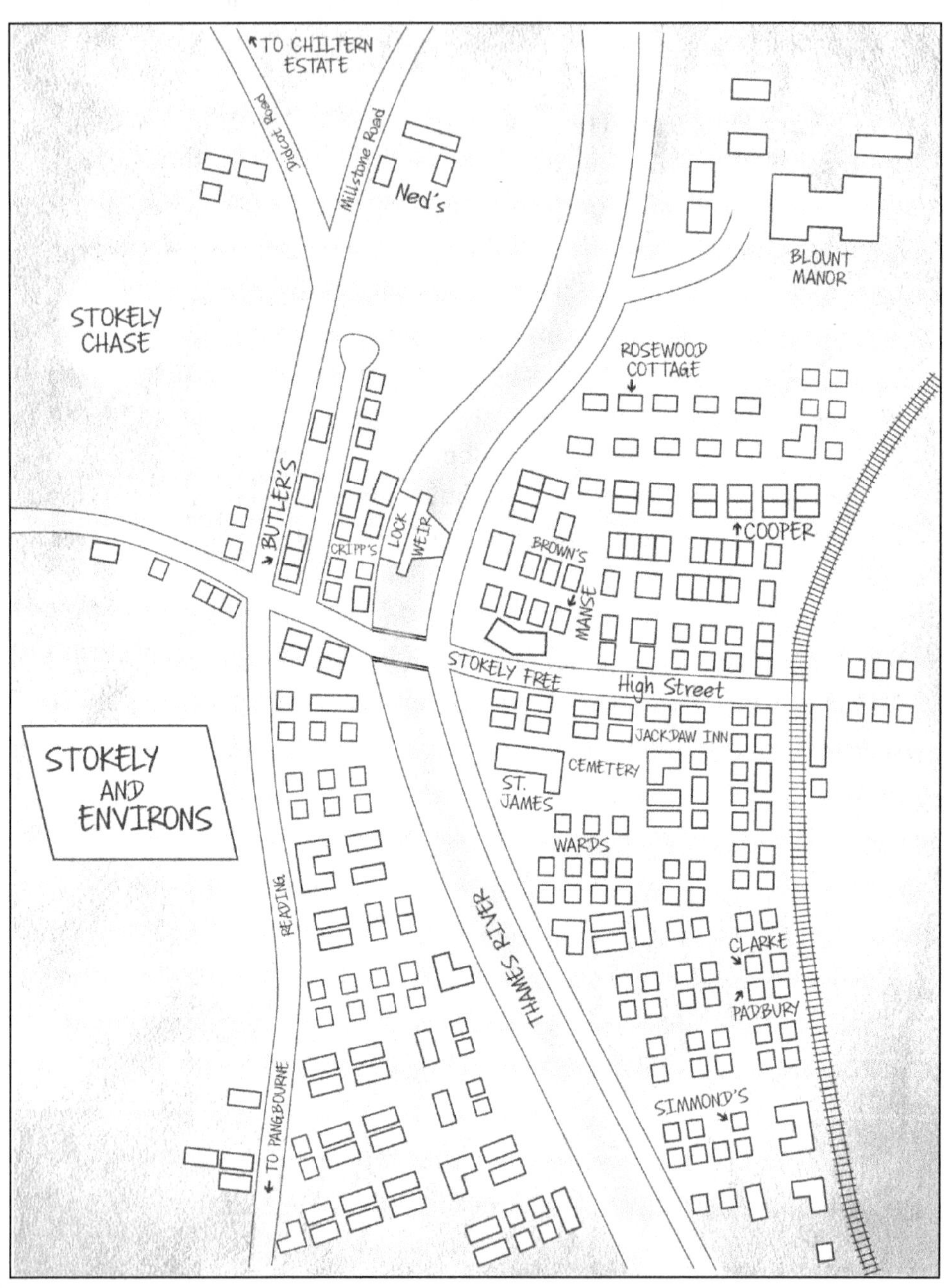

CHAPTER 1

25 July 1939

Lloyd hesitated as he approached the door. Inside he could hear Bert's voice raised above a high-pitched babble. Shifting the sack of tinned goods to his left hand, he knocked. The noise level dropped and footsteps clipped across the floor.

Meg opened the door a few inches and poked her head out. Her red hair hung limply to her shoulders and compressed lips had replaced her usual bright smile. "Good morning, Rev'rend Robins. It's bad just now. You might want to come later."

"Is there something I can help with?"

"I don't think so, Rev'rend." She sighed. "But come take a look." Lloyd followed her into the crowded sitting room. And chaos. The armchairs were filled with dirty laundry. A bookshelf leaned across the table and the books were spilled onto the floor.

But the dominant feature of the room was the children. Nellie, Meg's dark-haired niece, was sprawled on the floor, evidently cutting up old newspapers and cleverly making them into paper swans. Her brother Billy and Fred, Meg's oldest, were zooming around the room like airplanes, the swans in their hands engaged in a furious dogfight. Fred's little brother Harry had somehow clambered onto the side table and looked poised to jump to the chandelier.

"Fred, don't let your brother fall!" Meg spoke sharply. She was holding Emma, her youngest, on her hip. The three Butler children had all inherited their parents' red hair, while the Timms were dark-haired and dark-eyed.

Lloyd followed Meg across the room. "My, how she's grown! How old is she now?"

"A little over fourteen months." The baby squirmed and pin-wheeled her arms.

"It looks like she wants to join the party."

"It's always a party now that Tom's little ones are here, God rest his soul."

"How long do you think they will stay?"

"Can't tell. Muriel's still in pieces after my brother's death, she's caring for her parents, she's often sick herself, and she doesn't want to lose her job at Selfridges. Plus there is all this war talk. She feels better knowing they're safe here."

"Well, I'm praying you can make it work."

"We need all the prayers we can get, Rev'rend."

Meg led Lloyd into the kitchen. Bert was slumped in a hardback chair by the table, a belt around his waist holding him in the chair. His thin legs trailed on the floor. Several days' growth of red whiskers clouded his round face.

Walking toward him, Lloyd nearly slipped. His eyes tracked wetness across the floor to a pan. Above it, a fast drip was coming from a large dark spot in the ceiling, where a pipe came through.

"I hope you've brought your oar, Rev'rend Lloyd," Bert said. "If this keeps up you'll have to scull out of here."

"When did it start?"

"Started dripping Monday. Becoming a flood today. I think it's a joint but it's right up between the ceiling and the floor."

"Thank you for these," Meg said.

Lloyd had handed her the sack without thinking. He turned to see her putting tins on the shelf. "Looks like the cupboard's a little bare," he said.

Bert responded with a growl. "We haven't had bread in two days. The kids are hungry. I'm hungry. Meg's wasting away to nothing."

Meg broke in. "We had to pay the mortage this week, and it left us flat. Nellie and Billy's mum sends us a little bit each month, but it hasn't come yet."

Lloyd knew the church box had already been emptied for the week. He dug into his pocket and came up with but a single shilling and a few pennies, which he pressed into Meg's hand. "Here, get some bread, eat something."

Meg colored prettily and looked away. "Thank you, Rev'rend. We so need this … I hate to ask, but could you stay with Bert for a few minutes while I run up to Brown's for a loaf?"

"Of course," Lloyd said.

She went into the sitting room and Lloyd could hear her organizing the children for the short walk. He sat down next to Bert at the kitchen table, and they watched the leak. Even in the few minutes he'd been there, it seemed to have got worse. The soaked plaster of the ceiling was beginning to show ominous cracks. They speculated on who might be able to fix it.

"I could've done it myself, Rev'rend Lloyd, easy as pie, before the accident. I even kept my soldering kit for a while, hoping I'd get better. But I sold it all off two months ago to pay the mortgage." Bert leaned on his hands, rubbing his temples. "Don't know what I'm going to do now. Maybe I never should have bought this place. Above me, they said. And now . . . a man should be able to provide food for his family. And shelter. Seems like God has turned against us, and all my prayers just bounce off the ceiling."

At that moment a large piece of ceiling plaster disengaged, hung from one edge, and dropped between the table and the stove. Bert groaned. Lloyd adjusted the pan to the new center of the drip. "I'll clean up, Bert, but why don't we pray together first. Maybe the hole in the ceiling will allow our prayers to reach the Father's ears."

As Lloyd finished sweeping, Meg arrived home and cheerfully offered lunch. Lloyd's mouth watered at the warm smell of the bread, but when he looked at the little loaf and bit of jam, he decided they'd be better off if he excused himself.

Out in the wet air, he turned first one way, then the other.. His mind was too full and his stomach too empty to go back across the bridge to the church. His pockets were empty too, so he couldn't stop at the Jackdaw or the Calf for a quick bite. *Maybe I can kill two birds with one stone.*

He turned again and headed further up the road toward the Powells' farm. Though almost a mile out of town along the river, he thought it would be worth the walk to talk with Ned about the Butlers. And Alice, he thought, is the consummate farmer's wife. So the odds were good that she'd insist on feeding him.

Lloyd halloaed as he reached Ned's place. The farmhouse was one of three buildings around a square yard. Ned called back from the equipment shed, and Lloyd found him with his legs sticking out from under the old Fordson tractor. The sharp tang of electricity reached Lloyd's nostrils.

"I need to talk to you about the situation at the Butlers'."

"Talk away. I'm adjusting the magneto. If this thing shocks me one more time you can just bury me here and have my lunch."

Lloyd summarized the Butlers' financial straits.

"Hoo! That bad? Well, I commend them for trying to keep up the mortgage. I don't think either set of parents can help much."

"Agreed." Lloyd tended to fall into a military terseness with Ned, who had been his sergeant in the war. "But I don't see how they can keep going."

Ned made some lengthy obscure adjustment. Lloyd stared through the wide doors at the green and gold summer fields. The rain was back, but it didn't look cold from here. Finally, Ned's tall heavy frame unfolded itself from under the tractor, and he brushed himself off.

"I don't have an answer for you, Lloyd. But I guess we can start by getting the plumbing fixed."

He joined Lloyd in the doorway and cast a long calculating look at the men working in his fields. "I expect I could get to it this week, but you might ask Arthur Cripps. He's better at that stuff than I am, and can usually spare some time."

"Good thought."

Another pause. Lloyd had long since learned not to interrupt Ned's thinking. "Let's go up and see Alice. I know we've got a bit of fruit and stuff she preserved last autumn."

Before they reached the house, Alice came out, wiping her hands on her apron. She was only a few inches shorter than Ned, thin, with long dark hair braided down to the small of her back. She appraised Lloyd with a wry, friendly look. "Well, look who the wind blew in! I expect you're hungry, aren't you Lloyd; showing up at this hour?"

"Yes ma'am, I expect I am," Lloyd said with a grin.

"Well, fortunately for you, I made too much."

"She always makes too much," Ned said. "And too good."

"Wash your hands when you come in," Alice said.

She served them veal cutlets and boiled potatoes, and agreed with Ned that she could bring a few things down to Meg later that day.

As he approached the Thames, Lloyd scanned the lock and gate. He didn't spot Arthur. Squinting, he could see the sign that told boaters to operate the lock themselves, meaning the lockkeeper was away or busy. So Arthur might be in the house. But it was Rosie's booming voice that responded to his knock. "Oh bebother ye! Who's that coming around to interrupt a lady in the middle of her lunch?"

Lloyd heard heavy footsteps. The door swung open to reveal Rosie's red face, almost matching the large flowers on her shapeless dress.

She glared at Lloyd for a moment before her face softened. "Well, it's you Rev'rend Lloyd."

"Good to see you Rosie. How are you today?"

"Awful, if not worse. If you get the gout you'll see how it feels."

Lloyd was, as often with Rosie, at a loss for words. "I'm sorry … I was looking for Arthur. Is he home?"

"He's working on that boat of his, I think. Said something about a fuel line. Probably below deck."

"Well, I'll just go and look for him there. And I'll pray for your gout."

"One moment, Rev'rend," she said, "Come and look at this." She thumped back across the room to her chair, where her heavily marked up Bible lay open. She lifted it and pointed to a verse in the book of Revelation, chapter 17.

"It says here that the antichrist will gain allegiance from ten nations. Do you think I should count Czechoslovakia as one or two?"

"Excuse me?"

"Now, Rev'rend, I've been telling you for months I think Hitler is the antichrist. He's supposed to have ten nations, and he soon will. If I count Czechoslovakia as two …"

She dropped heavily into her chair, took up a piece of paper, and began to read the list "Germany, Austria …"

"I'll have to think about that, Rosie. Meanwhile I need to see Arthur. I'll just let myself out."

I wish she'd study Romans for a while, Lloyd thought. *Ah well. Father, please be with Rosie. Decrease her pain and give her insight into your Word.*

Arthur had just poked his bald head up from the hold of the *Guinevere*. His imperial mustache was a holdover from the previous century. Lloyd had been told that it was once flaming red. Now it was a dull white.

"Good day, Arthur! How are you?"

"Good day, Reverend. I'm fit, though I've no doubt this damp has had its effect on my Rosie."

"How's *Guinevere* coming along?"

"I finally got a lead on an engine. Six cylinder Sea Prince out of a wreck down south. Making a few modifications to accommodate it."

At that moment, a boat whistled at the gate.

"Hang on a sec. Got a customer," Arthur said. He jumped nimbly to the dock and waved off the captain of a boat bound up-river, who was tying off in response to the notice.

"Don't bother, Mr. Knowles," Arthur said. "I'll get it." He opened the gate at the bottom of the lock and Knowles guided in the trim motor yacht. Arthur cranked up the sluice gates and the lock quickly filled with water. Before long, the yacht moved off.

"Anyway," Arthur resumed, "*Guinevere* will be ready as soon as I get that engine pulled and installed."

"Well, I look forward to a ride on her one of these days. But I hoped you might have a little free time." Lloyd described what he'd seen at the Butlers'.

Arthur twirled the end of one mustache thoughtfully. "Bert's right. It sounds like a joint. Though I'd not be surprised …" He looked up. "I've got time. I'll get up there and see what I need."

Annie listened to the peculiar creak of the gate opening and closing and knew Lloyd had come back. She waited a few seconds, and when the vestry door didn't open, she announced, "Your father's home."

Lizzie and George leapt up from their tea to race to the door. Maggie, her face covered with jam, followed as close behind as her little legs would carry her. Norah jumped across the table to rescue a water glass Maggie had tipped. "You know, Mrs. Robins, you might warn me before you do that," she said.

"I'm sorry, Norah," Annie said. She helped the younger woman mop the spill while listening to the happy voices. Lizzie was telling her father about the good mark she'd got that day in school, George was asking if he could help him make a kite, and Maggie was just jumping up and down yelling "Dada, Dada."

Lloyd scooped the little one up, gave her a careful kiss, and spoke to Annie. "I've already had lunch, at the Powells'. I'm just going to get back to work. Can you pop over when you get a minute?"

His tone meant he wanted to chat outside the hearing of the children. "We'll be finished here in a few minutes," Annie said

She helped Norah clear the table and went to put Maggie down. This, inevitably, took more than a few minutes, but finally her energetic daughter nodded off. Norah was finishing up in the kitchen. "I'm popping over now," Annie said. "Lloyd wanted to talk. Can you stay until I get back?"

"I can. I was going to put up the new curtains in my flat, but the fabric didn't come in."

Annie entered the little church vestry, which was also Lloyd's study. His big Bible was open to John chapter 6 and his pen was in his hand. "Give me just thirty seconds, love … 'he that cometh to me shall never hunger; and he that believeth on me shall never thirst.'"

Annie looked out at the garden of the manse. The roses were in full bloom, and some well past. She would have to get outside again soon.

"So," Lloyd said. He stood and hugged her from behind. "I wanted to tell you about the Butlers." She turned in his arms, and met his affectionate kiss.

"Now, Mr. Robins, I told Norah we were going to talk."

"We're communicating." He kissed her again.

She laid her head against his chest as he described the Butlers' situation. "I'm wondering what else we can do," he said.

"Couldn't we pay their mortgage for them?"

He smiled. "Well, if you mean 'we, the Robins … no, we couldn't. I did give them what I had this morning for bread. If you mean 'we', the church … no, not at this moment. I gave the bottom of the church box to Percy yesterday."

"We'll just have to ask around." She thought for a moment. "Rachel is supposed to drop in a little later. I'll ask her to stop and talk to a few people on the way home. Food … and money for the mortgage."

"Do you realize how much that is?" Lloyd asked.

"It's not more than God has, is it?" She looked up into Lloyd's brown eyes. "Aren't you always telling us that he owns the cattle on a thousand hills?"

Her next thought deflated her. "Do you need me to call on Lady Blount?"

"Well … I hate to have you walk all that way, but …" He gestured at the desk. "If you can …"

"No, no, it's all right. Norah will be happy to stay with the children."

"Lady Blount would be offended if we didn't ask," Lloyd said.

Annie sighed. "But you know she won't give anything."

Rachel Busby let herself through the gate and went to Annie and Lloyd's door. She knocked briskly and then opened the door a few inches. "Hello. Anyone home?"

Annie came into the room from the kitchen, wiping her hands on a towel. "Hello Rachel. How are you?"

Rachel hugged the younger woman. "I'm better than I deserve … Didn't I promise to trim George's hair?"

"That's right. Perfect timing."

While Rachel worked, Annie told her about the plan to collect food for the Butlers. "Since you're out, could you possibly stop and pass the word to a few people?"

"Happy to," Rachel said as she fussed with George's cowlick. Finally, she licked three of her fingers and glued it down.

"Well, that'll do for the moment. So should I stop at the Coopers' and the Simmonds'?"

"Yes, thank you. I know it's out of your way. I'll run over and talk to Susan Ward, and then I'll go out to the manor and ask Lady Blount."

"Are you sure you don't want me to come with you? I'll give Eleanor Blount a few words. 'A squeezing, wrenching, grasping, scraping, clutching, covetous old sinner!' as Mother used to say."

"Rachel! I'm sure Virginia Townend would never have said such a thing."

"Of course she would. She was partial to Dickens."

Annie laughed and took Rachel by the arm to lead her to the door. "No, Rachel, I think I'd better visit Lady Blount."

"Doesn't she have a telephone?" Rachel gestured toward the instrument on a table in the front hall. "Surely she could afford one."

"No, I'm afraid the Lady of Blount Manor is a bit old fashioned."

Rachel zig-zagged through Stokely to Evelyn Cooper's house. She was unsurprised to find Lily and Phyllis in the sycamore tree. Evelyn's girls had twice as much energy as any boy in town.

Evelyn answered the door. Her straw-colored waves blew back from her fresh face as she invited Rachel in. "Lily, you be careful out there," she called.

Rachel followed Evelyn into the sitting room, where Ernest, Evelyn's husband, sat, slumped in his chair, his suit dusty.

"Is the Post Office working you hard, Mr. Cooper?"

"Good afternoon Rachel. Actually, yes. It's all this war work. London is insisting that we get the new Unit Automated Exchange installed at once."

"Well, whatever that is, I'll be praying it goes well."

"It's a telephone switching station, Rachel."

"Wonderful, I'm sure, Ernest."

Evelyn offered tea, and as she poured, Rachel explained the situation.

"I don't have much in the way of food in the house myself," Evelyn said, "but I'll get them some fruit and vegetables when at the greengrocer's in the morning."

"Just drop whatever you get at the manse."

Ernest sat up from his slouch. "I'll go around to the Jackdaw after dinner and ask a couple of the chaps for contributions."

Annie straightened her hat as she reached the gate of Blount Manor. She had made a point of enjoying the walk, stopping part way up the hill, where she could see the Thames. The flowing water and the sun setting through the scudding clouds spoke the peace her soul needed.

She went through the gate and up the long walk to the main house. From a distance, it retained its ancient beauty. Close up there seemed to be more peeling paint and deteriorating mortar than ever.

Before she could ring, Lady Blount's man, tall and reserved, opened the door. "Good afternoon, Mrs. Robins. We weren't expecting you, I believe?" The butler had a way of letting you know you were a distasteful intrusion.

"No, Thomas, but I would be grateful if I could have a quick word with Lady Blount."

"Yes ma'am. I will check with her at once. Perhaps it would be best if you came inside." Thomas led her to the beautiful sitting room, but the chair she sat in was worn to a velveteen polish in several spots.

"Anne, how nice to see you again. To what do I owe this unexpected pleasure?" Lady Blount, perfectly dressed and coiffed, swept into the room and offered her hand. Annie rose and took it for a moment.

"Please, sit," Lady Blount commanded. "Shall I have Vera bring some tea?"

"That would be wonderful, thank you."

Eleanor sat opposite, back straight, head high. Annie began to tell her about the needs of the Butler family. "They have the five children now …"

"I told Meg Butler she was a lunatic to take in her brother's brats. Hard enough for her to take care of her own and she's bringing in waifs."

"Lady Blount, please. Her brother is dead, her sister-in-law is overwhelmed. What else could she do? … And they're trying to keep up their mortgage."

"I've seen the same thing with many of these families," Lady Blount said. "They exceed their reach, get badly into debt, and then rely on handouts from honest hard-working people."

"Not the Butlers," said Annie. "Bert was a hard worker before the accident. It's not his fault an airplane engine fell on him."

"No, it's never these people's fault, but they ask for money anyway, don't they?"

"But … but …"

"Don't 'but, but' me, young lady. You know it's true. And this is no time for any of us to be giving our money away, is it?"

"Well, Jesus promised … "

"I know full well what Jesus promised. I've been going to Stokely Free since before you were born. You and Reverend Robins are the newcomers, aren't you?"

Annie looked down at her tea. "Yes, I guess so, Lady Blount."

"And you mark my words, this war is coming, and it will be worse than the first. Your two little ones will be hungry themselves before the year is out. You're taking food out of your own mouths to feed these wastrels."

"Three," Annie said quietly

"Three what?"

"Three little ones. I have three little ones. And I had better be getting back to them."

"Well, if you must leave with your tea half finished, it's no fault of mine. I'll thank you to tell Reverend Robins that Lady Blount regrets she is unable to help."

~ † ~

Henry Padbury sat at his usual table near the window of the Jackdaw Inn, working at a crossword puzzle, filling in answers almost as fast as he could read the clues. He set down his pen and checked his watch. Eleven minutes. *The Daily Telegraph* must have a new setter. The puzzle was getting too easy.

He looked up to see Ernest Cooper approaching. "May I join you, Henry? Quite a crowd tonight."

"Certainly, have a seat." Henry looked around. "I would say, statistically, that tonight's crowd is average or slightly below for a Thursday."

"Yes, Henry."

Henry caught the dry tone. "I'm sorry Ernest. I've spent the afternoon trying to cram some maths into dull minds and I find it hard to turn it off."

"Well, half a pint with a friend is a good place to start." They clinked glasses. Before long, they were joined by Charlie Simmonds and Philip Clarke.

"Good evening, gentlemen. Mind if we join you?"

"How's that new job going, Charlie?" Henry asked.

"Spot on. Mr. Shipperly says I'm a natural on the lathe. He's going to give me my own station, but I'll have to take night shift."

"Fantastic, Charlie. Glad to hear it!" Ernest said.

Henry considered his empty glass. Mrs. Waverly would leave his dinner on the table … nine minutes from now. It would take seven minutes to get back to the house. "Well, gentlemen, if I don't want a cold dinner I had better be off."

"One moment, Henry," Ernest reached out a hand to stay him.

"One moment is all I have." Henry sat back down and pulled out his handkerchief to clean his thick glasses.

"Did you hear about Bert and Meg?" Ernest said.

"No," Henry said. "Has something more happened?"

"Burst pipe," Ernest said. "And Reverend Lloyd's found out they're not feeding the kids."

"Not feeding the children? That's criminal!" Charlie said.

"It's not that they don't want to, Charlie. They're just flat broke. They can't pay the mortgage."

Henry thought he knew where this was going. "So we need to give something to help?"

"Right, old man," Ernest said. "The women are gathering food to take over tomorrow and I volunteered to gather a spot of cash."

Henry knew what he had in his wallet. He briefly contemplated what the Butler's mortgage payment must be and pulled out a pound note, then a second. "I can't pay a whole month, but give them this."

"Goodness Henry, that's generous" Charlie said.

Henry grinned. "Payday. Now that I don't have Mum and Dad's doctor's bills to deal with, it just burns a hole in my pocket. I thank God for the opportunity to give it away."

The following morning Lloyd was pleasantly interrupted several times by church members and friends bringing contributions for the Butlers. It began with Ernest Cooper, on his way to the train station, still exclaiming over the two pounds Henry had contributed. But others stopped by too – Harold Mills, Tom Waters and half a dozen others.

A procession of women passed by Lloyd's window, headed toward the manse with large or small packages, some clearly just purchased at Brown's. Finally, Lloyd's curiosity got the better of him and he headed for the manse. He almost bumped into Annie as she came out the front door headed for the church.

"I was just coming to get you …"

"Wait till you hear …"

They both stopped, started, laughed. Finally, Lloyd said, "You go first."

"Come in and see." She pointed at the kitchen table. "You'll have to go down and get one of Susan Ward's boys to help you carry it all."

Lloyd looked at the pile, huge and varied. "Praise God!" He pulled out the crumpled envelope. "And look at this . . ." The three pound notes were accompanied by many coins.

"My goodness! How much?"

"A month's mortgage! Close to two!"

Annie looked up "Thank you, Jesus!"

"Amen."

~ † ~

"Knock, knock." Lloyd's arms were too full to open the Butlers' gate. Wellington Ward stood behind him with more. Fred came and showed him in shouting, "Mum, look!"

Meg turned from her ironing. "Here," Lloyd said. Her eyes grew wide and her hands flew to her mouth. Joy sang in Lloyd's chest as he watched her.

"We'll just put this in the kitchen, shall we?"

He wasn't surprised to see a pair of legs standing on a ladder, head and torso all the way up through the ceiling. Arthur was humming as he worked.

"Bert, look! Eggs." Meg hummed as she sorted through the food. Wellington excused himself politely, and Lloyd went to stand by Bert, who was trying to help by handing Arthur any tools he could reach.

Lloyd spoke quietly. "There's this too."

Lloyd could see Bert estimating the amount in the envelope. He thrust it back. "No, Rev'rend, we can't accept this."

"Why not?"

"It's too much. People have already been so generous with the food and the help. A man ought to be able to provide for his own family."

"Oh, Bert! A man ought to be able to depend on his Lord and his friends," Lloyd said. "After all, don't we really depend on Jesus for everything?"

Bert snorted and looked down at his legs. "Well, I do at any rate." He looked up at the hole in the ceiling, put his hand on Lloyd's arm, and blurted out "Thanks!"

"So how are you doing up there, Arthur?" Lloyd asked.

"Coming along, Reverend. Do you know a spanner from a pipe wrench?"

"I think so."

"Well hand me the smaller pipe wrench and I'll tighten this last coupling … Noah's flood," Arthur paused to grunt, "is about to be ended."

CHAPTER 2

15 August 1939

Lloyd was staring out the window at the roses, trying to keep his mind on his sermon, when the sound of the door opening provided a welcome interruption.

"Hello," Lloyd said as he stepped into the sanctuary. "Can I help you?"

The stranger who had come in was neatly dressed in a decent London suit. He was a bit older than Lloyd, greying, and he walked up the aisle of the church with a canting limp. War wound, Lloyd thought.

"I don't really need anything, but I did hope to meet the pastor," said the man.

"You have, then." Lloyd introduced himself.

"Good to meet you, Reverend Robins. My name is James Grierson, and I'm out from London looking around for properties. But I looked you up because I believe we have a mutual acquaintance, Pete Miller."

"You know Pete?"

"Met him in Toronto after the war. I understand that you were there as well, though I don't think we ever met."

Lloyd looked at the man more closely. "No, I don't think so, but I'm glad to meet you now. Why don't we go across to the manse where we can sit comfortably and have some tea?"

"I don't want to impose."

Lloyd insisted. When they were settled, he asked, "So were you at TBC?"

"No, no. I regret that I have no Bible College training. I'm a vet. I was in Toronto doing post-grad anesthetics. I met Pete at Knox Presbyterian—"

"Teaching Sunday School," Lloyd said.

"Yes," James responded. "He made a huge difference in my spiritual life; introduced me to serious Bible study and prayer."

"He was already doing that when I met him in the trenches of France," Lloyd said. "He led me to faith in Christ."

"I wish I had known him then," James replied. He rubbed his right leg, but did not mention the injury.

"You said you were looking for properties."

"Right. I've been sent out by the Royal Veterinary College to look for an estate in case the war drives us out of London. Something with stables and space for the large animals and their surgeries, as well as classrooms and labs."

"Well," Lloyd said, "I don't know of any that are for sale."

Grierson rubbed his large chin. "Well, we're at an early stage. I'm not sure when I'll be authorized to buy. I'm just looking."

Ned watched Billy Parker chug off on the old tractor. Good thing it's running again, he thought. Shorthanded as he was, it would be hard to work the farm without it. *Lord, let Daft Billy not wrap it around a tree.* He hated to use nicknames, but in this case, it fitted so perfectly …

Alfred Brooks came into the shed. "Mr. Powell, can I talk to you?"

Ned nodded. Alfred took off his cap and twisted it in both hands "Mr. Powell, I've liked working here and I've learned a lot about farmin' and all, but I've got to leave."

Ned sighed. Not another one, he thought. "Why?"

"Well, Mr. Powell, I've been lookin' at the notices in those London papers and it seems I could get more money in those factories they're buildin'."

"Really? Have you included the fact that here you get room and board?"

Alfred twisted his cap harder. "I know, sir, and I will certainly miss Mrs. Powell's cooking, sir, but I don't want to stay in the country all my life."

"How old are you, Alfred?"

"Nineteen, sir."

"If war breaks out you'll be called up for military service. Tom's already gone to the Army."

"Yes sir, I know. But there may not be a war."

Ned could see he would get nowhere. "I pray you're right about that, Alfred. Can you give me the rest of the week?"

"Oh, yes sir. Thank you, sir."

Whitehall today reports that letters have gone out to conscript another 100,000 men, those born between April 1 and June 30, 1920. Robert Duckworth, Member from Kingston upon Hull reports that His Majesty's Government is preparing a bill to expand conscription to those aged between eighteen and forty-one years old. This brings a pool of four million men into possible military service.

"Rev'rend?" Ned's voice was tinged with sarcasm. "Did you even hear what I said?"

Lloyd snapped back to the present. "I'm sorry, no," he said to Ned. "They keep the BBC way too loud in here."

Ned looked around the Jackdaw. It was a relatively quiet Tuesday afternoon.

"So what was it I missed?" Lloyd reached up and rubbed at his ear.

The old injury acting up, Ned thought. "I said this war, if it comes, could be the death of the British farmer. I've been struggling for years to keep enough hands. Now I've got conscription and war factories to compete with."

"If it comes, it may well be the death of another generation of British young men. We barely survived our war."

"It might not be just the young. Did you hear that we're going to have to carry gas masks all the time, even here?"

Lloyd nodded. "And start having drills. I don't know that any of it will do any good."

"No. Gas is hard to deal with." Ned thought back to the Somme.

"And now Hitler can drop it from the air."

"Let's just pray he doesn't."

~ † ~

"Thank you for the invitation, Mrs. Robins." James said.

"Please call me Annie."

After James' second Sunday visit to Stokely Free, Lloyd and Annie had invited him home for dinner. He spotted the little ones watching him. "Hello, Lizzie. Hello George. Hello Maggie."

"Hello, Mr. Grierson," the older two responded.

James forced his stiff knee to bend. "So, Maggie, how old are you?"

Maggie disappeared behind her sister's skirt.

"Tell Mr. Grierson how old you are," Lloyd prompted.

Maggie held out two fingers. "Fwee," she said.

"Three. Wonderful. You are a big girl." He stood awkwardly, wondering for the millionth time why God had chosen never to give him a wife or children. Ah, well, there had been plenty of work and ministry. *And I have you, Lord.*

"Lizzie, please help the others wash up," Annie said. She and … *Norah was it?* … had just finished putting dinner on the table. The roast and potatoes filled the room with a lovely aroma.

Norah, James thought, must be something more than the hired help. She had been at church with them, and now sat down with them at the table.

"So how does London see the world these days?" Lloyd asked after they prayed.

"Not optimistically, I'm afraid," James said. "Did you hear about the huge blackout drill in Sussex and Kent over the weekend?"

"I talked to a preacher friend who said they mucked it up completely."

"Quite," James said.

"And your task in Stokely," Lloyd said, "is further proof the government expects a war."

"I suppose," James said. "We're only being told that these preparations are precautionary. Have you had any further thoughts?"

"I suppose you've tried Chiltern's?" Lloyd asked.

"Yes," James replied. "Already taken by the Army."

"Let's see … Have you talked to Harold Mills? He was at church the first time you came. Tall, skinny chap with rimless glasses?"

"No," James said. "Should I?"

"He's a broker's agent, knows the local market."

"Really!" James said. No stone unturned, that was his motto. "Could I possibly see him today before I leave?"

"He's away this weekend, I'm afraid."

James sat back. "Well, I'll see him next time I come out. Should be a week or two."

He forked up another large bite of cake. "But how's your personal life, Lloyd?"

"You mean my spiritual life?"

He nodded.

"You sound like Pete Miller. Not many here would ask."

"I hope I haven't offended."

"Not at all! Takes me back to the good old days."

"And?"

"Oh. I guess I'm getting along. Busy, of course, but that's typical." Lloyd sat back and rubbed his ear. "Under all that? … I think I'm anxious about this war. I didn't think it would hit me so hard … And you?"

"Much the same. The prospect of war grieves me. But it's driving me to Scripture and prayer, so that's good."

Before taking his leave, James sought out the hostess. "It was a lovely meal, Annie," he said. "Your cake was wonderful."

"Annie used to work in her aunt's bakery," Lloyd said. "Her bread and biscuits are also extraordinary."

"I hope to get the chance to sample them."

James shook the preacher's hand warmly, "I do hope to find something out this way. And I'll be praying for you."

Ten days later, Lloyd sat in the kitchen while Annie cleared up breakfast. "It reminds me more and more of 1914," he said. "It was the uncertainty that got to you. When the war broke out it came almost as a relief."

Annie watched him picking up and putting down newspapers from London and the Midlands.

"Here's what Eden said yesterday." Lloyd read, " 'We are in a period of a war of nerves and a prolonged testing time lies ahead of us … The Government is embarked upon a policy of building up a peace front to resist further acts of aggression.' "

"I wonder what 'a prolonged testing time' means," Annie said. "It seems to me Hitler won't wait long to snatch off a piece of Poland."

She regretted her pessimism immediately. Lloyd turned back to the papers and said in a weak voice "No, he probably can't be stopped by a 'peace front.' "

Change the subject, Annie thought. "So are you meeting with James Grierson today?"

"Yes, and with Harold Mills. Harold is going to help him look for an estate."

"Do you think he'll find one?"

"I hope so."

"I'll have a pint today," Lloyd said to the girl at the Jackdaw. "And one for my friend." Sometimes a little extra beer quieted the ringing.

Harold joined them a few minutes later. "Glad to meet you, Mr. Grierson. Sorry I'm late."

"No inconvenience, Mr. Mills. Reverend Lloyd and I were just catching up on old times."

"Have you known each other long?"

"No, we only just met last month."

"We have a mutual friend from Toronto." Lloyd explained. "He's now a missionary in China."

"Oh," Harold said. "Tough spot that. Have you heard from him?"

"No," Lloyd said, and James shook his head. "Haven't had a letter in over a year. But the post is non-existent at the moment. I just pray he's okay."

They ordered shepherd's pie, which the Jackdaw did well. It arrived hot and beefy-fragrant as they were talking about what the veterinary college needed.

"It will have to be a large estate," James said. "We'll have classrooms, dissection labs, a surgery, and outbuildings for large-animal care." He savored a large bite. "We'll open a clinic if the local population can support it."

Harold looked discouraged. "We have many such estates in the vicinity, but I fear none of them is currently for sale."

"No surprise there, Mr. Mills. But I wonder if any of these owners could be persuaded for the right price."

Harold counted on his fingers. "Elmcroft? No. Chiltern? Already gone. Grey? Almost certainly not. Blount Manor?— "

"She probably should sell," Lloyd interjected, "but I don't think she will."

"Please ask around, then," James said to Harold. "Let people know that His Majesty's Government is prepared to be generous."

Lloyd felt he had to ask. "And what if there are no places for sale?"

James rubbed his chin. "At this time, it means we don't get a place."

"And in the future?"

"I hate to resort to cliché, but we'll have to cross that bridge when we come to it."

Lloyd knew he should sit tight and work on this week's message, but he'd been trying most of the afternoon. And now it was really too late, wasn't it?

"I'm going for a walk, love. Anything I can pick up for you?"

"We could use some milk. And if you see any bananas or oranges grab them. Rumor is they've disappeared completely from London."

Lloyd felt in his pockets to make sure he had a few shillings. He would walk out along the Thames and shop on the way back. "Lord Jesus," he prayed, "help me to know what to say to your people this Sunday. Help me to focus."

Near the edge of town, he spotted Dot Simmonds standing at her door. Her wide, generous smile lit up her face in greeting.

"Rev'rend Lloyd, how are you today?"

"I'm all right Dot. Are you and Charlie enjoying your holiday?" Dot taught little ones at the primary school.

"Just so, Reverend. But Ned and Lisa are getting bored. Now that Charlie's on night shift we have to keep the house quiet night and day."

"Well that's hard for a … is Ned seven now?" Charlie was Ned Powell's nephew, and Ned had done a lot to help him get his life together after a rough patch in the twenties.

"Almost eight, Rev'rend."

"They grow up so fast, don't they?"

After a few more pleasantries Lloyd continued. The road on this side of the Thames ended at a path that followed the river all the way to the railway bridge. Through a thin line of trees, Lloyd could see a series of fields, golden with wheat and green with other crops Lloyd couldn't identify. The line ran through them, and Lloyd paused to watch the local puff across to Stokely station. The slowly westering sun glinted red and gold off the train windows.

Lloyd loved this land, these walks, this season. But, he reflected, he loved all the seasons of this beautiful place. He knew that God cared most for people, for the teeming cities of the world, but he felt closer to the creator out here in the unspoiled creation. He remembered the devastation of the Western front in the Great War, the land churned into a scene from hell by the engines of death. *Lord Jesus, please protect our cities and this land from the horrors of another war.*

As he was coming out of Brown's with Annie's groceries, Lloyd heard a familiar voice. "Rev'e Robins. Can I talk to you just for a minute?"

"Hello Percy." Lloyd waited for the aging man to catch up. Percy was dressed in his usual summer garb: pants ragged at the hem and a shirt with the sleeves torn off below the elbows.

"Hello Rev'e. Did you 'ear the one about the 'unter who came upon a tree with five doves in it."

"No, Percy."

"'e shot two of 'em dead. Now how many was left?"

"Three?"

"No, just the two dead 'uns. The others flew away."

Percy laughed revealing a mouth almost devoid of teeth. "'The others flew away.' Do you get it Rev'e? The three birds weren't left. They flew away."

"I get it, Percy."

Percy had a penchant for bad jokes, and a gift for the care of horses. When Lloyd arrived at Stokely, Percy had been the groom at Blount Manor. Lady Blount had sold the last of the stock not long after and Percy had been living hand-to-mouth in a little shed near the river ever since.

"I was wondering if you might have a little something for Percy today, Rev'e. Just a little something, and you being so good 'n all. The cupboard's awful bare. All the birds 'ave flown away." Percy laughed his joyful guffaw again.

"Let's just go up to the church and we'll see what we have."

Lloyd opened the church door and let Percy into the church entry, where the old carved poor-box hung on the narrow wall. Percy loved to open the lid.

"Less see, less see … coins, Rev'e, two shillings … no, one."

He fished a little more. "And four pence."

Percy put all the coins in Lloyd's outstretched hand. The old man's face was gaunt, his eyes sunk in their sockets. Lloyd reached into his own pocket and added the two shillings he hadn't spent at Brown's to the small pile. *No bananas, no oranges and now no cash.*

"Here," he said. "Get yourself something decent to eat."

"I will, Rev'e, I will. Thank'ee. Thank'ee."

Percy shook Lloyd's hand and shuffled out the open door.

"A fine lunch, Annie," Lloyd said. "Thank you." He followed her into the kitchen, carrying his plate. Annie had baked that morning and he had savored fresh bread with cold ham and freshly picked tomatoes. Lloyd had acquired a taste for them in Toronto and Annie indulged it with a few plants in their small back garden.

"I guess I'll head back to the vestry and see if I can finish the message."

"Still elusive?"

"Trouble concentrating. I'm leaving the papers here so I won't be interrupted rereading the bluster from Germany and London and Paris."

Lloyd had nearly completed what he knew was a mediocre message when he heard the main door of the church open and shut quickly.

"Pastor, are you here?"

"Yes, Alan." Lloyd tensed as he put down his pen and stepped out into the main sanctuary. Alan Ward's narrow face and long pointed chin were a contrast to his short, thick stature and bowed legs. His big Bible was in his hand.

There was room for only one chair in the vestry. "Can we sit in here?" Lloyd said.

"Does it seem right to you to use God's house that way?"

"I guess not … How about the church hall?"

"Certainly. I'm not picky."

They pulled up two hard backed chairs near one of the tall windows. The late afternoon light streamed in and illuminated the fine thin cloud of dust.

"Seems to me your Norah's not doing much of a job keeping this place clean, Pastor. Cleanliness is next to godliness you know."

"So I've heard," Lloyd said. He couldn't help enjoying the beauty of the streaming light in the high empty room.

"You're off work early this afternoon," Lloyd said. Alan was still dressed in the traditional uniform the Great Western Railway required clerks to wear.

"Had to bring the track maintenance schedules to all the station masters between Pangbourne and Oxford. Mr. Kingsley said I needn't bother coming all the way back to the office."

"That was generous of him."

"Did you hear the BBC this afternoon?" Alan asked.

"No, was there news?"

"The Germans and the Soviet Union have signed a trade and co-operation treaty. The BBC said it opens the door for a German invasion of Poland."

"Oh no! And just when it seemed the talks were going better."

"War is inevitable," Alan said. "I'm making my boys join up; I'd hate this to be all over before they saw any action."

Lloyd rocked back, rubbing his ear. He remembered that Alan had been denied military service. *Rickets, wasn't it?* He'd got his job with Great Western during the Great War, and had worked in Pangbourne ever since.

"But that's not why you've come," Lloyd said.

"No. I have a couple of items of church business to discuss … First, I'm wondering about this man, Percy."

"Why?"

"You seem to be giving an awful lot of charity to him."

"He's old, out of work, and nearly homeless. I help where I can."

"But isn't he Church of England? Shouldn't we be helping our own?"

"I don't think Scripture limits us to helping only church members, though I have been giving most of what comes in to Bert and Meg."

"What about Second Thessalonians? 'If a man would not work, neither should he eat.'"

"Percy works when he can."

"He also begs when he can," Alan said. "And I've heard he drinks when he can. We don't need that kind in this town and we don't need to be giving him all our charity."

Alan looked down as if consulting a piece of paper. "Second thing. I wonder if you've noticed Violet Clarke's behavior."

"No, I don't think I have." Lloyd grew even more wary. He often disagreed with Alan's definition of church business.

"You must have seen how she dresses. How much makeup she wears. Even to church. She's only, what, sixteen? And she's been seen with the wrong sort. Church of England girls. And that scoundrel Reggie—" Lloyd started to interrupt but Alan spoke over him. "Up to no good, I'm sure. You know how Edwin was before he ran away to London."

"Have you seen evidence of this rumored friendship yourself?" Lloyd asked.

A look of irritation crossed Alan's face, but he answered unemotionally. "No, technically not. But the stationmaster has seen them together, meeting the train when some of Reggie's low friends have come in. I have no doubt about what she's up to."

"Well, I do have doubts, Alan." Lloyd paused to control his irritation. "But I'll look for an opportunity to ask Philip how she's doing."

"Well, if you don't I will. He's not had a very good track record with his children."

"Oh, Alan!" Lloyd said. "You know they've tried hard with Edwin, and they pray hard for him. They can't be held responsible for all his choices."

"Children have to be made to follow the right path. That's what I'm doing with Nelson and Wellington and they're turning out fine." Alan got up stiffly. "You just talk to Philip Clarke and tell him to keep his girl under control."

Lloyd sat for a long time, praying for peace and wisdom – and thinking about Alan's other news, Germany's free hand in Poland. He rubbed hard at the ringing in his ear.

Annie and Norah walked with the children toward the Powell's farm. "I'm sure Aunt Alice will be glad to see us," she told Georgie. "It's not much further."

Annie had decided she needed to talk to Ned. He was the only one who had been with Lloyd through the last war.

"Thanks for helping me," she said to Norah. "It's hard to get out with three."

"I'm glad I could come. I love this walk."

Annie looked around. It was a beautiful view, with the misty river off to the right and the hills to the left. Everything had an end-of-summer goldenness to it that was accentuated by the ripe wheat in Ned's fields. But to the east, a line of clouds was building.

"So how are you?" Annie asked.

"All right, I think," Norah said. "I'm sometimes amazed how much anger and betrayal I still feel. It was more than a year ago." Norah's husband had run off with a local barmaid, and then forced Norah to divorce him.

"These things take a long time to heal," said Annie. "I think you're doing really well."

As they turned into the Powell's gate, a cry rang out "Lizzie!"

"Lily!" Lizzie and Lily met in the lane and spun around each other like a miniature cyclone.

"Well, that makes it more fun for all of us," Annie said.

Evelyn's older daughter Phyllis joined them. "Hello, Mrs. Robins, Mrs. Applewaithe. How are you today?"

"We're fine, Phyllis. Is your mother here?"

"Mum and Dad both. Dad got the day off to help Mr. Powell with the wheat. I wanted to help too, but Mum wouldn't let me."

Annie gratefully parked the pram under Ned's apple tree and took a wiggly Maggie out. George struggled to be free of Norah's hand.

"May I watch them while they play, Mrs. Robins?"

"Oh yes, thank you, Phyllis. I'll try to keep an eye out the window."

They found Alice and Evelyn in the big farm kitchen, squeezing lemons.

"Lemonade!" Norah said.

"I thought there were no more lemons in the south of England," Annie said.

"I found a few in Swindon last week," Alice said, "We'll have it ready in a moment."

"But we can't drink up all your expensive lemons!"

"Oh, why not?" Alice said. "We'll make it a party. I'm expecting the men any moment. I told Ned he had to come in out of the sun, wheat or no wheat."

Soon the women were sipping at the sweet treat. The children, despite every warning, had gulped theirs down and clamored for more. "No," said Alice, "the rest is for the men."

"And here they are," Evelyn said. Ned, Ernest, and Billy Parker came into the kitchen, wiping their brows. Slightly behind them was George Wilson, who normally worked on his mother's farm nearby.

"Wash your hands," Alice said. "Lemonade's ready."

"Well this is quite a gathering," Ned said. He took a deep swig of his lemonade.

"How is the harvest coming?" Norah asked.

"Slowly. We're doing as much as possible, but we're too far behind. If the rain comes we'll be in trouble."

Phyllis spoke up "Mr. Powell, I can help. I really can. I'm strong."

Ned considered for a moment. "Maybe you can at that. I'm expecting Welly Ward a little later, but maybe you can help until he gets here … Evelyn?"

Phyllis' mum nodded.

When the men had cooled off, Annie approached Ned. "I know this is a bad time, but could we talk just for a minute?"

Ned looked out at the field, but nodded. "George, Ernest, Billy, why don't you head back out? I'll be along with Phyllis or Welly in a few moments."

Ned stepped into the large sitting room, but he didn't sit down.

"I'll keep this short," Annie said. "I just wanted to ask you to pray for Lloyd. I don't know if you could see it in last Sunday's sermon, but he's not doing too well. It's the war, or the threat of war, or memories of the last war. Is there any way I can help him?"

Ned looked around. Annie was sure he was seeing another time and another place. "Nothing I can put into words. But he's survived worse hells. I'll be praying for him."

Annie sighed. She wished he had something more solid to offer. *Lord, you are the only one who can really strengthen my husband.*

When Annie and Norah gathered the children to head home, the clouds were building across a colorless sky. The wind had dropped and the air was tense.

"I hope they get the crop in before this hits."

~ † ~

There it is again. Lloyd put the paper down on the breakfast table, as the ringing in his left ear seemed to crescendo. It took him back to Morval, his second day in the trenches.

"Corporal Jeffries, can you come up here and tell me what I'm seeing?"

"Lieutenant, get your bloomin' 'ead down."

A loud whizz was followed by a huge explosion. Lloyd was thrown into the trench wall, and almost over it. He righted himself slowly. When he turned back toward Corporal Jeffries, all he could see was smoke and dust. Gradually he made out the man's body against the far wall of the trench.

Someone took hold of his arm and pulled him down. Lloyd twisted to see Sergeant Powell yelling, his words barely heard above the pain in his ears. "I said get down, Lieutenant. He's dead. You will be too if you don't get your caddie head down."

Lloyd began to hear the rounds whistling above.

"But I hardly knew him!"

"What does that matter, Lieutenant? Knowing a man won't keep him alive. Nothing will, if it's their time."

"It's not supposed to be this way!"

"How can it be any other? It's a war. People are killed. These men don't expect you to keep them safe, just to keep your wits about you … And when it all goes to hell in a hand cart, to keep your head down."

Ned had saved his life that day and many others, Lloyd thought. But his ear had never been the same.

He turned back to the paper. Britain had signed a mutual assistance treaty with Poland. Lloyd knew it was necessary, but it seemed to bring a new war one step closer. He stood, spotted Annie in the kitchen and went in. He took her into his arms and said. "I'm afraid it's all happening again. And this time we've got a whole church full of friends to mourn."

Annie tilted her head to look up at him. "We'll be okay, Lloyd. Jesus will not leave us, no matter what."

Lloyd looked away. "You're right, of course."

Outside, Stokely's lone newsboy began to shout excitedly. "Extra! Extra! Hitler's forces in Poland."

CHAPTER 3

3 September 1939

Annie sat on the edge of the bed and gently shook her sleeping husband.

"Dearest … Lloyd … It's time to get up … It's Sunday."

Lloyd groaned, then shot up.

"Sunday? What time is it?"

"Quarter past eight. I let you sleep in, because you were up so late."

Lloyd set his feet on the floor and took hold of his head, elbows on knees.

"Do you have a headache?" Annie asked. "Can I get you an aspirin?"

"No, I'll be fine." He shook his head. "Have you heard any news this morning?"

"No, nothing new. The Germans claim to be advancing rapidly. They've bombed Warsaw and the other cities."

"Chamberlain still plans to speak in the Commons?"

"Yes, this morning."

"It will be war then." He buried his head in his hands again. "But what else can we do? Hitler has to be stopped. If we can."

"Do you want me to get Ned or Henry to cover the church service?"

"No," he said, "I have to do it. I can't let these people down. I need to take care of them."

She knelt in front of him and took his hands. "Isn't it really Jesus who takes care of us?"

He sagged. "Yes, of course. But I don't want to let him down either."

Lloyd stood in the pulpit and looked out on the congregation. Nearly every member of Stokely Free Church was there. The room could only seat about 120 at a squeeze, and every pew was full. Even the Reynolds, who had moved to Pangbourne, and the Thompsons, who had drifted back toward the Church of England, were there. Beverly Wilson was there, with her oldest son, George. Her younger son, Adam, was already part of the British Expeditionary Force. "Lord," Lloyd prayed, "help me to help these people."

He lifted his eyes and spoke to the congregation. "For several weeks we have been studying the teaching of Jesus in John chapter 16. This morning we will look only at verse 33: 'These things I have spoken unto you, that in me ye might have peace. In the world ye shall have tribulation: but be of good cheer; I have overcome the world.'

"Jesus shocks us by promising that we will have tribulation, that testing and trouble will come. In Matthew's Gospel, he warns us that there will be wars and rumors of war, before he comes again.

"Today we enter into a kind of tribulation that may be unlike any before. Hitler's air force might soon be bombing and gassing our cities. But Jesus tells us that no matter how deep our distress, how tragic our trouble, he has overcome the world. Even today, as our world descends into turmoil, we can find peace if we are in Him. Are you 'in Him' today?"

He paused to let the question sink in. *Lord Jesus, am I in you today?*

"Rev'rend Lloyd, you gotta come! Alan and Welly's 'aving an awful row!"

Susan Ward was calling from the main door of the church. Lloyd rushed out. Susan was normally quiet as a mouse, partly to hide her London upbringing. What could have made her this desperate?

When he reached the sanctuary, she called "Hurry, Rev'rend," and fled.

The Wards lived only three streets away. Soon Lloyd could hear Alan shouting. "I don't care how old you are, you're my sons. You will do as I tell you. God's Word demands it."

"What's happening?" Lloyd said loudly, in as calm a voice as he could. Alan was facing away from him. Nelson and Wellington were backed against the cold hearth. Nelson, the dark-haired one, stood with clenched fists. Welly, also short and stocky but fair-haired, stood beside him, his hands splayed on the bricks of the fireplace.

"Pastor Robins," Alan said, turning. "Why are you here? This is a family issue, nothing to do with the church."

"Susan came to fetch me."

"Her too," he said. His voice lightened in an effort at self-control. "I don't believe anyone in my family takes seriously the command to submit."

"What is the argument about?"

"No argument, just a family—"

"It is an argument!" Nelson interrupted his father.

Alan spun back. "You'll hush if you know what's good for you!"

Susan spoke from behind Lloyd. "They don't want to join the services. He's trying to make them."

"My sons will not be labelled cowards for the rest of their lives."

"Is that what this is about?" Nelson said. "You're so ashamed of getting kept out of the last war that you'll make us fight this one for you?"

"Shut up! I haven't let my deformity keep me from feeding you, have I?"

Jesus, help me, Lloyd thought. "Alan, can you tell me what's behind this?"

Alan took a deep breath, his fists still balled at his sides. "Yes, Reverend." He shot a glance at the boys. "In light of the present crisis, I have repeatedly urged both of these fit lads to sign up for the armed forces. The Navy would be my preference, but I am willing to let them choose whatever branch they prefer."

"And?" Lloyd said.

"They're both … neither one of them is willing."

"I am willing," Nelson said. "But Reverend Robins, you know how well I'm doing at university. I'll go if I'm called up, but I don't want to be made to go before then."

Alan started to protest.

"Please, Alan, let the boy have his say," Lloyd said. "War isn't something to be entered into lightly. I've been there." He rubbed his ringing ear.

"Don't you flaunt your 'officer and a gentleman' at me Pastor. You're no better than I am, even though you fought!"

Lloyd's lips thinned. "Let the boy have his say, Alan."

Nelson spoke in a pleading tone. "I'm willing to go, Father, but if this war stretches out, I believe I can make more of a difference by becoming an engineer; designing and building what we need."

Alan responded, "And I say the Navy will teach you more than you can possibly learn among those professors and scatterbrains."

"Father, you don't understand."

Lloyd interrupted. "And Wellington? What about you?"

"I'm not like Nelson," the younger boy replied. "I don't want to fight at all. I don't believe in it. Rev'rend, does loving our enemies mean killing our enemies?"

"Not this again," Alan said.

"Well," Lloyd said, glancing from the boy to his father, "no, it doesn't mean killing our personal enemies. But in this case, the Nazis have already shown themselves to be evil murderers. As a just nation, shouldn't we work to contain evil?"

"I've read all the arguments, Rev'rend. I agree with the Quakers. There is no justification for responding to violence with violence. I want to become a conscientious objector. I'm willing to do anything, except take up a gun."

"You're a coward," Alan said. "I won't have anything to do with your slinking disobedience! You'll fight, or no longer be called my son."

Despair chilled Lloyd's heart. "Alan," he said, "do you really want to say that? Shouldn't you wait until tempers have cooled?"

"I wish you wouldn't accuse me of having lost my temper," Alan said. "I'm just trying to tell these boys what they must do in obedience to their father. That's scriptural, isn't it, Reverend?" He drew out the last word.

"Alan, there comes a time when a young man has to decide for himself."

"This is not that time."

"It is, Father!" Wellington pushed past him. "I've decided." The door slammed behind him.

Alan looked at Nelson. "And you?"

Nelson dropped the hand that had been reaching toward his brother. "I'll do what you want," he said. His tone was hard and flat. "But only because I'm a better son than you are a father."

He too walked out of the door.

Susan was sobbing behind Lloyd. "Oh, look what you've done!"

Lloyd wasn't sure whether she was talking to her husband or him.

When Lloyd returned to the church he could see Welly Ward pacing in front of the sanctuary door. He slowed down a bit to pray for the young man.

"That didn't go too well, did it, Rev'rend Robins?" Welly said.

"No. I'm sorry."

"I'm serious about the conscientious objection. I've looked into it. I have to go before a tribunal in Reading. They're just setting them up."

"Is there anything I can do to help?"

"Would you?"

"I don't agree with your choice, but I respect it and I'll support you."

"Thank you, Rev'rend Robins. They're talking about needing references from those who know my 'pacifist tendencies'. Do you think you could go down to Reading and fill in the form? They have offices in the courthouse."

"Of course. How soon do you need it done?"

"I don't really know. I think with the start of the war everything has moved into high gear."

"I'll go soon, Welly. What will you do in the meantime?"

"I won't go home." The boy's voice swelled with emotion.

"No, I see that … hmmm … I know that Ned Powell is short of hands. Perhaps if you explain the situation, he'll hire you – at least until you've heard from this tribunal."

"Yes, sir. Thank you, sir. I'll try that."

Lloyd pushed aside Tuesday's paper, full of bad news. He had slept badly again. "I think I'll go," he told Annie. "I can't concentrate anyway." He had planned to go into Reading to see what he could do for Welly Ward at the tribunal offices.

"You may not even be able to see anyone. They're just getting organized."

"I'll take that chance. I promised Wellington."

"What about the bombings?"

"There haven't been any confirmed yet. And Reading doesn't seem like a good first target. I'll be careful."

A little later Annie walked him to the door. "You've got your gas mask?"

"Yes." Lloyd patted the bag, remembering the last war.

It took only a few minutes to walk to Stokely station, but he found the trains behind schedule. He had hoped to catch the 9:11, but the 8:41 hadn't arrived yet.

While he waited, a train came in from Reading. A group got off; children ten or eleven years of age, with a few women who appeared to be their teachers. The bigger boys looked excited, but the cluster of girls, wearing frayed coats despite the heat, stood silently. One smaller boy crouched down on the platform. His teacher spotted him and hurried him away. Lloyd's nose told him that the puddle where the boy had squatted was not just water.

At that moment Lloyd's counterpart, the rector of St. James', came down the platform with a family from his church and one of the teachers from the Church of England school. They spoke with the evacuees and their teachers.

Mr. Bennett stepped across to Lloyd. "How are you today, Reverend Robins?"

"Pre-occupied with the start of this war, I'm afraid. As are you." He nodded toward the group.

"Yes, the Newells will house this group of evacuees. They were supposed to arrive on Saturday, but I understand they were sent to the wrong Stokely."

"'All Stokelys look the same from London,'" Lloyd quipped as his train pulled into the station.

"And just sign here, then." The aging court clerk pointed at a line on the deposition Lloyd had given. Lloyd had spent two hours looking for the right office, then more time waiting for those ahead to fill out their paperwork. Then the clerk had not been able to find Welly's file and Lloyd had had to wait for it to be brought over from the courthouse where he'd gone in the first place.

If the trains were on time he could still catch the 6:11 home.

But they weren't. The packed station seemed to be filled with people somehow already war-weary – a feeling echoed in Lloyd's soul. He stood by a wall, trying not to think about the destruction reported in Poland. His imagination and his memories were vivid, and the ringing in his ear from his old war wound intensified.

He walked back into the ticket office. "Any word on a local to Stokely?"

The stationmaster sighed and looked over to the telegraph operator, who shook his head. "No, sir, sorry. The line's bunged up in Maidenhead and the whole lot's shut down."

"Bombing?"

"Derailment. It'll probably be two hours before they get it opened up."

Lloyd rubbed his ear. *It's the noise in this station.* "Excuse me, but if I go over to that pub, can you send someone to fetch me when you have an outbound local?"

"Yes, Reverend, I'd be happy to do that."

Lloyd slipped off his clerical collar and entered the pub. The scent of old grease and stale beer assaulted him. *Not a high class place. Maybe I'd better stick with something cold.* He ordered a cheese sandwich and a bottle of Guinness.

He sat in the corner, by the front window. The Guinness tasted good and seemed to reduce the chaos in his head. His past told him that he shouldn't have a second bottle, but he ordered another anyway. Then another.

Then he lost track.

"We should replace Corporal Black."

Lloyd sat with his back to the muddy trench wall. Ned crouched beside him as they discussed the planned assault on Morval.

"There's no one to replace him with."

"He's reckless, Lieutenant. Too much time in the trench."

"We'll just have to send him toward the quietest part of the line."

"Yes, sir." Ned did not look convinced.

"You and I will take 1st section up toward the machine gun nest. Tom can take 3rd section up the middle. Sam Edwards can anchor the far end."

The artillery lit off at 0400, but it seemed weak and sporadic. When it ended, they went over the top. No man's land was a storm. 77's, rifle fire. The men were on their bellies in the mud. Slow work.

A big machine gun opened up from the right. "Sergeant," Lloyd yelled, "the gun's been moved." He signaled to two privates and screamed in Ned's ear. "Take the rest of the section forward. Be careful."

Lloyd could see Tom's men pinned down in a huge shell hole. Lloyd's little group hadn't been noticed yet. Maybe they could get far enough up to flank the gun. Then Tom stood and waved his men forward. "No!" Lloyd yelled, unheard. Eight men crested the far edge of the shell hole. Eight men tumbled back.

Lloyd scrambled along a protecting ridge of mud. The shell hole seemed to be filled with a mist of blood. Tom was dead. Head shot. No hope. Four others were bleeding out. Three were wounded. The machine gun continued to fire. Then a number of Mills bombs exploded. Ned! Lloyd thought.

1st section quickly put the nest out of action. Lloyd scrambled up. "Looks like we're the only ones to get this far." Rifle fire came from both directions.

Long minutes later a runner came through the firestorm with orders from the captain. Withdraw. Lloyd scrambled back toward the shell hole. "Withdraw!" he shouted. Ned and the rest of the platoon came crawling down behind him. "Take the wounded first. Bring the dead." Inching across the mud, covered in blood. Throwing a body over the trench wall. Falling.

~ † ~

A porter was shaking Lloyd. He was on the train. "Sir, Stokely."

The train stank and Lloyd's head swam. His ear buzzed and popped like rifle fire. He looked down. Someone must have tried to clean up the vomit. Oh, Lord, what was he going to say to Annie?

She was on the platform when he stumbled out. "Lloyd are you all right?"

'Do I look all right?" he grumbled.

"Lord help us," she gasped. "You're drunk!" She tried to take his arm.

He shook her off. "Leave me alone. I can walk by myself."

His shame was bile in his throat. He stumbled and she reached out again. He slapped her hand away.

"No!"

~ † ~

Annie dropped a plate of toast in front of Lizzie. "Mum, where's Dad? He never misses breakfast."

"He's not feeling well, dear." Annie said. "I expect he'll be down presently."

If he comes down at all. As far as she knew, he hadn't been drunk since the war; since Pete Miller had led him to faith in Christ. He had never before tried to strike her. He had woken up a few minutes ago with a headache, more nausea, and a pitiful litany of "I'm so sorry, Annie, so sorry."

While Lizzie and the others ate their toast, she took him an aspirin and a glass of water. He was on his knees by the bed with his Bible open in front of him. She hoped Jesus was giving him a good lecture. She knew she would.

~ † ~

He wasn't in the habit of kneeling, even for prayer, but a wave of nausea had driven him to his knees. He wondered how many bottles of Guinness he had consumed. He would have to check his wallet when he could move again.

"Oh, Lord," he cried. "Forgive me." He knew that part of his remorse was just the misery of the hangover. But the bigger part was the sheer disappointment of having let Annie down. She shouldn't have to see him like this. Letting the church down. "Our minister couldn't handle the war." Letting his Lord down. "Against thee, thee only, have I sinned, and done this evil in thy sight."

Why? What was it he couldn't handle? He thought of the days after he had come to faith. The war continued, but the despair hadn't been able to touch him.

Maybe it's been too easy lately. Jesus, are you trying to take me to a new place of dependence? He thought of the young men in his congregation, their parents, the little boy at the station. The months and years of this new war stretched out like no man's land. "No. This is too hard for me, Jesus!"

He looked down at the page where his Bible had fallen open. It was Isaiah 41. An internal laugh was accompanied by a new wave of dizziness. Pete Miller would tease him, his professors at TBC would correct him, for expecting to receive messages from God by random pointing at Scripture.

But Lloyd knew that this chapter was God's Word to him. "Fear thou not; for I am with thee: be not dismayed; for I am thy God: I will strengthen thee; yea, I will help thee; yea, I will uphold thee with the right hand of my righteousness."

"Lord Jesus, I can't do this! I've proven that already. Forgive me. Strengthen me," he whispered. The tightness in his chest eased a little.

His Bible had cross-references in tiny type. It hurt his head to focus on them. Joshua 1:9. This time he chuckled out loud. Joshua preparing to endure a war. He turned there. "As I was with Moses, so I will be with thee." The words poured into his soul like familiar music. "I will not fail thee, nor forsake thee. Be strong and of a good courage."

"Lord Jesus, I believe your promise. Help me be strong for Annie … for my children … for my church," he prayed.

"Only be thou strong and very courageous, that thou mayest observe to do according to all the law, which Moses my servant commanded thee." *Lord Jesus, I do repent of my sin. But be with me, Lord Jesus. I can't do this.*

After a while Lloyd bathed, dressed, and went downstairs. He embraced his wife. She was stiff and silent. He knew it was no more than he deserved.

~ † ~

A few days later Lloyd found Annie on the bed, in tears. "What's the matter, love? Maggie and George are crying downstairs, and Lizzie won't tell me anything."

Annie refused Lloyd's attempt to turn her toward him. "I'm a bloody awful mother. I've yelled at them all morning and now they'll hate me."

The words hit Lloyd like slaps. "Don't say those things, Annie." Lloyd said. "They would never hate you."

"Yes they will. I hated my father!"

"That was different. He was cruel to you."

Now she twisted toward him. "And I'm cruel to them. We're all cruel. You. Me. All of us."

Lloyd faltered. Annie's anger seemed to have grown every day in the week since his trip to Reading.

"Oh, Lloyd, how could you do this to me?"

"I'm sorry, Annie. I've said I'm sorry. Won't you forgive me?"

"Forgive you? I forgive you. I've told you I forgive you. I don't want you to grovel."

"I'm just trying to help you believe me."

The anger returned to her face. "Believe you? How can I believe you? You never told me you were tempted. I didn't know you were weak.

Oh Lloyd! I never in a nightmare dreamt you could hit me. I'm scared every minute."

She paused, her face and body stiff. "This can't happen again."

"It won't Annie. I promise."

"Can you really promise that?"

"Yes … uh. No." He felt his emptiness. "I don't know what I'm capable of, for good or bad. I just know I need Jesus more than ever – and you too."

~ † ~

Annie and Lloyd walked hand in hand along the Ridgeway. Below them, the village was touched with autumn colors.

"We have to make sure this doesn't happen again."

"How?" Lloyd said.

"I've been thinking," she replied. "You need to come home for lunch instead of going to the pub. You need to meet with people at home or at the church. You need to tell me where you're going, and let me know when you get there." She compressed her lips for an instant before continuing. "You need to earn my trust."

Lord Jesus, Lloyd prayed, is this right? "Annie, my love … I want to earn your trust. I'll do anything you say. But I'm not sure rules alone will be enough. I think I've had a change of heart, but I can't be strong on my own."

"You have to be, Lloyd. How can you be the pastor of this church if you're weak? How can you be a model for our children if you're weak? How can you love me if you're weak?"

"I'll try, Annie. I am trying."

"I've got to get back to the children. I think you need to go and talk to Ned."

She put her hand in the middle of his back, pushed him as she turned away.

"I will, love." He spoke weakly to her departing back. "But don't you think you ought to talk to Rachel or someone?"

She whipped round to face him. "I think this is our problem!"

~ † ~

Ned spotted Lloyd coming up through the field of rotting wheat. He didn't know whether to blame the loss of the crop on the weather, the war, God, or himself. His nose told him that he'd have to turn the field under soon.

"How are you doing?" Lloyd asked.

"I hate all this." Ned pointed to the fields.

"I understand."

Anger flared. "Do you? Everyone sympathizes with my loss of income. I can survive that. I just hate seeing all this fail to be what it was supposed to be. I—"

He stopped. "How are you?" he said. Lloyd had already told him of the episode in Reading.

"I'm afraid I feel rather like a failed crop myself."

Ned and Lloyd had a favorite spot to sit: a bench someone had put up near the Thames. The setting sun cast the two men's long shadows across the quiet water.

"I don't know what to do, Ned. Annie wants me to live by a set of rules. And I have to do that for her. But I don't know if it's going to help."

"What will help?"

"I don't know. I do know I can't do this. I keep thinking of the verse that says 'my strength is made perfect in your weakness.'"

"Good one."

"Do you remember when we first believed? The middle of a war, the middle of hell, struggling with drink. But when we met Jesus … everything changed."

Ned picked up a stray stalk of wheat near his feet and sat back. He knew Lloyd knew the answers. After a while, he thought of something. "I read a sermon once."

"Yes,"

"It was called 'The expulsive power of a new affection.'"

"So?"

"You ought to look it up. Or don't. The title really says it all."

~ † ~

Annie sat in the old rocking chair in the children's room, Maggie in her arms, softly humming a hymn. Maggie was getting too big for a morning nap, but Annie was trying to hold on to it because the nap, when it happened, was often the only time she had to herself, her only time for Scripture and prayer.

She sang quietly, "Be still my soul, the Lord is on thy side. Bear patiently the cross of grief or pain."

Lord Jesus, am I? No, I'm not. Lord, I'm scared and angry.

Maggie was asleep. Annie laid her gently on her bed. "Sleep well, little hen." she whispered.

A few minutes later, there was a gentle knock at the door.

"Hello, Rachel. How are you?"

"I'm better than I deserve, but I'm concerned for my friend."

"Are there rumors going around? Gossip?"

"Not that I know of, Annie, but it didn't need an Oxford don to see that you were miserable in church Sunday."

"Oh, well … Shall I put the kettle on?"

"Yes, thank you."

When they were settled, Rachel asked, "So, what's going on?"

"I don't know if I should tell you. It's really between Lloyd and me."

"Something Lloyd hasn't told anyone?"

"No, he's told Ned."

"Well then."

"And he actually said that I needed to talk to you … but I'm not sure I can."

"You can."

Annie did.

"But I would never have guessed you struggled with anger," Rachel said.

"Oh I struggle," Annie said. An image, never long absent, came into her mind …

She was a little girl, maybe eight years old.

"Annie," her father said. "Run and get me my paper from the kitchen."

The shelf was high, but she saw the fold of the paper sticking out a few inches. She reached up and pulled. It was heavier than she thought.

Suddenly her father's favorite teacup tumbled over the edge. Panic burst like fire in her chest. She tried to catch the cup. Boiling heat poured over her, her hands, her arm. She didn't hear the cup and saucer smash, but saw the pieces fly. One shard cut her leg as it flew by her knee.

She sat heavily on the floor and screamed.

"What in heaven's name is going on?" her father yelled. He stormed into the room and towered over her. "You clumsy, stupid child, can't you do the simplest thing? I'll give you something to scream about."

He grabbed her by her burnt arm and sat in the kitchen chair. He spanked hard, harder with each stroke. Four. Five. Six. Finally, he stopped and propelled her across the room. She fell hard, impaling her hand on a fragment of the cup.

"Now you stand in that corner until your mother gets home."

She tried to get up, but couldn't.

He turned away with a snort, lifted the paper from the shards of china, and stomped into the sitting room.

Another image.

She was fourteen. She had been caught drinking beer and kissing an older boy behind the church. She was already screaming when her father dragged her into the house. "Leave me alone! I hate you! I hate you!"

"I'll teach you hate!" he said. He waved his Bible before her face. "God hates those who disobey his law. God hates drink. He hates little whores like you. You're a disgrace to this house." He shoved the Bible at her gut while simultaneously landing a roundhouse slap on the side of her face.

Annie crumpled.

Years later.

Writhing in Aunt Emily's loving arms. "I hate him!"

"I know, pet, I know. But your hatred and anger don't help, do they?" Tears coursed down her aunt's strong face. "Jesus is the only one who can bear this grief and carry this sorrow!"

"Jesus hates me too! Dad always told me that!"

"Jesus loves you! He suffered in your place – and He suffers with you. He says, 'Come to me you who are weak and burdened and I will give you rest. Take my yoke upon you and learn from me for I am gentle and lowly in heart and you will find rest for your soul.'"

"Thank you for coming, Dad" she said quietly. They stood outside Swindon Chapel. Her father had just greeted the young preacher, Mr. Robins. After years of healing, years of learning the grace of Jesus, Annie had finally felt strong enough to invite her father to Aunt Emily's church.

"You know, I remember why I can't stand these dissenting churches," her father said. "There's no order in the worship. No liturgy a man can count on. And that young man," he pointed at the door, "has got to learn to make his sermons about half as long."

She fought to control herself. "Dad, stop. Don't say those things."

"What things? What's wrong? I was just commenting on your service."

Her vision filled with a red mist. "Yes, which you despised just like you hate everything about me."

"Annie," he said, arms stiff, "You will not speak to me like that."

"You hate me!"

His hand flew out. She never could avoid those hands.

The garden behind the church. Pastor Robins awkwardly offering her a clean handkerchief. "Here, Miss Woodward. You need to wipe your face." Only a little blood came away with the tears.

"Has he gone?" she asked.

"No. I walked him away from the situation and talked to him. I've calmed him down."

"You calmed him down?"

The pastor looked away "Well, God did, I guess … He wants to apologize. And I think you should apologize to him."

She remembered Aunt Emily's words: "The question is not whether you can do what is right, but whether Jesus can do it through you."

Pastor Robins was offering her his hand. She took it and stood.

Rachel wrapped her arms even more tightly around the sobbing young woman. "Oh, dearie, I'm so sorry."

Annie dabbed her eyes. "I really didn't mean to say all that. I don't know where I'd have ended up without Aunt Emily. And Lloyd. And my father has softened. He even walked me down the aisle at our wedding."

"Well, praise God," Rachel said. She considered her words carefully "So you're angry now because you're afraid Lloyd is going to be violent if he drinks?"

Annie froze. Very softly she said, "I guess that's it."

"But he's never threatened you or hit you before?"

"No. Never. That's why I fell in love with him … because of his gentleness, because he knows God's grace."

"So now your only hope is to keep him from ever drinking again."

"Exactly!"

Rachel sighed. "Annie, you won't do it. If you try to keep him in too small a box, you'll either crush him or drive him away. He needs you to be on his side."

"But he's weak! I can't trust him!"

"No, I don't think you can," Rachel said. Annie's eyes widened. "It seems to me that the real question is not whether you can trust Lloyd, but whether you can trust God with him."

"What?"

"Lloyd is a sinful person, just like all of us. But God's faithfulness does not depend on Lloyd's trustworthiness."

"Trust God with him," Annie said.

She sat a long while.

Henry Padbury was standing on the sidewalk with Philip Clarke. He considered the angle of the sun, the time of year and the brief delay in today's train ride and said, "Well, I'd better get inside. The news will be on the Home Service at any minute."

"Ah, would you mind if I joined you?" Philip said. "I'd love to hear the latest on the Russian movements."

"Feel free, old chap."

As they entered the library, Henry was gratified to find that Mrs. Waverly had turned on the receiver before she'd left.

"Russian troops crossed the Polish frontier along its whole length early yesterday. The Poles state that they are resisting what they describe as this flagrant act of aggression ..." The announcer went on. Henry looked over at Philip, who was rubbing his cheekbone with two fingers.

"Well, that's finis Poland, then." Philip said.

Henry nodded. "The Jerries on their own were too much for them, but the Red Army is the largest in the world."

Philip sighed, "Well, I need to go home, Henry"

As the two reached the door, Philip placed his hand on Henry's arm. "Can I ask you to pray for us, Henry?"

Henry saw the trouble on his friend's brow. "Certainly."

"I'm about to have a difficult conversation. Ed is joining the RAF. He's eighteen. I won't stop him, but I asked him to come out this evening for a talk."

"How's he doing?"

"He's working in that wireless shop, and apparently he's quite good at the repairs. But he's running with a bad crowd. He seems to be drinking a lot. Holly says he's boasted about his friends dragging him home dead drunk."

"Do you think the RAF can straighten him out?"

"It could, Henry, but I don't know why it should."

He half turned at the bottom of the steps. "If you get a chance, can you ask Lloyd to pray for us?"

"I will," said Henry.

"Lloyd!" It was Henry Padbury, calling from behind him.

Lloyd turned and waited. He was on his way to see Arthur and Rosie Cripps. Rosie was feeling particularly unwell, and had asked for prayer. She was also upset about her nephew Stanley, who had come to live with them at the start of the war. When Lloyd had told Annie this simple plan, she had started to protest, but stopped herself, and nodded. She even gave him a sad smile. He wondered what it meant.

When Henry caught up with Lloyd he asked, "Can I buy you a pint? I need to talk for a minute."

Father God, give me wisdom. "Hello, Henry … let me run back to the house for a minute."

Annie was still in the kitchen. He took her shoulders and turned her to him gently. "My love," he said, "I love you more than life itself."

She turned her face away.

"But this is not going to work."

She looked up sharply.

"We need to talk. But right now, I am going to go to the Jackdaw with Henry Padbury, who has just asked for a minute of my time. I will have just one half. I'll tell him he needs to hold me accountable, and that he may need to talk to you."

She stiffened, looked up toward the ceiling, relaxed. "All right, Lloyd."

~ † ~

Henry was waiting on a bench that would have been in the sun on a nicer day. While they walked the short distance to the Jackdaw, Lloyd gave a brief explanation of what had happened in Reading. "I feel like I'm fine right now, but I need you – and others – to hold me accountable."

"I understand, Lloyd."

"And I'm sorry for my weakness. I wish I didn't have to do this."

"I said I understand."

They entered the pub. Henry shared the request for prayer for the Clarkes with Lloyd. "I asked Philip whether he thought the RAF might straighten Edwin out," Henry said. "What do you think?"

Lloyd sighed. "Well, obviously, for me the military was a mixture of discipline and temptation. I'm still struggling with what it drove me to

…" He lifted his barely sipped beer. "But God also used it to bring me to faith."

Henry paused to clean his glasses. "Well, I didn't say it to Philip, but I've seen far too many boys give in to the bottle at university."

"Can we stop now and pray for Philip and Marjorie, and Ed?" Lloyd asked.

Henry nodded. "And for you and Annie," he added.

"Lloyd?" Annie rolled over and snuggled up next to him. He responded sleepily "Um … yea?"

"It's almost time to wake up, but I was hoping we could talk."

He shook a little sleep from his brain and rolled toward her. She looked him in the eye, and then away toward the corner of the room. "I've been thinking a lot about this whole thing."

"Me too. I think …"

"You were …"

They always laughed when they both spoke at once.

"You go first, love." Lloyd said.

"Lloyd, I've been so angry, so hurt, so fearful. I love you so much and I never want to lose you." He had missed that compassion to the depths of his soul. "And I've been so ashamed of you. How could you do such a thing, to me, to the church, to our Lord? How could you raise your hand to me?"

"I know. I don't have any answer except weakness."

A tear slid down Annie's cheek. "Did I do something to make you weak?"

"No, dearest. The weakness is in me. It's mixed up with old horrors, and old pride – not wanting to let anyone down. It's too much of me, not enough of Him."

"And I've hurt you while you were struggling. I'm so sorry, Lloyd." Her tears were flowing freely now. "Will you forgive me?"

"Forgive you? Yes, if you want. But I never blamed you. I deserved much more than I got."

"Deserved? No. Not from me. I'm supposed to be here for you. And I'm praying I can trust God for that, every day of this awful war."

He held her close for a long time.

"It's not about rules, is it Lloyd?"

"I don't think so, Annie. Rules help, but it's really about grace, and trust—"

"Trust in God," she finished. "Rachel told me I needed to trust God with you. That's what I need to do."

"What we need to do," he said.

CHAPTER 4

26 March 1940

Lloyd swung open the door to the manse but didn't step in. "Annie?"

"Yes," she called from the kitchen.

"James and I are going for a walk."

"But it's so muddy. And it looks like rain."

"Spring at last," Lloyd said. "But James' leg is stiff. He's been cooped up for days." He joined the older man outside of the gate. Lloyd was grateful for this new friendship that had developed as the vet looked for properties in the Stokely area – with no success so far.

"Let's go out Millstone Road. The Thames is beautiful even on a dreary day."

Before they had gone far, they met Alan Ward coming the other way. "Good morning, James, Lloyd." he said. "I was just coming to see you."

"Nothing urgent, I hope. James and I were just stepping out for a walk."

Alan glanced at James' leg. "War wound doesn't keep you from walking?"

"It requires me to walk. Gets stiff if I don't."

Alan turned back to Lloyd. "I hope it's not urgent. I'm concerned that the offerings are down. If things keep on as they have the last two weeks, we could have to make some hard decisions before the summer."

Lloyd knew that meant a cut in his salary, the church's only significant expense. "Well, then, let's pray that two Sundays do not make a trend."

He changed the subject. "How are the boys doing?"

Alan's face softened for a moment. "We got a letter from Nelson this week. He's on a destroyer, the HMS *Keith*. Seems to be doing well."

"And Wellington?"

"Still lazing about. He's got that coward status he wanted, but they haven't assigned him to anything, so he's now a farm hand, living out with the Powells."

The disdain in Alan's voice was heartbreaking.

"Well, Ned really needs the help."

At that moment, a column of military lorries rumbled loudly down to the bridge. "One gets the feeling this won't be a phony war much longer," James said.

"There's a report that an agreement has been reached in Finland," Alan said.

"The Soviets apparently got as much as they wanted."

"The Finns made a remarkable show of it," Lloyd said. He turned to Alan. "Thank you for your concern. Let's pray for a while and see what happens."

Alan looked like he wanted to protest that idea, but nodded.

Lloyd and James walked in silence. The snowdrops along the verges of the road were mostly gone, but the celandine was in bloom, and bluebell shoots were abundant. The river below was a smooth dark reflection of the grey sky.

"Heard anything new about the war?" Lloyd asked.

"Nothing that hasn't been in the papers," James said.

Ahead they heard the noise of lorries, the sound of raised voices. They found men working at the entrance to the Chiltern estate, using an old road roller to flatten new pavement. The engine noise thrummed the air.

"What's being worked on here?" Lloyd yelled to the closest laborer.

"Macadam, guv'nor," the man replied.

"Yes, but for what?"

"Blessed if I know, guv'nor. Someone movin' into the old 'ouse, I 'spect"

James was smiling. "Here, let me try." He walked across the mud to the lorries, where a man in a suit was talking to the driver. "Excuse me my man, can you tell me who's moving in here?"

The man turned, dark eyes in a creased face. He regarded James for a moment, then said "Alexandra Orphanage, sir. They hope to bring the children as early as next week, though how it will ever be ready is more than I can tell."

"I thought the estate had gone to the Army," Lloyd said.

"Apparently they didn't need the buildings," James responded. "I wish they had thought to tell me."

"So you still haven't found anything?"

"We have our eye on Blount Manor."

"But it's not for sale."

"No, it's not," James said. "I have visited the acerbic Lady Blount on two occasions already. She is not, one might say, warm to the idea."

Lloyd laughed. "I imagine not … It would probably be perfect, though."

"It would be. Nearly eighty rooms. Eight or ten outbuildings. Huge stables. I haven't found anything within thirty miles that's even close. And … I now have the power to force the situation."

"What?"

"Well, yes. I've been trying to avoid it. But it's been months and the pressure is building. Bombing could start any time." James looked off in the distance.

"All right then," Lloyd said, "Spill the beans."

"Right." James brushed at his jacket. "I need you to help me persuade Lady Blount to sell."

Lloyd's heart sank. "I thought you said you could force her to sell."

"I can, but I prefer to buy the property with her agreement. I don't want to use the powers I have. I don't think it would suit her."

"No, probably not."

"Well, will you help me?"

"I'll pray about it, James."

~ † ~

Lloyd's feet dragged like lead as he walked with Annie up the hill to Blount Manor. James had called from London the day before. "I can't say exactly what's going on, but things are afoot that mean there's increased danger to London," he had said.

Lloyd let the big knocker drop three times. There was no immediate answer. He knocked again. Finally, Annie heard a door close in the house. "Someone's here, at least," she said.

Moments later, the door opened a fraction of an inch. Lady Blount looked out "Thomas? Vera? Are you back?"

"No, Lady Blount," Annie answered. "It's Annie and Lloyd Robins."

"Annie and Lloyd? … Oh, Reverend Robins …You'll have to go away. I'm not dressed."

It was two in the afternoon.

"Can we come back in an hour or so? We'd really like to talk." Annie said.

"About what?

"About … the manor."

The door opened a few inches more. "Again? I've given that rude man from London my answer."

"Yes, Lady Blount," Lloyd said. "But I don't believe he's made it clear how much authority he has. If you can't work something out, he can simply take it."

The door swung open. Lady Blount was in a flowered silk dressing gown. Annie had never seen her with her hair down. She looked fifteen years older, almost incompetent. An unpleasant smell flowed from the house. But her voice did not admit any weakness. "Take it. No! That can never happen. I must preserve this estate!"

"Well then, you'll have to talk to Mr. Grierson," Lloyd said.

"Why? He can't just take my property!"

"He can. The Emergency Powers Act gives him the right to do pretty much whatever he feels necessary."

"Over my dead body!"

Annie interrupted. "Lady Blount, I know it sounds awful, but it's true. We want you to talk to them so things work out the best for you, and for Blount Manor."

It took another ten minutes, standing in the doorway, before Lady Blount finally said, in an undefeated tone, "Now, Mr. Robins, I can't possibly see them this evening. I must get Vera to clean up this place. Oh, wait! Vera and Thomas are … out."

She looked around, a trace of confusion appearing on her lined face. "Not this evening, anyway. Would tomorrow evening be acceptable?"

"I'm sure it would."

"Lady Blount," Annie said gently, "would it help if I came out after tea tomorrow and helped you to get ready?"

"No! They'll be back." She half looked over her shoulder, then stood with her head down, and spoke quietly. "Or maybe not … In which case I must accept your gracious offer, Mrs. Robins. Thank you."

"I'll be glad to help, Lady Blount. I'll see you tomorrow."

"Lily!"

"Lizzie!"

Annie smiled as the two friends did their traditional hug and spin in the front garden of the manse. The garden was coming along. No roses yet, of course, but the leaves were opening on the apple tree, the grass would need mowing soon, and the geraniums were already thinking of flowering. It had dried out a bit in the last few days, so the children could play without getting muddy.

Annie set the plate of biscuits on the wrought-iron table and went to greet Evelyn and Phyllis at the gate. "Come in, ladies."

Evelyn carried a plate of cheese-and-cucumber sandwiches. "Thanks for helping me put this little party together so quickly," Annie said.

"Well, it's a blessing that Muriel is able to come out."

They heard a babble of children's voices.

"Here they are," Annie said. "Hello Billy, Nellie." The two children were towing their mum up the sidewalk. Muriel Timms was in her early thirties, pink-faced and dark-haired like her children. She was neatly dressed, as all the department store girls in London were required to be.

Meg Butler came in behind Muriel, pushing an ancient pram. Harry and Fred trailed behind, kicking stones up the sidewalk and bickering about who was winning. "Hello Annie," Meg said. "Thank you for inviting the barbarian horde."

Nellie let go of Muriel's hand and ran to the two older girls, who were playing with Lily's doll. But Billy held on tight, his gaze fixed on his mum.

Dot Simmonds came through the gate last, carrying a covered tray. "Scones," she said, "with dates!"

"Oh lovely," Annie said.

"I used the last from Christmas. Who knows if we'll get any this year?"

Annie looked up the walk "Did you bring the children?"

"No. From what you said they already had us outnumbered. I left them with Charlie."

The women served milk and milky tea to the children, and then sat with their own tea in the garden chairs. The warmth of the sun offset the slight chill in the air. Muriel seemed to fit right in with the three townswomen, though occasionally her Cockney accent would make one of them smile.

"So are you very lonely with the children gone?" Annie asked her.

"Oh, I miss 'em terribly, Mrs. … Annie. But I don't know how to bring them back. I've got Mum and Dad to take care of, plus the work.

And I'm not too well myself." Annie realized that Muriel had been coughing discreetly into a handkerchief since she arrived.

Muriel was unsurprised to find that the children had also been fighting spring colds. "Even a little chill an' Billy gets trouble in 'is lungs," Muriel said. "It eases 'im if you let him breathe mint steam. Takes after 'is father, I 'spect. It was the consumption that took 'im."

"I'm so sorry," Dot said. "How long has he been gone?"

"It's almost a year. It was April the ninth he died." Muriel wiped her eye with the back of her hand. "But he's with the good Lord now, and doesn't have the pain. And someday Billy and Nellie and me will get to be with him again."

Lloyd was sitting in the Jackdaw with James and Harold Mills. The half pint in front of him was barely touched. He had just described the conversation at Blount Manor. " … So, reluctantly, she agreed to meet you tomorrow night."

"Right," James said. "I have to run into town tonight to assist at an operation, but I can be back anytime you say."

"The 6:51, then. Harold and I will meet you at the train." Harold nodded.

At that moment, Ned Powell came up with a half pint in his big fist. "Do you gentlemen mind if I join you?"

"Not at all, Ned. Pull up a chair." Lloyd said.

As Ned settled in, he gave Lloyd a quick private glance. "First, I presume."

"First and only."

"Good." Ned nodded almost imperceptibly.

Ned spoke in a more public version of his always-quiet voice. "Carry on, gentlemen. Don't let me interrupt."

Lloyd spoke up, a little reluctantly. "We're going to see Lady Blount tomorrow night about selling the manor to the veterinary college."

"She won't sell," Ned said.

"No, probably not," Lloyd said, "James will offer her a lease."

"And if she won't?" Ned asked.

"If she refuses, we'll have to seize the manor," James said.

Ned choked, the glass held to his lips. "You're going to take her property against her will?"

James spoke quietly. "Only if she refuses. And not permanently."

"But it's her property. Been in her husband's family for generations."

It had been a while since Lloyd had heard Ned speak with such force.

James rubbed his bad leg, stuck out his jaw. "It's a national emergency, man. I know we're only a veterinary college, and the Army's gone mechanized, but we still depend on animals – for labor, for food, for friendship. We can't let our research be pounded to bits."

James had obviously given this heartfelt pitch before. "I won't argue with that," Ned argued. "I still use horses every day. But there must be properties that people want to sell. Why would you take away an old woman's inheritance?"

"Are you listening, man? She can lease it to us for the duration of the war. Doesn't have to sell it. Doesn't have to lose it."

"She won't do it." Ned said.

"She will," James shot back. "She has no choice."

Harold addressed Ned. "Why won't she? We know she needs the money."

"Did any of you know Lord Blount?" Ned asked. The rest shook their heads. "Blount loved that land more than life itself. Only one of the gentry I ever knew who poured himself into farming."

"But he's gone and she's done nothing with the land."

"Granted," Ned said. "But she loved that man deeply. You'd never know it from her hard shell, but it's true. He rescued her from … something … to marry her, and she was devoted to him."

"So you're saying she's keeping the manor to honor his memory?"

"Yes! Is there something wrong with that? Or any other reason? It's her property." Ned rounded on Lloyd "I can't believe you'd even be involved in this. It's no more than legalized thievery. Isn't there a commandment about that?"

"Ned, I don't want to take it from her. I—"

"So just leave the poor woman alone!"

There was a long silence. Both James and Lloyd started to respond, but thought better of it.

Ned set down his glass. "I appear to have finished my beer. Good day, gentlemen."

Rachel had set her grocery basket down and paused at the turning for the cottage. She chided herself for her breathlessness. "I will not give in to my age. It's just a little hill." And the view made up for it. She and her mother had bought Rosewood Cottage because it nestled up against the hill topped by Blount Manor. "Ninety percent of the view for one percent of the price," her mother had said.

Just as she was about to turn away, she saw Annie Robins starting up the road. She waited the few minutes it took the younger woman, not out of breath at all, it seemed, to reach her.

"Well hello," Annie said. "How are you this fine day?" She turned to look at the view. And she was breathing a little heavily, Rachel noted with satisfaction.

"I'm better than I have any right to be. And you? Did you come to see me?"

"No, I'm sorry. I'm on my way to the manor to help Lady Blount prepare for guests this evening."

"Help!" Rachel said. "I would have thought she already had plenty of help."

"Vera and Thomas seem to be missing," Annie said. "I don't know what's become of them. Lady Blount said that they were out."

"Out or missing?" Rachel said. "And who are her guests?"

Annie told her about the meeting with James Grierson.

"Annie, can I come and help?"

Annie raised an eyebrow. "I shouldn't let you … But I might need you. I smelled something in that house that I didn't like at all."

"Well, I'm immune to all smells." Rachel said. "Let me put my groceries inside the door and we can be off."

Together they climbed to the manor. Lady Blount answered quickly. Her hair was up, though imperfectly, and she was dressed in a dark, out-of-style dress that hung loosely on her large frame.

"Welcome, Mrs. Robins." She squinted in the bright afternoon light. "Oh, you're not alone."

"No, Lady Blount. It's Rachel Busby. I came to help Annie with whatever needed to be done."

"Mrs. Busby, I don't need … Oh, never mind!" she said. "Come in."

As Lady Blount closed the door, the odor Annie had mentioned twisted Rachel's nostrils. Rotten. *Something is rotten in the estate of* … She chuckled.

"I'm in great difficulty, Mrs. Robins," Lady Blount said. "I have never been ashamed of the fact that I haven't had to cook or clean." She raised her hands, pointing vaguely and waving them back and forth like leaves in a stiff breeze. "I am not unaware that with Vera and Thomas … out, I am managing these things badly. But I will not allow that to threaten Blount Manor. You must help me be ready to repel this attack."

She seemed to sag when this prepared speech was done.

"Where should we start?" said Annie.

"The most important thing is to find the source of that stench," Lady Blount said. She led them toward the back of the house. Rachel was relieved to find that she had at least noticed it.

The kitchen was a disaster. The mess wasn't just the sort that came when you cooked and didn't clean up; this looked like a whirlwind had gone through, opening drawers, sweeping shelves onto the floor, spreading flour and sugar and tea in heaps around the room. Some of the bricks had even been ripped from the fireplace and lay in a heap on the floor.

"Oh dear!" Annie said. "Did you do this looking for the source of the smell?"

"No … I've looked, of course. But it was like this after Vera and Thomas … went out."

"Why would they have done this? And what do you mean 'went out?'"

"They went out, just as they always do on a Thursday. It has been their day out for twenty-five years. Only … they haven't come back."

"Thursday? Last Thursday?"

"No. No it was … let me see …" Her hands stopped fluttering for a moment as she touched her fingers. "It was Thursday the twenty-second."

"Last month?"

"Yes."

"What have you been eating?"

Lady Blount waved her hands. "I found some cheese. And biscuits."

Rachel looked around and spotted a large old icebox. "Have you opened this?" she asked.

"No," said Lady Blount. "What is it?"

"Rachel, no!"

But Rachel had reached the icebox and pulled open both doors. The stench leapt out and hit her in the face like a blow. Blinking away tears, she saw that on the left side was a pool of blackened vegetables and the right crawled with maggoty meat.

"It's an icebox," she said.

Half an hour later, Rachel and Annie had buried the spoiled food in the back garden. Rachel hoped no foraging animals got a whiff. All the windows were open, and the late afternoon breeze was freshening the house.

"I wish we could have moved the icebox. I don't believe we'll ever get the stink out of it."

"When will the men arrive?" Rachel asked.

"In about an hour, I expect," Annie said.

"All right then." Rachel thought for a moment. "There's nothing edible here, but I just shopped, so I'll run down to the cottage and get tea and things. Annie, if you don't mind dusting and straightening the sitting room."

Annie nodded.

"And Lady Blount, you retire to your bath, change into a fresh dress, and try again to put up your hair. Put on some jewelry."

"Um … yes … I'll see what I can do."

"Do you need me to help?" Annie asked.

"Certainly not! It's just that … there is no jewelry."

"What do you mean?"

"Well it seems that when Vera left … she took all my jewelry. And Thomas took the little money I had left in the safe … and … everything."

"What? How much did they take?"

"All of it. About twenty pounds in notes, and a little more in silver."

"That's all?" Rachel asked. "Where is the money Lord Blount left you?"

"Humph … I'm not sure you have any right to know. But it wasn't very much. This house and the land were his legacy."

"But why haven't you called the police?" Annie asked.

"It's just that they have gone out before, for a few days. But they have always come back! And they have been here since Lord Blount's time. I don't think Cyril would have approved of getting the police involved in our affairs."

"What?" said Rachel. "Lady Blount, you really are too much! Tomorrow morning we'll report this."

The men were predictably late. Rachel had returned breathless from the cottage, brewed the tea, and set out a small cake. Annie had put the sitting room to rights and had gently insisted on redoing Lady Blount's hair. In doing so, she had discovered that there were almost no clean clothes. "Vera did all that," Lady Blount had explained.

The laundry room, Annie told Rachel, was almost as big a disaster as the kitchen. "But much better smelling – laundry powder everywhere."

The train had been late and James' leg had slowed them on the uphill walk from the station. He was winded when they reached Lady Blount's door. As he caught his breath, Lloyd asked what had made the college's move so urgent. "I'm afraid I can't say. But it has Whitehall in a bother. Some kind of escalation on the continent, no doubt, and a fear that bombing will start."

Lloyd was about to knock when the door opened. He half expected the lean form of the butler, Thomas. But it was Annie. Her smile was a bit artificial.

"Hello, Lloyd. James, Harold. Come in."

"Is everything all right here?" he asked.

"It is at the moment," Annie replied. "Come into the sitting room."

Before Lloyd and the others could sit, Lady Blount sailed in, looking very much her imperious self. She was followed by Rachel Busby.

"Annie allowed me to recruit myself to help," Rachel said.

There were six cups on the tray. "Lloyd," Annie said, "do you want Rachel and me to stay?"

"I guess that's for Lady Blount to decide," Lloyd said.

"They will stay, of course," Lady Blount said.

Lloyd was surprised to see the three women sit together on the sofa. The three men ranged themselves on the other side of the table.

"So what is all this about?" Lady Blount opened. "I have heard your offers twice before and I have told you clearly that I am not interested."

"Lady Blount," James said, almost with a bow, "I understand your position and the great attachment you have to this place. I would remind you, though, of the generosity of our offer."

"Tosh!" Lady Blount interposed.

"You could set yourself up in a lovely house, invest the rest, and live just as you always have," he continued.

"No!" she said. "I must not and will not sell the Blount heritage. All over England the great estates are falling, one by one. Lord Blount saw it coming. 'It must never happen here,' he said. I will not betray him."

"Well, that's settled then," James said, with a sad look on his face that told Lloyd this was just an expected preliminary. "Are you, Lady Blount, familiar with the Emergency Powers and Compensation Act which was passed last year?"

"Certainly not, Mr. Grierson. I do not make it my business to pay attention to the vulgar politics of the lower house."

"It's not the politics, but the war," replied James, "that will force me to make you relinquish this property."

"You mustn't."

"I have the authority to buy, lease, or simply move onto the property."

"No!"

"One of these things will happen in the next forty-eight hours. I have lorries lined up along Camden Street waiting for my telegram."

Lloyd studied the opponents. Lady Blount was stiff, her head erect, her eyes blazing. James was leaning forward, his face stern but not angry. It was clear that he was not enjoying this. To Lloyd's astonishment, Lady Blount looked away first. Staring at the ground, she asked, "What would be the income from such a lease?"

Harold spoke up. "It is generous, my lady. It is calculated based on similar leases in the area and includes compensation for lost production. The college will fund any modifications needed and repair any damages."

"Don't shilly-shally, young man," she said, still staring at a point on the floor. "You have calculated all that and you can make me your offer. Do so."

"Three hundred and ninety pounds per year, my lady, payable quarterly."

"Three hundred and ninety pounds? Why … why … a lawyer can make that much."

"Yes, my lady," Harold said. "But this is a competitive lease price and, as I said, generous compensation for the worked value of your land has been included."

Lloyd thought it was very generous. But, he reflected, he had never been privy to upper-class incomes. Lady Blount sat for a long time, holding one wavering hand over the other in her lap. Eventually she looked at Annie, who shrugged but then nodded. She looked at Rachel, who nodded firmly.

"I would get the estate back at the end of the lease?" Lady Blount said, turning to make eye contact with James.

"At the end of the war, yes," James said.

"And how would I live while you are despoiling Lord Blount's home, Mr. Grierson."

"We are prepared to leave you a spacious set of rooms in this building."

"And what of my possessions?"

"We will carefully store anything that does not go into your apartment."

"I'm sure. And how will the rest of my property be molested?"

"We'll use all the outbuildings for the larger animals. Horses and cattle. Goats and sheep. The classrooms, the labs, the surgery, and accommodation will be in the main building. We'll also do the smaller animal care in here."

Lady Blount bristled "You're telling me that my beautiful home will be used for dog kennels? For laboratories? For surgeries? For rabbits and rats?"

"I'm afraid so. We are a research college."

"And you expect me to live with all this? The noise? The noxious smells? The chemicals? The animal … defecation."

"We will of course keep the entire enterprise sanitary."

Lady Blount's hands had started to flap over her knees. She sat for what seemed an eternity. "No, Mr. Grierson."

"Excuse me?"

"The answer is no. You may rape my house if Parliament gives you the power. But I will not voluntarily sign anything that desecrates my husband's memory. I will not accept your money and I will not live here with that shame."

She stood. "The moment your lorry pulls through my gate I will walk off this land, and I will not return until the last whiff of your vileness has been erased."

To Lloyd's astonishment, both Annie and Rachel were quietly applauding. In truth, he felt a little like applauding himself.

Rachel was on the brink of tears when James Grierson and Harold Mills left. How could the man do this? He had told Lady Blount that the payments she refused to accept would be held for her, that she could take any of her possessions she cared to and the rest would be stored, but that the first lorry would arrive on Friday afternoon.

When Lady Blount came back into the room, traces of the tears she had not cried in front of the men lined her face. Rachel's heart went out to her and she took her hands gently, stilling the flapping. "What will you do?" she asked.

"I don't know." She sagged toward Rachel for a minute, and then pulled herself erect. "But I've done the right thing. The man is a thief, but I had no choice. Dogs. Rats. Chemicals. Blood. I could never live with it."

"I understand," Rachel said. "Do you have a relative you can go to?"

"No one. You know we were childless. A gaggle of distant cousins will inherit. None of them cares a royal hoot about me."

"What about your side of the family?'

"Gone. All gone. No one knows that story now."

Rachel turned. "Lloyd, Annie, we've got to find her ladyship a place to live."

"I've been racking my brains," Lloyd replied, "but I can't think of anywhere suitable."

"Nor I," Annie said. "It must be inexpensive, clean, and quiet, with someone willing to provide practical care."

"Now don't you trouble yourselves about me," Lady Blount said. "I will pack my things in one or two bags and totter off. I'm sure something will turn up."

"We need to pray about this," Rachel said. She had a great discontent in her soul that only prayer could touch.

The next morning Constable Elliot interviewed Lady Blount about every aspect of Thomas and Vera's behavior and wrote a detailed list of every item that she was sure had been stolen. Then he asked Annie and Rachel what they thought of the missing couple's characters.

"Slippery," Annie said.

"Slimy," Rachel said at the same moment. "At least Thomas was."

"Well, don't expect a quick result," the constable concluded. "The trail, as they say, is a bit cold."

Annie stayed with Rachel to help Lady Blount think through what she might take with her when she moved out. Together they tried to identify someone who might take in the evacuee.

"It's so simple with children. Why is it so hard with adults?" she said.

"Well," Rachel finally said, "I must confess that I have had an idea."

"What?" Annie turned and looked at her, but Rachel went over to where Lady Blount was sitting, sorting through a large pile of hats. Stiffly she got down on both knees so that she could look her directly in the eye.

"Lady Blount, I would like you to come and live with me."

CHAPTER 5

8 May 1940

Ned came in from the morning chores to find Lloyd in the kitchen talking to Alice. "Hello," he said. "Sorry it took me a so long this morning. I left the milk cows out last night and Flossie didn't want to come in. I'm getting too old to chase women." He flopped down at the table.

"I would say so," Alice said. She dropped generous plates of eggs, sausage, and toast in front of the two men.

"Smells wonderful," said Lloyd. "And so much! Thank you, Alice."

"It helps that we raise most of it ourselves," Alice said. Ned," she went on, "wash your hands before you eat."

"I washed before I milked," Ned teased. She gave him a wry smile.

He spoke to Lloyd from the sink. "If she had seen how we lived during the war she wouldn't be so concerned about the dirt under my fingernails."

"No, but I thank God we're here, clean and well fed, rather than there, hungry and filthy."

"Amen," Ned said.

"But I shouldn't eat much this morning." Lloyd said, "I'm having lunch with Harold Mills."

"Stealing someone else's property?"

Lloyd took a deep breath. "No … He feels he's missing something of the reality of the presence of God. He's seen it in others at Stokely Free since he moved here, but he says he doesn't know how to get it for himself."

Ned regretted his sharp words. "Sorry. What are you going to tell him?"

"I don't know," Lloyd said. "If there was a formula for closeness to God I'd give it to everyone. I'll just listen and pray, and remind him of some of the basics."

Ned was reminded of the heart for ministry that lay beneath Lloyd's casual words. "Listen," he said, "I'm sorry I've been angry with you and the others about Lady Blount's property. Will you forgive me?"

"It's all right. I forgive you," Lloyd said. "You would have been proud of the stand she took."

"But did it do her any good?"

"If the war doesn't outlast her, she'll get the manor back and she's getting a decent amount meantime."

Ned chewed silently for a while. Finally he said, "It's the principle of the thing. My family has had this farm about as long as the Blount's have had their land. But now the nation can decide that my land ought to be used as a training base or an aircraft runway or a … shipyard. And there's nothing I can do."

Lloyd nodded slowly, "I guess that's about the size of it."

~ † ~

Lloyd came out onto Millstone Road. The spring was in full bloom now, and he reveled in the sunny morning, the full stomach, and the peaceful heart. He knew it was because of Ned's apology. He walked briskly back to the church and dived in to preparing his message, but he didn't get very far: the Scriptures lured him along several nice rabbit trails of thought, which he indulged.

He was startled by a knock at the vestry door. Seeing Harold Mills, Lloyd fumbled for his watch. "Am I late?"

"No, not at all. But I ran into Meg Butler on my way to the pub. She would like you to call in to see her right away. They've had a telegram."

Promising to come to Harold's office after he saw Meg, Lloyd went across the bridge to the Butlers'. Along the way, he thought about what might be in the telegram. He wondered if Muriel Timms had changed her mind and was coming to take the children back to London.

Meg answered the door looking a bit tearful. "Thank you for coming, Rev'rend."

Lloyd walked through the sitting room noting the piles of clothing, some neatly pressed, which still filled the place. Billy and Nellie were sitting together on an overstuffed chair, clutching each other's hands. The three Butler children were on the couch. All looked somber.

Bert sat in his usual place at the kitchen table, holding the thin paper of a telegram. "Here it is, Rev'rend." He handed Lloyd the form.

"Muriel Timms stop pneumonia stop St Thomas stop Bring children soonest." It had been sent by Muriel's father.

Oh, Lord, no! This was not what Lloyd had prepared for. An image of Muriel joyfully singing at church during her visits from London filled his mind.

"It arrived this morning, Rev'rend. Bert said we needed to talk to you. Should I take the children and go?"

"I say she should. We'll be fine here."

Lloyd considered for a long moment. "I agree. The children have to have a chance to see their mum … just in case."

Meg began to weep. "Oh Rev'rend. God wouldn't take her from them, would he? Their dad's already gone."

Lloyd wished Annie were here to give the young woman a hug. He pulled out a fresh handkerchief. "A minister's kit must always include a fresh handkerchief, for one of his chief functions is to offer comfort." Doctor Carver's practical advice at Toronto Bible College had served Lloyd well over the years.

"She'll probably be fine, Meg. But we do need to get you and the children there. I'm sure Annie and some other ladies can bring in meals while you're gone … You can probably make the 2:36."

"Rev'rend Lloyd," Bert said. "I hate to ask, but could you go with her? Meg's not very familiar with the city."

"Well … I'd like to, but I've got a couple things that need to be taken care of. Let me pray about it, and if I don't think of someone else, I'll go."

Lloyd found Annie sitting on the bench in the front garden, watching Maggie play. He quickly filled her in on the situation.

"Oh Lloyd, how awful! Will you go up to town with Meg?"

"I probably can," he said. "But as I came up from the bridge I wondered whether I might be able to get James to meet them."

"Is he in London still? I thought he had moved into Blount Manor."

"The college has, but James is still going back and forth. I think he's there today."

"It can't hurt to phone him," Annie said. "I'll organize meals for Bert and the children … I wonder if we could have a prayer meeting?"

Lloyd smiled. "I was thinking the same thing."

"We could meet tonight, but it's a bit short notice. Do you think tomorrow would be too late?"

"No, I certainly hope not."

"I'll get the word around, then."

"Great, Annie. Thanks." He gave her a hug, loving the old truth that they were one. He let his gaze linger on little Maggie, playing happily. *Lord God, thank you for all the goodness you've shown to me. Why do some people have to suffer? Lord, I pray for Muriel. Please God heal her and let her see her children grow up.*

While Annie fixed him a quick lunch, Lloyd called James Grierson, who readily agreed to meet Meg. "What train will she be on?"

"I think we can make the 2:36." Lloyd grabbed a timetable from the little table near the phone. "That puts them in Paddington at … 3:51 … I'll call you if they're on a later train."

Lloyd hurried back to the Butlers. "If you can make the 2:36, James Grierson will meet you at Paddington and take you to the hospital."

"Oh, perfect," she said. "I was hoping something would work out."

Nellie was subdued on the walk to the station, but Billy danced like a kite at the end of Meg's arm. "He's too young to hold a sad thought," Meg said as she ruffled his hair. "Can you pray for us? My stomach is in knots with worrying."

"Lord, we pray that you will be caring for Muriel in hospital," Lloyd said, "and that you will protect Meg as she travels. Lord, I pray for Billy and Nellie: that you would be with them and comfort them."

As the train chugged in, Lloyd asked, "Do you have any money?"

"Not a lot, Rev'rend. I used our grocery money to pay for the tickets."

"Here, take this." Lloyd had raided the church box on the way out.

"Thank you, Rev'rend," Meg said. "I wish we could pay back all this generosity."

"No need to pay it back, Meg … But do use some of it to let me know how she's doing."

James looked up from his paperwork. Meg Butler would be arriving at Paddington in less than an hour. "Sam," he said to his assistant, "I've got to go out. Take this lot down to Farnworth and bring back this afternoon's post. I'm expecting the ration requests from Stokely and I don't want to have them hanging around here a minute longer than necessary."

"Yes, Sir James."

James slung his gas mask over his shoulder and emerged to the oddly cheerful sight of silver barrage balloons rising into the late afternoon sky. So far these had been little more than pretty baubles on the city skyline, but if the warnings proved true …

He arrived at Paddington early and picked up *The Times*. Many of the stories focused on the withdrawal of British troops from Norway, which the Germans were trumpeting as an unalloyed victory. James was inclined to agree.

One American commentator noted the extensive German propaganda, which claimed that "Britain, foiled in Norway, will now seek compensation by extending the war to other parts of Europe." The commentator said this was a way to prepare the German public for "a sudden thrust of their forces to the southeast." James was inclined to agree with him too.

James folded the paper as the train pulled in. It wasn't hard to pick out Meg as she stepped off the train, herding the two distracted children. "Meg," he called. She turned. "James Grierson. Lloyd asked me to meet you and help you get to the hospital."

"Oh, Mr. Grierson, thank you," Meg said. "I believe we need to find the Waterloo underground station."

"Bakerloo line, yes, to Waterloo." James replied. He took Nellie Timms' free hand, little and cold. "Down here … and down again there."

When they emerged on the deep platform, a train was just pulling out. "We'll have to wait a few minutes." Meg clutched Nellie against her side and patted Billy on the back.

"Reverend Robins has told me all about your mum," James said to Nellie, hoping to break the tension. "She sounds like a wonderful woman."

"Yes, sir," Nellie said. "How long, sir?"

"I believe that's the train pulling in now."

A short walk from Waterloo station, St. Thomas' Hospital loomed over them. As they entered, James asked the first person in medical garb where they might find a pneumonia patient.

Apparently there were several pneumonia wards, widely separated. After a frustrating amount of trial and error, they finally entered a large ward on the fourth floor.

"We're looking for a patient named Muriel Timms," James told the stiff, blank-faced war Sister at the desk.

"Muriel Timms." The woman consulted a chart. "She's here. Bed 6. Critically ill. Is she a relative?"

"Yes, these are her children."

"Are either of you related to her?"

"I'm not, but this is her sister-in-law."

"Sorry. Immediate family only; no children." She dismissed them with a turn of her head. Billy started to whimper.

"Madam," James said in a hardened tone, "these children are evacuees. Their father is dead. They have not seen their mother in months. She is, as you say, critically ill. They must be permitted to visit."

Fire flashed from the ward Sister's eyes, but he did not allow his own to waver.

"I cannot expose children or non-relatives to the risks of this ward," she said.

"Move her to a private room."

"On whose authority?"

"I will take responsibility."

"And who are you?" She studied him from under a furrowed brow.

"I am Sir James Grierson, principal of the Royal Veterinary College"— the Sister snorted—"and a member of the London City Council."

"Sir James?" Meg emphasized the first word.

James waved her away. "I will see this patient in a private room or I will have the Matron call Whitehall and ask about my authority." The nursing Sister broke eye contact.

"Highly irregular. No reason why this woman should have a private room."

James softened his voice. "Do it for her children, Sister."

~ † ~

James and the others watched from the hall as Muriel Timms, looking small on the trolley, was wheeled into a private room.

"Sir James?" Meg asked again.

"Yes. CBE, if you must know. For some work I did on anesthesia during and after the last war. Turned out to have wider usefulness."

"Member of the London City Council?"

"Technically I have resigned that position because of the move to Stokely, but yes."

"Does anyone in Stokely know all this?"

"It's public knowledge. Anyone who cared to find out could do so."

"We're ready, sir," the porter said.

"Praise God," Meg said. "Let's go and see your mum, children."

They went into the small room. Blackout curtains blanketed the window. Muriel Timms lay … breathing. All her strength seemed to be focused on raising her chest for the next rasping breath, which was followed by a pained cough and a weak groan.

Meg held two little hands tightly as they approached the bed. She had warned the children to speak softly.

"Mum," Nellie said. "Oh, Mum!"

James caught hold of Nellie's free hand as she reached out. "Please don't touch her Nellie. We're already defying the hospital's rules on contamination, and pneumonia bacteria are very real, though you can't see them."

The child glanced at him in incomprehension.

A few moments later Muriel turned her head and opened her sunken eyes. "Nellie" she mouthed voicelessly. "Billy."

"Mama, mama, mama, mama," Billy whined pitifully. He squirmed to go to her. Tears ran down Muriel's cheeks, but she did not reach for the boy.

After a few awkward minutes, Meg said "Well, children, you can see that mum is working hard to get better. We should only visit her for a little while at a time."

James was about to add some words of support when two aged Cockney voices cried out from the door, "Billy!" "Nellie!"

The children responded in unison, "Nanna! Grandpa!"

There followed a chaos of hugs and tears, introductions and explanations. The woman was tiny and round, her face red like Muriel's, her grey hair wrapped in the tightest of buns high on her head. The man was thin and stooped, his pants several sizes too large, belted almost under his armpits. Behind them stood an elderly man in a minister's collar. "I'm Reverend Hillsway," he said. "Minister at Moorfields Methodist."

They suddenly realized that the patient was being ignored. They found Muriel still laboring to breathe, her head turned toward them, her eyes shining.

"Per'aps I should stay and take care of 'er," Mildred said. "Some of you lot could take Alf for a walk or somefing. 'e don't 'old much with 'ospitals."

"Meg and Reverend Hillsway can sit out here with the children," James said. "Alf and I will go find the post office and send Lloyd a telegram."

Lloyd wiped the last of Annie's excellent bangers and mash off his plate with a slice of fresh bread. "Lovely meal," he said. "I nearly fainted this afternoon watching Harold Mills wolf down a whole shepherd's pie while we talked."

"How did that go?"

"Well. I think. I was able to explain some of the basic disciplines of the Christian life that draw us into God's presence – prayer, Bible study … It's amazing how much of my ministry comes directly out of those first few months with Pete Miller."

"Did you tell him about the prayer meeting?"

"I did. He thinks he'll be able to come."

There was a knock at the door, the telegram from James. It reported Muriel's serious condition, her 'racking breaths.' 'Pray,' it said.

He read the words to Annie, who was clearing up. "Let me get this bit of washing-up done and I'll come and sit with you."

At the sitting room window, Lloyd watched the last of the evening light fade in the garden. *Lord, be with Muriel's parents. I don't know them, but you do, and you know their needs. Let them be strong for their daughter in this.*

"Lloyd, could you help Lizzie with her maths for a few minutes?"

"I thought we were going to pray?"

"I'll be a few more minutes here."

Lloyd stepped back into the dining room where Lizzie sat with her exercise book. She was struggling to enter the world of division.

"Let me look at a couple of them with you," Lloyd said. *Lord, help Lizzie with these things, and be with Nellie right now. Sustain her as her mum struggles.*

Several minutes later Annie stood at the door, drying her hands on a towel.

"All right, then, I'm ready."

At that moment shouting broke out upstairs, where George and Maggie were supposed to be playing before bed.

"What's going on up there?" Lloyd called.

"Georgie broke my doll!"

"I did not. Her old doll is just falling apart."

Lloyd turned and looked at Annie. "I'll get it," he sighed. "Sit down for a minute and wait for me."

The doll was easily restored, and Lloyd gave George and Maggie a familiar few words about playing nicely. *Jesus, be with these two as they grow and help them to find strength in you for the hard things in life. Like kindness. And Lord, be with little Billy in London. Give him peace even as he watches his mum suffer.*

When Lloyd came downstairs, Annie was nowhere to be seen.

"She went outside, Dad. I think she's talking to someone."

Lloyd looked out the door and saw Annie with Susan Ward. Lizzie was chewing on the end of her pencil, obviously engrossed in her sums, so he walked back into the sitting room. *Lord, be with the Wards and help Susan and Alan as their sons struggle with their place in this war-torn world. Help Nelson and Wellington to grow close to you no matter where they find themselves.*

He heard the door open behind him and turned to see his wife's sweet shape framed against the evening light. *Thank you, Lord, for my Annie. Please keep her from the dangers of these days. And Lord, be with Muriel. Strengthen her, body, soul and spirit for the enduring of this illness. Raise her up, Jesus.*

"We'll need someone to watch the children tomorrow night," he said.

"Already covered," Annie said. "Phyllis Cooper and Violet Clarke."

"Great, thanks."

They sat next to each other on the little couch. "All right then, let's pray."

Lloyd received another telegram in the morning. Reverend Hillsway appeared to have an overdeveloped sense of economy: "Muriel same stop parents flat stop meg children hospital stop tired stop pray."

Annie helped him interpret. "I think Muriel is the same, her parents must have gone back to her flat. The others stayed at the hospital and they're tired."

"Well, I guess that's better than Meg and the children being admitted to the hospital."

"Or Muriel's parents having been run over by a road roller."

Annie cleared the table and encouraged Lloyd to go to the vestry and work. "When Norah comes," she said, "I'll take lunch up to Bert and the children. On the way back I'll visit a few people and tell them about the prayer meeting tonight: the Simmonds, the Chandlers, maybe even Helen Waters."

"Thank you," Lloyd said. He held Annie close for a moment, comforting and taking comfort.

Henry's telephone rang as he stepped into the house. It had been a fine walk, and he looked forward to a cool drink. Mrs. Waverly had been saving the last two lemons for his day off.

She picked up the receiver just before he reached it. He would have been happy with a little less efficiency.

"Stokely 341," she said.

"Yes, he's here. May I tell him who is calling?"

"Very good, Mrs. Robins. Just a moment."

"It's Annie Robins."

"Yes, I know," he said as he took the phone. Sometimes, Henry thought, these modern devices drained the brains out of people.

"Hello, Annie, what can I do for you?"

"Hello, Henry. I was wondering if you'd heard about the prayer meeting tonight. I tried to call last night but didn't catch you."

"No, I was late home yesterday. What are we meeting to pray about?" Henry drew in a breath as Annie gave him the details. *Father, help the doctors to have wisdom in caring for Mrs. Timms.*

"Well, I'll certainly be there. Is there anything I can do?"

"No, thank you—Oh, Lloyd did mention that he'd like to sing a hymn or two, so I expect he'll ask you to lead that."

"Right. Glad to."

Rachel had got a telephone call from Annie the previous afternoon. Now she was trying to persuade Lady Blount to go. The constant rumbling of lorries and equipment going up and down from Blount Manor was not helping.

"My nerves are too unsettled to see people this evening."

"*Au contraire*," Rachel chided. "It will do you good to get out and think of someone else's problems."

"But I'm not dressed."

Lady Blount was wearing an old flowered tea dress that must have been expensive when new. "You're fine as you are."

"Now Rachel, you know I've been opposed to this whole business from the beginning. I told Annie Robins I would have nothing to do with it. I'm sorry for the children, but they shouldn't have been here to start with."

"We're just praying."

"Well, go ahead then."

Rachel stifled the temptation to snap. *Lord, give me patience.* "Let's do it this way," she said. "I'll make us an early dinner and we'll see what you think after we've eaten."

Lady Blount smiled knowingly "I'm happy enough to have you wheedle me with your cooking, Mrs. Busby. The good Lord knows it's better than what Vera's been giving me all these years. But I'm still not going."

~ † ~

Ned yelled from the engine compartment. "Right ... Right ... Right, that should do it. Hold it there while I tighten it." *If I don't pass out first.* "Goodness, it stinks down here."

"Bwa?" called Arthur's voice.

"Nothing," Ned yelled louder.

"Stanley," he said, "pass me down a washer."

"This one?" Fourteen-year-old Stanley had been living with his Aunt Rosie and Uncle Arthur since the panic in London last fall.

"Yes. Now the five-eighths spanner."

"Which one is that?"

Ned stood out of the hold and stretched toward the wrench. "This one," he said. Stanley put it in Ned's hand.

"Arthur, back off just a fraction of an inch. Okay, now come back. No, toward me."

"I'm … bwa … gen … twin … kdo," came the muffled voice from the other compartment.

"Fine, just hold that."

After a while, Ned was able to come up. He wiped his face on his sleeve and looked up to see Arthur emerging from the other hatch. His bald forehead was the color of day-old sunburn.

"Whew. You look worse than I feel, old man."

"But I think we've got her." Arthur stood thinking for a moment, fussing and smoothing both sides of his mustache with his greasy hands. "Aye, I think we're good," he said. "Stanley, can you run to the shed and get the can of petrol?"

Stanley grunted and took off like a shot. "Nice kid," Ned observed.

"Yes. He's had a hard life," Arthur said. "He lost his mother years ago and his father is a lazy rogue. The boy hasn't heard from him in months, doesn't even know if he's dead or alive, still in London or off in New Zealand."

"New Zealand?" Ned asked.

"Apparently he always talked about moving to New Zealand. Stanley says he had some swindle working in London that went bad about the time the war started. His dad used the war as an excuse to ship Stanley out and disappear." Arthur twirled one of his mustaches around his finger. "Ah, but he's a Payne."

"Excuse me."

"My wife's maiden name." Arthur showed evident glee in rehearsing what must have been a very old joke. "I knew when I married her that she was a Payne. Her brother Archie is definitely a Payne. And Stanley is a bit of a Payne himself."

"How so?"

"Oh, his father dragged him through every dive in London and taught him language to make a sailor blush. He's got a temper on him. He's clueless about religion. Despite all that, he's somehow got a decent education, and he certainly works hard. I suspect that's a reaction to his father's laziness."

Stanley came back, lugging a five-gallon can. "This one?" he asked.

"Yes, thank you, Stanley … Let's see how she goes."

After a prolonged period of fussing, adjusting, false starts, and clouds of smoke, the engine seemed to be running smoothly.

"Righto! Let's take her out," Arthur called.

Ned shook his head. "Not me, Arthur. I learned during the last war that a farmer's stomach is not intended to go to sea."

"This is not the Channel, Mr. Powell," Arthur gestured at the smooth river.

"Still …" Ned said.

"How about you, Stanley?" Arthur said. "I could use a deck-hand, since this dyed-in-the-wool farmer is too queasy."

The eagerness on the boy's face made him look years younger. "Can I?"

Arthur and Stanley pulled away from the quay. The engine died. Ned was holding a line and hauled them back in. A while later they pulled away again. The engine died before they reached the main current. On the fourth try, the engine seemed to want to keep running. Stanley cast off the long line and Ned coiled it. He sat in the shade of a poplar, idly reading a soiled copy of *The Times*. Hitler's invasion of Holland and Norway seemed to be going too well. Soldiers falling from the air like rain, he thought. Glad we didn't have that in our war.

Half an hour later, the *Guinevere* reappeared, still under power. Ned applauded as they pulled alongside.

"Good work, Arthur. You've really done it."

"Well, the steering's a little off, but that's easily fixed. I took her out almost to full power above the town, and she held together. Course that's when the rudder stuck hard to starboard."

"It was great!" Stanley said. "Almost killed a whole flock of swans."

"Oh, I hope not, Stanley," Ned said. "This river belongs to them. We're just visitors. God made them to show us his beauty." That was awkward, he thought.

"Don't know anything about that." The boy's face darkened.

"I had to hit the rudder with a stick to free it," Arthur said. "It stuck again at about three-quarters power. I have some ideas, but for now, we've got to clean up. When did you say that prayer meeting was starting?"

"Seven o'clock," Ned said. "Which means I'd better get along. I've got a good deal of cleaning up to do before my Alice will let me step inside the house – let alone the church."

~ † ~

Lloyd was grateful to see quite a large group, fifty or so, gathering in the sanctuary of Stokely Free. "Alice, could you and Henry lead us in a hymn?"

"I'm sure we can," she answered. "Do you have something in mind?"

"No, sorry."

Alice picked up a hymnal and walked over to where Henry was standing, cleaning his glasses. A few moments later, she came back.

"Henry says he was thinking of *O God our Help*?"

"Perfect."

"Rev'rend Lloyd," a voice called from across the room, "do we need to keep little Tommy with us?"

"No, Helen. If you want to take him to the fellowship hall, Phyllis and Violet are going to care for the little ones there."

Lloyd went to the front. "Well," he said, 'it looks like most of us are here."

At that moment, Rachel came in with Lady Blount, followed closely by Arthur Cripps who had Rosie on his arm. The two pairs entered the same pew from either end and Lloyd smiled to see the aristocratic lady in her proper hat next to the lockkeeper's rough wife.

"We're here to pray for Muriel Timms," Lloyd said. "And for little Billy and Nellie, for her parents Alf and Mable Cotton, and for Meg and Bert Butler."

"Mildred," Annie said.

"I'm sorry. Yes, Mildred Cotton."

"Just before I came over here I got another telegram from James Grierson. He says that Muriel has had a quiet day, has been able to express her love to the children and her thankfulness to Meg for bringing them, but is still having real trouble breathing. And a lot of pain. It seems to be getting worse."

They sang the hymn and then began to pray, taking turns. Most of the people prayed the same things they had been praying all day, some in flowery old language, a few with something akin to despair, some with deep confidence in God's healing power. Henry Padbury prayed as Jesus had in the Garden of Gethsemane: "You know what we desire, O Lord, but thy will be done."

As Lloyd listened, he tried to echo each prayer in his own thoughts. Sometimes his mind wandered. He couldn't help but notice that Alan and Susan Ward were there without either of the boys. But at other times, he felt that he was truly conversing with a very present Savior.

As the congregation disbursed, Harold Mills caught hold of Lloyd's arm. "I don't know how this is all going to work out, Rev'rend, but whether Muriel lives or goes to be with Jesus, I truly sensed he was hearing our prayers tonight."

Early the next morning Lloyd received another telegram from James, who, apparently, did not go for economy of words. "Muriel struggled all night but became quite peaceful toward morning stop breathed her last labored breath 4:30 a.m. stop Meg and Muriel's parents are comforting the shocked children stop Billy asks 'but will she get better now?'"

Lloyd felt a huge pang of grief twist at his heart, a weight on the top of his stomach. Why Lord, should such lovely children lose both father and mother? Where will they go now? *Lord, let them sense your love even through this pain. Be with Meg as she cares for them.*

~ † ~

Nellie buried her head in her knees and sobbed. Meg would have liked to take the stiff young girl in her lap. She settled for wrapping her arms around her. *Lord Jesus, be with these little ones.*

Billy sobbed in his grandmother's arms. He had cried and screamed when the hospital staff had come to take Muriel's body.

James had gone with Alf and the Methodist minister to make the arrangements for Muriel's burial. Now they returned.

"How are they doing?" Reverend Hillsway asked.

"About as well as could be expected," Meg said.

James cleared his throat. "I'm afraid we're going to have to give back this room now. We can go back to Alf and Mildred's flat. The funeral will be tomorrow at Brookwood."

"Before we leave," Reverend Hillsway said, "can we pray?"

The group gathered in a huddle. Reverend Hillsway put a hand on each of the children. "Lord Jesus, we don't understand times like these, losses like these. We cry out to you now for help, comfort, and strength. We pray especially that you will be with Nellie and Billy, and do not embitter them against you, but let them cling to the one who loves them."

Meg's heart embraced the words even as distress clenched her insides in waves and squeezed tears from her eyes.

When they walked out into the bright midday sun, the newsboys were shouting on all the corners. "Hitler invades Netherlands and Belgium! Latest details from Europe. Chamberlain's response expected tonight."

CHAPTER 6

20 May 1940

As Lloyd walked into the sanctuary early on Sunday, he heard loud, elaborate whistling. Alan Ward, no doubt, and this morning's tune was 'A Mighty Fortress is our God.' Lloyd had never figured how the man could whistle polyphonically.

He found Alan in the vestry. "Good morning," Lloyd said. The whistling paused. "You're here early."

"Do you like to take a chance on not getting your job done, Pastor?"

Lloyd winced and wished Alan had kept whistling.

"We need to talk," Alan said.

Why did people always try to talk to him on Sunday morning before church? No one except Annie realized how hard he worked to focus on the words God had laid on his heart for the morning message.

"Go ahead."

Alan caught Lloyd's eye with his own narrow gaze. "Reverend, I've been hearing rumors that I find very disturbing."

"What rumors are those?"

"Well, I hope none of its true, Reverend, but it's about you."

Lloyd felt a sudden emptiness in his chest, a vacuum so strong his ribs wanted to collapse. He tried to take a deep breath. "Go on."

"Well, to put it bluntly, I've heard that you've got a problem with drink. In fact I've heard that when the war started you went on a blind."

"Well …"

"Now you know what I believe, Reverend. Drink is of the Devil. 'Wine is a mocker and strong drink is raging and whosoever is deceived thereby is not wise.' Paul says, 'do not be drunk with wine but be filled with the Spirit.'"

"How did you hear this rumor?"

"I have a friend who works at the station in Reading. He says he fished you out of some pub and poured you on a train."

Lloyd sighed "That's right."

"You don't deny it?"

"No, Alan. The start of the war brought back horrible memories of the last one, this ear was acting up, and that one time I tried to drown it all in drink."

Alan turned red in the face. "There you go again. You and everyone, always so high and mighty about what you did in the war, how horrible the war was, how you're scarred for life …"

"That's not what I—"

"Well, Reverend, I don't think being everyone's hero gives you any excuse to sin. Furthermore you've tried to cover this up."

"I've told Ned Powell. I've told Annie. I've told Henry."

"You didn't tell me."

"And what would you have done if I had?"

"Demanded your resignation. Which is what I'm going to do now."

"Alan …"

"Look Reverend, I've got communion to take care of here."

"So then we went out to Brookwood on that little death train, and held the service," Meg said. Annie stood in Meg's crowded sitting room, helping her catch up on her ironing.

"Doesn't the London Necropolis Company give you the creeps?"

"Though I admit, they did their job. Found a plot right near Tom's grave, and even put up a tent for the burial. It rained, of course." She paused. "Rev'rend Hillsway did a nice memorial."

"What will her parents do?"

"They have a little pension. Rev'rend Hillsway says the church will help."

"And how are the children?"

"Oh, Annie!" Meg said. "That's why I asked you to come. I don't know what to do with them. Nellie has always been quiet, I suppose … but now she will hardly say a word. 'Yes' and 'no' are all I can get out of her. I find her crying, but she's stiff as a board to me."

Lord, Jesus give me wisdom, Annie prayed. "Hmmm. After losing her mum I wonder if she's . . . not ready for closeness to anyone else. Is she eating?"

"Not much. She likes sweets, but we can't afford much."

"Well, thank you for this, then." Annie took a bite of the teacake.

"Gift from Alice Powell."

The noise level in the back of the house suddenly rose.

"Excuse me, Mrs. Butler." Violet Clarke appeared at the door, twisting one strand of her long dark hair around a finger, "It's Billy. I can't deal with this."

Annie followed Meg to the back bedroom where Maggie and George were standing on one bed, saying 'Ew … Ew." Nellie sat on the other bed. Fred and Harry stood against the back wall, stifling laughter. And Billy stood between the beds, sobbing. At his feet on the wooden floor was an expanding puddle.

"I'm sorry, Mrs. Butler. I asked him if he needed to go and he said no." The girl's voice seemed to have an edge of anger.

"It's all right," Meg said. "He's been doing this."

With Billy changed and the floor mopped, Annie and Meg sat back down to their cold tea. "He's been like this ever since she died. He says 'mama, mama' constantly, except when he's whining or weeping. And this …"

"I'm so sorry, Meg," Annie said. "Didn't he have the same problem when he first came?"

"He did. It took him almost till Christmas to get it under control."

"Well, I wonder if he's regressed? Maybe if you treat him more like a baby and less like a five year old he'll come out of it."

"Oh, I hope so. But I don't like hearing that. All I can do is wait. I want them to be comforted now."

"Whoa!" Ned yelled to Bluster, his second-best plow horse. He stepped back from the cultivator and wiped his face. Across the field, he could see Welly Ward driving Buster, the better plow horse.

Alice appeared at the end of the row with … water? No, that looked like lemonade again. *I don't know how she does it.*

"Welly, take a break," he called.

The two men walked to the end of the field and gratefully took the cold lemonade glasses.

"Almost done, Welly. Good work."

"I'm still not a big fan of that horse. I'd much rather work with a tractor."

"Can't use the tractor for this. The Americans have tractors that can cultivate row crops. But I couldn't afford one even if I could get it."

"Ah well, I'm glad to be able to give you the work for another couple of weeks. Given the news from France I expect I'll be assigned to something soon."

"What do you think you'll do?"

"I'm hoping for ambulance driver or medical work. Some of the CO's are getting ARP duty."

"If Hitler starts air raids those spots will be dangerous as being in France."

Welly took a deep breath. "Mr. Powell, whatever my father might say, I don't think I'm a coward. I just don't believe war solves anything."

Ned looked at the young man steadily. "Didn't say you were a coward. Just said France wasn't the only place in danger."

He emptied his glass. "Alice, you are the queen of farmer's wives."

"That's as may be," she said, "but I suspect I will be queen without lemons from here on."

"Well, then, I will endeavor to remember this moment forever." He met her eyes, and felt the comfort of their shared life.

"Okay, Welly, let's finish this. I will not lose this crop!"

Lloyd sat with Henry, Philip, and James Grierson, listening to Churchill's speech on the BBC. "Side by side, the British and French peoples have advanced to rescue not only Europe but mankind from the foulest and most soul-destroying tyranny which has ever darkened and stained the pages of history. Behind them –behind us – behind the Armies and Fleets of Britain and France – gather a group of shattered States and bludgeoned races: the Czechs, the Poles, the Norwegians, the Danes, the Dutch, the Belgians – upon all of whom the long night of barbarism will descend, unbroken even by a star of hope, unless we conquer, as conquer we must; as conquer we shall."

"The man is brilliant," James said. "Did you hear what he said to Parliament last week? 'I have nothing to offer but blood, toil, tears and sweat?'"

"And yet," Lloyd said, "we have all but lost in France."

Philip nodded. "He says we will stabilize the front, but there is no front, only masses of Jerries on the move behind their tanks. *Blitzkrieg*, the papers are calling it." He took a long swig of his beer.

"This morning Lord Gort mentioned the possibility of a fighting withdrawal of the BEF," Henry said.

Lloyd rubbed his ear. The buzzing was like a thousand honeybees, and every dismal word stirred the hive. He swirled the foam on the bottom of his glass. No use thinking about a second one. He tried to change the subject. "Philip, what do you hear from Ed?"

"Not much," Philip replied. "He's finished his training in radio repair. He apparently just squeaked by. He got picked up once for being drunk and disorderly, but he avoided a discharge because the Warrant Officer took a liking to him."

"Now is this your oldest son, Philip?" James asked.

"No, the oldest one is Lenny." Philip said. "He's graduated from university and works for the government in London. Some hush-hush science thing. Then comes Holly. She's married and living in Coventry. They have two little ones, our first grandchildren."

"Congratulations," James said. "Boys or girls?"

"Beautiful little girls." Philip smiled broadly, then sighed. "Ed's the third born, but he's our problem child. We're pretty sure he was already drinking here, but it got worse in London. We're hoping the RAF straightens him out." He looked around for the landlady. "Angela, bring us another round, please."

"No, I . . ." Lloyd stopped. After all, it was a drink in sympathy with his friend. And it might help this infernal ringing.

"How are things going with the college, James?" Philip was asking James.

"I would say we've had about every problem that could happen, but we've got most of them straightened out now. This morning we carried out our first operation on a horse in what was Lady Blount's drawing room. I showed the students the finer points of large-animal anesthesia, and Dr. Black repaired a herniated colon."

"Poor Lady Blount doesn't seem to like you much, James," Lloyd said. "Last Sunday she told me again how you stole not only her house but her money."

"I still don't understand where her money went," Henry said. "I knew Lord Blount for a long time and I could have sworn he was saving money for her."

"What makes you think so?" Philip said.

"I believe, old boy, that I have some mathematical skills," Henry said. His pomposity made everyone laugh. In a normal voice he said, "I've estimated his income over the years, from rent and such, and his spending. It seems to me he must have been salting away at least a hundred pounds annually, even in the bad years. I have no idea where it all went."

With sudden loathing, Lloyd stared at his half-empty glass. "Well," he said, "I'd better get on home."

Away from the noise of the pub, the noise in Lloyd's ear calmed to a dull roar. He took a moment to step out onto the bridge. The eddies downstream of the weir built and broke. *Oh, Holy Father, I confess that I went beyond the boundaries we put in place to keep me safe. Forgive me. Give me strength to confess to Ned, and Annie.*

He toyed with the idea of confessing only to Ned. Annie would be so disappointed. No! He'd made a commitment. As he turned, he saw Percy shuffling toward him. "Beautiful evenin', what, Rev'e Robins?" Percy said, doffing an imaginary top hat.

"Beautiful, Percy. How are you?"

"How does Hitler tie his shoes, Rev'e?"

" I don't know, Percy. How does Hitler tie his shoes?"

"With little Nazis!" Percy guffawed. "Little knotzis. Do you get it, Rev'e?"

Lloyd laughed at the man's good humor.

"I was wondering if you might have a little something for Percy, Rev'e. Just a wee coin or two?"

Lloyd still had the small change from the church box. "Here you go, Percy. Now I heard a rumor that you've been drinking what I give you."

"No, no, Rev'e. Percy doesn't drink anymore. Makes Percy see little Nazis. None of that Rev'e, only nice bangers and mash."

"Right then. Enjoy your dinner. Lord, be with Percy and provide for him."

"Amen, Rev'e. Amen."

~ † ~

"Excuse me, sir, is that boat seaworthy?"

Ned looked up from the hatch of the *Guinevere.* After a full day of fussing, Arthur had been unable to correct her steering problem. He had, he told Ned, rebuilt nearly the entire steering system at this point, but she still refused to return from starboard at speed. He had called Ned for help, but so far, Ned had not had any brilliant ideas.

"Excuse me?" The voice came again. Ned turned to see a young Royal Navy Warrant Officer on the quay. He looked no older than Stanley.

"Nearly seaworthy," Ned said.

"Are you the captain?"

Ned laughed. "No, sir. He's down there."

"Ned!" Arthur's voice called "I think I've got it. It's a little bit of interference where it comes through the bulkhead under torque."

At the back of the boat, Stanley was in the river with his legs wrapped around the rudder, simulating said torque.

"Righto, Stanley," Arthur called, poking his head up through the hatch. "You can come up now."

"'bout time. Cold down here as a witch's—"

"Stanley!"

"Oh! Yes, sir." The boy swam to a piling and pulled himself shivering onto the dock. Ned wrapped a blanket around him.

"And who are you, young sir?" said Arthur, finally noticing the officer.

"Wight, Royal Navy."

"What can I do for you?"

"Sir," the officer said, "I've been sent to look for large river craft capable of crossing the Channel. Is your boat capable of that?"

Ned was chilled by the request. There was only one reason for the RN to send a small boat across the Channel.

"Of course she is," Arthur said. He was smoothing both mustaches. "The *Guinevere* is capable of anything."

As long as it involves going in a circle, Ned thought.

"You'll have to man her yourself to get her down the Thames," said the officer. "You'll turn her over to the Royal Navy at Ramsgate."

"Turn her over? I can take her across myself."

"No sir, the RN is providing crew for the rescue … for these ships, sir." He offered Arthur a form. Ned watched with agitation as Arthur filled it out. "*Guinevere.* Forty feet. Three feet. Maximum passengers? Hmmm? I'd say twenty."

Ned felt compelled to interrupt. "Twenty? Arthur are you sure you want to do this – to put twenty lives at risk with a boat that hasn't even been tried."

Arthur stroked his mustaches. "She's been plying these waters for twenty-five years. I've just spruced her up. She's tried and true."

He turned back to the form. "Size of crew? Hmmm … two."

He signed the form and handed it to the Warrant Officer. "Now what?"

The young man looked it over, signed it at the bottom, and neatly tore off the bottom third. As he handed it back he said, "Thank you, Captain Cripps. They will expect you at Ramsgate at your earliest convenience. Tomorrow, if possible."

"We will be there." Arthur returned the officer's salute.

"Captain?" Ned said.

"The master of a vessel is always called captain."

"You were RN, though, weren't you?" Arthur nodded. "And were you Captain Cripps?" Ned asked.

"Always hated the way that sounded – Admiral would have been better."

~ † ~

Ned and Arthur got right to work, installing a heavily greased sleeve to guide the steering rod through the bulkhead. "This could still seize up," Ned said.

"Now that I understand the problem, I'll be able to release it."

"Could take too much time in hostile waters."

"What do you mean hostile? Ramsgate is just down the coast. Our coast. It's not like I'm going to be crossing the Channel." Ned was wise enough to hear the "unless" in Arthur's voice.

"No, it's not like that at all, is it? … You know," Ned said, "this feels an awful lot like the last war: good men going over the top. Most of them never came back."

"Uncle Admiral?" said Stanley, apparently awed into politeness by what he'd overheard. "Can I come?"

"It's Captain. No, it's just Uncle. And no, of course you can't come. You're only a boy."

"Uncle, I've been helping. I'm the one who went in the river for you. I can do it."

"No. I will not take you into danger."

Anger flared in the boys eyes. He credibly imitated his uncle. "What danger? Ramsgate is just down the coast. The Germans are all the way across the Channel."

He's got you there, Ned thought.

Stanley appeared to sense he had gained ground. His voice softened to a pleading whine. "I'll do good, Uncle Arthur. I promise."

Arthur rubbed both mustaches. "Your aunt would have to approve."

"She will."

"And only as far as Ramsgate. If we do anything after that we're sending you home."

"Thank you, Uncle. I'll work hard. I promise."

Ned shook his head, frustration mixed with admiration. The boy bounded off to use his winsome powers on Rosie.

"So who was 'we' in that sentence?" Ned asked Arthur.

"I have someone else in mind for my crew."

~ † ~

Wellington was cleaning up in the equipment building when Arthur and Ned walked in.

"Mr. Powell," Wellington said, pointing, "I finished that repair on the tractor. I knew you'd want to look before I started it up, so I've left the covers off. Mr. Cripps," he continued, wiping his hands on the greasy cloth and then shaking the almost equally greasy hand extended to him. "Good to see you, sir. How are you? How is Mrs. Cripps?"

"Hello, Welly," Arthur said. "I'm fine. Rosie's a bit under the weather. How are you?"

"Well, thank you. Learning to be a farmer."

"Glad to hear it, but I'm hoping to interrupt it. You remember when you crewed for me on *Evangeline* a few years back?"

Wellington had loved the river cruises they had run that summer. "Of course, sir."

"You were a good tar."

"Thank you, sir."

Arthur briefly described the plan to take *Guinevere* down to Ramsgate. "I want you to crew for me."

"But sir, I've only ever been on the river."

"You'll be fine. I know the knack when I see it. I spent enough years looking for it."

Welly asked the real question that had constricted his throat. "But wouldn't this be combat, sir?"

"Ned and I thought of that, Welly," Arthur said. "I know your position, and I respect it." He paused, smoothing his mustaches. "The *Guinevere* will, of course, be completely unarmed. But if we get the chance to cross the Channel, I intend to take her. The morality of that, a rescue mission, is for you to decide."

"How long do I have to think? And pray?"

"Not long, lad. Right now I only have my nephew, Stanley. I can probably get to Ramsgate with him, but if I'm asked to cross the Channel I'll have no one."

Ned spoke up. "Let Alice make the boy some dinner, Arthur. I'll send him down to tell you his answer as soon as he's been fed."

"Right, then. Back to the *Guinevere.*" He rubbed hands together in anticipation, then turned and left at a clip.

Alan Ward's accusation had one positive outcome: Lloyd lost all reluctance to keep the return of his struggle from Annie. "I don't want to make excuses, dearest one, but this ringing in my ears drives me nuts. I keep thinking just one more sip of the beer will drive it away."

"But Lloyd, it won't. It only leads to greater problems. It might lose us this ministry that we've worked so hard at all these years. It's going to bring dishonor on the name of Christ!" Her shame and anger were like a knife in his heart. His anger responded to hers, but his shame eclipsed it. He turned and walked to the front door. There he stopped.

Lord Jesus I need you and I need her.

He turned to go back, found her already there. They embraced, held each other for a long moment.

"No," he said, "I will not let shame rule me. Jesus has forgiven me, and I have to trust him to get us through this."

"Oh, Lloyd, me too. I'm sorry I'm so easily angered. Will you forgive me?"

"Forgive you? I beg forgiveness of you."

Wellington knocked softly on the door of his parent's house. His mother opened it. He rejoiced to see the sudden light his presence brought to her eyes.

"Oh gracious, it's Welly!" She looked about to faint.

Over her shoulder, Wellington saw his father stump into the room.

"Hello, Wellington. Have you come home, then?"

"Hello, Father. I can't come in." He saw the descent of his father's dark eyebrows, the set of his mouth. He took a step back, away from the threshold. "But I did want to tell you that I'll be away for a few days." He described the plans for the *Guinevere*. "We'll be leaving tonight." He lifted the small sea bag his father had given him that summer on the *Evangeline*.

"So you have changed your mind." His father's eyes shone with a hard gleam.

"No, Father." The gleam went out like a candle snuffed between two fingers. "I've thought and prayed, and Jesus seems to have given me freedom to do anything that is not actually combat. I know some will condemn me. But if taking the *Guinevere* to Ramsgate, or any act of mine, can save a life, I will do it."

"But you will not fight?"

"I will not kill."

"Be off with you then."

Wellington felt his heart empty and slump. He stooped to lift his bag. His mother enveloped him in a brief hug, her tears too copious for any word to escape.

He gently pushed her away, forced himself to straighten, turn, take a step.

"And Godspeed."

~ † ~

When Welly arrived at the *Guinevere* Arthur was below the deck making a last minute adjustment to the rudder pull. "Stanley, pass me down that grease gun one more time."

"Aye, Aye, Uncle Captain Cripps."

Arthur poked his head out of the hatch. "On this trip you can call me Captain, but not Captain Cripps, please."

Welly stopped at the rail. "Permission to come aboard, Captain."

"Granted. Thank you for coming. Stow your bag forward."

A few minutes later Ned appeared on the dock with an armful of blankets and a huge basket.

"Ah," said the captain, "the mess has arrived."

Ned brought the supplies aboard and helped Welly stow them. Then he said, "Arthur, can I pray for you?"

"Sure, Ned."

"Lord Jesus, please be with these men. Guide them safely to Ramsgate. Let them trust in you and find strength every mile. Let this old boat run well, let it do its job at Dunkirk. In Jesus' name, Amen."

"Dunkirk?" Stanley asked.

"That's where the BEF are embarking," Ned told him, "Thousands of them, every ship the RN can send."

Arthur nodded. "Right, Welly, here's the drill." He gave Wellington a thorough review of the engine and its controls as he started it up. "I wouldn't normally run at night, but we know the middle river so well, it won't be much risk. Probably only go as far as Henley, then sleep for a little bit. Start for London at dawn and we should be at Ramsgate tomorrow night."

He looked around. "That's it then. Shipshape. Let's be off. Bow line."

Welly ran forward and threw the line to Ned.

"Stern line."

Stanley threw his line onto the dock. Welly watched Ned coil the ropes as Arthur applied a little power to get them moving down the river.

~ † ~

Late the next morning James sat in the Jackdaw with Lloyd, waiting for Ned. He noticed that his friend was sipping a soft drink. "What's with this?" he said.

Lloyd smiled, maybe a little grimly. "I'll tell you after Ned gets here."

While they waited, Lloyd asked James if he had ever met Percy Wilkins.

"No, I don't believe so? Someone local?"

"Yes." Lloyd told Percy's story.

"Right," James said. "That's the third time you've mentioned how good he is with horses. Do you want the college to hire the man?"

"You're sharp, James. Yes that's what I'm leading up to."

"Well, I have a couple of people who specialize in equine care, but more on the medical side. They're complaining about being stable boys. They would appreciate the help."

"He'll work hard," Lloyd said. "But he has an awful sense of humor and not much upstairs."

"Right. Of course, I'd have to let him go if it doesn't work out."

They sipped their drinks. "You know," Lloyd said, "this stuff is really not very good."

"No. Fit only for Americans. I don't know why you're drinking it."

A few minutes later Ned showed up. As he sat down he said, "I can't stay long, I've just lost another farm hand."

James was amazed as Ned shared the story of Arthur Cripps and Welly Ward. He'd always had the impression Arthur was a hen-pecked old salt. "We should toast those two – cheers and Godspeed."

"And we should pray for them," Lloyd said. They took a moment to lift up the voyage of the *Guinevere.*

Ned stood to leave but Lloyd caught his arm. "Before you go, I need to get you caught up on this." He raised the glass of cola.

"Uh-oh."

Ned obviously understood Lloyd's implication.

"James," Lloyd said as Ned sat back down, "I need to tell you a story." He quickly outlined the temptation he was struggling with, his wife's fear not only of his drunkenness but of his anger, and their decision to trust Jesus but be accountable. "And that's why I wanted to see both of you this morning. James, I want to widen the circle of those who know and watch out for me. Ned, I need to tell you that as this European situation has heated up the ringing in my ear has come back, maybe worse. A couple of days ago I slipped over into a second glass."

"So the cola is punishment?" Ned said with humor in his voice.

Lloyd sipped at it. "Yes … It's to remind me that I have a struggle on my hands. If I could get used to this stuff I'd switch to it, but …"

Lloyd put the glass down and said, "But there's another issue …"

James was saddened by Alan Ward's attitude. "Do you think there are many in the church who will agree with him?"

"I really don't know, James. Not many, I hope, but there are some who have never been comfortable with any alcohol."

"What do you think, Ned?" James asked.

Ned paused for a moment. "I think having people who know, and a wife who cares, and a substantial victory leaves room for forgiveness when a man struggles."

"What will the church think?" Ned continued. "My guess is most will offer forgiveness and grace. Not all, maybe, but most."

Ned turned to Lloyd. "But if Alan goes ahead with this, it will be very hard on all of us, hard on the church body … I think I need to talk to Alan."

"Would you, Ned?" Lloyd said. "I'd be grateful."

Welly peered over the bow of the *Guinevere*, looking for the entrance to Ramsgate. The blackout certainly seemed effective, though the cloudy night and bit of fog probably helped. He saw a lighter shade of darkness a little to his right.

"Starboard. Fifteen degrees. That's good."

They had made good time until they reached London. An RN officer there was checking the credentials of the boats moving east. They were sent on in a group, which had become strung out as each ship made its own speed.

"Keep a good eye out," Arthur called. "If I was running this show I'd send a convoy across the Channel about now."

A few minutes later, he was proved right. Welly heard the destroyer before he saw it. "Hard starboard. Hug the shoreline."

The destroyer loomed huge, towering above the little ship. She was followed by a flotilla of smaller boats. "There they go," Arthur said. "Let's get her into the harbor and see what we find."

What they found seemed to be chaos. The docks and moorings were filled with little ships – ferries, fishing boats, yachts smaller than *Guinevere*. They had to nose their way in at the end of a long dock.

"Welly, see what you can find out. I'll hold her here."

Welly wasn't excited about jumping across the moving space between the boat and the dock. He saw a boat about their size backing out of a slip.

"Captain," he said, "could we pull in there?"

"Good eye," Arthur responded.

When the boat was tied off, Welly and Arthur left Stanley to watch her. They followed their ears to a warehouse near the center of the dockyard.

"We're trying to hand over a boat." Arthur said to a sailor in uniform.

"Over that way, sir. Table at the far end."

"*Guinevere*. Forty feet." The officer at the table inspected the form. "A little small for crossing. I'm reluctant to put men on a boat that will make so little difference. But leave her. We'll find someone eventually . . ."

He turned his head away, dismissing them.

"Wait a moment, Lieutenant. My name is Cripps. I'm a retired RN captain. I can take her across myself and get men off the beach."

Welly was unsurprised, but his stomach began to churn. "But sir, you said we'd only be delivering her."

"Hush, youngster. I told you we'll do whatever we can."

The officer sized Arthur up. Possibly it was the imperial mustache. "All right. You can talk to Captain Grimes. There at the end."

"Grimes," Cripps said. "I think I know the man."

Sure enough, when they approached the busy officer, Arthur said. "Grimey. I see you're not an admiral yet."

The man looked up "Captain Cripps! Why am I not surprised? Good to see you, sir." He shook hands heartily. Welly noticed that his right hand was missing the last two fingers. "Have they called you back in?"

"No, I'm too old. But I've got a little ship here, the *Guinevere*, and I'd like to take her across." He handed the officer the slip.

"Well, Williams is right. I don't have anyone I can spare at the moment for a vessel this size." The captain considered Arthur for a moment, then turned to look directly at Welly. "This young man capable, Captain?" he asked.

"Yes, sir."

"All right then." He reached under the table and held out two folded packages. "Fly one on each side. Join the 0400 flotilla."

"Thank you, Captain. One other thing. I have a third young crewmember, my nephew, who needs to wait for us here. He's only fourteen."

"Fourteen? What am I supposed to do with him?"

"Put him to work? He's got raw edges, but he can make himself useful."

Grimes looked distracted. "All right." He hastily scribbled a note. "Turn him over to the petty officer on the dock."

"Thank you, Captain."

"Thank you, Crippy. Be careful. It's a mess over there."

Arthur saluted.

~ † ~

Welly watched Stanley walk off with the petty officer. Stanley had protested angrily, as expected. "You're a bloody great tyrant, Uncle Arthur."

"I'm sorry, Stanley, but I'm not taking you. And watch your language."

The boy continued to rant as the sailor half dragged him away.

"That went well, I think," said Arthur. Welly prayed that God would take care of Stanley and reveal himself to him.

The briefing was brief. "You will cross in convoy. HMS *Sabre* will escort you. When you arrive, report to the embarkation officers on the beach, and follow their instructions. There are likely to be enemy aircraft and artillery, so use caution. We are also told that the soldiers on the beach are getting desperate, so be careful not to overload. That's all. You depart in an hour. Make ready."

Welly and the captain were quiet walking to the *Guinevere*. Welly wrestled with his own soul. Was he a CO because of conviction, as he believed? Was it to spite his father, as he sometimes thought? Or was he a coward, as his father claimed? That assertion loomed large. What if he failed the captain, the soldiers?

"Start her up, Welly, we're forming up."

Welly pushed the thoughts aside, but the weight of them was like a rock in his soul. *Lord Jesus, help me to live by faith. Give me strength … and courage.*

The *Guinevere* was small compared to most of the ships in this flotilla, but not the smallest. That record appeared to go to a little fishing boat named *Tamzine* who lined up near them. She was at most fifteen feet long.

They left the harbor before dawn, but soon the sky lightened. "Keep a sharp eye, Welly," the captain said. "We'll be as plain as ink in a few minutes."

Welly wondered what they could possibly do if an aircraft did spot them.

~ † ~

A few hours later he had ceased worrying about anything other than the rise and fall of the waves. In his time on *Evangeline*, the harshest weather had been a brief storm. Now the Channel breezes were blowing the engine exhaust into his face and creating waves the size of trains, coming from every direction, jolting his stomachache in one direction and his headache in the other.

"Just look out to the horizon, Welly. You'll be fine." The captain seemed maliciously happy at the wheel.

Suddenly a new noise was added to the pounding of the engine. Welly spun around; an unfortunate action, for his stomach spun in the other direction and bile rose in his throat. He saw the hatch over the fuel tank rise, and the top half of Stanley Payne who stood straight up and vomited toward the rail.

This sight was too much for Welly. He lunged to the rail and imitated the younger man violently.

"What in the world are you doing here?" the captain said.

"Uh throwing up." Stanley said.

"I see that. But how did you get aboard?"

"Gave the sailor the slip and hid here while you were gone."

"Why?"

"I want to help. I want to be involved."

"Some help you'll be!" Arthur looked over his shoulder. "Do I break formation and turn back?" he said.

"No, Uncle Arthur," Stanley said, straightening.

"Well, I'll at least let you help clean up. There are some rags in the engine compartment, and a bucket. Clean that deck. Welly, are you done?"

"I think so, sir." Welly felt remarkably improved.

"Get back in the bow. I think I see action ahead."

Before long Welly saw that the captain was right. There were ships on the horizon, smoke above them, yellow flashes, an occasional low thump like thunder.

"We're headed right into it."

Welly spotted dots in the sky. "Aircraft, Captain?"

The captain squinted. "Stuka. No bombs. They'll strafe."

Light winked from their destroyer. "Scatter. Make for beach," Captain Cripps interpreted. He eyed the aircraft. "Hard to port, boys. Hang on." He spun the wheel. The little ship canted violently as a wave caught her. They separated from the other little boats, and the captain turned her back in.

"Try to look small," he said. "Not worth their trouble."

It seemed to work. The dive-bombers avoided the destroyer and strafed the main convoy. Lines of bullets splashed in the sunlight, a few clearly hitting some of the small ships. But none of the aircraft turned their way.

Welly's heart was stuck in the foulness of his throat. He looked around for something to do. Stanley was on hands and knees, ineffectively wiping the vomit around the deck. Welly leaned over the rail and filled the bucket with salt water. "Stand up, Stanley, I'll rinse it." The young man clung to the structure of the cabin while Welly splashed the yellow slop off the deck.

"Look sharp, boys, beach ahead. I don't think we'll need to go ashore."

Welly saw a mass of men and equipment. It reminded him of a beehive he'd seen broken open as a boy. Then he was able to make out half a dozen, no, a dozen lines of men making their way out to small craft like the *Guinevere*. Many of the small boats were heading out to a larger ship, possibly a troop ship that could come no closer.

"Right. Go forward. Welly to port. Stanley to starboard. Help the men aboard. Count, loud, when you bring a man on. I've got to stop at twenty."

The captain chose his spot well, at the end of a snaking line of men that had just had its head cut off by the departure of a lifeboat. Hands reached up to Welly. He grasped an arm, slippery with sweat, water – and blood. He pulled, and the man came aboard, writhing on the deck, blood spurting from a jagged cut on his forearm.

"One."

Stanley yelled, "Two."

"Three."

It seemed only moments before they reached twenty. Welly turned to see almost that many more crawling over the railings on each side.

"Enough," Captain Cripps shouted. He backed up briefly, wiggling the ship to shake men off the rail, then brought the engine to full power and turned to port, toward the waiting troop ship. Welly felt tears of relief flowing down his cheeks. He turned to help the wounded, but saw that the other soldiers were already ripping apart pieces of their uniforms to help their brothers.

The troop ship was surrounded by little ships like bugs around a light. Every few moments one would pull away and another would dart in to take the dangerous place by the constantly shifting hull. Climbing nets hung down on both sides, and soon the *Guinevere* was discharging those of her passengers strong enough to climb up to the deck far above. Those too weak clung to the backs of burly ratings. *God, that must be exhausting.*

As they pulled away, a Stuka took a strafing run right along the length of the troop ship. Welly saw one of the men who had just reached the deck cartwheel off, a pinwheel of blood spurting red in the sunshine.

Guinevere and her crew repeated the performance twice in the next ninety minutes. The second time they unloaded the crammed decks onto a Dover ferry under a dense cloud of smoke.

"It's coming off a destroyer to starboard," the captain yelled. "She's in trouble. I'm going to go see if we can help."

They chugged along into oil-slicked waters. The destroyer was down hard at the stern and listing to port. Flames shot high above her stern. Sailors were lined up in life jackets, jumping into the water as it rose, and swimming hard to get away.

Welly was almost too numb to notice the markings on the side of the destroyer. He shook his head to clear it. D06 was the pennant number of the *Keith*, his brother Nelson's ship.

"Captain," he shouted. "Captain, Nelson's out here somewhere. We've got to find him."

"No use for it, Welly. We'll take as many as we can hold and trust these others to do the rest." A minesweeper and several tugs were circling the doomed destroyer, plucking life from the water.

Captain Cripps maneuvered the little boat to the head of a line of swimming men, and Stanley and Welly began the now familiar routine of pulling them aboard and counting. They were oil-soaked and exhausted and, with no bottom for them to push off, Welly had to lift every man aboard. When he heard Stanley yell a number, he took as many chances as possible to steal a glance at the man tumbled to the deck. Nelson was not among them.

Eighteen … Nineteen …Twenty. They had learned the wisdom of the captain's limit. The combination of maneuvers and swell had already set the *Guinevere* almost on her side. Only the captain's skillful response had kept her from capsizing.

"All right boys, I'm backing off. Let's go."

The thought of leaving his brother behind in this sea of death brought Welly to the edge of panic. "No, Captain! Wait."

"Stuka!" Captain Cripps yelled. "Hang on to something." He pushed the throttle to full and the engine responded with a smoky roar. He spun the wheel to starboard and she heeled over in response. He spun the wheel back.

And nothing happened. "Rudder's stuck," he yelled, pulling back the throttle to idle. He spun the wheel back and forth, but the boat continued to circle. "Stanley," he yelled. "We're sitting ducks. Go over the stern and free that rudder." He killed the engine. "Welly, go and get ready to restart her on my word."

Stanley ran to the back of the boat. He vaulted the rail and lowered himself into the water. Welly clambered over the greasy exhausted sailors to the engine hatch, yanked it open, and jumped down next to the engine. He connected the battery and held his hand over the starter switch.

Out of the corner of his eye, he caught a movement. A new line of sailors was making for the *Guinevere*. Beyond them, a Stuka was turning to line up on the wallowing craft.

"Stuka!" he yelled. He reached for the starter.

"Not yet, Welly," the captain cried. "Give Stanley a chance."

Time slowed. The dance of the moments took on a deadly graceful rhythm. In the water, Stanley struggled with the rudder. The Stuka grew slowly larger, its wings blinking as splashes marched toward the ship. The first of the men in the water reached for the boat's rail. But it was the sound of his own name that stirred him. "Welly, it's me, Nelson. Help!"

Welly focused on a familiar shape. His brother was close to the rail, supporting a man with no life jacket. Their eyes met.

"Now, Welly. Start her now." He jerked round to see Captain Cripps pulling Stanley over the stern.

It took all the discipline of an accused coward to stand by the starter and press while the engine slowly found life. The roar of the Stuka filled his ears. The line of splashes closed in. The boat surged forward. His brother screamed.

Welly leapt from the engine well and threw himself almost over the rail. "Nelson!" he cried. His brother's hand reached out. The two connected with the strength of childhood's grasp as the boat gained speed. An eternity later hands reached over the rail and gripped the two sailors. At that moment, a blow like a fiery hammer struck Welly. He pulled his brother in. Blackness engulfed him.

Lloyd stepped off the train and waited for Alan to follow. They had received a telegram from Nelson Ward, instructing them to go to Sutton Emergency Hospital in South London. This was the first they had heard of Welly since Arthur had returned, telling them he had loaded the brothers onto a ferry. The *Guinevere* had been pretty shot up. With Stanley bailing, Arthur had nursed her back to the British coast but had to abandon her in shallow water as far up a coastal canal as he could get.

Lloyd stopped a sister in a white uniform. "We're looking for a Ward."

"It's a hospital, Rev'rend. We've got twenty wards here." Lloyd had worn his clerical collar because it opened doors at times like this.

"No, not a ward of patients, a patient named Ward."

"Bloody likely that," said the woman. She had deep red circles around her eyes. "Did you ask the floor warden?" She pointed to a desk at the far end of the hall from the stairs.

"No, we only just arrived. Thank you, Miss."

They went to the end of the hall, only to find that there was no one named Ward on that floor. They went up one floor at a time, walking the length of the long hall to the warden, receiving the same answer, and walking back to the stairs. Alan began to limp, a lifelong effect of his childhood rickets.

"I suppose they could have designed it worse," Alan said. "They could have put the first-floor warden on the seventh floor, and so on."

The fifth-floor warden finally recognized the name. "Mr. Ward and his nice brother are in Ward 6, back by the stairs on the right," she said pleasantly.

They spotted Nelson immediately. He wore the starched blues of a petty officer. After Arthur's description of him covered in oil and blood applying pressure to his brother's leg, his appearance was a pleasant shock.

Wellington lay in the bed next to him. His leg was elevated and he was very pale. The wheezing of his breath could be heard across the room.

"Dad!" Nelson shouted in a whisper. He got up and padded in stocking feet between the two rows of patients. Some groaned as he passed. The smell of hospital and decay mingled in the air.

"He's asleep." Nelson gave his father a hard hug. "I'm so glad you came. I've been with him day and night, but I've used up all the RN's good will. I've got to be back in Portsmouth at once."

"How bad was his wound? How is he doing?"

"It was a clean shot; 7.9 mm bullet through the thigh. It missed the bone. Thank God, it wasn't the second Stuka. Almost sank us with its 20 mm cannon."

"But he's struggling," Nelson continued. "He had a high fever yesterday. It's gone back down, but he's not sounding good. Maybe pneumonia now. You can talk to the doctor this afternoon. That's really as much as I know. Now I've got to go."

"Nelson, can't you stay a little while? We haven't seen you in months."

"I can't, Dad." He grabbed a new, almost empty kit bag out of the corner of the room. "I've got a war to fight, remember?"

CHAPTER 7

30 July 1940

Ned and Alice were finishing dinner when there was a soft knock at the door. Wellington Ward stood there, looking thin but fit.

"Whoo hoo! Alice mine, come and see who's back … Come in, come in. How are you?"

"I'm doing pretty well, Mr. Powell. I've only got back today and I've been making the rounds … well, just to my parents and Captain Cripps and now you."

"Come in and sit down. Alice and I were about to have a little of her treacle tart. I'm sure I can tempt you – you look like you need to put on a couple of stone."

Wellington sat, with a relief evident to Ned's eyes. "A bit less than that, I think. But yes, the doctors told me to eat as much as I can. But most people don't have anything to spare."

Alice brought in the rich, fragrant tart and a pot of tea. "My mum always taught me to keep the pantry stocked. Except I can't keep hold of lemons."

"How long has it been since Dunkirk?" Ned asked Welly.

Welly's face clouded. "Two months on Thursday."

"Are you still in pain?"

"No, not physical pain. The wound was never that bad." He gestured toward his leg. "Passed through the thick part of my thigh, which was a lot thicker then. Most of my recovery was spent fighting off infection. I hope never to have a fever again. I was out of my mind a lot of the time, re-living those horrid few hours."

Ned saw pain in Wellington's face. "So will you be coming back to live with us here? We have plenty of room. Billy Parker, bless his befuddled soul, is the only hand I have at the moment, though Stanley Payne does come in to help."

"No, sir. My mother said I must, please, stay there, and my father relented."

"You haven't changed your views, then?"

"No, sir. After what I saw at Dunkirk my opposition to war is greater than ever. So is my commitment to save lives. Most of the CO's have already been assigned. They passed me over until I was well. But I reported in this afternoon, and they said I'll be assigned to a bomb disposal unit that begins training soon."

Ned tried to decide if the next question was necessary. "So, do you think you've recovered enough emotionally and spiritually to face that?"

"I believe so, Mr. Powell," Welly paused. "I asked Mr. Cripps much the same question, and he said he thought I had what it takes. 'Cool under fire,' he said. 'Terrified under fire,' I told him. 'Courage,' he said, 'is doing the right thing at the right time, even while terrified.'"

Ned mulled that over for a moment. "Old Arthur's got it in spades."

"You've got that right," Welly said, enthusiasm creeping into his voice. "Although, if I hadn't been there I wouldn't have believed it. Shame about the *Guinevere*, though."

"Well, Arthur says he can put her right if he can just get her back."

Alice served Welly a second helping of the tart.

The line was full of static. Annie raised her voice so Rachel could hear. "I said I was wondering if you could go down the hill and speak to

Evelyn Cooper for me. If it's too much trouble I can have Lloyd take care of it, but I hate to interrupt."

"Oh, no problem, love. What am I to tell her?"

"Just that Lily's not feeling well. I think she needs to go home, but I can't leave the other children to take her myself."

"Poor dear. Fever?"

"Yes. Not high, but she's also complaining of achiness and a little nausea."

"Right. I'll hop right down to Evelyn's."

"Thanks so much, Rachel."

Annie replaced the telephone and went to the bedroom. Lily and Lizzie had been playing with the dolls' house, but now Lizzie was doing all the playing and Lily sat on the floor, hugging her knees. But she was laughing at Lizzie's silly voices and making an occasional suggestion, so she couldn't be feeling too bad.

"Mama! Mama!" Maggie was awake. Maybe she should take everyone and walk up the hill to meet Evelyn. But before she could get them organized Evelyn came to the door.

"Rachel said Lily's sick."

"Maybe. She has a little fever and she's complaining of aches and pains. Could be the flu, though I wouldn't expect it this time of year. It may be nothing."

Evelyn felt Lily's forehead. "I hope so. She was sick all spring it seemed, but she's been right as nine pence this summer … She does seem warm."

"I have some aspirin."

"No, thanks. I have some, but I'd rather see how she does without it."

Lloyd was leaving for his study the next morning when the telephone rang; quite insistently, he thought. It was Rachel Busby.

"What can I do for you, Rachel?"

"Nothing for me. It's Lily Cooper, Lloyd. She's had fever and vomiting all night and she woke up this morning with a stiff neck. Evelyn and Ernest are on their way to the station, they're taking her to hospital in Reading. I think you ought to go with them." Lloyd prayed silently for a moment and agreed.

He found Ernest at the station, with Lily cradled in his arms. She was limp, feverish, and lethargic. The sixteen minutes to Reading West seemed like an eternity. When the train shifted Lily's head side to side, she moaned like someone whose pain has made them too weak to scream.

It was a little over a mile from the station back to Battle hospital. Lloyd hired a cab. Ernest and Evelyn crowded into the back seat, cradling the girl's body across their knees like a pieta. "C'mon little one, stay awake," Evelyn crooned. There was an edge of panic in her voice, wildness in her eyes.

They went through the main doors. "Emergency care," Lloyd called. "Can someone show us where to find emergency care?"

A soldier with an elaborately bandaged arm said, "This way."

He led them down a corridor and around a corner, to the casualty ward. The room was crowded with children, parents, and the elderly. Fortunately, a competent looking nurse took one look at Lily and said, "Come with me." She threaded them through the room and called for a porter and a trolley.

"Take her to room sixteen. I'll bring Dr. Brownley."

In the small dim room, Lily was transferred to a bed. The nurse and a young doctor entered. "I'll have to ask you to leave while I examine her."

Lloyd, Ernest, and Evelyn paced the hall. Not many minutes later, the doctor came out. "I need to know the history," he said. "When did she begin to feel bad?"

Evelyn wiped her eyes and straightened up. She answered the doctor's questions crisply but wilted a bit when he asked whether Lily seemed sensitive to light. "I don't know doctor. What does all this mean?"

The doctor looked at Evelyn and Ernest, then Lloyd. He raised an eyebrow, which Lloyd interpreted as asking if these parents could handle bad news. Lloyd nodded. "Spinal meningitis," the doctor said. "All the symptoms point that way."

Evelyn gasped. Lloyd remembered stories of the meningitis epidemics from the early 1900s – it had been fatal.

"We are preparing to do a tap to check for bacteria in her spinal fluid. We will also send Dr. Hill to London to requisition four vials of Flexner's anti-serum."

"What's that?" Evelyn asked. "Does it work?"

"In cases where the disease has not been active for long, the anti-serum is quite good, reducing the mortality rate to as little as thirty percent."

"Thirty percent." Evelyn suddenly looked like a lamb trapped in a cage with a wolf. She staggered and reached out for her husband's arm.

Grief flashed across the doctor's face. But he took a long whistling breath and resumed a professional tone. "Thirty percent at best."

"When can we see her?" These were the first words Ernest had spoken.

The doctor turned. "I'm sorry but she may be highly contagious. If it is meningitis, she will need to be isolated until we're sure the serum has been effective. And we won't know until the fever breaks if her mind has been affected."

Lloyd decided to push, depending on the special relationship between ministers and hospitals. "I'm her minister," he said. "May I go in and pray with her."

Suddenly the doctor seemed older, infinitely weary. He spoke softly. "You know the risks? You could catch this. You could pass it on."

"I'm willing."

"Yes, Reverend," he sighed. "I'll have the nurse fetch you when the tap is complete. You must wash with surgical solution before and after your visit."

Not long after the nurse came and took him back to a tiny isolation room. Poor Lily was curled up on the bed in a fetal position. "The lights," she murmured. "Mum, turn off the lights, they hurt."

Lloyd looked around. There were no lights on in the room, and the light from the hall was diffuse. "I'm sorry, Lily, your mum can't be here now. Maybe soon. It's Pastor Robins and I want … I want to pray for you."

"Play … lights … Oh." Lily convulsed and put both hands over her ears.

When Lloyd laid his hand on her shoulder, she seemed to relax. "Lord God, help this little one. Heal her. Raise her up …" When he had finished, Lloyd watched the little girl in silence for a few moments, then left quietly.

Ernest and Evelyn were sitting, tightly side by side, on a bench. They looked up expectantly. "She's resting," Lloyd said. "She asked for you, and I told her you would see her soon." He gestured upward. "She was definitely sensitive to light."

"Yes," Ernest said quietly, "The doctor seems quite certain it's meningitis. The anti-serum should arrive from London by late afternoon."

"Right." Lloyd sat thinking and praying for a minute. "I think we should try to gather the church to pray – tonight. Should I telephone Annie and have her get Ned and Henry to do it, or should I go back myself?"

"Oh, Rev'rend, it's good that you're here," said Evelyn.

Ernest said, "But we've already talked about this. We want you to gather the people and pray."

"Right," he said. "There's not another train until 1:15. Let me go and get the two of you something to eat, then I'll leave."

Moments later Lloyd blinked in the hot sunshine on Pangbourne Road. The tavern that had been the site of his disgrace was over a mile away, near the station. He went across the street to a pub called The King's Haven. He looked longingly at the Guinness behind the counter. When the barman turned to him, he said, "Could you possibly do me some food to take over to some people at the hospital? Oh, and a couple of bottles of lemonade."

"Lemonade's extra." The barman said.

Lloyd re-counted his coins. "Right. No problem." Soon a plate of bread, cheese, and salad came out. The tomatoes and cucumber looked fresh.

"Can I bring you back the plate?" Lloyd said.

The barman looked at him suspiciously. "If you do," he said.

"I promise."

Evelyn and Ernest had not moved. "Thank you, Lloyd," Ernest said. "I don't know if we'll be able to eat anything."

"Well, let's at least pray."

"Lord, Jesus," he began, "we come to you in complete dependence. Even as we give thanks for the provision of this food, we cry out for your provision of healing. We lift Lily to you and ask you to restore her. Strengthen Evelyn and Ernest for these hours of waiting."

When they had finished praying, Lloyd hugged both of Lily's parents and went back out to the sunny street.

Handing the plate to the barman, he looked again at the row of bottles.

"I'd like another of those lemonades to take away."

Annie sometimes felt her ears had a life of their own; listening, listening, for a need among the children, or, especially, for Lloyd to come home. At last, later than she would have liked, she heard the distinctive creaking of the gate.

"Hello, dearest," she said. He leaned in to kiss her, then backed away. Immediately fear gripped her by the throat. She hated this new habit of smelling his breath, but she could not break it.

"You might want to hear my story before you get too close to me."

She saw no guilt in his face, only gravity.

He told her of Lily's pitiful condition and of the diagnosis. "Tentative diagnosis, but the doctor is acting on it. Ernest and Evelyn would like us to gather as many people as we can to pray, tonight."

Annie nodded. "I can make a couple of telephone calls right away."

"The other thing you need to know is that I went in to see her. I didn't stay long, and I washed thoroughly. I didn't think it made much difference considering we all traveled down with her."

"No, probably not."

"But there's an outside chance I've picked it up. And I could pass it on."

"Well," she said, folding herself into his arms. "I'll take that chance."

Annie called all those with telephones: Alice, Rachel, the Simmonds, and Henry, though she could only reach Mrs. Waverly, who promised to tell the Clarkes. Rachel and Alice both agreed to spread the word to a few other families.

A few minutes later Lizzie burst through the door, pulling George by the hand. "Mum, I'm home," she yelled, "Is Lily okay?"

"How did you know Lily was sick?"

"She wasn't at school. The teacher said she was in hospital."

"She is. Let me get your father to explain it to you."

She fetched Lloyd and the three of them went to the sitting room. This scared Lizzie and she huddled close to her mother.

"It's called spinal meningitis," Lloyd told Lizzie. "It's an infection mostly in the fluid around her brain and backbone."

"I thought the backbone was a bone."

"Well, the way I understand it, our spines have many bones with pads between them, surrounded by a fluid. That fluid can get infected, like a cut does."

"It is very serious, Lizzie," Annie said. "Many of the children who get sick with this die."

"But Lily can't die." Lizzie's voice rose almost to a scream at the end.

"We don't know, Lizzie," Lloyd said. "She might … and she might not be the same even if she lives."

"What do you mean … not the same?" Lizzie's spoke between sobs.

"Her brain might not work the same. She might not be able to walk, or to talk, or even to recognize her mum or her dad – or you."

"No!" Lizzie grew angry. "She will always know me. She will always be my best friend."

"That's what we're praying for, Lizzie."

"Then that's what God will do."

"He doesn't always do things the way we ask."

"He will." Her face changed to a look of peaceful determination. "He will."

Annie was amazed how much like Lloyd she looked.

"We have to pray right now," Lizzie said.

Arthur saw Alice Powell heading up the path to the house. He flipped the 'self-service' sign down and followed her. Rosie was feeling the gout today and refused to leave her chair by the radio. She was convinced the invasion was going to start any moment.

He caught up with Alice at the door. "Hello, Alice. Good to see you. Come in." The little house was barely presentable.

Alice stepped inside and greeted Rosie. "How are you today?'

"Oh, it's the gout as usual, Alice, though if it wasn't it would be something else I'm sure. Everything's going to be worse after the invasion."

"Oh, I hope not, Rosie," Alice said.

"Now don't be playing Pollyanna, Alice. You don't think Hitler's going to let a little bit of sea stop him? I tell you the man is the antichrist, come to torment us."

"So what brings you by today, Alice," Arthur said.

"I'm just on the way into town, but Annie asked me to spread the word about a prayer time tonight at the church."

"Oh?"

"It's for Lily Cooper. She's in hospital in Reading. Spinal meningitis."

"No! Poor girl. Are they treating her?"

"They will. Starting this afternoon, according to Lloyd."

"I pray it's effective, Alice. I have a cousin who survived meningitis. Bright young man, before he took ill. Lost his sight, too. Very sad."

"Oh, that would be terrible. She's such a lovely girl."

All three were silent for a moment.

"Well," Alice said, "I'd better get along."

After Alice left, Arthur made Rosie comfortable. "I hope your pain will be less, so we can go to the prayer time tonight."

"Not likely, is it love?" Rosie said.

Annie always felt like she was flying three kites when she took the children out by herself, so now that Norah was volunteering out at the Alexandra Orphanage, even urgent visits like this were daunting and time consuming.

Lizzie and George ran ahead. Maggie tugged on Annie's hand.

"Hello! Hello!" the children chorused. Meg's two oldest, and Billy and Nellie gathered at the front door. "Mrs. Robins! Can Lizzie and George come and play in the field? We've got a fort."

Meg stood in the doorway. "Hello Annie. Good to see you. Can you stay a little?"

"Only for a few minutes, I'm afraid."

All the children groaned.

"But there's just time for you to go and see this fort," she said. "Maggie and I will come and get you when we're ready."

"Come in," Meg said, "and say hello to Bert. He gets so lonely cooped up here."

Annie stopped short as she came into the kitchen. "My goodness! Your chair has wheels," she said.

"Hello, Annie." He backed the chair away from the table, turned it on a sixpence, and propelled himself by pushing on the big back wheels. He held out his hand and she shook it.

"Well, that must make so many things easier! Did you do it yourself? Annie could see that the front and back wheels had been added to a simple chair.

"I did. I'm working on something even better."

"It's about time for tea," Meg said. "Will you stay?"

"Well, I can't stay long, but as the children are well occupied, I could manage a cup."

Annie enjoyed the brief, pleasant conversation with the couple. When she mentioned the prayer meeting, Bert said, "Oh, poor girl. I wish we could all come and pray, but I'm not that mobile. I'll stay with the kids and let Meg come."

"Oh, Bert," Meg said. "I wish we could all go."

Annie thought for a moment. "What if we asked Ned Powell to come by with his car? Could we help you in and out of the passenger seat?"

"Oh, that's no problem."

"If you could be ready at … um … around seven?" Annie said.

"We'll try. If Ned comes, we'll make it work."

Annie sipped her tea, then asked, "What else have you found to do with yourself, Bert, besides inventing chairs and caring for kids?"

"I help with the washing," he said. "I can't iron. But then, I couldn't iron before the accident."

"Wonderful."

"And I've been spending a lot of time studying the Word. After that episode last year, I decided I really needed to get close to God. I'm in

Ephesians at the moment. Fascinating stuff and great for my soul, as well as my marriage."

"Fantastic, Bert! You're making the most of this hardship, aren't you?"

"I don't know how I survived before this hardship."

~ † ~

"Violet!" The young girl wrenched her attention away from the old magazine.

"Yes, Mum," she called.

"Can I see you for a minute?"

"Yes, Mum." *Why does she always have to interrupt?* Violet hauled herself off the bed. She paused to look in the mirror. Dowdy old dress, she thought. The girls in uniforms were getting all the attention these days. *But at least black is my color.* She grabbed a lipstick and re-applied the bright red she liked best.

"Come down, Violet."

"Coming."

When she reached the bottom of the stairs, Mum explained. "I just talked to Mrs. Robins. Rev'rend Lloyd is asking us to come to a prayer time at the church. Little Lily Cooper has spinal meningitis, and today and tonight are critical."

"Lily! Poor baby. Is there a chance she'll …?"

"Yes, a good chance she won't make it."

"Oh! What will Phyllis do? You have no idea how much she loves her sister." *More than I love stodgy old Holly.* "Where is she?"

"She's in the hospital in Reading. Her parents are with her."

Violet had meant Phyllis. *Why couldn't Mum ever think things out?* "And is Phyllis with them?" she said. She knew a bit of exasperation had entered her voice.

Mum sighed. "No, Violet, she's with Rachel Busby. She'll be at the church. But so will some of the children – Ned and Lisa Simmonds, Billy and Nellie and the Butler children, and maybe others. Mrs. Robins was wondering if you could care for them."

"Will Phyllis be helping too?"

"No dear, she will be in the prayer meeting. It is her sister, after all."

"Well then I want to be in the prayer meeting too. She's my friend. I won't desert her in the biggest crisis of her life."

"No," her mum said. "I understand that." Clearly she didn't. *Doesn't she know that no one else who could comfort Phyllis in a time like this?*

"Well dear," Mum said, "We'll see. Maybe someone else will be willing to look after the children."

We'll see, thought Violet, means I have to whether I want to or not.

~ † ~

Lloyd was just about done with dinner when Ernest Cooper called from the hospital. "Ernest, good to hear from you. We were about to go over to the church to pray."

"Good. Evelyn wanted me to keep you up to date, though there is not much to report."

"Go ahead."

"Evelyn finally persuaded them to let us in to see Lily. But we weren't allowed to touch her." His voice cracked and he caught his breath.

"I'm sorry, Ernest, that must have been hard."

"Especially for her mother. But Lily seems quieter. She moans terribly when they touch her or turn her. She hasn't woke up at all, far as we can tell, and her fever is high. But the big thing is that they've started her on the anti-serum and they say the next twelve hours are crucial. If she doesn't begin to turn around …"

"I understand, Ernest."

Ned pushed back from the table. "Well, let's see if the old Morris will start."

"I'm sure it will be fine, dear."

"Billy, Stanley, do you want to come to church? We're going to be praying for little Lily Cooper," Ned asked.

Ned watched Billy blush at the thought of being among so many people. He shook his head. "N … N … No, sir!"

"Stanley?"

"I don't know. Dad didn't believe all that church stuff. Still …"

Looking at Stanley's face, Ned could almost see the fires of Dunkirk.

"I'm thinking that what you saw in France has made you question things."

Stanley started. "I guess so, Mr. Powell. You can't imagine what it was like."

"Thank the Lord I can't," Ned said. "I've got enough images of my own from the last war."

"But didn't all that lead you to God?"

"Not directly, Stanley. It was a recognition of my own sin and how helpless I was to do anything about it that led me to Jesus."

Stanley seemed to look deep inside himself. "Yes, sir. I think I'll come. See what it's like to pray. What's Lily got?"

"Spinal meningitis."

"Blimey!"

They cleared the table and went out to the equipment shed. The old Morris was a bit dusty. *When was the last time I drove the old girl?*

Ned got behind the wheel. "Lord, let this work," he prayed.

Krrmpph … krrmpph … krrmmmpph … krrrrrrr.

"And we'll adjust the choke …"

Krrmpph … krrmpph … krr … phmmp phmmp phmmp phmmp.

"That's got it."

As Ned parked at the Butlers', a gaggle of children burst from the gate.

"A car! A car! We get to drive in a car!"

"Not all of you," he said. "Stanley, Meg, Alice, I think you'll have to walk across the bridge. I'll take Bert and as many children as I can fit in the back."

Ned helped Bert swing into the car. Fred, Harry, Nellie and Billy filled the back seat. Meg decided it was safer to carry Emma than to entrust her to the boys.

James piloted his Daimler out of the too-narrow gate of Blount Manor and turned onto the too-narrow lane to Rachel Busby's Rosewood Cottage. He wondered how the next few minutes would go. This would be the first direct encounter he'd had with Lady Blount. Rachel Busby had sounded reluctant to ask him to give Lady Blount a ride, but could think of no alternative.

He walked through the thriving cottage garden to the door of the little house. It opened before he knocked.

"Good evening, Mr. Grierson." Rachel said. "Come in. We're almost ready."

She left him standing by the door as she disappeared into the back of the cottage. James heard her tell Lady Blount that it was a perfect hat. Phyllis Cooper came to the door, twisting and smoothing a damp handkerchief in pale hands.

"I'm so sorry to hear about your sister," James said. "I've been praying all day for her and your family. Have you heard anything from them?"

The young girl nodded. James waited for her to continue, but she focused on the handkerchief. He tried to speak gently "Did they have any news on her condition?"

Suddenly the girl spoke in a rush. "They said she hasn't woke up at all and her fever is higher and they've only just started the medication and Mum got to see her and no I couldn't come down there because they would never let me in and anyway they didn't want to expose me to the stupid bloody germs and I'll never see her again." Great sobs took her and stopped the flow of words. She jammed the handkerchief into her eyes and turned away, her forehead against the wall.

That went well, James thought. He touched the girl's shoulder and prayed aloud. "Lord Jesus, please be with Phyllis and comfort her in this difficult time. Lord, we do pray that you would heal Lily and keep her from any harm or damage. And that you would strengthen Phyllis and her parents and give them peace."

As he said, "Amen," the women came into the hall.

"Very nice, Sir James," Lady Blount said. "It's nice to know that even a rapacious land-grabber can pray under the right circumstances." He couldn't tell if she was being sarcastic or sincere.

"Thank you, Lady Blount. You look nice this evening." The traces of confusion and hunger that had marred her face at their last meeting had gone.

She nodded as if accepting the compliment at first, then appeared to change her mind. "You have no place speaking to me that way. I'm only accepting a lift from you because I no longer have a chauffeur."

"Yes, Lady Blount," James said, tipping an imaginary hat.

Lloyd went across to the sanctuary right after dinner. Alan was already there, turning up the lights. Lloyd had opened all the windows earlier and a bit of a breeze had made the temperature tolerable.

"Good evening, Pastor."

"Good evening, Alan. Thank you for coming. Have you heard anything from Nelson?" Lloyd carefully chose what he hoped was a safe subject.

"He's in Portsmouth, waiting to be re-assigned. The Navy has more than enough sailors for the ship it's got. That will all change if the Americans give Churchill his destroyers. Wellington leaves next week for bomb disposal training …" Alan paused. "A coward wouldn't volunteer for that, would he? I just don't understand that boy."

"Alan, I think you have every reason to be proud of both boys."

Lloyd turned to see Ned and Stanley rolling Bert Butler through the main door.

"I heard about that chair," Lloyd said. "It's fantastic."

As Bert was maneuvering to the end of a row, Alice and Meg came in. Alice immediately asked Lloyd if he wanted a hymn.

"*It is Well with My Soul.*"

"Good choice. I'll find Henry and let him know."

Phyllis came in a moment later. Lloyd moved toward her, but Annie spotted her first and embraced the weeping girl. Rachel, coming in behind her, shook her head sorrowfully at Lloyd. "She's really struggling," she mouthed, before turning to help Lady Blount find a seat by the aisle. James, a few paces behind, joined them.

Ned walked in behind Arthur and Rosie, with the famous stowaway, Stanley Payne. *First time in church.* Lloyd went and greeted Rosie warmly.

"Drop the mush, Rev'rend and find me a place to sit my aching bahookie."

Lloyd almost laughed. "Right over here Rosie."

Lloyd found that Ned, Arthur, and Stanley had been joined by Welly Ward. "Well, here are our three heroes," he said.

"And as proper a mutual admiration society as has ever been formed," Ned said. "Each thinks the other is the true hero."

"Nice to see you, Stanley," Lloyd said. "Glad you came."

"Uh … yeah … I mean, no." The boy looked uncomfortable.

"No, I will not do it." Violet Clarke's raised voice caught Lloyd's attention. She was clinging to Phyllis.

"Look, she's been crying her eyes out. She needs me to stay with her."

"I know, Violet," Marjorie Clarke said, "but the children need someone to care for them."

"I can do it if I need to, Lloyd." Annie said quietly at his elbow.

"No one has asked what I want," Phyllis said. She was pushing Violet away.

"No, dear, I'm sorry, we haven't," said Marjorie.

"Well, first, I want to be in Reading. But if I can't, I want to care for the children. I'll die if I stay here and listen to all these prayers."

"I think I understand, dear." Marjorie said. She turned to Lloyd and Annie. "Would that be all right?'

"I think so," Annie said. "But not alone."

"Violet?" said Marjorie Clarke. The girl looked ready to refuse. It was clear she was not happy with Phyllis for making no pretense of depending on her.

"If that's what Phyllis wants, I guess I'll go."

"Good girl," Marjorie Clarke said. Violet shot her a look that should have drawn blood, but Marjorie appeared not to notice.

"Mum, can I stay?" Lizzie asked from Annie's elbow.

Annie looked at Lloyd, who nodded. "Yes, Lizzie," she said. "Sit with your dad and me."

~ † ~

Lloyd called the crowded room to order. "Ernest says the next twelve hours are crucial. After we sing the hymn, we'll pray. Feel free to pray silently or aloud."

When peace like a river attendeth my way.
When sorrows like sea billows roll.
Whatever my lot, thou has taught me to say,
It is well with my soul.

"Lord, we ask you to be with us tonight and hear our prayers. But more than that, be with Lily, Ernest, and Evelyn. Comfort and strengthen them. And Phyllis."

"Holy God," prayed Arthur, "we know that each of our lives is in your hands. We know that you love Lily. We pray that you will restore her and give her back to the love of her parents."

"Jesus," Lizzie prayed. "Please heal Lily. Don't let her die. And don't let her be … different."

Tears formed in Lloyd's eyes. *Childlike faith. Lord, I don't feel it. Do you really answer prayer? Are you really here with us? Why are we going through all this?*

"Amen, Lord," Annie prayed. "We ask that you not only heal Lily, but that you keep her from any of the damage that can happen with this awful disease."

"Lord Jesus, you have been with us so many times as we've prayed. You have not always answered in the ways we want," Rachel said. "But we pray that out of love for our church and for this sweet family, you would heal this time."

"Jesus, please help this little girl," Dot prayed, "and raise her up to follow you, knowing that she is a miracle."

"God in Heaven," Alan prayed, "please heal Lily. And if there is any sin she has done to bring this on …" A soft protest stirred the room. "Let her confess it and receive forgiveness and healing."

Henry prayed. "Jesus, Son of God, we know that you are the High Priest who stands before God on our behalf. We pray that you will bring these cries and pleas to your Father's throne and allow him to act, not on our behalf, but yours."

Philip Clarke prayed, "Raise up this dear daughter to her parents."

Others prayed. There were times of silence. Lloyd sensed tears. As the praying wound down, he said, "Lord Jesus we lift all these prayers to you. You taught us to pray 'your will be done.' So we close tonight by saying as you said, 'Lord, if this cup can be taken from Lily, please remove it. But your will be done.'"

Early the next morning Lloyd stepped off the train in Reading. He helped Rachel and Phyllis alight, and the three walked in the warming morning sun to the hospital. "Remember, Phyllis, it's too early to expect to know anything."

"I know, Rev'rend Robins." She clung tightly to Rachel's arm.

"Slow down a little, Lloyd," Rachel said. "The old and the young can't keep up with the nervous."

"Does it show?" Lloyd paused.

"If foot-tapping could drive a train we'd have been here twice as fast."

"Sorry." If dread could power it, he thought, we'd have been here instantly.

As the lift doors opened, Lloyd saw Evelyn and Ernest sitting on the same bench. *She's alive, at least.*

Phyllis broke into a run and threw herself into her mother's arms.

"How is she, Ernest?" Rachel asked.

"About the same. A little better," he said quietly. He straightened. "Could still go badly, but she is a little better. She is."

"Have you seen her?"

"We both have. Two hours ago. They're still trying to let her sleep. Wish they'd let us sit with her."

"Did she seem to recognize you?"

"No way to tell, Lloyd, no way to tell."

Lloyd gripped his friend by the shoulder. "Let me see if I can go in."

He found the ward nurse. "The doctor let me see her yesterday."

"Yes, I know. Same rules, same risks," she said brusquely.

"Yes ma'am."

When Lloyd walked in, he found Lily still lying on her side. As he got closer, he saw in the dim light that her eyes were open. She stirred the slightest bit. *Oh Lord, please!*

"Hello, Rev'rend Robins," she whispered. "Where's Lizzie?"

Tears overflowed Lloyd's eyes. He refused to wipe them with his sterile hands. Considering all that might have happened to her, body and mind, Lloyd thought this was one of the most brilliant questions he'd ever heard.

CHAPTER 8

2 September 1940

AIR BATTLES IN LONDON AREA
DIVE-BOMBING AND MACHINE-GUN ATTACK
LAST DAY OF AUGUST MARKED BY FIERCE CONFLICTS
R.A.F. SMASH ATTEMPTS TO RAID AERODROMES

"I wonder how much truth there is in all these reports." Lloyd folded Sunday's *Observer*. Despite the assertion that the RAF was destroying immense numbers, the intense new air war continued. Lloyd remembered the last war. If you had believed the first reports, you would have thought the Allies won a hundred battles they actually lost. His heart sank and the ringing in his ear grew, like the buzz of a dying electric lamp. *Lord, strengthen the men who are going up in these machines.*

"What's wrong, Lloyd?" Annie could squeeze love and fear into three words.

"Just discouraged by these newspaper reports. I feel sorry for Nelson Ward and Adam Wilson and all those on the front line."

"I understand." She placed her hand over his ear.

"Thanks, love." He turned and cupped her hand to his lips.

The telephone rang, and his heart jumped. The black device was more and more an instrument of bad news. "Hello, this is Lloyd Robins."

"Henry Padbury."

"Good morning, Henry, what can I do for you?" Lloyd forced his voice to sound cheerful.

"I'm afraid I've got bad news …" Lloyd shook his head and gritted his teeth. "Philip Clarke just called in to tell me they've got a telegram. Apparently Edwin's been injured – or worse."

"Oh, Lord Jesus, no!"

"He'd like you to come as soon as you can."

"I'm on my way. Henry, do you have time this morning to telephone a couple of people? Get some folk praying?"

"I don't tutor until this afternoon. I'll call around."

Annie wanted to come, but she had to get the children to school. "Maggie and I will be back shortly. Telephone if you need anything."

It was a grey morning. Fog lay thick over the Thames. On another day Lloyd might have found it beautiful, but today it only seemed ominous. On the short walk to the Clarke's house, Lloyd thought about Edwin.

What was that noise? The door to the little communion cupboard sat open. Lloyd found a tousle-haired nine-year-old boy crouched behind a chair, his eyes wide, his hand full of crumbs from communion wafers, his mouth stained with grape juice. And this little miscreant was? Edwin Clarke. Lloyd chided himself for not knowing the names of all the children yet, even after five months at Stokely Free.

"Hello, Edwin."

"Mphhph rvdth rbbttth." The boy stood up, but didn't raise his head.

"Yes, well, perhaps we'd better go find your parents." Lloyd reached out to take the boy's hand, thought better of it, and guided him gently by the shoulder.

"Rev'rend Lloyd?"

"Hello Marjorie. What can I do for you?"

"Edwin wants to talk to you.' The boy stood fidgeting at her side.

Lloyd thought about the message waiting on his desk. *Now, Lord?*

People first, came the silent answer in his heart.

"Certainly. Can we sit in the sanctuary?"

"I'd like to leave him with you for a few minutes. I'll pop in and say hello to Annie."

"Quite. Edwin, let's sit here. What can I do for you?"

"Uh … nothing."

Lloyd smiled, trying to make the boy comfortable. "I doubt your mum's brought you all this way because you wanted to talk to me about nothing."

"Uh … no."

Lloyd waited.

"Uh … I want to know what I need to do to be good … uh … I'm not good … I do things my parents tell me not to, and I don't do what they tell me, and I'm nasty as can be to Violet and … and … I hate Lenny – I really do."

"Why do you want to be good?"

Edwin gave Lloyd a baffled look.

"Because … I want to go to heaven?"

"So you think you have to be good enough to go to heaven?"

"Uh … yes?" Lloyd suppressed a chuckle. The boy must feel that Lloyd wasn't much of a preacher to have missed this basic truth of theology.

"Edwin," he said, putting a hand on the boy's shoulder, "it turns out none of us is 'good enough' to go to heaven. I'm not, your dad's not, your mum's not. I've disobeyed God and been mean to others, just like you."

"But you say all the time you're looking forward to heaven. How can you say that if you're not good enough?"

"I think you know the answer already, Edwin. What did God do to rescue us from our sin, from our not-good-enough-ness?"

"He sent Jesus to die for our sins?"

"Good answer. Do you believe it?"

"Yes … I think so."

"Well, if you believe Jesus paid the price for your sins, you also believe that you don't have to be good enough to pay the price yourself."

"How much do sins cost?" Edwin asked.

"Well, the Bible tells us that the price of sin is death. You earn death by your sins, but Jesus died in your place. The price is paid with a life, yours or His.

"And if I believe he makes me good enough?"

"He was good enough. You get that goodness as a gift."

"And I'll never be bad again?"

"Uh, no. Sorry. I wish it worked that way. You may still sin, but he forgives even those sins and starts to change you day by day."

Edwin looked crestfallen. "I don't understand."

"It's about trusting him. You trust him first to rescue you from your sins, and then you trust him every day for the strength to obey. And when you fail, he forgives you and helps you to try again."

Edwin lapsed into silence.

"Do you want to tell Him you believe He died to pay for your sins?"

"Do I have to pray out loud?"

"Well, not necessarily out loud, but it helps."

"Well … right … will you tell me what to pray?"

"Hello, Edwin." Lloyd and Edwin met as Lloyd entered the church hall. The lad pretended not to hear him. He put his head down and tried to sidle past, but Lloyd decided to block the door. "How are you?"

"I'm fine.." Edwin mumbled.

"Is there some way I can pray for you? You haven't looked very happy."

"No, Rev'rend. There is no way you can pray for me. Everything's super.." He tried again to sidle out the door.

"How is that friend of yours? Reggie is it? The one who used to come to church with you?"

Edwin finally made eye contact, with eyes that were as narrow and hard as a knife. "He doesn't want to come anymore. He says church is bloody stupid. He hates this place because everyone tells him how awful he is. They tell him what to do and how to dress and talk and breathe. They won't even let you walk where you want to."

Edwin turned on his heel and stalked out of the door he'd come in.

Lloyd's gloomy memories accompanied him to the Clarkes' door. He knocked gently, then again, but there was no answer. Listening hard, Lloyd was sure he could hear sobbing from behind the door, and from the open window above him. Violet's room?

He clenched his soul, clenched the doorknob, and turned it. Unlocked. He poked his head in and was about to call out when he saw Philip and Marjorie. They were huddled on the couch. Philip had his arm around a sobbing Marjorie, but he was staring into space at the wall. He didn't seem to notice Lloyd's arrival. Lloyd quietly knelt in front of the couple and asked, "What's happened?"

Philip jumped, but said in a tightly controlled rasp, as if his throat was raw, "Edwin's been killed." He gestured vaguely toward the end table. There were two buff-colored telegrams, one on top of the other. "Top one just came," Philip whispered.

Lloyd picked it up and read. "Deeply regret to inform you your son Edwin Paul Clarke P/VX47762 killed on war service August 31 1940 stop letter follows stop Commander 11th Group Fighter Command."

Lloyd hung his head. "Oh no! Oh no!" He could think of nothing else to say, so he just knelt in front of Philip and Marjorie, put his hands over theirs and his head on his hands. After a long time he prayed aloud. "Lord, you alone know the depth of this hurt. We cry out to you as the God of comfort, and we take refuge in you. Lord, we don't understand how this can be your will, but we ask you for comfort that surpasses our understanding. Lord, strengthen this family. Enable each one to turn to you in the hard hours and days that are to come …"

Lloyd looked up into Philip's face. His friend had aged twenty years since church yesterday. He shook his head slowly, paused, shook it again, repeatedly. "I can't do this," he rasped. "I don't even know if he was saved."

It wasn't the time for that conversation. Lloyd asked the simplest question he could think of. "How's Violet?"

Philip looked at him uncomprehendingly and continued shaking his head.

Marjorie looked up. Her normally bright blue eyes were dull. Lloyd thought of the phrase 'dimmed by tears.' "She's in her room. I'll go up to her now."

"Do you want me to talk to her?"

"No, Rev'rend. She will need to talk, but she's in no shape now." Marjorie bowed her head, grasped his hand, and spoke in a whisper. "Neither are we. Thanks for being here."

She raised her head. "But, Lloyd, Lenny and Holly don't know. We need them, need to call them, but we can't leave each other – or Vi. Lloyd, could you call them?"

Lloyd sighed and wiped his eyes. "If you think it's the right thing, I'll do it. I know they'll want to talk to you straight away."

"Tell them to come as soon as they can."

Ned walked up from the bridge hand in hand with Alice. Henry had called them. "How long have we known the Clarkes?" he asked Alice.

"More than twenty years. Philip joined old George Bennett's law firm a little after the war."

They turned onto the Clarkes' street. A small crowd was already there, surrounding Henry Padbury. As they walked up, he was telling

Rachel Busby he had seen a second telegram delivered, but he didn't know what it said. Alan Ward arrived just as he finished, and Henry patiently rehearsed the story again.

At that moment, the Clarkes' door opened and Lloyd stepped out. He paused to direct a question into the shadows behind him, nodded, and came down the path.

"Hello, Ned." Lloyd looked relieved to see him. Never a good sign.

"Hello," Lloyd said in a louder voice. "Could we gather for a minute?" When Rachel and the others had drawn close, Lloyd told them about the second telegram. His words were met with a mixture of nods, gasps, and tears.

Before Lloyd left, he grabbed Ned's arm. "Could you gather these people and pray. Pray for Philip and Marjorie. Pray for Lenny and the girls. You know what to do." Ned did not feel at all confident that he knew what to do, but he knew an order when he heard it. "Yes, Lieutenant," he said, catching Lloyd's eye and giving him a nod. *Lord Jesus, help me.*

Lloyd walked quickly back to the house. It felt like he'd been gone forever, but Annie was not yet back from the school. He hesitated over the phone, praying for the right words, then called Lenny. The connection crackled badly but finally went through.

"Hello, Lenny. This is Rev'rend Lloyd. How are you?"

"I'm doing fine." Lenny's voice was clipped. Lloyd knew he'd already realized this was no casual telephone call.

"Lenny, there is no way to make this easy. Your mother and father asked me to call to tell you that Edwin's been killed at an airbase."

"Killed? Are you sure?"

"Yes Lenny. Your parents have a telegram."

"Damn!" Lenny said. "I told that idiot he'd break Mother's heart." Lloyd had experienced many reactions to death, but the angry ones still shocked him.

After a long pause, Lenny said in a much gentler voice "Right. What can I do to help?"

Lloyd had always loved the young man's heart. "Come home as soon as possible. Your mum needs you. Your dad maybe even more."

"I've got a meeting … but I can work it around. I'll be home this afternoon."

Next Lloyd dialed the number of the post office where Holly's husband worked. After a few minutes, Robert came on the line, and Lloyd quickly broke the news.

"Oh no, this'll kill her Rev'rend."

"I'm sorry," Lloyd said. "I know how hard it will be to tell her. But her parents need her here. I'm guessing she'll comfort Violet as well."

"We'll be there soon Rev'rend. Tell her family we love them."

Violet felt she had fallen in a well, a pit of darkness that was her own heart. Black as coal, mined out, abandoned, but crawling with cold memories. It's so dark in here, she thought. There's nowhere to go. I'll lie down. I'll sleep.

"Violet?" Mum's voice came from a long way off, echoing down the walls of the pit. "Violet?"

"Violet, sit up please, dear." She opened her eyes, but saw only blurs, spinning images. Nausea. Slowly one of the images resolved into Mum's face. A second was the window. She turned her head and everything blurred again.

"Violet, tell me what you're thinking."

She reached into the darkness, looking for her voice, but found only an infinite pool of tears. Suddenly her mother's presence was the most important thing in the world. She hugged her, burrowing her head, and wept. Mum wept too.

Apparently she had slept. Mum must have covered her. She was drenched with sweat. She threw the eiderdown off, felt the cool air chill her. She wiped her forehead. Her hand came away soaked and clammy.

She was alert now, but felt she was standing on a needle of rock, surrounded by the pit. Anything could make her fall.

She walked cautiously to the window. It was late afternoon. There were still people in her front garden. A table had been moved out there. It was covered with food. Her stomach crawled at the sight of Mrs. Busby's steak and kidney pie. Someone had cut out a large slice, and the filling oozed out like gore from an animal carcass. It seemed to reach for her. She backed away.

At a noise from the door she spun, arms raised to protect herself. The light was too bright, but the shape was not threatening.

It was Holly. "Oh, thank God! Holly, you're here." Her voice sounded strange in her ears, as if it had been distorted forever by the blackness.

"Violet! Oh, I'm so sorry."

Holly sprang from the far edge of the pit and landed on Violet's needle. There was barely room for them both. They had to hug to maintain balance.

"It's my fault, Holly. It's all my fault." Suddenly she knew this was the name of the blackness, of the pit, of the falling. "It's all my fault."

She fell.

Holly and Mum sat with her, bathing her forehead. The lamp on the dressing table was lit. The window was dark. It was night. Today or yesterday?

Suddenly a third shape was in front of her. She reared back but her mother and her sister held her tight.

"Hello Violet," said an ugly, familiar voice. "It's Reverend Robins." When had his face begun to drip off like that?

She found her voice, but ignored the man in front of her. "Thank you, Mum." She turned and hugged her, fighting the tears that hung just over the edge of blackness.

"Holly, I love you."

"I love you too, Violet … Do you know what's happened?" Without intending to, Holly had got behind her and pushed her toward the pit once more, asking again, "Do you know what's happened?"

"He's dead." Violet screamed as she tumbled into blackness. "He's dead and it's all my fault." She seemed to fall forever. Suddenly the face of the preacher appeared in front of her, falling with her. She screamed at him, sharp certainties, accusations of darkness as she fell.

"Why does God hate us?"

"Why is he doing this?"

"It's all my fault."

The preacher's face faded. The walls of the pit rushed past.

"I hope she'll be better now." Dr. Nesbitt said. "I've given her a different sedative, much lighter, and I think she's sleeping naturally. Call me if I need to come out again."

Lloyd stood by the Clarkes' door. "Thank you, doctor. We appreciate your help." He turned back to the family, sitting in the front room.

Holly had always struck Lloyd as mature, handling motherhood and even the move to Coventry with dignity and charm. Now she looked terrorized. Her face was pale and blotchy, her makeup scrubbed off by her tears. Her dress was wrinkled from the hours tending to the children in the little car Robert had borrowed.

Lenny, by contrast, was carefully dressed in a dark suit, not matching the image of a science wizard at all. At twenty-six, he was old enough for his face to be making the transition from smooth boyhood to a more rugged manhood. He had arrived from London with a bag in one hand and a Bible in the other, and whenever the family was occupied, he pulled out the Bible and read. He already seemed to radiate a hard-won peace, like a flame in the dark room.

With the arrival of the older children, Lloyd felt he could go home. In bed, he found himself wrestling with the family's questions. Had Edwin rejected his faith? Had he really been a believer, or was that nine-year-old faith only a child's conformity? Why had God allowed someone in such spiritual conflict to be taken?

The next morning he knew he had to try to get the family thinking about what must happen next. He clutched a telegram in one hand and the morning post in the other. "Perhaps we can gather and read this," he said, holding the telegram out toward Philip. He waved it away, but nodded. "Gather … gather." The only people there at this point were the family, Lloyd, Annie, and Henry Padbury, whom Philip kept asking to stay.

Holly and Robert's beautiful children had already proved to be a sweet distraction from the stress. As they sat, the women passed the baby, Ivy, from arm to arm. She looked like a miniature version of Violet, dark-haired and pale with translucent skin. Rose toddled back and forth, loving the attention, lifting arms and saying one of her few words "Up … Up?" She looked more like her father, with light curly hair and bright blue eyes.

"Can we start with prayer?" Lloyd said. Philip, Marjorie, and Lenny all nodded. Lloyd asked Jesus to be with them, to give strength for the day, and to speak words of comfort and peace into each aching heart.

He held up the telegram. "This is from the war office in London. It informs us that under the provisions of some army regulation for deaths on domestic soil, Edwin's body will be transported by the British Army

Graves Commission to a military cemetery, or, at the request of family, to a local cemetery of their choice. We need to reply to this at once. I assume we want his body brought here?"

Nods all around.

"To be laid to rest in White Hill?"

More nods. Marjorie wept, and Lloyd paused, praying, while Philip and Holly comforted her.

"Do you want me to send the reply?"

Nods.

Lloyd took a deep breath. "I also have two letters that came this morning. The first is from Edwin's commanding officer."

Lloyd pictured himself at the crude trench table in Vimy, writing letters just like this one. He always tried to have something positive to say about each soldier, though he recalled fighting the temptation to write in despair: "Your son is dead because he was stupid," or, worse: "Your son is dead because I was stupid."

To the parents and loved ones of Edwin Clark;

It is with great sadness that I repeat the news I'm sure you have already heard, that Ed was killed in action on 31st August 1940.

I was Ed's commanding officer and I spent considerable time with him in August. I admired his skills and I'm proud to report that he was on his way to becoming a fine soldier.

Ed was killed during a heavy raid by German bombers. I ordered Ed and several others from the repair shop to a bomb shelter. Unfortunately, and to my sorrow, the shelter took a direct hit. All within were killed instantly. Please comfort yourselves with the fact that Ed did not endure prolonged suffering.

I enclose a letter from one of Ed's closest friends in the unit. I have not read it, but I trust the author, and I understand its intent is to bring comfort.

Again, you have my deep condolences,

Rodney A. Hill
Flight Lieutenant, RAF.

~ † ~

September 1, 1940

Dear Mr. and Mrs. Clarke, and family;

My name is Tom Brooks. Ed and I were comrades at [here several words have been cut out]. He was a good friend and I sympathize with your deep loss.

Ed and I met at [more words cut out]. We shared a deep love for tinkering with radios. Also, unfortunately, a deep love of drink. This got us into many tight scrapes. Ed often said his family was deeply disappointed by his drinking.

I wanted you to know that both Ed and I were trying to get free of this. Before our transfer, we had been attending a local church and meeting with the rector, who had been a drunkard himself after the first war. This man gave us great assurance of God's help in our struggle, and by God's grace, Ed had been sober for several weeks when we moved.

Unfortunately, the presence of a convenient pub in our new location meant Ed once went on a bender. The Sunday after that we sought out a church and listened to a fine sermon which Ed said strengthened his soul. I was optimistic that he would be permanently free of this temptation. I would like to ask your family to pray for the same for me.

I hope it is a comfort for you to know that, even in his struggle, Ed was constantly turning back to God. I assure you that I look forward to seeing Ed again in eternity.

Sincerely,
Tom Brooks

Lloyd looked up from the second letter, wiping his eyes, and found that Phillip, for the first time, was smiling. Marjorie too, although with tears running down her face. Lenny was bent in an attitude of prayer. Holly was taut, looking like she had things to say.

And at the door stood Violet. Her face was ravaged and pale, the tracks of her tears glossy against the whiteness of her skin. She stood in rapt attention as if the images of bomb-shelter carnage, pub dissolution and stained-glass repentance filled her eyes.

Philip spoke "I think we should pray for this young man …"

"Tom," Lloyd interjected

"Tom. And praise God for this testimony."

After the prayer Lloyd listened to the stream of reminisces that poured forth from the family. He always treasured these moments in the midst of grief. The memories of the good times and the bad, the habits and foibles and escapades of loved ones, seemed to him balm in Gilead.

One of Marjorie's first memories was of that day she had brought Ed to Lloyd's study. "We sang hymns all the way home. Ed had such a nice little voice. 'My chains fell off, my heart was free.'" She buried her face.

Holly, it turned out, had been waiting for a chance to talk of Ed's faith – not only of that of his childhood, but of later glimpses. Once, she had been invited to a birthday party Ed's friends had held for him. Ed had spoken to one friend who was heartsick over a breakup with his girl. To Holly's amazement, he had told this friend that the only one you could rely on in life was Jesus.

Lenny recounted to loving laughter the time when he had saved Ed's life. Ed had been reading about Benjamin Franklin's experiment with a kite and, on the next thundery night, had decided to try it. Lenny had woken up and followed him to their favorite spot on the ridge. He was running hard, soaked to the skin, his shredding kite whipping in the wind. 'Let it go,' Lenny had shouted, but Ed had refused. Finally, Lenny caught up with him, ripped the string out of Ed's hand, and flung the kite to the wind. At that moment a flash had exploded in front of them.

"And Ed saved my life," Violet said, sitting in the doorway. "We never told anyone. When I was only little, I snuck out of the house. When no one came after me, I wandered down to the river. I became fascinated by the white streams of water flowing over the weir." Marjorie and Philip were staring. "I guess I decided to touch the water. Before I knew what was happening I'd tumbled in. Dad always said 'don't breathe the water,' but I was too little. It rolled me round and filled my mouth and nose." Violet's face had taken on a semblance of life and energy as she told the story. "Ed and Reggie and some of them were playing on the bank—."

"They shouldn't have been there!" Marjorie broke in.

"Ed could hardly swim yet, but when he saw me, he jumped into the water and paddled after me. He caught me where the current slowed, and dragged me to the shore. I couldn't breathe, so he sat on me and pushed on my stomach until I threw up."

Lenny took the telegram from the delivery boy, scanned it quickly, and brought it to his father. "They say his body will arrive on the fifth," he said. "They want our undertaker to meet the train."

"We'll have to take this to Mr. Russell," his father said. "We can do that after we've seen Lloyd."

A little while later Lenny accompanied his mother, father, and sisters into the manse. Robert had stayed behind with the little ones.

"May I get anyone tea?" Annie asked.

Everyone assented. Most of them were surviving on strong tea.

Philip said, "I suggest we have the … funeral … on Saturday … the seventh." Lenny felt that his father was bouncing back, but he seemed to have to thrust out every word. "Marjorie's family … could come down from Birmingham."

"Agreed," said Lloyd. "I'm assuming we'll have the service at church before the burial?"

Philip nodded.

Lloyd said, "We'll check with Mr. Russell, but let's assume that's the plan."

Lenny tried to get to the point. "And what will you say about Ed?"

"That's the key question, Lenny," Lloyd said. He turned to the family. "I'd like to get everyone's ideas. How should we speak of Edwin? How much of his life, his circumstances, his struggles, should we share?"

When his father didn't answer, Lenny spoke up. "I've thought and prayed about this ever since I got Reverend Robins phone call. I didn't know as much as I do now about Ed's continued seeking after God – that makes it easier. But I think we tell the whole story. He was rebelling. He made bad choices, and they made him miserable at times. But he didn't lose his faith. It kept showing up. And even though his death is a tragedy, it's also a rescue from suffering, from sin, and from his own doubts and weaknesses."

"I agree." It was Holly. "We don't need to lie about his struggles and make him some kind of stained-glass saint. People know. Some people need to hear that story as a warning. But, Reverend Lloyd, you have to believe that he is with Jesus now. You've got to say that part too."

"I do believe it. I wish he had made some better choices sooner, but we're all sinners, we're all weak. That's why we need a Savior … I've been thinking about a passage of Scripture that speaks to this, speaks to both your loss and your hope." He paused, and then added "Our loss and our hope."

He picked up his Bible. "It's the climax of the story of Lazarus."

Thank you, Lord Jesus, Lenny thought.

Lloyd began to read from John 11. "Then said Martha unto Jesus, Lord, if thou hadst been here, my brother had not died."

Violet cried out, her voice rising in a keening moan. She dashed the few feet from the door to sit next to her mother.

Lloyd paused again. It was obvious he didn't want to cause her pain. But Lenny felt God wanted this said, especially to his sister. "But I know, that even now, whatsoever thou wilt ask of God, God will give it thee."

Lenny got up. Feeling every eye on him, he almost quailed. But he felt another eye on him as well. He knelt in front of Violet and took her hands.

"Jesus saith unto her, Thy brother shall rise again. Martha saith unto him, I know that he shall rise again in the resurrection at the last day. Jesus said unto her, I am the resurrection, and the life: he that believeth in me, though he were dead, yet shall he live: And whosoever liveth and believeth in me shall never die. Believest thou this?" Violet turned up her tear-worn face. His baby sister's beautiful dark eyes looked in his. "Believest thou this?"

She closed her eyes, bit her lip … and nodded.

"She saith unto him, Yea, Lord: I believe that thou art the Christ, the Son of God, which should come into the world."

The room was hushed. Lenny looked around. There were tears on every face. Still no one spoke. Finally, he said to Lloyd, "I've been memorizing that."

His father spoke, quietly but firmly, in his old voice, "Even in the midst of war and destruction, death is not the end. Death does not have the final word. Jesus himself rose to life, and He himself is the promise of eternal resurrected life. If we had asked Ed whether he believed this, wouldn't he have said yes?"

They nodded through their tears. Lenny didn't think he had seen Lloyd smile yet. Now he did, and asked, "So is this the text I should use? Is this the message we should try to bring?"

Lloyd walked back with the family after the meeting with the undertaker. "Lenny," he said quietly, "I think it would be wonderful if you could read the text for us on Saturday. Even better if you could recite it."

"I'm not sure I could, Reverend. I get nervous in front of a crowd."

"You could have it open in front of you. But you won't need it."

"All right, then."

As they approached the house, they could see Arthur Cripps, standing in the front garden, pulling on his mustaches and fending off more visitors. There had been a constant stream, some total strangers, since the obituary had appeared in the Oxford paper. Arthur, Ned and others had organized themselves to deal with the arrivals.

Lloyd took a step to catch up with Philip, who walked with his arm tight around his wife's shoulder. "Philip, I wonder if the church is going to be large enough for this service? Would you mind too terribly if I talked to the vicar to see if we could use St. James'?"

Philip sighed, putting his head close to Marjorie's. She first shook her head, then nodded and whispered.

"That would do, Lloyd. We love our place, but St. James' is beautiful … and after all Ed was helped by a Church of England rector near the end."

When they reached the house, Arthur handed Philip the morning mail. "I couldn't help but notice the one on top." It was from Buckingham Palace. After Philip read it, he gave it to Marjorie. "How beautiful," she said through her tears.

When she handed it to Lloyd, he saw that it was written under the Royal Seal: "The Queen and I offer you our heartfelt sympathy in your great sorrow. We pray that your country's gratitude for a life so nobly given in its service may bring you some measure of consolation." It appeared to have been signed by the King himself.

Later, Lloyd called in to see the rector, Mr. Bennett, thankful that the historic animosity between the state and dissenting churches was often overlooked in Stokely. It helped that Bennett was sincerely devout, though he always seemed to have a shortage of pronouns.

"Yes, Lloyd. So grieved to hear about your loss. Intended to come to the service. Be fine to hold it here. When do you plan?"

"Saturday, mid-afternoon, if that works for you."

The rector looked up as if consulting a calendar written on the ceiling. The Anglican's small study was ten times bigger than Lloyd's. But the only thing he really envied was the rich collection of books lining the walls. He wasn't sure why he hadn't ever tried to borrow any.

"That works. Will speak to the warden. Make sure everything is prepared."

Violet woke with a start. She had again tossed and turned all night, but was instantly grateful that she could not recall her dreams, good or bad. Then she realized that today was the funeral. Despair threatened to open up beneath her, but she remembered the words her brother had quoted, "I am the resurrection and the life." Today, she must cling to those.

She went to the window. The day was calm and bright. Quiet, high clouds filled the sky. At nine, the beautiful tenor bell in St. James' tower sounded the hour. As the echo of the bells subsided, the setting could not have been more peaceful, and yet her fears and memories gnawed away the edges. She pulled on the first dress that came to hand and fled the room.

The morning hours passed as yesterday's had, at once eternal and fleeting. She refused more food than she normally ate in a week.

"Violet, when are you going to dress?" Holly asked.

She looked down at the dress. She could see that it was worn and stained. But she didn't have the energy. "No," she said.

"Oh Vi! I know this is hard. Here, let me help you pick something a little nicer." Holly took her by the hand and led her upstairs. They stepped onto the point of the needle. Violet froze, but Holly's faux-cheerful voice still reached her.

"How about this one? This one?"

Focus, Violet, focus. Lord Jesus, help me.

The darkness faded, the floor of the room re-asserted itself. Holly was holding out a lightweight winter dress, dark green. She hadn't worn it much even last year. She nodded.

"Now for a little makeup."

"No."

"At least a little lipstick."

"No. I just can't, Holly."

Now they were at the church. They stood in a cold, stone side room with Rev'rend Lloyd and the Anglican priest. Violet leaned on Mum and shivered. "It's so cold," she said.

Her brother slipped off his jacket and wrapped it around her. She reveled in the life warmth it held. "I'll have to take it back for the service," he said.

That came too soon. Violet looked only at the floor, but she could not avoid the realization that almost everyone from Stokely was there. Halfway up the aisle, she heard familiar snickering whispers and stole a sideways glance at Reggie and several of Ed's old school chums. Blackness billowed from their midst and threatened to consume the sanctuary. "Jesus, help," she whispered. She knew that the others had prayed Ed's friends would come. She ached for them to be gone.

The family was seated on the front row and she was the last one in. For seventeen years that had meant sitting next to Ed. Now her shoulder pressed against Holly's. Annie Robins appeared on her right and put her arm around her. Violet whispered, "I don't like this place … don't like this place … It's cold. It's so cold. And it's dark. Why is it so dark?"

She realized the service was starting. Stood. Looked at the meaningless marks on the hymnbook's page that should have been words. But when Lenny began to recite the Scripture, the same passage as yesterday, there came a quiet sense of light through the darkness. She took hold of it. It was strong, a cord of hope, lifting her yet again from the pit. "I am the resurrection and the life." She clung to it as Rev'rend Lloyd spoke, even laughed when he shared her story of Ed saving her life. He described Martha's despair, Jesus' comfort, and the words of promise. For a moment the light spread.

Rev'rend Lloyd didn't avoid the hard questions about Edwin's faith and behavior, but kept returning to Christ as Savior, Christ as life, the promise of eternal life that came through grace. He ended by saying, "This is our hope, 'whoever lives and believes in me shall never die.' Edwin believed and, though he has died, physically, yet he lives and shall live. But this is also a promise to us: despite loss, despite grief, despite war, we have life, Christ's life in us to sustain us. He gives the Comforter to be with us in sorrow. He gives us the light of his presence, the promise of eternity."

Oh, Jesus show me that light, Violet prayed. She saw it in Mum and Dad, surrounded by friends and hugs. She saw it in Lenny and Holly, and the gold of little Rosie's hair.

But the darkness gnawed sharply at the edges. She knew its name. Guilt.

CHAPTER 9

19 September 1940

The bomb was lying on its side, half buried in the dirt. With great caution, the bomb disposal crew had rotated it so that Welly could reach the fuse cover.

Welly oriented the Crabtree, the device that would allow him to take hold of the fuse. He began to sweat. He attached a line to the ring on the Crabtree and threw the other end across the hastily erected blast barrier.

Now came the delicate part. Welly adjusted the wrench to fit the slots of the locking ring. The fuse was tight and Welly's hands were slick. He twisted the wrench cautiously, stopping at every sound of metal against metal. Not that stopping would mean anything if a bomb decided to explode, but Welly could not convince his trembling arms of this truth.

Counting carefully, Welly loosened the fuse nine full turns, the number of threads. A flood of relief hit him as he finished, and then a counter-flood of concern. Had he really counted to nine?

He backed away, then crawled over the berm, where he was handed the end of the string.

Had he done everything right? His head said yes, but it could not convince his gut. He had to pull the fuse sharply so it cleared the bomb case when it fell into the sand. He gripped the line with both hands and jerked.

"Bang … You're dead."

Welly jumped and turned to his instructor. "Why? What did I do wrong?"

"Nothing. Not a bleeding thing. We've just discovered a modification that detonates the bomb when the fuse lifts. Discovered it the hard way."

Welly was appalled. One of the reasons he hated war was the idea of applying God-given intellect and creativity to the science of death. The Germans seemed to excel at it.

"What was I supposed to do?"

"We don't know yet. We've lucked into an intact version. If we find a way to identify it, and sort it out, we'll let you know."

Henry had been looking for a chance to call in on Bert. He knocked briskly at door of the Butler's little house. After a moment Meg called, "Come in then, my hands are full." Indeed they were. She was trying to fit a huge armful of ironed clothing into an old kit bag. Arthur stepped in and grabbed the bag to hold it open.

"Good afternoon, Meg. How are you?"

"I'm well, Henry. Bert's through there."

"Hello, Padbury. How are you?" said Bert.

Henry walked into the kitchen to find Bert in his wheeled chair. It looked even more complicated than it had at church. To Arthur's delight, Bert had a big Bible open in front of him and pages of notes in his large sloppy handwriting covered the table.

"What are you studying, Bert?"

"Suffering."

That brought Henry up short.

"Do you know that suffering is a promise, just like eternal life or comfort? Listen to this … where did that paper go? … Here it is. Jesus says, 'In the world ye shall have tribulation: but be of good cheer; I have overcome the world.' That's two promises – suffering and Christ's victory."

"Fantastic, Bert! When did you get to be such a student of Scripture?"

"Sitting in this chair. I may not have my legs, but I have my brain. I'm even thinking of asking Rev'rend Lloyd to let me preach some of these things. How would that look, the preacher at the front of the church stuck in a chair?"

"I think it would be great. I'll put in a word with Lloyd."

"No! No! Don't do that." Bert seemed suddenly shy. He ruffled the papers nervously. "I don't want to do anything till I'm ready. Don't want to share any half-baked ideas."

Meg's voice sounded from the next room. "Have Lloyd let him preach, Arthur. He's been doing it around here for months." She poked her head around the corner. "And I'm loving it."

Violet stood at her bedroom window and looked out at the roiling clouds. Lenny's words from John were true, she told herself. Jesus promised life from death. Ed had believed that, had that life. *So what?* Ed had believed, but she obviously didn't. The roiling guilt that churned her soul was unrelenting. She didn't have peace, had not even changed her ways.

"Come on," he had said last night, after she finally pushed away his kisses. "You're a tart. You always will be. You know you want it." He had grabbed her roughly and pressed himself against her before letting her flee to the house.

"Good morning, Violet," Mum said. "How are you?"

Violet looked out of the kitchen door. "Awful black day, isn't it Mum?"

Her mum came, hugged her shoulders, and put her face next to hers. "Not so dark, dear. See …" she pointed "… there's a patch of blue. I believe it's growing."

"If you say so, Mum."

Mum led her to the dining-room table and got her a cup of tea.

Violet took a deep breath. "Do you think I could call on Mrs. Robins?"

"I'm sure she would love to see you, dear. Can I ask why?"

"I think I need … I could talk … about Ed … and stuff."

"Can't you talk to me, dear?"

"I want to, Mum, but no, not yet."

"All right then. I'll ask Annie to see you soon."

Lloyd would have liked some company on his walk, but a quick mental survey had failed to turn anyone up. James was in town, Ned was busy with the harvest, Henry was at the university, and Arthur had a seemingly endless stream of boats to let through the lock.

I guess I'll just go by myself. He needed the exercise, needed the quiet, needed the time with God. But he found himself not really getting the latter. The news from bombed-out London distracted him, and the ringing in his ear only made things worse. He had been working on his sermon but was having no success discerning God's heart in the opening chapter of John's first letter. He'd picked the passage before the bombing started, and now he couldn't seem to find anything to say.

"Lord," he said to the scattered clouds, "help me." He couldn't even find words to pray.

Still, the walk did him good. The air was chilly, but not as damp as it had been. He could see a golden haze above the river, off to his left, and the trees were hinting at autumn, though it had been too rainy lately for them to show true colors. He tried to empty his mind of everything and just enjoy.

Maybe I'll stop at the Butlers', he thought on the way back. He wanted to see if Bert was really willing to preach.

The Butler's door was standing open when he arrived. Fred and Nellie were unloading dirty clothes from a cart. Nellie worked with precision, but Fred had tried to take a huge armful, and dropped at least half of it into the cold mud.

Lloyd scooped up the damp clothes and, with a hello, followed Nellie into the house. Meg stood behind an ironing board, pressing clean shirts.

"How are you, Meg?"

"Busy, as you see. And trying to cope with all the help the Lord has given me." She nodded toward Fred, who was gathering the clothes he had dropped inside the door.

"Well," Lloyd said, "I won't interrupt. I really came to see Bert."

"Usual spot," Meg said from behind a cloud of steam.

Bert was writing furiously on what appeared to be scraps of used paper. "Just a moment, Rev'rend Lloyd," he said. "Had a thought."

Lloyd listened to loud, whining voices coming from the front of the house. Eventually Bert picked up the piece of paper, looked at his words critically, and threw it down on the table.

"Preparing to preach, I assume," Lloyd said.

"Henry talked to you?"

"With great enthusiasm."

"I'm willing, but …" Bert pointed to the scattered and piled papers on the kitchen table. "Every time I think I know what God wants me to say, I get distracted by something else. Something equally wonderful."

"That's not a bad thing, Bert. I remember the first time I preached. High Street Chapel in Birmingham. My pile of ideas was at least that huge. Of course, paper was easier to come by then."

"But how did you decide what to say?"

"Reverend Marley said, 'Pick something that touches your own heart. That's what people really want to hear.'" Bert looked unconvinced.
"Which passage has the tallest pile?" Lloyd asked.

"Probably Philippians, on finding peace." Bert lifted a thick sheaf.

"Great. That's perfect. When can you preach it?"

"It's nowhere near a sermon."

"Do you think you could be ready in October?"

Bert shook his head. "No way. Maybe November."

Lloyd smiled. "You're sure?" Bert nodded, looking both enthusiastic and terrified. At that moment Meg came in, wiping her hands on her apron, then lifting a wisp of hair behind her ear.

"I know these children are trying. It's just that they can be *so* trying."

"What's happened?" Bert asked.

"Oh, the usual. Fred said something and Nellie shut down. Went off to read a book, left Fred with all the washing. Now Billy and Harry are fussing about something. Billy I can understand, but Harry's just a whiner."

"It's no surprise Billy and Nellie are struggling." Lloyd said. "They're still shell-shocked after the loss of their mum. And their father, for that matter."

"I know," Meg said. She thought for a moment. "I wish I could make it all better for them right now."

"Have you stayed in touch with their grandparents?"

"Not to see them, but Mildred writes. Draws the sweetest little pictures for Billy, though her hand's kind of shaky. They both love to hear from her."

"Well, I'll be praying for them – and for you. Pretty exhausting, isn't it?"

"Bert does all he can, but … yes."

Lloyd walked slowly back to the church. Before he reached the door, he saw Alan Ward, waiting with his characteristic knee-knocking impatience.

"Hello Alan."

"Pastor. You know, for a man drawing a salary, you aren't here much."

"I was visiting Bert Butler."

"Long visit."

Why was Alan always able to make him feel defensive? "I took a walk before that, to clear my head."

"Oh? Been having the old problem again?"

"No, Alan!" Lloyd bit back any further words.

"Temper, temper, Rev'rend." Alan shook his head. "Ned Powell talked me into letting that go, but I'm watching. First sign of dissolution I see and we'll be letting you go. Be good for the church budget."

Lloyd shook his head in frustration, making his ear ring. "Did you have something you wanted to talk to me about?"

"Just wanted to warn you to keep your eye on that Norah of yours. She's been seen talking to Harold Mills."

"So?"

"She's a divorced woman, Reverend. It's not her place to be getting friendly with a single man."

Maybe I won't take any more walks, Lloyd thought.

Annie watched the children play in the garden. It was cloudy and cool but not raining, and Annie felt a little fresh air would do them good. She returned to the kitchen to put on the pot. She had baked a small cake, using most of the sugar ration, and would share a piece with Violet then serve the rest to Lloyd and the children.

Violet was even paler than usual when Annie invited her in. Annie prayed silently for wisdom. After a bit of small talk, Annie said, "Tell me how your family is doing."

"Mum and Dad are okay, I guess. They have each other. I think Mum cries a lot, but mostly at night. She's … cheerful during the day.

Lenny has been writing often, and never fails to mention some good memory of Ed.

"Holly and the girls went back to Coventry. It was so good to have them with us, Mrs. Robins. Rosie played with me all the time and Ivy is so beautiful."

"And how are you doing?"

Violet looked away and seemed to shrink in on herself. "I'm awful, Mrs. Robins. It's not just Ed dying, it's this war: the rationing, the bombing, and … and …" Violet flung her arms around Annie's neck and burst into tears.

"There, there," Annie said as she held her. "God can get you through."

"But you don't understand! I'm bad. I'm awful. God hates me. I can never undo what I've done, Mrs. Robins."

"What dear? Tell me what you think you've done."

"I … I … I …" Violet's sobs came like drumbeats. Annie pulled out her hankie and Violet mindlessly traded it for her own soaked one. She took a breath. "I have to tell you. That's why I came."

"Go ahead, dear."

"Well, it's about Ed and his friends, and … me, Mrs. Robins." Violet sobbed again. "Ed was my hero when I was growing up. He could do no wrong and he always told me everything. When he started to drink I knew right away. I knew all the outrageous things he and his chums did. That paint on the bridge? That was them. And most of the mischief in town." Annie and Lloyd had long suspected some of this.

"It really wasn't until Ed went away last year that I started to go bad." Violet continued. "Ed's mate Reggie started to invite Winnie and me to their parties. There were a couple of other girls too. I lied to Mum and told her I was going to Winnie's house to listen to the wireless."

"Which one is Winnie?" Annie asked.

"She's the tall, thin girl in my class. Doesn't go to Stokely Free."

"Oh yes, I remember her. Very stylish."

"Anyway, it wasn't long before I began to drink a little. Beer at first. It was only a year ago I got drunk for the first time. I don't know if you remember Mum telling you how sick I was. I told her it was something I ate at the fish and chip shop in Reading … Oh Mrs. Robins, I've been so horribly bad. I'm on the same road as Ed."

Annie responded instinctively "No, no, Violet. God can get you through this. You have to be strong to tell your parents, but they love you. They'll forgive you."

"But that's not the worst of it. It's Reggie."

Annie felt a chill sweep across her. "What about Reggie?"

"Well … I've always despised how he is with the girls – really, I have. Honestly, I don't know what they've all done but he knew I was a good girl and left me alone. Until about six months ago when he began to go all sweet on me. He'd break away from his girl and hang around with me at parties. He started to take Winnie and me home in his dad's old car. And he'd drop Winnie first. He's told me he loves me. I've tried not to believe it, but … so I … oh, Mrs. Robins."

"What have you done, child?" Annie whispered

"Not the worst, Mrs. Robins. But … but … more than kisses … Too much more than kisses."

"But you're not with child?"

"No, ma'am. Not that. Winnie's mum is a nurse and Winnie knows all about it, and … no ma'am. I've always made him stop, even when it makes him mad."

"Well, praise God for that. Still, we'll have to tell your parents. And you'll have to stop seeing him."

"I tried to stop, after Ed died. But I'm not strong. And everything's so dark. Reggie almost … but not … but he made me …"

Annie didn't want to ask.

"He says I want it and I think he's right. I keep going back."

Rachel shook her head in frustration. "Yes," she said, "I'll be there in a minute." *How did I get myself into this?* She finished washing the dinner plates and put them on the rack to dry. Then she walked into the sitting room where Lady Blount sat in 'her' chair, the chair that had been Mum's.

"It's cold in here. Close the window and top up this cup of tea."

Rachel looked at the ceiling in mock despair and real entreaty. "Lady Blount, much as I admire your stand on the manor house, and happy as I am to share my home, I will say one more time. I. Am. Not. Your. Servant. If you want to close the window, close the window. If you want a cup of tea, get a cup of tea. If you want my help, remember the basic courtesies all British children are taught. We. Say. Please. And. Thank you."

"Rachel Busby, you watch the way you speak to me. I can have you …"

She trailed off, her stern anger fading to a look of confusion.

Rachel continued in a softer voice. "Have me what? Dismissed? That's what I'm saying. I don't work for you, Lady Blount. We share this house, and it would do my heart good if you would do what you can to contribute to your own care."

"But I can't do most of these things."

"I know, and some of them you never will. But a gentle 'please' and a sincere 'thank you' do not take domestic skill. Only Christian kindness."

Lady Blount shrank down in the chair. "You're right … I will try to do better."

Rachel walked over and closed the window.

"There. I will put the kettle on. When it whistles you can come and make yourself a cup of tea."

Five minutes later the water had nearly boiled.

"Rachel?"

"Yes, Lady Blount."

"Bring me a cup of tea at once. Mine is cold." Rachel rolled her eyes. She went back into the sitting room.

"Lady Blount, do you remember what we just talked about?"

"I remember you were impertinent."

"Rightly so. Here, let me help you up."

"Where am I going?"

"You are coming into the kitchen to make yourself a cup of tea … If we can't change your mind, maybe we can change your habits."

Lady Blount brewed the tea without mishap. She looked around.

"Thomas, come here and carry this out to the … the other room."

"Thomas isn't here, Lady Blount."

"Well where on earth is he? Is it Thursday? Has he gone out?"

"No, Lady Blount," said Rachel. She didn't want to go through it again. "Here, let me take your tea in for you."

Rachel helped the older woman into her chair. As she turned to go to the kitchen, Lady Blount spoke again.

"Rachel."

"Yes, Lady Blount."

"Has that criminal couple been caught yet? Didn't they steal my things?"

"Yes. And no, they haven't been caught yet."

"Have the police all gone on holiday? Isn't it their job to catch them?" Lady Blount began to wave her hands nervously.

"I'm sorry, Lady Blount. I'm sure they are trying. They've even contacted Scotland Yard. But with no result so far."

"Well they must be found. This impudence and disrespect is an outrage. When I was a girrr—"

Lady Blount's voice stopped abruptly. Her hands dropped into her lap. Rachel turned to face her. She seemed to be in a daze or a trance.

"Lady Blount? … Lady Blount, are you all right?"

Suddenly both of Lady Blount's hands flew to her head. She bent forward and cradled her temples. "Oh! Oh! I have such a headache."

Rachel ran over and put an arm around her. "Oh, I'm sorry, Eleanor."

"Get me a powder. At once." She looked at Rachel and her hard features softened. "Please."

~ † ~

James pulled the Daimler up in front of the church and helped Rachel fold Lady Blount into the passenger seat.

"Where is your gas mask?" James asked her.

"I don't like those things. Always getting in the way." Lady Blount said.

"She had it when we went into the building." Rachel said. "It's in a … rather wonderful old bag she found. I'll go and get it."

James watched people leaving the building. Was it just his imagination or had the congregation been smaller lately? Maybe it was the sermons. Lloyd had seemed rather flat again this morning.

Rachel came back, carrying a huge beaded bag. James could not see anything even remotely wonderful about it. He helped Rachel into the back seat.

"Thank you again for the lift," Rachel said. "I miss the walk, of course, but Lady Blount is grateful. Not many have petrol rations these days." Her tone of voice made James feel like a necessary evil.

"Yes, thank you, Sir James," Lady Blount said. "Though I still don't understand why you don't have a driver."

"I just like to drive," he said, trying not to sound offended. He felt an obligation to help, but the hostility of the two women was wearing.

"It's not much of a drive, though, is it?" Lady Blount said. They were already approaching the little side street that led to Rosewood Cottage.

"So, what will you two ladies be doing this warm afternoon," he ventured as he helped them out of the Daimler.

"Nap," said Lady Blount.

"I'm going out to Ned's to help Alice feed the men. They're back in the fields this afternoon trying to get the potato crop in."

"Who has he got helping him?"

"Only Stanley Payne. Billy Parker got it into his head that he needed to join up. Didn't even get a notice, and I've no idea how he was accepted."

James chuckled. "He's a big lad. Sometimes that's all a recruiting officer sees. In the first war I worked with some lads who made the horses seem brilliant."

"Billy makes a cow seem brilliant."

"Now, Rachel!"

"It's true!" He chuckled at the feigned sincerity in her voice.

"So some of the men are helping?"

"Yes. Ernest, Philip, Henry, even Lloyd. All the young men are gone."

"I suppose I should go out and help as well."

"With your leg the way it is? I don't think so!"

James was offended by the implication of aged infirmity. But he had to admit that his leg hurt more with the coming of autumn.

James waited at the door while Rachel settled Lady Blount in her chair. "I'm just going to walk Sir James out to the car, my lady."

"Oh you are, are you?" Lady Blount gave her best imitation of a grin.

"Yes, I am. Nothing more." Rachel's voice failed to make the statement humorous.

Outside, she said, "I wanted to ask you about Lady Blount. I know you're not a real doctor but—"

"My vast experience with stubborn mules might give me insight?"

"Sir James! Be kind."

She described Lady Blount's strange headache earlier that week. "It hasn't happened again, but …"

James considered what he'd observed. "Probably nothing except age. You've noticed that she's starting to deteriorate mentally?"

"Yes, I've noticed." Rachel said with a roll of her eyes.

"I'd keep an eye on it though. Vacancy followed by headache can be a bad sign. If it happens again you ought to take her to a doctor – a real doctor."

~ † ~

Henry felt a bead of sweat run down the inside of his shirt. "I thought Sunday was supposed to be a day of rest," he said to no one in particular.

Ernest stood up from bending over the earthed-up row of potatoes. He pushed against the small of his back. "When my back breaks I'll get all the rest I need."

Ned was lifting huge baskets of potatoes onto the wagon. "Now you know why farmers die young." He sighed, gazing at the unworked length of the field.

Henry looked at the sun and calculated that they would finish this field before sunset. But there were two more this size. He moved over and began working next to Philip. "How are you doing?" he asked.

"Legal training is the perfect preparation for picking small potatoes."

Henry laughed. "I meant in general."

Philip wiped sweat out of his eyes with a corner of his dirty sleeve.

"It's hard, Henry. Missing Ed's only part of it. With all this bombing, we're also worried about Lenny. He's right in the heart of the city."

"What did he have to say on Wednesday?" Lenny had been calling Henry about once a week so he could talk to his parents who would come through from next door.

"He's well. He helped out for a couple of days in bombed-out areas, and he spends a good deal of time in the shelter near his building. He says they may be moved out of town. That would suit Marjorie and me."

"And how is Violet?"

Philip was quiet while he fished three largish potatoes out of the soil.. "We don't know what to think. Her reaction has been so extreme. She's asked to talk to us later tonight. Maybe we'll know more after that."

Henry's basket was nearly full. He pushed on the ache in his own back before lifting the basket and taking it to Ned.

"Well, here's a few more."

"Thanks." Ned nodded. His face looked worn and old. Dirt lay in the grooves where sweat had deposited it. "There's Alice," Ned said, "with a jug of something. I wish it was lemonade, but it's probably apple-peel juice."

"With blackcurrant, I think," Henry said. He had gone to the kitchen earlier. "It's not too bad, actually."

The men gathered in the shade. Alice and Rachel had brought out two kitchen chairs. Uncharacteristically, Ned collapsed into one of them. He rubbed his chest just below his collarbone.

"It's probably no use. We've already lost the wheat. Now the potatoes are past their best, and all of you will be going to your desk jobs in the morning."

"I don't have any lectures tomorrow, Ned. I could come back out," Henry said.

"And I'll come after work." Ernest said.

"Me too," said Philip.

"Monday's my day off anyway," said Lloyd.

Ned smiled for the first time that day. "Thank you."

"Breakfast looks wonderful, Norah," Annie said, "but Lloyd's not ready yet. Norah was grilling a hard-to-find sausage to go with eggs.

"So how was the trip to Oxford?" Annie asked. Norah had gone with Harold Mills to visit the university city after church.

"It was lovely. The trees are getting their autumn colors, and the colleges are beautiful. So much history. I wish I could have pursued that life."

Annie didn't feel ready to ask how she had enjoyed spending time with Harold. Norah had long said that she would never think of marrying again after the divorce.

The creaking of the stairs, along with a groan, announced Lloyd's descent. Annie watched with amusement and sympathy as he came stiffly to the table.

"Well, I don't think I'm going to be able to go out and help Ned today."

"Too much pain?" Annie said.

"No, no, not that. I've got to get started on my message … and Philip, Marjorie, and Violet are coming for tea, aren't they?"

Annie laughed. Male pride was so transparent.

Lloyd laughed with her. "Well, I've got to admit I welcome the excuse … I think Ned will be able to get in the rest today without me."

"I'm worried about him, Lloyd … Alice says he's been working round the clock and lately he's had chest pains. She's trying to get him to go to the doctor."

Lloyd grimaced. "I don't know what to do to help him. He's totally committed to making that farm work."

"We can pray for some kind of help," Annie said.

She was more than a little troubled by the skepticism in Lloyd's voice when he said, "I guess we can do that."

"Grierson," James said as he picked up the telephone.

"Sir James? It's Rachel Busby. There is a man here from Scotland Yard. He says the information he has concerns you."

"I'll be down in a moment," James said. "Do you think he has found Thomas and Vera?"

"Just come and talk to him, James. He's making Lady Blount nervous."

Ten minutes later James arrived at Rosewood Cottage, rather breathless despite the downhill walk. Lord, why do I have to endure this leg? he thought.

A plain black car was parked in front of the cottage. James knocked lightly and Rachel answered at once. James found Lady Blount ensconced in her chair, a well-dressed older man with a tiny mustache seated opposite her. He rose and introduced himself as Detective Coleridge.

"I have some new information on the thieving couple, and it may involve you, since I understand you are the current occupant of Blount Manor."

"Yes," James said. "Royal Veterinary College. I am the Principal."

"Right," the detective said. "Let me begin by saying that I believe your two thieves are dead, killed in an air raid in the East End."

"Dead!" Rachel and Lady Blount said at the same time.

"Yes. There were bodies discovered in the rubble of a cheap hotel. Matched the description you gave perfectly, though they seem to have registered under a different name. They were found with this …" He pointed to a box on the low table. James saw that it was a metal ammunition box, probably from the first war.

"What's in it?" Rachel asked.

"Several papers, a small bit of silver, some pound notes. The notes were traced to Lord Blount, who drew them from a Reading bank in …" The detective consulted a small notebook, "…1928."

"Mine!" said Lady Blount.

"Yes. In many ways, case closed. However, what intrigued us was this…" He opened the case and took out a piece of paper, a diagram of some sort.

"Can you tell us whether this is a drawing of Blount Manor?" He showed the page to Lady Blount, who shook her head.

"I'm not good with diagrams and such – show him." She waved vaguely in James' direction.

James looked at it with interest. It was clearly a floor plan of the Manor. Several spots were marked with circles, but some of the circles were crossed out.

"Yes," he said. "Ground floor. What do you make of these markings?"

"We're not sure. That's why we're consulting you."

"Can I see it?" Rachel asked, in a tone of poorly repressed curiosity.

"Certainly." Detective Coleridge handed her the paper.

"Yes, I see. Kitchen. Fireplace … Isn't that the laundry room? Oh."

James saw it too. "These are some of the places that were destroyed when Thomas and Vera left the house."

"It's like they were looking for something," Rachel said.

"Ahhh!" said the detective. "That's what we suspected. But what would they be looking for?"

"My money," said Lady Blount. "I always suspected that Lord Blount was putting away cash for me. He hinted several times that I would be well cared for when he died. But he never told me where to find it. And he died so suddenly …"

Lady Blount wiped tears from her eyes with both fluttering hands. Rachel left her seat and went to comfort the old woman.

James said, "A local university professor, a mathematician, also mentioned that he felt Lady Blount should have received more at Lord Blount's death."

"That's probably it, then," said the detective. "We don't know, of course, if they found what they were looking for, but it would seem not."

"No," James said. He lowered his voice. "The manor is in a considerable state of disrepair at this moment, since we are building facilities … Perhaps I can direct a discreet search of the remaining places."

The detective looked James over, as if assessing his integrity. "Yes," he said. He handed over the paper. "You will let us know immediately if you find anything. In the meantime, the contents of this box can be returned to her ladyship, as the criminal case is closed."

He brought out a small receipt book from another pocket, listed the contents, and got Lady Blount's shaky signature.

Lloyd put down his pen and propped his head in his hands. Writing a sermon was hard enough these days, but the added aches and pains brought on by picking potatoes made it almost impossible. Furthermore, he was hungry. Annie was doing amazing things with their rations, but sometimes it just didn't seem there was enough.

He was relieved to hear the gate open. This conversation with Philip and Marjorie was likely to be difficult, but it offered the opportunity to linger over tea. He hoped Annie had found a miracle of sugar and butter to go with the flour that was, at least for the moment, abundant.

Annie was greeting the Clarkes when Lloyd stepped across. "I'm glad you were able to come. I'm afraid the cupboard is a little bare, but there were some apples at the grocer's, so I made what we'll call a sour apple cobbler – sweetened only by the fruit."

Marjorie was gracious. "That will be lovely, I'm sure, Annie."

"Why don't we begin with prayer," Lloyd said. To his shame, he found himself speaking to the Lord for nearly the first time that day, in words as stiff as his back. After some pleasantries, mostly about Ned's potatoes, Philip turned the conversation.

"Lloyd, I'm sure Annie has shared Violet's confessions with you." Philip had seated himself in the middle of the love seat, with Marjorie on one side and Violet on the other, and now he squeezed both their hands. "As Annie suggested, Violet came and talked to us on … Sunday?"

"Yes," Marjorie said faintly.

"We were – and are – tremendously saddened by all this. We don't understand what would cause you …" he looked at Violet, "… to do all this."

Violet buried her head in her lap. Philip raised his knuckle and wiped a tear from under his eye, then wrapped his arm around Violet. "But we are very proud of her for confessing to us and seeking our help." He wrapped his arm around Violet. "We forgive her and love her so much."

He pulled out a handkerchief. Seeing his wife's tears, he wiped her eyes as well. Then Violet's. "We talked again yesterday, and again last night, and we've tentatively come to a decision that we want your opinion – opinions – about.'

Violet sat up and looked at Annie. "I want to go away. I need to go away, Mrs. Robins … to Coventry, to stay with Holly."

"Oh! I see," Annie said.

Marjorie spoke up. "We think it best. We know she'll try hard to stay away from … that crowd. We'll do all we can to help but … but she's that tempted."

"I wish I could do what you said, Mrs. Robins. I wish I could walk with Jesus all the time. But it's so dark, and I'm so sad, and sometimes just giving in, going to the parties and the drinks and … Reggie seems like the only way out. I think I'll do better with my sister."

"She's always looked out for you, hasn't she?" Annie said.

"Always. I've spoken to her. She knows everything and she's willing to help."

"Does she have space?"

"Not much," Marjorie responded. "Violet will have to sleep in the sitting room. But Holly and Robert don't think it will be a problem."

"And I would get to see the babies. And help her with them."

Lloyd spoke up. "Well, it seems reasonable to us."

Violet looked to Annie, who nodded firmly. "When will you leave?"

Philip answered. "I'll take her up there on Saturday. I do have to do a little legal work, even though it appears I was designed to be a potato farmer."

Lloyd felt a lot closer to the Lord as he prayed. "We do ask that you would keep Violet safe, not only from outside temptations, but especially from the inward temptation to despair. Strengthen her parents to trust you while she's gone."

Violet hugged Annie. "Thank you so much, Mrs. Robins."

"I'll be praying for you every day."

At that moment the air raid siren sounded. Violet looked worried and reached for her mother's arms. They discussed whether they should go to the only municipal shelter, the basement of the town hall. Lloyd thought he heard aircraft far off and high up, but the town's two anti-aircraft guns remained silent.

~ † ~

Lenny sighed. His boss, R. V. Jones, had given him an impossible job and expected immediate results. Jones was so brilliant that his intuitions bordered on certainties. Now he was certain that the Germans were using a second, more sophisticated, target-aiming system for their bombers in place of their already-defeated Knickebein. Jones thought the new system would be pioneered by one, or at most two, German bomber groups. Lenny's job was to determine which, if any, showed above average accuracy. Observer reports, radio intercepts and reports of downed aircraft poured into his office, and the girls turned it into summaries and maps. But there was only him and Tom to piece it together.

And these bloody raids were infuriating. How was a man to concentrate? He was closing his door, as if that would make any difference, when Tom stepped in.

"Bit of a row, old chap, what?" Tom had been reading Wodehouse again.

"Too loud to think." Lenny replied.

"Got a call from the old man. He thinks this one's for real. Tells us to head for the shelter." Damn! Lenny thought. He paused to give an objective listen. The noise did seem to be increasing every moment.

"All right then. Have you told the girls?"

"Yes, they're waiting for us."

Lenny swept his papers into a rough pile, tucked it under his arm and grabbed his jacket. Tom and the dozen girls from their section were waiting in the outer office. "Everyone go to their desk and get today's dispatches. They're irreplaceable. Keep them with you."

Some of the girls tried to protest, but the others chivvied them on.

As they started down the stairs, an enormous explosion shook the building.

"Getting closer. Let's get a move on here." Tom said.

They emerged onto the street and ran the fifty feet to the next building. The shelter was in the basement, and Lenny knew it had been reinforced. It was one of the few shelters that gave him any confidence.

They descended the steps and pounded on the metal door. The large room with its stout pillars was already nearly full. The dozen of them squeezed in and found a spot near the wall, where Lenny had just enough room to leaf through his papers. There it was again. Kampfgruppe 100 appeared to be operating independently of other bomber units. Now if he could just show that their attacks were more accurate. Before he could ferret anything out, the noise and smell of the shelter broke his concentration for good.

Lord, he thought, let this be over quickly. Keep the people up there safe, especially the ARP and the anti-aircraft crews.

The noise drew a picture of a wave of bombers approaching and dumping their loads. First to the left of the shelter, then to the right, then, blessedly, mostly beyond it. Lenny thought the raid would be over soon.

Then there was a rending crash. A wave of pressure and a blast of grit drove Lenny back against the wall and entwined him with a score of bodies. He struggled for breath and sight. Breath came first. The lights were out, but a few torch beams were scanning around. The ceiling appeared to have held.

"Tom? Louise? Angela? Are you all right?"

Tom answered. "I'm fine Lenny. Some of the girls are hurt. Come and have a look at Angela's arm." Lenny crawled across the debris-filled floor. Judging only by touch, he thought the arm was badly broken. "Compound fracture," he said. "We need to straighten it and stop the bleeding." He took off his jacket, then his shirt, and began to rip it into strips by feel. "Anyone got a torch?" he called, but there was so much chaos that no one responded. When he and Tom straightened Angela's arm, she passed out. He wrapped the limb tightly where it bled and splinted it with his jacket.

"Sir, can you come over here?" The man with the torch had found the new girl, Susan, lying against the wall, unresponsive. When they turned her over, they found her skull crushed at the forehead, oozing something. She was dead. *Oh Lord, no!*

Most of the occupants of the shelter had gathered where the door had been. It had collapsed inward, and much of the building above now covered the stairway. A couple of big men organized a crew to carry debris away from the entrance, hoping to tunnel up to the surface.

Lenny and Tom cared for the wounded. Two more had been killed outright, and another two didn't look like they would make it. A dozen were less seriously injured.

As they worked, the drone of the planes continued, waxing and waning. After a while, it appeared another wave was right overhead. The bomb blasts from this wave sounded deeper. The ground shook. Debris fell from the ceiling. At one point there was a deep, solid thump.

But no explosion.

The bomb was lying on its side, half buried in the dirt. The air raid siren was sounding, planes were droning overhead, the crump of anti-aircraft fire was nearly continuous and pierced at frequent intervals by the baritone rumble of an SC50 or the long bass shake of an SC250.

This was a 250, five times bigger than the practice bombs. It seemed to crouch in and menace them from the pit they had dug around it. A smaller bomb had fallen earlier, crushing the only entrance to a shelter. They could hear cries for help from within. If this bomb exploded those people would be goners.

The lieutenant pointed at Welly. "Right, Ward, Hudson, you're it." Welly already knew that. He and John took their kits and crawled cautiously down to the bomb. The 250 had two fuses. Either one could be ready to set it off.

He took the fuse closer to the tail. They each attached their Crabtrees, threw the lines, then prepared to unscrew the fuses.

Before they could get very far another wave of planes begin to unload. It was sheer idiocy, Welly thought, to be crouching behind five hundred pounds of high explosive for shelter from flying debris. Fires raged all around. The raid had included incendiaries. The fire brigade was dragging hoses past them to try to stop an inferno reaching from building to building. Ambulances were queued up to take the injured out of the bomb shelter, but they kept being called away.

Finally the droning bombers passed. Welly and John got back to work. Fifteen turns, Welly told himself. When he got to the fourteenth turn, he carefully rotated the fuse by hand. In the orientation it was in, it could slip out, which could be a ticket on the express to heaven. He stopped at fourteen-and-a-half turns.

John was exactly as far along as Welly. They crawled up out of the hole and perched behind a pile of debris that had been hastily constructed. It would provide almost no protection in an explosion.

"Another wave coming in," the lieutenant called. "Do this now."

"They're not booby trapped," Hudson yelled. "Tool markings are wrong."

"Are you sure?" Welly asked. Hudson shrugged.

Side by side, they took hold of the lines that attached them to the fuses. They counted to three and pulled at exactly the same moment. They would never know which one of them had killed the other.

No explosion. It took Welly a long moment to realize it. He and John clapped each other on the back as the rest of the team rushed up and put the two fuses in a blast box. Others set up a lift rig over the crater, while still others began to dig at what had been the entrance to the shelter.

Welly just sat on the pile of debris and watched. The last wave of Heinkels dropped their loads a few streets away, but no one even flinched.

Finally, the hole reached the entrance to the basement. A medic put his head to the opening and yelled. "How many critically injured?" He held up two fingers.

The hole was rapidly enlarged. Soon the medics were able to start passing in stretchers. The critically injured came out first, followed by the bodies. As the hole grew, the occupants of the shelter were able to leave. By this time, Welly and his crew had just about finished packing up and were ready to move on to the next bomb.

A young man with no shirt on came out of the shelter, carrying a girl whose arm was encased in a bloody bandage. An ambulance driver ran up and spoke to him, then went for a stretcher. The young man laid the girl down, appeared to pray with her for a minute and then stood watching as they carried her away. Welly wondered if he was a minister. Then the young man turned. Welly was shocked to recognize him. It was Lenny Clarke.

CHAPTER 10

3 October 1940

Arthur wound the gear to allow water from the upper river to fill the lock. There were still cargo boats on the middle reaches of the Thames these days, but the private traffic had almost died out. Arthur recognized this boat, a fifty footer, as belonging to a businessman whose estate was up near Oxford.

To his surprise, Captain Grimes jumped off the yacht as it waited for the lock to fill. He looked uncomfortable in a tight civilian suit.

"Grimey! What are you doing here?"

"Just checking up on an old friend. Have you recovered from Dunkirk?"

"I'm doing well, Captain, though I still haven't got my boat back."

"If you have a minute, perhaps we could find a pub and have a pint."

What's this going to be about? Arthur thought. "Certainly," he said.

Arthur saw the yacht through the lock, and watched it tie up next to the towpath. He joined Captain Grimes on the bank. The naval officer asked after Wellington and Stanley as they walked up into the town, and Arthur told him about Welly's assignment to a bomb disposal unit. "Stanley's working out at a friend's farm. He stays there most nights. Itching to join up himself, but he's still only fourteen – no, he turned fifteen last month."

Arthur assessed Grimes' face as they sat at a corner table with their drinks. His hands suggested he was nervous. "So. What can I do for you?" Arthur asked.

"Yes, well … We think well of what the three of you did last spring, and we've got a proposal."

Arthur leaned forward intently. "And who exactly is 'we' in this context?"

"You don't really need to know. Let's just say I've been seconded to an organization concerned with the possibility of an invasion."

"Oh, ho, rather old news, that. Hitler's not likely to cross the Channel now, with the weather closing in and his planes all tangled up over London."

"That's as may be," Grimes said. "But one wants to be prepared. There will come another spring."

Arthur sipped his bitter and waited.

"Many preparations have been made, of course." Grimes said. "Some of them not widely publicized."

"As is to be expected. I didn't think it was entirely rhetoric when Churchill had his say about the beaches and the streets and the fields and the hills."

"No? Good man!" Grimes said. He waved his three-fingered hand and lowered his voice even further. "Even this side of London, there are those who have been recruited to provide active resistance if the invasion should come."

"Active resistance?"

"Information, troop counts, movements." Grimes paused. "Sabotage."

"Ah."

"His Majesty's Government is inclined to provide resources in preparation for such patriotic activities."

"And you'd like to provide me with such resources?"

"You put a lot of work into *Guinevere*, didn't you?" Grimes asked.

"I did."

"And you'd like her back?"

"Quite. She is, of course, a little the worse for wear right at the moment."

"Yes," Grimes agreed. "Shot up on deck and a few holes straight through. Must have made getting back across the Channel a bother."

"I had an adequate pump and a willing hand."

"But she's really still in fine shape," Grimes continued. "Patch up a couple of holes, new oil and such in that fine Sea Prince engine and you'd soon have your little side business back, running tourists up and down the river."

"Not much tourist business at the moment."

"You might be surprised."

"So are you saying it could be done?"

"It is being done even as we speak." Grimes said. "A few good mates will bring her up the river to Reading, shipshape, this week. Don't want to bring her any closer for fear of raising talk."

Arthur leaned in. "And what exactly am I supposed to do with the old girl?"

"Well, from time to time you'll be quietly asked, to transport a party from here to there, or to drop a modest bundle discretely under the deck in one little town and unload it downriver. I can't give you any details, of course."

Arthur smoothed both mustaches. He knew he'd already decided. He wanted his boat back. And … well, he had to admit that things had been rather boring since Dunkirk. Here was a chance to make a contribution, however far-fetched the invasion scenario.

Ned coughed violently, and then laid his head back against the chair. He hated being sick, and he really didn't have time for it at the moment.

Alice answered a solid knock at the door.

"Why hello, Arthur. Come in."

Ned didn't have the energy to get up. "Hello, Arthur," he called.

"Ned's not feeling well," she said. "He's got an awful cold, and he's exhausted."

"Sorry to hear that, old chap. I can come back later."

"No," Ned said. "Have a seat. Let Alice get you a cuppa."

"Right then, I won't keep you long. Did you get the potatoes in?"

"We did. Thanks to a lot of help from the church," Ned replied. "And I heard that you're getting the *Guinevere* back."

"Picked her up in Reading yesterday. Bet those Navy chaps couldn't stand her cluttering up the coast. Decent of them to give her back." Ned was not so sick that he couldn't smell something false in this, but if Arthur wanted to tell him more, he would. "That's partly why I've come. She's not quite shipshape and … not to put too fine a point on it – I think I need Stanley back for … a few days – to help me tidy her up."

Ned slumped. Lose Stanley? How would he get the wheat planted? He got as far as exclaiming, "Arthur!" before he was wracked with coughs.

"I'm sorry, Ned." When the fit had passed, Arthur continued. "I know he's being helpful here, but I have to have at least one hand to get *Guinevere* back into shape."

"What's the rush, Arthur? Winter's coming, there's a war on. No one is going to hire that boat."

"We've had enquiries."

"From whom?"

"Can't really say, but enough to justify a little urgency."

Again, Ned felt the falseness in his friend's words. "Surely it's not more urgent than getting the wheat planted? I had to leave it rotting in the field last year. I can't afford to lose Stanley when it's time to plant."

"When is that?"

"Sailor boy, aren't you?" Ned roused himself, stood, shook off his frustration. Out of the window, he could see Stanley on the Fordson, tilling. Good lad.

"Could be this week, but it can wait as long as next week."

He turned and looked Arthur in the eye. "But no later, Arthur. I need him back."

~ † ~

"She looks great, Uncle Arthur," Stanley said.

"They did a passable job, considering the damage and the gore. Can't say I like the color scheme." *Guinevere*'s hull had been painted midnight blue.

"But I heard you say she's not shipshape."

"We'll strictly speaking, she's not. I want to break down and inspect the engine before we run her. And I want to put a hatch in the lower deck so we can store some things against the hull. Quite a bit of wasted space there."

"Righto, let's go. I want to get back to Mr. Powell. I think he needs me."

This is a good lad. And too bright to leave completely ignorant. "Before we do, I want to tell you something."

Arthur gave a carefully worded summary of their role. "It could be dangerous. We'll be moving people from one place to another. And we'll be moving supplies. Maybe military supplies. I hope I don't need to tell you that all this needs to be completely secret. And voluntary."

"Yes, sir," said Stanley. "I volunteer."

"Why do you so willingly put yourself into danger, Stanley?"

"Why do you?" Stanley retorted.

"I'm an old man. Serving my country is a habit. But you've got your whole life ahead of you."

Stanley was thoughtful as they gathered tools for the engine work. "My dad's a spiv. I'd rather do something useful."

Arthur saw an opening, but groped for the right words. "Do you ever worry about what happens to you when you die?"

"My dad said that all that pie in the sky was for sissies and old women."

Arthur responded gently. "And how good have you found his opinions?"

"Dad's? No bloody good at all."

Arthur decided to ignore the epithet. "Do you think Welly Ward's a sissy or an old woman? Mr. Powell? Rachel Busby?"

"But she is an old woman!" Arthur smoothed his mustaches and raised one eyebrow. "Well … not really, I guess," Stanley said.

Arthur thought of a lot more, but he contented himself with "Maybe you should get their ideas on what happens when you die. And maybe you should read that Bible I gave you and see what kind of sissy Jesus was."

Lloyd was finishing the final draft of his message when he heard the garden door of the church open. A voice quietly said, "Lloyd?"

"Yes. Is that you, Alice?"

"It is. Do you have a minute?"

"Certainly. Just a moment." He scrawled the rest of the sentence, but he knew he had yet to explain, or even understand, Peter's command to count it all joy when meeting diverse trials. "Hello, Alice, how are you?"

"Good, I think."

"Do you want to go back over to the house to talk?"

"I was just there. Annie said I should stop by and ask you to pray for Ned."

"I've heard that he's struggling to get the wheat planted."

"That's part of it. Arthur came by this week and stole back Stanley. Ned's been sick, so he hasn't had a lot of energy. But ten years ago he'd have jumped into it, him and his horse, sunup to sundown."

Alice paused. She chewed the tip of her tongue when she was nervous.

"But there's more?"

"I don't know, Lloyd. I've never seen him like this. He doesn't want to do anything. He's become a total pessimist. He's convinced the

Germans are building up strength to invade in the spring, or that they'll starve us out with the blockade. 'Don't you know,' he keeps saying, 'that Britain imports seventy percent of its food supply.'"

Lloyd smiled at Alice's imitation of her husband's deep, slow voice. Then he thought about it. "Is it really that high?"

She nodded. "I think that's why the loss of the wheat hit him so hard."

Jesus, Lloyd prayed, please do something to lift Ned's eyes, to energize him. And me. Lloyd forced himself to say the right thing. "Is there any way I can help?"

He hated that she brightened. "Come and visit him," she said. "He's officially still recuperating from this chest cold, but I think he's just unwilling to make the effort. Come and encourage him."

How?

Arthur approached his own house with some caution. Rosie had been feeling a little better, which made life easier, but this morning she had complained of her gout again and couldn't move from the bed.

"Hello, Rosie, I'm back," he called from the door.

"I'm right here," she said from her chair in the sitting room.

"Hello, dearest," he said. "I didn't expect you to be up."

"Come see what I've found this morning." She had her big Bible in her lap.

"Can I spend a moment getting lunch started?"

"No need. I've already got it on the table."

He looked through to the kitchen and saw a steaming pot on the table, bread already sliced, and two bowls.

"Rosie, Rosie," he said, "you must really be feeling well today." He rejoiced when the girl he'd married showed through the pain that bedeviled her.

"I am." A weak smile reversed the habitual shape of her mouth. "But, I've also become convicted of something." She motioned to the chair near her.

"What have you been studying?" Arthur asked. *Lord, let her have found some heart truth in your Word this morning.*

"Matthew 25."

Arthur knew this was one of her favorite chapters, with its mysterious and complicated second-coming prophecies. "What have you seen?" he said with as much enthusiasm as he could muster.

"It all starts with the parable of the talents," she said, pointing to the middle of the chapter. "Jesus tells a similar parable over here …" she flipped to the place she was holding with her finger, "… in Luke 19. He says to the servants 'occupy until I come.' I'm quite sure that means that they should put whatever he gave them to work. Then …" she flipped back, "… he tells the story of the sheep and the goats, and says that he's going to judge when he comes based on how we've met the needs of the hungry and the naked and prisoners and strangers."

"And what did the Lord say to you from that?"

"It's simplicity itself, love," she said. "I think he's telling me I need to be caring for others, not just rotting my bahookie in this chair."

"But you're so often in pain."

"True. But Jesus endured pain to care for others." Long pause. "Arthur, I'm sorry I don't pull my weight in this organization."

"I know how hard it is."

"But I selfishly make it harder. I'll try to do more: for you, for Stanley, and for others. If Hitler's the antichrist and these are the last days, I want to be found doing what Jesus wants when He comes."

He took her hands. This sincere heart beneath the bluster was one of the reasons he loved her. "Amen, Rosie, Amen."

"Now help me get my bahookie out to the kitchen," she said.

Arthur devoured the soup. The old girl could really cook when she put her mind to it. He wondered why she put up with his burnt sausages and runny mash. Pain is a funny thing, he told himself.

"So Arthur," Rosie said. "Can you tell me the real reason they brought you back that old boat?"

Philip sat with Marjorie, and the train sat on a siding. Their trip to Coventry had started well enough. The local to Oxford ran almost on time. But the train to Coventry had been late and crowded. They'd only found seats after Banbury.

"Oh, I hope we get there before dark," Marjorie said for the third time.

"It's more than three hours to sunset. And as I said, these night bombings don't really get started until hours after dark. And except for London they've only hit the industrial cities."

"What about trains?"

"Well, occasionally." Philip knew that railroad tracks, often visible in the moonlight, were a secondary target when the Jerries could not find their primary target.

Just then the train started to move with a jerk. "Here we go, then. By the way, the postman dropped this off just before we left," Philip said.

"It's from Lenny. Why didn't you give it to me sooner?"

"Slipped my mind." It was the kind of little white lie intended to keep one's beloved from pain. Marjorie nodded solemnly and turned to the letter.

Philip wondered how much of the letter was the same kind of lie. Lenny reported that there had been a spot of trouble at his building, but that he had been safe in a bomb shelter, and had bumped into Wellington Ward. He also mentioned that he had attended a funeral for a co-worker killed in a raid.

"Oh, he's moving out of town. That's good, isn't it?" Marjorie said. Tears, never far away, had begun to slip down her cheeks as she read the letter. "Do you think he has been in much danger?"

"Yes, I expect so."

"Well, we can thank God He has spared him thus far."

And curse God that he took Edwin? Philip was astonished how quickly bitterness could leap to the surface.

Rachel was sitting perusing the newspapers with Lady Blount. "It's the little things you have to look for," she said. "All this talk of the Tripartite Pact doesn't mean a thing – it's only meant to keep the United States out of the war."

"And you don't think that affects us?" Lady Blount answered. "In the last war it was America that swung the tide."

"Oh, I agree," Rachel said. "It could be bad long term. But if you want to know what's happening now, you have to look at the little stories."

She folded the paper and showed it to Lady Blount. "Here is a list of merchant seaman receiving awards from the King for meritorious service. Most of them are for heroic escapes from bombings and from submarines. In other words, the Germans are wreaking havoc with our merchant shipping."

"That's as may be. But you're avoiding the question I asked earlier. Why don't you like Sir James? I think he's perfect for you."

"Perfectly horrible. An unrepentant thief, wrapped up in his work, high and mighty with his CBE."

"Now you know you don't believe that. He's a fine Christian man. Though he is an unrepentant thief. Stole my manor for his stinky sheep." She paused and scrunched up her nose in a way that made Rachel laugh.

Father, why have you given me another old lady to take care of? Watching her dear mum die had been one of the most painful experiences of Rachel's life.

"Do you smell them?" Lady Blount said. "They must pile the sheep shit right against your back fence."

Rachel laughed again. This woman was definitely a caution. "Lady Blount," she said, "that is not a very ladylike thing to say."

"I'll say anything I like." Her voice was playful. "Sheep shit … sheep shit … sheep … shiii…"

Rachel's heart leapt in her chest. "Eleanor!" She leapt up, took Lady Blount by both hands. Her face was lifeless, her eyes glazed. *Lord Jesus, help!*

As suddenly as the fit had started, it changed. Eleanor's eyes rolled until all Rachel could see was bloodshot white. She crumped in on herself, almost sliding out of the chair, perfectly limp.

"Eleanor! Eleanor! Can you hear me?" Rachel took a limp wrist in one hand and felt for a pulse. It was there. *Thank you, Lord.* And … yes, she was breathing.

Rachel hesitated a moment then ran to the telephone and dialed Dr. Nesbitt. The phone rang and rang. Eleanor's hands were beginning to flap weakly. Rachel dialed the operator. "I need Dr. Nesbitt to call me immediately. Can you keep ringing him? … Thank you."

The old lady was breathing heavily. *What do I do?* Finally, she dialed Sir James at the manor.

"Grierson's office. Walter Pennessy speaking."

Blast! Rachel thought. Help, Lord!

"This is Rachel Busby. I need to speak to Sir James. It's rather urgent."

"I'm sorry ma'am, but he's in a conference. I expect him to be free in a few minutes. May I have him telephone you?"

Rachel looked over to where Eleanor was starting to stir. "Yes. Please. Rachel Busby." She replaced the receiver and hurried to Eleanor's side. Her eyes were open, and her mouth was moving as if trying to talk around a wad of cotton.

"Let me get you a drink." Rachel said.

After a few sips of water, Eleanor said "Wha … hwa … hap … happened?"

"I don't know, my lady. You seem to have had a stroke or a seizure. Can you move your head?"

"Yes." She rolled it around, then stretched out her arms, hands and finally her legs.

"Good," Rachel said. "Let me help you sit up a little … Has it stopped?"

"Yes. Did I pass out?"

"For a few moments. Before that you seemed to just stiffen up."

"Well … I seem to be feeling better now. Thirsty." As Eleanor downed a second glass of water, the phone rang.

"That will be the doctor. Now don't you move … Hello."

"James Grierson here."

Argh! Faster than the doctor. "Thank you for calling, Sir James. Lady Blount has had another stroke or seizure, and I couldn't get hold of Dr. Nesbitt."

"Does she need to go to hospital?"

"I don't know. She seems to be recovering now, just a little weak."

"Right. Let's take her to Nesbitt's office. If we don't get him we'll go straight to Reading."

But Dr. Nesbitt was just entering his surgery when they pulled up. A few minutes later Rachel found herself sitting uncomfortably with James in the small waiting room.

"The good news," Dr. Nesbitt said when he had examined Eleanor, "is that she's recovering. You'll be able to take her home. The bad news is that I'm not sure what it was. She hasn't had a stroke. She doesn't have symptoms of diabetes and says she has no history of seizures. My best guess is some kind of growth in the brain."

"Oh, no!" Rachel said.

James thought for a moment. "Course of action?"

"Are you aware that we can now diagnose intracranial tumors with X-rays?"

"No."

"They've been doing it in America for almost four years. One of my colleagues in London, Cheswick, has tried the procedure."

"Ralph Cheswick? I know the man. Brilliant. Does he think it works?"

"No proof yet, but he thinks if there's a tumor he would see it."

"And if it's not a tumor?"

"If it's not a tumor it may be something we can treat."

~ † ~

Arthur and Stanley stood up after Rosie's wonderful dinner. They would need their energy tonight.

"Thank you, my Rosalinda, for an excellent repast." Arthur could not have been more thrilled by Rosie's attitude these last few days.

"You're very welcome, sir," she said in her best imitation of a saucy barmaid. "Now it would be most ungrateful of the customers to go out and get themselves killed, wouldn't it? Terrible bad for business, like."

Arthur laughed and embraced her large frame. "We won't be long."

When he broke the embrace, she took his hands. "I wouldn't know what to do without you."

He shrugged. "You'd get by. You've got my little pension."

"That isn't what I meant, you old rogue."

"I know. I'll be careful." He gave her a kiss and ritually bowed his head so she could kiss the center of his bald forehead. Out of the corner of his eye, Arthur saw Stanley shake his head at the demonstration of affection by the old people.

As they prepared the *Guinevere*, Stanley asked, "So what's the plan?"

Arthur considered the rapidly maturing lad. "It's the real thing tonight. We go downriver past Reading. Our cover is that we're going to spend the night at a private dock and take a party of gentlemen out for a little hunting along the banks. In reality, they unload what I've got in the new hold."

"How did it get there?"

"Can't say. But I'll be happy when we get it out."

The night was cool, the clouds low and thick – perfect for concealment from anyone watching overhead or from the banks. The fresh river breeze and the feeling of the open country on each side spoke peace to his tight soul. As they wound their way along, Arthur brought up the subject they had been discussing for weeks. "Have you been reading the Gospels, lad?"

"Aye, aye, Captain." Stanley replied.

"And what do you find?"

"Jesus … I guess."

"Do you like him?" At the odd question a thoughtful furrow creased Stanley's forehead.

"Yes." Stanley's whisper grew in intensity. "He's amazing. I love it when He confronts the Pharisees. 'Blind guides! Hypocrites!'"

"And do you know why he calls them that?"

"They're liars. They don't really believe anything. They're just out to be seen. Like my dad."

"And Jesus?"

"He's not like them at all. He's always helping people. What'd he say? 'I came to seek and save the lost.' And he's a man. Went up to Jerusalem knowing he'd be killed."

"Very good, Stanley. I didn't know you were such a reader."

"Had a teacher in third form. Miss Summers. Dad was mostly gone that year. She helped me stay in school."

"Good for her."

"But I've a question, Uncle Arthur. Who did Jesus save? And from what?"

Arthur paused to thank God for the question. "Us. From sin, lad, from rebellion against God. Do you remember in Matthew when the angel says that Jesus will save his people from their sin?"

"Yes … first chapter I read, I think. But I'm not a sinner."

"Are you sure? Have you ever been selfish, or said things to hurt, or hated someone?"

"Well, my dad, but …"

"I admit your dad's a bad sort. But does that give you permission to be angry with him or to hate him?"

"Maybe not." The lad turned his face away, and spoke roughly. "But I'm not sorry for it."

"I understand. But keep reading, lad. The Gospels are only good news for those who see their own sin."

Not long after, Arthur went forward to scan the banks. In the pitch dark there was the flash of a torch. Two blinks, a pause, two more.

Arthur sent back one blink, then two, then one. They crept slowly up to a dock. A lone figure stood there, dressed in hunting garb. Arthur leaned out of the boat in response to this man's silent gesture. He whispered "All off. We're not ready. Couldn't assemble the men. Tuesday night."

Early on Monday morning James pulled up at Rachel's gate. They had decided to drive into London rather than take the increasingly unreliable train. Lady Blount was nervous and snappy. "C'mon young man. We don't have all day. I don't know if you've ever driven to London, but it's a long way."

She criticized every aspect of James' driving. "Didn't you see that hole? It was the size of a police box. I'm surprised you didn't break an axle.

"Have you been drinking this early in the day? You're all over the road. Try to leave half of it for someone else." James felt a twinge of sympathy for Thomas.

The streets of London were a shambles. Many were closed, and James had to re-route, re-route and re-route again.

"Look!" Rachel said. "That building is still on fire."

James glanced to his left. "It's the Carlton Club. I've dined there."

"So have I," Lady Blount said in an almost wistful tone. But then, "My back hurts in this awful automobile of yours. Why are you wasting time chasing fires?"

The hospital, St. Bart's, appeared substantially undamaged, but as they descended to the basement, they were met with a wall of noise, and the stench of hospital, fire, decay, and broken bodies. They walked past hall after hall of the injured and wounded, often surrounded by family.

"Where is the X-ray department?" James asked. "Dr. Cheswick?" Finally, a nurse in a soiled uniform pointed them toward a long dark hall, one side lined with trolleys on which injured patients struggled to rest while waiting for their turn at the big X-ray machine. In the intersecting hall, nurses were writing diagnoses on white paper, pinning them to the clothing of the victims. These patients, it seemed, would be taken to hospitals out of town.

James found a seat for Lady Blount, who was bewildered and dismayed by the destruction, stench, and noise. Soon James spotted a familiar silhouette. "Ralph?" he said. "Dr. Cheswick?"

"Yes." The doctor turned slowly. For a moment James thought he had made a mistake. The man's face sagged with fatigue and the bags under his eyes were as black and blue as bruises. By contrast, his skin was an ashen shade of grey.

"Yes, can I help you?" Ralph had not recognized him.

"It's James Grierson, Ralph. I've brought a patient for an X-ray."

"Hello, James." Cheswick said without emotion. "Join the queue. What kind of injury?"

"It's not an injury. Suspected brain tumor."

To James' surprise, Cheswick perked up. "A tumor. Tell me all about it."

He raised his voice and yelled over the din, "Jones, I'm taking five minutes."

James led the exhausted man to Lady Blount and got him a chair. He and Rachel told the doctor what had happened.

Gently, the doctor said, "Let me look into your eyes, my lady." He shone a bright light into each eye, and carried out a few other simple tests.

He wrote a note on a scrap of paper and handed it to Rachel. "Why don't you take your friend to the front of the queue there?" As the two walked away, he turned to James, every bit the fascinated doctor. "Yes, very likely, and it could be quite advanced. Let's see if my machine can see it."

They almost didn't get the chance. Lady Blount refused to step up to the machine. Rachel had to agree to stand next to her, holding her hand, as the big film canister was placed behind her. The doctor insisted on three pictures.

"I'll send these off to the darkroom," he said. "Lady Blount, if you can sit over there, we'll have the answer in just a few minutes."

It was more like an hour. The doctor's grey pallor seemed even more pronounced. "James, Mrs. Busby," he said quietly, "can I show you something?"

"The good news is, my machine worked perfectly. You can see the tumor in all three of these photographs." James didn't actually think he could, but he took the doctor's word for it. "The bad news is that the tumor is advanced and deep into the area between the two halves of the brain. No known treatment."

"And?" Rachel asked.

"Apart from a miracle – and I still believe in those – it will kill her. Not as fast as a bomb," he gestured around, "but just as thoroughly ..." He sagged. "I would take her back out of town and care for her. She might last several months. She will probably have more symptoms. Loss of hearing, or sight, or speech, or use of her limbs. The lower back pain suggests it will be that, but it can strike anywhere." He held out his hand. James shook it. "Thank you for bringing her. If this madness ever ceases I hope give some attention to treating these things."

James looked again at the chaos of St. Bart's. "Can I pray for you, friend?"

"Absolutely, James."

"Lord," James said, "thank you for Ralph and for all these people here risking their lives to save others. Please strengthen them and keep them safe. Let this horror cease. Help the wounded to be cared for, and help them recover. In your name, Jesus. Amen."

"Thank you, James. Prayer may be the only thing that makes a difference here."

~ † ~

Violet hugged Mum fiercely.

"Let me look at you," Mum said. Violet looked her in the eye as long as she could and tried to smile. Then she turned away.

"Better," Mum said quietly, "but not all better."

Violet watched as Mum greeted Holly and the precious babies.

She walked over to her dad, who was watching the greetings with a smile. "Hello, old dad," she said and gave him a hug. "How are you doing?"

To her surprise, he shut his eyes, grimacing in pain. A tear escaped and began a long slow journey down the rifts and crevices of his face. After a while he shook it off, hugged her around the shoulders, and said quietly, "It comes in waves. But it's getting better. And I do believe Ed is with the Lord. That helps."

"Me too, Dad, me too." Her own guilt flared at the assertion.

"So, how long can you stay?" Holly said.

"We don't want to impose," Mum said.

Holly laughed. "Well, we don't have much room, but it's no imposition. You can put your bags in here." She opened the door to her bedroom.

"But that's your room. You and Robert deserve a little privacy."

"We'll be fine right there under the table. Safest place in the house, if you believe the reports."

"And where does Vi sleep?" Mum persisted.

"In there with the girls." Holly answered.

"Come and see," Violet said. She had a mattress at the foot of Rose's bed.

"How sweet," Mum said. "Don't the babies keep you awake?"

"Sometimes they wake me, sometimes I wake them." It was a comfort to wake from a dark dream and hear Rose breathing peacefully, or to soothe the little girls' tears when the sirens sounded.

James hurried into his office on Camden Street, miraculously as yet untouched. Rachel and Lady Blount were down in the Daimler, and he wanted to get out of town quickly, but he thought he should call first. Annie answered the telephone and gasped when she heard the diagnosis.

"Well," she said, "we'll just have to pray for a miracle. Maybe we can organize a prayer time tomorrow?"

"That's what I was hoping. We're about to head back. Pray for stamina for Lady Blount. It's been a long day already. But if she sleeps tonight I think she can make a prayer time tomorrow."

He hurried to the car. "The first problem, ladies, is finding petrol." He had a full book of ration coupons, but where would he find a filling station?

In the end, he didn't. They endured an hour of blocked streets, bombed pumps, and garages with no stock.

"I just want to get home and lie down, Thomas. My back is killing me."

"I'm sorry Lady Blount. I'm doing the best I can."

Rachel said. "Eleanor, you just need to be patient. Here, let me tuck in this lovely rug."

Finally, James gave up and decided to try to make it to Reading. He knew the filling station there, or they might find one on the way.

They had not gone far when the siren sounded.

Annie set down the receiver and sighed. She was not having much luck contacting people. Henry's housekeeper said he was going to stay in Reading for the night, having a tutorial there early in the morning. The housekeeper had gone next door to the Clarkes' but found no one home.

Alice had said that she and Ned would try to come, but he was working alone trying to get the wheat planted, and might be too exhausted.

"Where is Stanley?"

"Arthur needed him again. I can't understand why. Arthur knows the spot Ned's in … Anyway, pray for us, and we'll make it if we can."

I'll have to take a bit of a walk with the children after school, Annie thought. It was a nice day, dryer than it had been, and cooler.

When she arrived at the Cooper's Phyllis had just got home from school. She opened the door tentatively, Annie thought. "Mum, Mrs. Robins is here."

"Just a moment."

Evelyn came into the sitting room. Her skin was pale. A network of fine wrinkles surrounded her eyes. Annie couldn't recall having seen them before.

"I'm sorry, I was just making Lily lie down."

"Oh no! Is she ill?"

"She says she feels fine, but I'm worried about her. She hasn't regained her strength. I insist she takes a nap every day."

"I wanted to play with her." Lizzie whined.

"That's not going to be possible today, dear." Annie said.

Annie could hear voices behind the house. "Are you having work done?"

"Yes," Evelyn sighed. "Ernest is indulging me. We've men from Reading preparing the back yard for our Anderson shelter."

"You're getting an Anderson?"

"The sirens have gone off almost every night. Who knows when Hitler may bomb us?"

"We're not a very important little town." Annie told herself this every time. Apparently, the Jerries flew near Stokely on their way to targets in the west. But that was all – so far.

"I'm just trying to keep my babies safe," Evelyn said.

Phyllis, standing behind her mum, rolled her eyes.

Annie explained about the prayer meeting, but refused the offer of a cup of tea, explaining that she had a few other families to visit.

The children fussed at the wind when she crossed the bridge to go to the Butlers'. "Hello, Meg. How are you?"

"I'm doing well, Annie. And you?"

Annie considered answering honestly. *I'm tired, discouraged. Death and despair are always on my horizon. Everyone I care about is struggling with some burden, and my heart can't bear them all.* "Carrying on, you know."

"Come in and have a spot of tea. Bert and I were about to sit down."

"Not that I'm ever not sitting down," Bert called from the kitchen.

"Where are the children?"

"Oh, out and about." Meg stuck her head out and looked both ways. "There. Fred! Nellie! Come play with Lizzie and George for a few minutes."

This time Annie accepted the tea. She hadn't realized how tense she was until she relaxed for a moment. But when she mentioned the plans for the prayer meeting, Meg said, "Oh, I don't think we'll be able to come. Bert has some bigwig from his old factory coming round for dinner. I don't know why, exactly, but Bert's hoping he's going to talk about taking him back on."

"But what about his legs?"

"I don't know, Annie, but I don't want to bash his hopes."

When Annie left, she checked off names on her fingers. She was out of time, but so far only Dot Simmonds, whom she'd met at the school, seemed positive about attending. She hoped Alice would persuade Ned to come.

"We'll just drop by Arthur and Rosie's house," she said to the children.

"Rosie," she said when the door opened wide, "you're looking well."

"Well, if I look better than I feel, that's not half bad." When Annie had untangled this, it seemed to come out positive.

"Would you like to come in for some tea?" Rosie said.

Surprised again. "I'm so sorry, I can't stay. I just dropped by to tell you and Arthur that we're going to have a prayer time at the church."

She explained Lady Blount's diagnosis. "Prayer is the only thing we can do."

Rosie said she would try to make it, if she felt well enough. She didn't think Arthur could, because he and Stanley were heading out on the boat.

"At night? Why, whatever are they doing?"

"Ah, mum's the word, isn't it?" She gave Annie a broad conspiratorial wink.

Lloyd stood at the door of the church. He had received a worrisome telegram from James the previous evening, warning that they might not make it back. But where could everybody else be? When he turned, Annie was behind him.

"Have you heard from Ned or Alice?"

"Not since this afternoon. It sounded like Ned was exhausted. I expect Alice kept him home to get him to sleep. Arthur Cripps keeps taking Stanley Payne from him to mess about on that old boat."

"Well, I guess we'll have to start without a hymn."

At that moment, Lloyd heard a large familiar voice. "Ho, Rev'rend," Rosie said. "Don't you shut that door in my face."

"Good evening, Rosie." She stepped in and, to Lloyd's surprise, gave him a suffocating hug. "The Lord be with ye," she intoned.

"And also with you." Lloyd said automatically.

The only other people in the room were Dot and Charlie Simmonds and Alan and Susan Ward. Lloyd knew that the small turnout was mostly due to circumstances, but it didn't feel that way. Every missing face felt like a personal judgment, a feeling reinforced by Alan Ward's smirk.

Nonetheless, they prayed. They prayed for God's intervention in Lady Blount's illness, His peace to be on her and for Rachel as she cared for her, His healing if that was His will, and freedom from pain if this was her calling home. They prayed too for some who were missing. Rosie prayed a long obscure prayer of thanks and protection for Arthur and Stanley. Annie prayed for Lily to regain strength, and for Evelyn to have peace. Lloyd prayed for Ned to get help with the farm, somehow.

After he prayed the 'your will be done' and 'amen' he looked up to see James Grierson standing there, hands limp at his sides, his face wearing a look somewhere between grief and anger. "Hello James. Is Lady Blount all right?"

"Yes, but weary beyond reason. I left her and Rachel at the cottage. I hope Rachel can put up with her long enough to get her to sleep."

"Have you just got back?"

"Just about. We had quite a trek. Didn't get out of town before Jerry came. Had to spend the night in the Piccadilly tube station. Wall-to-wall bodies. Then it took the whole day to get back here. Ran out of fuel this side of Maidenhead. Had to leave the women in the car while I begged enough to get us to Reading. Lady Blount was half out of her mind with fatigue. It was no picnic."

James sat heavily. "And now … this." He spread his hands to encompass the tiny group. "I had this image of a whole group lifting her up before the Lord." Suddenly anger flared in his face and his voice. "I was here when you prayed for Muriel Timms, for Lily Cooper. The room was full. What kind of people are you? You can't pray for Lady Blount just because she has a title in front of her name? Or is it because she's old, like me? Worn out, so why waste the prayers? Or are you just a little mutual affection society and anyone who doesn't quite fit doesn't get the benefits?"

Lloyd was dumbfounded. Grief and anger wrestled in his heart. "Lloyd, I expected better of you – of all of you," James said. Lloyd held James' fiery eyes for a long minute, then bowed his head in defeat.

"I don't know, James. I just don't know anymore."

~ † ~

The waxing moon was already up, and the stars shone brightly. If the Jerries had really owned the riverbank, it would have been hard to avoid detection. As it was, Arthur feared some ARP warden or plane spotter would sound an alarm. It wasn't forbidden to travel by night, but their cover story had a few holes.

"Light on starboard shore, Captain." Stanley said.

Arthur set the motor to idle and drifted with the current near the far bank.

"Wonder why that's there?" he asked the boy. "Haven't these people heard about the blackout?"

But there were no other incidents on the long slow ride.

"Torch," Stanley said. He flashed the response.

They pulled into the landing. Their contact met them. "It's on. The men will come every five minutes."

For a long half hour men came out of the darkness, gingerly took a sack full of wrapped lumps, and slipped away. After the last courier disappeared into the darkness, Arthur said to Stanley "We'll stay here until the moon is down. We still have plenty of time to get back."

A long slow hour followed. Arthur and Stanley sat low in the boat so it would look unoccupied. Arthur prayed for wisdom and then said, "So did you read any more today?"

Stanley nodded. "I'm reading John."

"Good. Anything stand out for you?"

"Well, Jesus seems to just want people to believe in Him."

"Exactly," Arthur said. He thought of an important clarification. "But when Jesus says believe, he's not just talking about believing that he existed, or was a good man. It's more like trusting, like … like trusting a rope to hold you." He gestured at the taut line that tied them to the landing.

"And he says that when you do you don't perish, but have everlasting life. I learned that verse back when Mum used to take me to church."

"Lots of verses like that," Arthur said. "It's Jesus' answer to the whole what-happens-to-you-when-you-die question. 'He that heareth my word, and believeth on him that sent me, hath everlasting life, and shall not come into condemnation; but is passed from death unto life.'"

Stanley sat quietly. "Condemnation. That's for sin right?"

"Yes," Arthur said.

"I think you're right about all of us being sinners. My dad hurt me, but I hated him back. Jesus says it's like murdering him in my heart. I've done that."

"Jesus paid the price of your sin on the cross. Believe in Him, lad, call on Him, and you cross from death for your sin to life in Him."

Stanley turned away and said no more.

They had to run the engine louder to make headway against the current on their return.

"Light on port shore, Captain." Stanley said.

"Same light, I'd think." Arthur slowed and maneuvered to the west bank of the river. He got the boat into the blackness of the trees.

Suddenly the boat stopped with a sharp hard jerk. "Blast," he whispered. "Fouled on something." When he shut the engine down the boat swung all the way around and pointed back downstream. "I'm going to have to go down and cut her free."

"No, Captain," Stanley said. "I'll do it. I've been under this boat a dozen times."

Arthur considered it. He hated to put the child at risk, but Stanley was more agile and possibly stronger. *Blast age!* "All right. Take the shorter knife from the toolbox."

Stanley grabbed it and came back. "And close the toolbox." Stanley sighed and turned back. "If she heels or spins, I don't want things flying around."

"Yes, sir."

"Go over the side. Swim to the stern and check the rudder. Quietly."

After a few moments, Stanley reported that the rudder had caught on a net that was looped and knotted around it. Arthur thought for a moment. "Dive down and cut whatever's anchoring it. That will probably get us some steerage."

"Yes, sir," the boy said.

He dived beneath the water. Arthur listened to the quiet sound of the current running past the anchored boat. His mental count grew. It was about time for the boy to come up. He hoped Stanley wasn't pushing himself too hard.

A few more long seconds passed. "Come up, boy." *Lord, let him come up.*

Even as he was praying, Arthur was opening the toolbox to get the other knife, tucking it into his belt, closing the box. He jumped over the side of the ship and swam to the stern. No sign of the boy. He dived. The net was bigger than he feared. He circled it, pulling and poking, but he finally had to come up.

Arthur waited a moment on the surface, taking some deep breaths. Should have done that the first time. Then he dived again. This time he found the boy, caught in in a huge tangled mess, struggling weakly.

Arthur backed off and swam a little deeper. He ran into a taut line, trailing downward. He slashed at it and it parted.

But there was no upward pull. He swam forward. He would have to surface soon if he was going to survive this himself. His chest was tight. His heart pounded. Dizziness assailed him. But he found another line. It took three clumsy slashes of the knife to part it. Then he kicked – hard.

The boat was drifting freely. No sign of Stanley. Gasping, he swam, head up, to her stern. He pulled at the net, hand over hand, until he drew Stanley to himself, faced down, motionless. Quickly he turned the boy over and dragged him to the stern. Stanley began coughing and gagging. *Praise God.* Arthur grabbed the stern rail and gradually they both found breath.

"Thank you … Thank you, Uncle Arthur."

He untangled the boy and the two dragged themselves back into the boat. A few minutes later Arthur began to carefully work the net off the rudder.

"I think God can hear through water," Stanley said as they got underway.

"What?"

"You told me that anyone who calls on the name of the Lord would be saved. While I was flailing away down there I cried out to Jesus – and I was saved."

"Do you mean just from drowning?"

"No, really saved, Uncle Arthur. If I died, I wanted to be sure what would happen next."

CHAPTER 11

28 October 1940

"My story!" Ned said. "I'd like to hear your story."

"I can't really say." Stanley said. "Uncle Arthur made me promise. But I'm … um … I believe in Jesus now, and I know you've been praying for me."

"Yes, as early as Dunkirk." Ned said. *Though I haven't been praying for anybody much lately.*

"I … I want to thank you. I didn't know I needed Jesus until I met people like you and Uncle Arthur who really know Him."

If he knew how cold and tired my heart is, he might not think so. Lord, help me to be what this boy thinks I am, not what I've been lately.

"Uncle says that you and Rev'rend Robins became believers together during the last war. Can you tell me about it?"

"Well," Ned said, "Lloyd's the wordsmith. He really ought to tell you."

"Over the top." Lieutenant Fowler explained the plan to the men. "A massive artillery barrage will silence the German trenches. Should be a walk in the park."

Ned looked at the lieutenant and shook his head. He hated these rah-rah types. "Over the top" meant only one thing. Death.

"What's our objective, sir?" Ned asked.

The lieutenant pointed vaguely forward. "Mametz Wood."

They expected to go in the morning, when the artillery peaked, but the order was delayed all day. As the sun was setting, the artillery kicked in again. "Go! Go! Go!" Lieutenant Fowler ordered.

The first fifty yards were slow, but enemy fire was sporadic. Crawl in the park, thought Ned. Bloody muddy park.

They were half way across no man's land when the artillery stopped. Fowler ordered a sprint to the German trench. No! Ned thought.

They stood and began to run. Machine guns at the edge of Mametz Wood responded with ripping fire. Men began to fall right and left. The lieutenant kept screaming the survivors on. My turn next, Ned thought.

Fifteen feet ahead, the lieutenant turned. He counted the pitiful remnant of the platoon. Then his head disintegrated. In slow motion, blood and gore flew.

"Get down," Ned yelled. "Back to the trench."

"Corporal Wilkins, you're a good man." Ned looked at the basket of bottles the corporal had dragged into the tent. He and Wilkins were the only NCOs left in the platoon since the death of Tom Black.

"I'll just start with one of these." He pulled out a bottle of some cheap French wine, worked the cork with his knife for a few minutes, and then drank deep and deeper, liquid oblivion washing down into his soul.

When the pain had dulled, he lifted two more bottles and swayed to his feet. "I'll just take these to Lieutenant Robins. I know he'll appreciate it."

Ned pretended to do paperwork, but listened intently to what the Canadian was saying to Lieutenant Robins. "You and your sergeant are walking into darkness, Lloyd. You won't survive. Ned hasn't the will for it, and you care too much."

A few minutes later Ned walked in for the lieutenant's signature. "Sit down, Sergeant … Lieutenant Miller here has just been telling us what's wrong with us."

Miller went on in his fast Canadian. "Everyone has their own brand of sin: lust, drink, anger, hatred, pride. It's all sin, all rebellion against God, and deserving of judgment. But," he said, "God sent Jesus to take the punishment of our sins. He died on the cross and defeated death in resurrection. Now, by faith in Him you can be rescued. You can find light in this darkness, peace in this turmoil."

It would be nice if I could believe that. But it's probably just another form of trench fever, a fantasy woven from too much time in the horror.

"The day after tomorrow you'll go into battle," the padre was saying. "You're as well prepared as any army has been in this foul war. I'm confident you'll take Vimy Ridge. But many will die. Are you prepared for that?

"Today is Good Friday. The day after tomorrow is Easter. Today we remember how Jesus died for our sins. Sunday we will remember that he rose to conquer death. Only by faith in him can you be sure of eternal life."

The padre looked around at the attentive men. If this is a trench fever, Ned thought, it is one that appeals to many.

"God offers you peace and light in place of turmoil and darkness. He offers His Son, who can reign with peace in your hearts even while you endure the hell of this war. You can have the peace you've seen in Pete Miller and others if you will give up on yourselves and put your faith in him."

Ned and Stanley had walked into the barn and put away their tools while Ned was sharing the bare bones of his story. "And that's what Rev'rend Robins and I did that Good Friday. The padre asked anyone who wanted special prayer to see him. I went, and he helped me to pray my first believer's prayer. Lloyd prayed with Pete Miller."

"And did it make a difference?" Stanley asked.

"A huge difference, Stanley. I wasn't looking for death anymore because I wasn't scared of it. Rev'rend Robins and I were able to stop drinking. We began to grow as believers." Ned smiled. The muscles felt rusty. "Pete Miller was fanatic about two things: studying God's Word and praying. I recommend both."

They walked into the stable. "Right, let's see about Buster. You said he wasn't eating?" Ned studied the big bay. His head seemed to have a slight shake, and his stomach was a bit distended. "Come here, big fella." The horse shied away slightly from Ned's hands. Curious. Ned looked at his eyes and teeth. Nothing. But when he touched the horse's midsection, Buster whinnied and pawed.

"This could be colic." *Lord, I can't afford to lose this horse. In the maelstrom of your world, can you take a moment to touch and heal him?* "Let's put that bit of molasses I've been saving in his feed, see how he does tonight."

~ † ~

"Ned," Alice called from the yard. "James Grierson's here."

"Give me two minutes." Ned quickly straightened and hung up the tack. He'd had to use Bluster for cultivating this morning, as Buster was in obvious pain. He was sweating, pawing at the ground, trying to bite his stomach. He turned to find James entering the barn.

"I heard you've got a sick horse?"

"Good morning, James. How did you know?"

"I ran into Arthur at the Jackdaw last night. He said Stanley was worried. The symptoms sounded a bit like colic, so I decided to come out."

They walked to Buster's stall. The vet looked at the water bucket, touched the feed trough. "Hasn't been eating – even molasses. Has he been drinking?"

"Yes."

James asked a few more questions, looked in the horse's mouth, checked his feet, examined a dropping. "Almost certainly colic," he said. "But his teeth are sound. He has great tone. Have you been working him too hard?"

Ned felt his shoulders sag. "Yes." *No harder than I've been working myself.* "Buster's a lot easier than Bluster. I'm afraid I make him carry a lot of the load."

"Could be a twisted intestine then."

Ned felt his energy drain like the last blood from a wound. "I'll have to put him down?"

James rubbed his chin a few times. "We've got a nice surgery set up at the manor. I've brought the latest anesthetic equipment. If we can get him up there without foundering, Ron Black and I can try an operation. Ron's the best."

Ned took the easy path of pessimism. "Cost more than a new horse, likely."

"No charge. His Majesty's Government pays us to test these techniques."

He felt a faint stirring of hope. *Lord God, I need this horse.*

Lloyd stepped out onto the street, shoulders hunched against the cold. He remembered how inadequate his coat was. "Are you sure you want to do this, Annie?" He pointed to the threatening clouds.

"Yes. You need the walk, and Norah's happy to watch the children. She's going out to the orphanage this afternoon."

I probably do need the walk. Ever since the prayer meeting for Lady Blount, Lloyd had been battling a desire to just sit in his chair in his little vestry. He told everyone, Annie included, that he needed to pray, to study. But in reality, not much prayer or preparation was being done. *It's better than hanging out at the pub.*

"Well," he said, "north, south, east or west?'

"Let's go uphill first," she said. This was a kindness, Lloyd knew. For some reason his long marches in the war had given him an almost obsessive preference for starting any journey with the uphill leg.

"Past the manor, then, and up into the hills."

Lloyd was content to make small talk. "I wonder if Roosevelt will win today's elections."

"They say Willkie has been gaining ground," Annie responded.

Lloyd could see Annie's heart wasn't in the conversation. She seemed discouraged. Probably by his apathy, he thought. She took his hand as they walked, and seemed about to speak, when Lloyd heard the sound of an engine approaching. It looked like Ned's tractor, pulling a wagon. James Grierson was leaning over a makeshift stall to pat a horse's head and neck.

"What's going on?" Lloyd yelled.

Ned shook his head and killed the engine. "Things all right back there, James?" he said.

"Fine. He's restless, but I'm able to keep him fairly quiet."

Ned turned back to Lloyd. "Colic. James is going to try an operation."

"Can you do that with a horse?"

James answered. "We can try. We've had some success." Lloyd did not relish the mental picture of cutting up the huge horse.

"Well, I'll let you get on with it then."

Ned nodded. He seemed drained and numb.

The engine started with a rumble. The horse whimpered and stamped. When the sound had died a little, Annie said, "Which horse was it?"

"Buster? Or maybe the other one?"

"Oh, Lloyd! Normally you would have asked."

"Well … it's just a horse."

"Normally you would have prayed before you let them go on."

"I would have prayed for a horse?"

"Of course you would. You know how important that horse is to Ned. You know what stress he's been under."

Justifications sprang to Lloyd's mind. *What about the stress I've been under?* He dropped Annie's hand to rub at the ringing in his ear. "Well, I just didn't think of it … It's only a horse for goodness sake."

Immediately Lloyd regretted his sharp tone. Annie didn't deserve that. They walked in silence past the gate to the manor.

Lord Jesus, Lloyd prayed. I hate this. You've got to do something to draw me back to you. I'm drifting.

It started to rain.

Ned paced nervously. He had been fascinated by the surgical set-up – a crane mounted on the ceiling was attached to a wide harness. Buster was heavily sedated. When he went limp, the bellyband held him.

"Now we lift him, Mr. Ned." Percy said. He was perfectly comfortable with the big horse. "Mr. Ned, what did the pony say when he had a sore throat?"

Ned just shook his head.

"'Sorry, I'm a little hoarse'… Get it, Mr. Ned? A little horse?" Percy cranked the lift until the horse's feet left the ground. With some effort, they moved him to the operating table and lowered him onto his side.

"Ned," James said, "this is Ron Black, who will do the operation." Black was taller than Ned, thin as a rake, with long, long hands. He introduced the two students who stood behind him.

"Now you should leave," James said. "The anesthetic is tricky to administer and the operation is delicate. We don't need a nervous daddy in here."

Ned had paced for almost three hours when James and Ron came back out. "It went well, Ned." James said. "It was a massive twist in the intestine—"

"A double knot, we call it," Ron said. "But I was able to unravel it without cutting the intestine."

"Then he cleverly re-arranged things so it won't knot again." James said.

Praise God, Ned thought.

"But we're not out the woods. Any number of things can happen during recovery. He's coming round, but we'll keep him down for a few more hours to allow him to get over it a bit."

"Percy's keeping an eye on him," Ron added. "We'll probably try to get him on his feet early this evening. How well he does then will tell us a lot."

"Why don't you take the tractor home now," James said, clapping Ned on the back, "and come back in a few hours?"

Rachel looked in on Eleanor. *Asleep. Good.* Eleanor had invited James Grierson to dinner and Rachel had prepared the Lady's favorite meat pie. It even had a little meat in it. But James had called to beg off because of the operation and Rachel had reluctantly agreed to take the rest of the pie up to the manor. She suspected Eleanor of trying to be a matchmaker.

Rachel lugged the basket up the hill, breathing hard as she got to the door. A young man in an army uniform answered. *When had they begun staffing the veterinary college with … corporals?*

"Good evening," he said, "How may I help you?"

"I understand Sir James is working late this evening. I've brought him some dinner."

"Yes, ma'am. If you don't mind waiting, I'll run up to his office and tell him."

"I believe you'll find him in the surgery."

"Oh? I'll check there first then."

The corporal walked around a reception desk that had been set up in the entry hall. He turned left toward the morning room.

Why would the Army be at a veterinary college?

The corporal returned. "Right this way, ma'am." He led her through the door and pointed down the hall. "Through the double doors at the end, then to the right."

Rachel lifted the heavy basket. If the corporal were as polite as he had sounded, he would have carried it.

She knocked. "Come," said James' voice. As she opened the door, her nostrils were assailed with the smell of horse and hospital. She set the basket down outside. The men were clustered around Buster, who had a large bandage wrapped all the way around his belly. The morning room was partly covered in hay, with the surgical table and crane filling one corner. If Eleanor saw this …

"It's me, Rachel Busby. Lady Blount asked me to bring you the dinner you missed," she said. "How is he doing?"

James came over. He smiled broadly but his face was weary. "Well," he said, "weaker than we would like, and he hasn't started eating."

"But he'll be all right?"

"Too soon to tell." James regarded the horse. "An operation like this is very risky. He needs to eat, gain his strength, and avoid infection."

"Right. That's how I'll pray, then." She turned to Ned and Percy. "Would you two like some dinner? I've brought plenty."

"Hello, Miss Rachel," Percy said. He turned back to talk to the horse. "Ho there, Buster, Miss Rachel brung us some dinner. But you need to eat first, me boy. C'mon, let's walk a little more and see if we can get you a little bit hungry."

Ned was quiet, watching the horse with folded arms. Rachel walked over. "How are you?"

"All right, Rachel. Hoping this works out."

"Can I talk you into some dinner?"

Ned thought about that way too long. "Guess so."

"James," she said, "Is there someplace less … fragrant … you can eat?"

"If Percy watches Buster, we can eat in my office. Are you joining us?"

"No, I ate with Lady Blount. But I can stay while you eat and take away the plates. She'll sleep for a bit."

They went down the hall and up a flight of stairs. James cleared his desk as Rachel set out the food. "So," she said conversationally, "why do you have a corporal guarding the entrance?"

James moved a pile of papers and said nothing. Under the pile was the drawing of Blount Manor. Rachel pointed. "So have you looked in any of these places?"

James quickly folded the paper and placed it with the stack. "One or two."

"One or two?" Rachel said. "Is that all? I'd have thought that, if you really cared about Lady Blount, you'd have made it a priority."

James looked away. "Of course." he said. "But I don't actually have access to the whole building."

"Don't have access!" The pieces of this little puzzle were falling into place. "You've moved some army … something … into this house haven't you? Without telling Lady Blount."

James' face flushed red and he turned away. "I can't say."

"And I can't stay. Enjoy your dinner. You can send the plates and basket back with Ned or Percy."

"Thank you so much for looking after this horse so well," James said to Percy. Buster was in the stables and had eaten both that morning and the night before. "Mr. Powell will be here shortly. You need to go get some rest."

"Yes, Mr. James. Percy has his little room at the back of the stable, thank you. He can hear if Mr. Ned needs any help … Mr. James, what kind of horses go out at night?"

"I guess I don't know Percy. What kind of horses go out at night?"

"Nightmares. Get it? Night mares?"

"I get it, Percy." *Did the jokes get worse when Percy was tired?*

A few minutes later Ned appeared in the stable. He was relieved when James told him of Buster's progress. "Thank you, Father," he said, looking up. "And thank you Percy for looking after him. You should rest now. I'll be here for a while and make sure he's cared for."

As Percy walked away, Ned said. "But I'm not going to talk Percy-talk.'

"Quite right." James said. "And as things appear stable here, I'm going to attend to a pressing bit of business."

James went back up to his office and gathered the dirty plates and dishes from last night's dinner. Then he went to the manor kitchen and washed them up. He didn't want to give Rachel any reason for further sharp words. He wasn't sure why he needed to resolve this little conflict. *I expect because it's just the Christian thing to do. After all, she is taking care of Lady Blount, and I feel responsible for that situation. I ought to at least try to help her. But it won't work if we can't get along.*

Rachel heard footsteps on the gravel walk of Rosewood Cottage. Probably Ned she thought. "I'll just get the front door, Eleanor. You try to finish that soup."

"It's cold. It doesn't help the pain in my back unless it's hot."

"I'll reheat it in a minute."

As she opened the door, a knocking hand almost hit her in the face. "James," she said. *What was he doing here?*

"I apologize, Mrs. Busby. I didn't know you were there."

"Well I am. Shouldn't you be up at Lady Blount's manor caring for a horse or conspiring with your little army friends?"

Inwardly, Rachel groaned. *Where did that come from? Am I that angry with this man? Hasn't he gone out of his way to help Eleanor?*

James' lips hardened. He straightened to his full height and said, "I merely came to return these dishes …" He held out the basket. Rachel reached for it, and their eyes locked. I don't owe you an apology, Sir James! she thought. Or do I?

He looked away and spoke softly "… and to apologize."

"What?"

"Apologize," he said, a little louder. "I'm sorry I kept the presence of … Colonel Blake's unit … from you. And from Lady Blount."

"Is that you, Sir James?" Eleanor's voice called from the dining room. "Stop letting the cold air in and let Rachel heat my soup."

"May I come in?" James said.

Rachel didn't know what to do. To let the man in would somehow be conceding something, accepting something about his presence, his apology, his person, that she did not want to accept. In the end politeness won out.

"Come in then," she said. "Tell Lady Blount what you've done and give your apology to her. I'll reheat the soup." She turned her back on him and walked into the kitchen.

When she came back with the hot soup, Lady Blount was saying "The Army … how exciting!" Oh, no, Rachel thought. She had fully expected the dignified lady to be appalled, and horrified.

"Is it some kind of secret, hush-hush, unit?" Lady Blount asked.

James, looking immensely relieved, said in the same conspiratorial tone "Yes, my Lady, I'm afraid so. Even I don't really know what they are doing in the east wing." His voice changed back to normal. "But I can assure you it is nothing messy. It seems to involve truckloads of paperwork moving to and from London."

He turned to Rachel, obviously making an effort to include her in the conversation. "I thought the college was overrun with bureaucracy, but the Army seems to take it to a new level."

"That's as may be," Rachel said, her own tone softening, "but you should have told us – should have told Lady Blount – what was happening."

"I agree," James said. "And I apologize. In my own defense, Colonel Blake gave me strict instructions to tell no one."

Rachel fought with herself for a moment. Lord Jesus, do I want to not like this man? she prayed. She took a deep breath and said "Apology accepted. I understand … And I need to apologize to you for my anger. There is no excuse for speaking to you the way I did."

"Apology accepted."

"Is someone going to give me some hot soup, or must I wrest it from you bodily?" Lady Blount said.

"Oh, of course," Rachel said. She was surprised to find the bowl still in her hands. She set it in front of Eleanor. "Sir James, would you like to join us? There's plenty."

"It's wonderful, Sir James," Lady Blount said, and slurped loudly.

James looked between the two women, apparently evaluating the sincerity of this invitation. "Yes," he said. "It looks and smells delicious."

"Rachel, you should join us," Lady Blount said. "She hasn't eaten yet." Rachel recognized the impish 'matchmaker' grin and sighed.

"Yes, join us," Sir James said, pulling back a chair.

Rachel felt resentment rise up in her heart, but beat it down.

"I will," she said.

When James left, Rachel began to clear the dishes.

"Just a moment, young lady," Eleanor said. "Sit back down and let me give you a piece of my mind."

Oh, no, Rachel thought. Now what? She remembered her mother's frequent claim that she had given someone "a piece of my mind I can't afford to lose." Eleanor really couldn't afford to lose part of hers.

"That Sir James," Lady Blount began, "is a very nice young man."

"What do you mean?" Rachel said. "He stole your manor. He's populated it with sheep and rats. And now with the Army. He isn't nice at all."

"Tosh! He is too. I could see that even when I was fighting him." She shifted in her chair and moaned. "It's my back again today. But my brain is clear."

"Can I get you some aspirin?" Rachel said. Dr. Nesbitt had said that the painkiller would do her no harm.

As soon as Lady Blount had swallowed the pills, she spoke again. "You may not want my opinion, but I think you would make a perfect couple."

"What? Me and that old, broken-down, puffed-up thief."

"Oh, stop the name calling. It doesn't become you. And you're not fooling me in the slightest. I could see that day in London that you admired him. And I can see it now."

Rachel was taken aback by the old lady's insight. "What if I do admire him? That doesn't mean I want to marry him."

"Why not? Have you got a better reason?"

"Lady Blount, this is a stupid conversation. I'm too old to get married—"

"Are not!"

"And I don't want to."

"Why not?"

Rachel paused to think about that. *Why not?* She thought of sweet Roger, of the girls … and tears began to flow. "Because everyone I've ever loved has been taken from me. You know I lost my family to the Spanish flu …" She was sobbing now, but she couldn't help it. "… I lost my mum who became my best friend after Roger died. And now …" she sobbed again. "And now I'm losing you …" She lowered her head to the table, laid it on her forearms, and wept.

"There, there," Lady Blount said. "I know what it is to love somebody and lose them. We all do, if we live long enough. But God gives us strength to go on … He's given you great strength. And I believe he wants you to love again."

~ † ~

Ned stepped back into the now familiar stables of the veterinary college. He looked toward the stall where Buster had been recovering, but saw no one there. Percy was fussing in front of a different stall.

"How is he doing, Percy?"

Percy turned and saw Ned, then shrank back against the door of the stable. "Oh Mr. Ned. Please don't be angry with Percy."

"What?"

"Mr. James says Buster has a fever. Maybe Percy hasn't been giving him enough water. But Percy has tried, Mr. Ned. Percy has tried."

Ned's flash of anger dissolved into a fog of discouragement. You couldn't be angry with the sincere little man. "I'm sure you've tried, Percy."

Ned looked in on Buster. The horse was still up, but his head hung almost to the floor. He was breathing heavily and sweating.

"I was just about to rub him down again." Percy said, gesturing at a pail of clear water and a sponge.

"Let me do it," Ned said.

"It's wet in there, Mr. Ned."

Ned saw that there were several inches of water on the floor, which appeared to have been constructed with a basin, like a shallow bath. Sometimes cold water kept a colicky horse from foundering.

"I can handle that."

He stepped into the stall with the bucket. Buster snorted softly in greeting. As Ned rubbed the horse with the cool water, he prayed. *Lord, I can't do this.*

Before he finished he heard James talking to Percy.

"Hello, Ned." James said from the door to the stable, "I'm sorry that Buster has taken this turn for the worse."

"Not near as sorry as I am."

"There is still hope. Many horses recover from these post-operative fevers."

"He doesn't look good," Ned said.

"No, he doesn't. His bowels seem to have shut down again. Percy's doing everything possible to get him moving," James said, without any apparent thought of a double meaning. Ned managed a small inward grin.

~ † ~

Annie watched Lloyd from the kitchen. He was sitting at the dining-room table in what had become a common posture, leaning forward on his left hand, elbow on the table, rubbing his ear and reading one of the numerous papers he now bought every day.

Lord, I can't do this, she thought.

"It's the inconsistency that bothers me," Lloyd said, raising his head for the briefest moment to acknowledge her presence. "This one says the Greeks are holding off the Italians and even counter-attacking. This one …" he lifted another paper, "… says that the Italians are advancing deep all along the front." *The Times* has no comment at all on merchant shipping losses. The *Birmingham Gazette* says they are enormous and getting worse. This one …"

"Oh, just stop, Lloyd!" Suddenly her weariness and frustration got the better of her. She stormed out of the house, across to the vestry and grabbed Lloyd's big Bible. When she walked back in Lloyd was still at the table, looking at her, she thought, like a stunned fish.

Approaching the table, she tucked the Bible under her left arm and used her right to sweep the papers away. She paused to pick up two that were left behind, one at a time, between thumb and forefinger and dropped them on the floor with the others. Then she put the Bible on the table in front of him and opened it at random, somewhere in the Psalms. Her anger ebbing but still not gone, she said in a quieter voice. "What does this one say, Lloyd? What does this one say?"

She turned and walked toward the kitchen, but a rush of shame chilled her before she could get there. She turned back to see Lloyd still staring at her, one hand on the open book.

"I'm sorry," she said. "You didn't deserve that."

"No," he said weakly. "I did … I know what I need … but all the other words get in the way. Pray for me, dear Annie. Pray for me." He grasped his forehead with both hands and lowered his head over the book.

Eleanor cried out in the now familiar moan that indicated the onset of one of her headaches. Rachel rushed into the bedroom to find her pressing both hands into her eyes and forehead. Her legs thrashed as she squirmed from the pain.

"Ohh, make it stop! Make it stop!"

Hoping for the sudden release that had characterized these headaches so far, Rachel knelt by the bed and tried to cradle the writhing old lady in her arms. After what seemed a long time, the pain had not gone away, though Eleanor could talk in gasping cries.

"I'm seeing colors … lights … it hurts … help me … Oh, I have to go … take me to the bathroom … Oh, too late, you're too slow … I've done it." She subsided into childlike tears. Rachel worked quickly to change her nightgown and bedding. Fortunately, Dr. Nesbitt had anticipated this development and they had made up her bed with a rubber sheet.

"Are you feeling a little better now?" Rachel asked.

"No …" Eleanor looked up for the first time. "Yes … thank you … but the pain in my head is horrible and I can't see straight."

"I could give you the morphine Dr. Nesbitt prescribed?"

"No." She tried to sit upright. "I've told you I hate that stuff. It took my Cyril away from me before he could even say good-bye."

"I'm sorry, then. I don't know what to do."

"Oh, stop fussing, girl. Get that James person. Maybe he'll have an idea."

"James?"

"Yes. Are you deaf?"

"No, it's just that—"

"Then go to the telephone and call him ...Oooh." She clutched her head.

Rachel made the call, though it was early for James to be at his desk.

"Grierson," he answered with a morning-gravelly voice.

"Sir James, it's Rachel Busby." She described the events of the morning.

"I still wonder if I should give her the morphine Dr. Nesbitt gave us."

"No," James said. "Not if she doesn't want it." He paused. "I just got a little package of coffee from Toronto. I had friends there who used it for migraines—"

"Yes! My mum liked coffee and said it was good for her headaches."

"If you can find a way to grind it—"

"I have a little coffee mill that Mum used, somewhere around here."

"Get it. I'll be right there."

"Yes, sir," Rachel said, smiling a little at his military air.

"Well, that seems to have helped a little," James said.

"Yes, thank you." Lady Blount had protested that she couldn't stand coffee, but had drunk the cup Rachel had made.. Half an hour later they watched as she nodded off. They filled the time with small talk about coffee.

"It was quite the rage in Oxford when Mum taught there. I was too young to appreciate it, though I enjoyed a cup from time to time in her later years."

"My friends in Toronto live on the stuff," James said.

"Do you suppose there is enough for us to have a cup?" Rachel asked in a playful tone.

James smiled. He was gratified to hear a little warmth. "That would be lovely," he said. "But, no. Given the scarcity I think we had better save it for medicinal purposes."

Lady Blount's voice interrupted them. "I'm dying, aren't I?"

"I beg your pardon?" James said.

"Rachel said she was losing me. I know that doctor found something in my head, but nobody has said if it's killing me."

James looked at Rachel. She paused, nodded, but gestured to him. He took Lady Blount's hand. It was cold and thin, as fragile as a winter leaf. "The doctor in London reminded us that we still believe in miracles. And we have been praying. But … yes, without a miracle the tumor will take you from us."

She sighed. "At least I'll be free from this bloody pain … And with the Lord. And with Cyril." She made to straighten herself and Rachel adjusted the pillows so she could sit up more in the bed.

"Would you like another cup of coffee?"

"Heavens, no. It's done wonders for my head, but isn't it horrid stuff?" She looked at the two of them with a gleam in her eye. "As I'm dying anyway, can I tell you a story about true love that no one remembers anymore?"

"Certainly, my Lady." James wondered what was coming.

"It's about me. And Cyril … Oh, Cyril! … I'm sure you think I'm from a good family, but it's not so. My father was a poor tenant who worked the fields closest to the manor. I grew up with Cyril, and we were friends. Both sets of parents tried to keep us apart, but when I was fifteen our friendship developed into a romance. We became … intimate. A few months later I realized I was expecting a child."

James stared at the old woman with wondering fascination.

"When old Lord Blount learned of this he tried to make Cyril send me away. But my love refused. Instead, he persuaded his father to let him to marry me and have a proper wedding. I have been playing the part of a real lady ever since."

"Playing the part?" Rachel said. "You are a real lady."

"Only because of Cyril's love, dear girl. And I know I took the 'haughty lady' role too far. I never wanted to dishonor my husband's name."

James was trying to fit this story into what he knew. "But you and Lord Blount never had children," he said.

"No. Our baby boy was delivered stillborn. I never conceived again. But Cyril remained my faithful friend all his life."

She looked at James, then at Rachel. "That's what marriage is all about," she said. Then she laid her head back on the pillow with a satisfied grin.

Lloyd had dropped in on Meg and Bert to confirm that Bert could preach on the fifteenth of December. Lloyd was looking forward to the Sunday off.

"Before you go," Meg said, "could we talk to you for a moment?"

Lloyd saw eagerness on Meg's face, reluctance on Bert's. "Is it about Billy and Nellie?"

"Not exactly. They finally seem to be adjusting. They miss their mum and dad, of course, but there is nothing to be done about that. It's their grandparents we're wondering about."

"How so?"

Bert spoke up. "Alf and Mildred barely have enough to keep their little flat, even with their church helping. Now, with so many buildings destroyed, their landlord says he could get much more if he rented the flat to a displaced family."

"Well, that's a bit greedy."

"And any night they could get bombed out," Meg said. "Or even killed. So Bert and I are thinking of asking them to come and live with us."

"In this little place?" Lloyd gestured around.

"At least they'll be with their grandchildren. And safe. And cared for."

"I know, Meg, and I commend your good heart, but where are you going to put them?"

"Well, Reverend, I've got it all figured out." She checked off points on her fingers. "Bert mostly spends his time in the kitchen or our bedroom. We can move Billy and Nellie up under the eaves with Fred and Harry, and bring Emma back down to our room. Then we can make up the sitting room for the old folk, and let them sleep there at night as well."

"And what about all of this?" Lloyd gestured at the piles of laundry that seemed to fill the room.

Meg smiled. "We'll have to fit it into the nooks and crannies, won't we?"

"Meg," Lloyd said, "you're a wonderful foolish woman. Who's going to take care of everyone when all this makes you sick?" To Lloyd's chagrin, Meg's face fell at his attempt at good-natured humor.

"Rev'rend Robins, we've just got to do this. I have the constitution of one of Ned's horses. We'll be fine."

Buster or Bluster? Lloyd thought. "Well, then, I'll pray that the Lord provides a way."

"Mr. Ned, Mr. Ned, Buster's feeling better. He is." Percy almost danced with excitement as he met Ned at the stable. "He's been, Mr. Ned. And he's eating and drinking. Mr. James says he's going to be fine."

Praise God, Ned thought. The relief he felt was all out of proportion to the actual value of the horse. *Jesus thank you for this favor. Thank you for your love still shown to the least of your children.*

James walked in. "Great news, isn't it? Come and see."

Buster's head was up and he stood with his usual stolid stillness. The bandage on his side was smaller and neater.

"When can I take him home?" Ned asked.

"I would wait another day or two; the trip back in the wagon might jar him. Percy will take good care of him, of course."

"Right." Ned said. He was suddenly filled with gratitude and admiration for the vet. He turned and held out his hand.

"Sir James," he said, "I have to confess that I held it against you when you commandeered Lady Blount's estate. I knew you had no choice, but I blamed you anyway. I'm sorry."

"Apology accepted." James said seriously.

"And I'm grateful to you and Dr. Black for saving my horse. You've done wonders."

"I'm afraid the Lord was the one who intervened to save the horse."

"Yes," Ned said, "He's done wonders as well."

CHAPTER 12

14 November 1940

Violet and Holly had just got the little ones into bed, hoping they would get a few hours of sleep before the air raid warning sounded. Of course, some nights it never came, but lately Goering had been sending small flights of bombers over the cities nightly, terrorizing. Last week a string of high explosives had caused twenty deaths in a row of houses not far away.

Still, Violet was more irritated than afraid when the siren sounded early. Little Ivy had been cranky all day and would not let anyone comfort her. She really needed the sleep, but the alert wound her up to a full-throated howl. Rose, in the next bed, was sleepily repeating 'Ivy, no … Ivy, no.'

"Let's get them into the shelter," Holly said, "before we try to settle them down." The shelter was in the cellar. Robert had built a small half-high space with railroad ties for columns and a plate of steel for the top. He was rather proud of it. He was on the other side of Coventry this evening, helping a friend build one.

Inside there was just enough room to lie down on damp mattresses. There were not enough blankets to go around, so Violet grabbed Rose's bedding as she scooped her up. Within a few minutes, they were settled in the cramped space. Holly rocked little Ivy and Violet sat against the rough wall opposite, mechanically patting Rose.

Violet was especially prone to the darkness of her soul in this black damp place. During the day, reading her Bible, she caught glimpses of hope, but at night she wrapped herself in guilt and fought despair. Images floated in her head. For some reason she kept seeing Edwin's coffin – with Reggie sitting on it saying "Come on. You know you want it."

A dim buzz was growing louder. "I think I hear planes," Violet said, more to herself than to Holly.

"I wish Robert hadn't gone out."

Violet forced herself to share Holly's concern. "Mr. Edwards' shelter is almost done. They'll be safe there."

The droning grew louder. Then the anti-aircraft guns started up, their crump-crump shaking the darkness. Violet imagined a black wedge crawling across the night landscape, pointed straight at Coventry, pointed straight at her dark soul.

"Holly, pray for me," she said. "Please. It's bad."

Her sister reached across and took her hand. "Lord Jesus, please be with us and keep us safe. Keep Robert safe. Protect Vi from the darkness. Pierce it with your light and help her to trust in you."

Holly's prayer seemed to build a thin wall around Violet's fears. But the noise of the planes crescendoed, and the damn Nazi death whistles began to shriek from the sky. There were a few explosions, mostly the sharp pops and faint hisses of incendiaries. Violet could imagine the fire watch, some of them now her friends, running through the darkness with buckets, shovels, and stirrup pumps, seeking the blazing constellation of fires, snuffing them one by one amid the crump-crump, crump-crump of the anti-aircraft fire.

She shuddered and curled up on her blanket. The first wave of planes passed. The noise of a second was close. She thought she could hear a third wave.

~ † ~

Hours later, Violet cried out in agony. "I've got to get out, Holly. It's all around me. It's all inside me."

"Oh, please settle down Violet," Holly pleaded. "Nothing has touched us yet. The HEs seem to have stopped."

The sixth or seventh wave of bombers had brought the high explosives. Some had seemed to be aimed straight at the house. At any moment Violet had expected to see her last blaze of light before judgment. The narrow windows above their shelter had blown out.

The pressure wave from every blast buffeted Violet's defenses. Thick darknesses roiled around her, leered at her naked soul and body, screaming, "You know you want this! You know you deserve this!"

Finally, she couldn't take it. She wrenched free of Holly's grasp and crawled to the shelter door. She retained just enough sanity to shut it behind her. There was glass under her hands, piercing her palms. She felt, rather than saw, her dark red fluid begin to flow.

She stood up. The small basement windows were filled with flame. "It's all burning, all burning," she yelled, hoping Holly could hear through the chaos. Not that Holly would believe her. She had said much more alarming things already.

She slowly climbed the stairs. At the top, her feet encountered hard objects. Holly used the landing as a pantry, and all the cans and bottles had fallen and shattered. She shuffled her way through and opened the door, half-expecting to see the kitchen ablaze. But there were no flames there. However, the gutted windows were filled with them, wave upon wave of burning buildings like lines of hills. Through the back window above the sink, where Holly had once rejoiced in her view of the tall cathedral spire, there was now a skeleton wrapped in smoke and light.

She ran from it, ran to the front of the house and out onto the street. To her right a blazing wall of fire consumed the houses like an oncoming wave.

Think, Violet. Think. She pounded her head with her bloody hands. She felt herself a comet of darkness, the nucleus of murk thick inside her brain, the tail trailing away into the house.

To the north, the firestorm seemed less intense, broken by streaks of darkness. She turned back and the wall of fire towered over the house. "Holly!" she screamed. "We've got to get them out."

She stumbled through the door, across the house. She slipped and fell, breaking the fall with her bloody hands. A broom stood at the top of the stairs. She swept furiously, clearing a path through the glass to the door of the shelter.

Dropping to her hands and knees, she tore open the door. "Holly, we've got to get them out. The fire will have us!"

In the flickering light from the window Violet saw Holly's eyes, wide as those of a trapped animal. "Believe me, Holly. You have to believe me."

Finally her sister moved, gathering up Rose and handing her out of the shelter, then scrambling out with Ivy.

The drone of planes began again. *Lord, how long?*

"We need to go north, away from town," Violet yelled.

"But Robert is in the other direction.!"

"Come and look." They stumbled up the stairs, through the house, out onto the street. The flames were attacking their row of houses from the side and rear. Waves of heat poured out at them. Holly took one look and ran up the middle of the street, the light of the flames casting grotesque shadows before her. Violet followed. A building collapsed behind them, sending clouds of smoke rolling toward them, lit hideously red. Violet choked and gagged.

Darkness rolled toward her as well. "Stop," it said. "Give up. You know you want this. You know you deserve this."

"No!" she shouted. She clung tightly to the heavy screaming toddler in her arms.

The walls of flame slowly fell back behind them, but the roar of the planes grew louder. As the death whistles started again, a figure loomed up out of the darkness. A flash of light illuminated him. An air raid warden. The roar of an explosion back toward the house washed past them.

"The school!" he yelled into the relative silence. "Follow me." He ran across a wide-open space toward a long building. Before he was halfway across he was transformed into a flash of light. A roar. A wall of heat and pressure.

With her last conscious thought, Violet welcomed the darkness.

~ † ~

James laid the late edition of *The Times* down in front of Ned. They had just transported Buster home to Ned's barn, and Ned was buying James a half pint in the Jackdaw. "Look at this," James pointed to the top of page four.

BIG ATTACK ON COVENTRY: an air raid, officially described as being comparable with that of the largest night attacks on London, was made on Coventry Thursday night. Relays of German aircraft arrived over the city from dusk to dawn. Casualties were heavy, and many buildings, including the fourteenth-century cathedral, were destroyed. Preliminary reports indicate the number of casualties may exceed 1000.

"Isn't that where the Clarkes' girl is?" James asked.

"Yes, Holly." Ned had been feeling a little more hopeful with Buster's recovery. Now his spirit drooped like a plant in a heavy rain. "Violet's there too."

"No! Why?"

Ned realized he really didn't know. He hadn't seen Lloyd much lately and even when he had, not much had been said. He wondered briefly if Lloyd was trying to spare him. "Went to help with the little ones, I think. And I don't think she was handling the loss of Edwin very well."

"Understandable," James said. "I pray this doesn't make it worse."

"I just pray they survive it."

~ † ~

Annie sat in the family pew. By some miracle, all three kids were quietly occupied. *Lord Jesus, please put your blessing and power on your Word this morning. Help Lloyd to hear your heart. And touch your people.*

After the hymns and the offering, Lloyd stood for the pastoral prayer.

"I have two things I'd especially ask you to pray about this morning. First, please pray for comfort for Lady Blount, and relief from pain.

"Second, please pray for the Clarkes. You all know what they've been through, and I suppose most of you have heard of the blitz this week in Coventry. Philip and Marjorie haven't heard yet from Holly and Robert or Violet. Pray for their safety, and pray for comfort and strength for Philip and Marjorie."

Lloyd prayed, then brought the message. He was completing a series in the book of Ephesians. "You may think," he concluded, "that this present war is against Hitler. And it is. But Ephesians 6 teaches that our ultimate war is not against flesh and blood, but against Satan and his demons, the rulers of this present darkness. So our armor is not tanks or planes, but spiritual armor by which, though it may not feel like it, I believe we can stand against the evil of this day."

Not bad, Annie thought. But she wasn't sure Lloyd believed it.

After the service, Lloyd stood greeting people by the door. Lately Annie had stood with him every week. She hoped Alan would temper his remarks in her presence.

Meg and Bert were there with all five kids. Billy and Nellie looked innocently happy today. Then came Marjorie and Philip Clarke, worn as could be. Marjorie gratefully received Annie's hug. Philip said, "Could we talk for a few minutes after …" He gestured with his head toward the short line of churchgoers behind them.

"Of course," Lloyd said. His voice was weary.

Annie said, "Why don't you go across and wait in the sitting room. I'll ask Evelyn to stay here a little while with my three."

Marjorie and Philip walked slowly down the path, worn, almost elderly. When Annie and Lloyd arrived, the couple were deep in a discussion that sounded a little like an argument. "But you just can't," Marjorie was saying. "You'll only be putting yourself in danger. I can't lose you too."

"But there are no reports of any more bombings in Coventry."

"So, Philip," Annie said, "are you saying that you're going to try to go to Coventry to find them?"

"Yes. If they're alive they may be homeless, without any resources. I'm sure they'll be taken care of, but I want to bring them back here."

"I agree." Annie said. She looked for – and found – the surprise on Philip's face. "I've talked to Violet. I know how fragile she is. She'll need to leave."

"I hate to disagree," Lloyd said, not meeting Annie's eye. "But I think it's too dangerous. The authorities have been saying since September that people should stay out of the bombed areas."

"But the authorities don't have any reason to care for my children."

Marjorie stirred. "Annie's right … you're right, Philip. It's not what I want, but you need to go and bring back Violet. Bring Holly and the babies too." She clutched at his sleeve. "But you can't go alone."

"We've already talked about this Marjorie," Philip said. "Lenny is completely out of touch. They've moved him someplace out of London and we don't even know where his letters are coming from."

"There must be someone here."

"I could ask Arthur, I suppose. But he's already done his bit. Ernest can't leave his job—"

"I'll go," Lloyd said.

Annie's heart wrapped itself around a sudden vacuum in the pit of her stomach. "No," she said. "Lloyd, you know you shouldn't. You're not doing well."

"I'm not doing anything, you mean."

"Oh!" Anger flared. "So you feel you have to prove yourself by going off and being some kind of hero? Didn't you get enough of that in the last war?"

She stifled a sob, felt the anger drain away as fast as it had come. "Oh, Lloyd, I'm sorry. I'm just so worried about you."

"It's not about me, Annie." His voice was stiff and his gaze went over her shoulder. "Philip needs someone to go with him. I grew up near Coventry. I'm the obvious candidate. It's not like I'm helping anyone here."

The afternoon train was delayed. The surprise, Lloyd thought, was that they could buy tickets to Coventry at all. Put it down to the efficiency, or idiocy, of the railway system. When the train rolled in an hour late, it was almost empty.

The journey through the November countryside was quiet. From the window, no one would ever know there was a war on. The nearly bare trees, their few leaves devoid of color, matched the brown fields.

After they changed trains in Birmingham, they began to see signs of the storm that had descended on Coventry just days before. In the road approaching one village, men were filling in huge bomb craters. Must have been HE that some Jerry dumped without finding the target. Further along, the train was shunted onto a siding for a while and then continued at a crawl. This close, every church, every major building seemed to have suffered. Blackened beams and timbers poked at odd angles from piles of rubble, many of them still smoking. The few people they spotted seemed equally smoke-blackened, poking feebly through the ruins.

They stopped several hundred yards short of the station, near the London Road. Hundreds of people stood at the bottom of the steep bank, carrying bags and bundles of every size and description.

"They'll spend the night in the country," said the porter, in response to Lloyd's question. "You will too if you know what's good for you."

Lloyd and Philip stood at the top of the bank and scanned the crowd. Many of the faces were too sooty to see clearly, some had bloody bandages wrapped around hands or arms. Still, Lloyd expected Philip would have easily picked out his family if they had been there.

"They may be doing the same thing on the north-west side of town. That's where their house is."

Coventry was not very big, but the journey across seemed interminable. The roads were blocked with the rubble of collapsed buildings or roped off against unexploded bombs or leaking gas mains. A few places seemed relatively unscathed, but most were blackened or blasted.

"Oh, Lord! There's the cathedral." Only the spire, and the skeleton of the nave stood, the dark sky visible through the empty arches of windows.

"We need to head left a bit," Philip said.

Holly's part of the city had been consumed by flames. Here and there, fire crews were pumping pitiful streams into smoldering or still-burning buildings.

"That's the theater," Philip said. "Their street will be …"

Lloyd's heart, which had been sustained by some senseless hope, collapsed. "Oh Lord Jesus, no!" he said.

"Let's find the house."

Philip thought he was on the right street, but he couldn't be sure. Everything was blackened, burnt, or covered in rubble. "They may be here. They may be here. I've got to find them."

Lloyd stopped him when he began to wade into one smoldering pile. "Philip, if they are here we're too late. Let's talk to one of the fire crews."

"Survivors? Ha!" The crew chief appeared on the verge of laughing maniacally, but then sobered. "Where are you come from?"

"Stokely," Philip said. "We're looking for my daughter and her family." Philip's voice broke. Tears ran down his ashen face in the dying light.

The man nodded. "Some who escaped are at Bablake." He pointed vaguely, further to the west. "Most are out in the countryside. Trains running in as far as Radford Road."

"Thank you," Lloyd said, taking Philip by the arm.

"Hope you find them, mister."

It was fully dark, but Lloyd knew his way to Bablake with the unerring compass of boyhood memories.

They reached the broad playing fields that separated the school from Coundon Street. The gate was open and Lloyd led Phillip to the main hall. When they went in, they were assailed by noise and stench. People were moving back and forth purposefully in the dim light of a few burning candles. They walked along an aisle between crowded rows of sleeping or restless figures, mothers kneeling to comfort their children, injured lying still or writhing in pain.

"Foolish to have them here at night, isn't it?" Lloyd said. "The school is one of the few remaining targets if Jerry comes back."

"We'll have to check every family," Philip said.

But they didn't. A nurse with a clipboard came up to them and said "Looking for someone?"

"Yes." Philip said. "Robert and Holly Allen. They have two children, Rose and Ivy. And my daughter, Violet Clarke."

"We have no record of a Robert Allen." Lloyd's stomach revolted violently at this announcement. He couldn't imagine what Philip was feeling.

"Hold on a minute. What did you say the woman's name was?"

"Holly Allen. And Violet Clarke."

The nurse flipped to the back pages of her stack.

"Yes, I remember them. Two women and two babies. They were here the first nights. They were sent out yesterday."

"Where did they go?"

"Couldn't tell you." She turned her stack back to the front page. "Probably took the train from Radford."

In moments they found themselves back out in the dark street. "They're alive!" Philip said. "Praise God! Now we've just got to find them."

"I wonder why Robert wasn't with them?"

"Doing relief work, maybe? I hope we'll know soon."

It was a clear night and stars shone above, except where columns of smoke still blocked them. The waning moon rode high in the eastern sky.

"The station is north on Radford Road," Lloyd said. "If we go through the park to the east, we'll hit it."

They hurried past darkened buildings in the rapidly cooling air. With the blackout, it was hard to tell if any of them were still occupied. At the small station, the waiting area was full of ragged families.

"What are you all waiting for?" Lloyd whispered to a man standing in the aisle. His wife was seated on the bench, cradling a sleeping toddler.

"The last train, though I don't know it'll hold all of us."

"Where will it take you?"

"Nuneaton. Hinckley perhaps," the man said. "We'll sleep in the station and then come back in tomorrow."

Philip was fidgeting. "Hurry," he said. "They might be in this room."

But they weren't. After checking every family group, Lloyd asked at the ticket window. "Are there any other families here?"

"Platform."

A few groups huddled in the dim lights. Philip looked both ways, then started swiftly toward a group Lloyd wouldn't have picked out from any other.

"Holly! Violet!" A head turned, then another.

"Dad!" The two women scrambled to their feet, babes in their arms.

Philip reached them and wrapped his long arms around both. "I found you."

Lloyd stopped a step away, warmed to tears even as he shivered in the cold.

"But where's Robert?" Philip was saying.

"We don't know." Holly clung to her father. "We can't find him."

~ † ~

Violet stood still as Dad and Reverend Robins talked to Holly.

"Where have you looked?" Dad was asking.

"We've been all around the city," Holly replied. "We went to where he and Mr. Edwards were working, but their place was worse than ours. We tried the soup kitchens and first aid stations, but no one had seen or heard from him. We tried schools, churches, shelters. We've spent two days. We only just came back to see if he might have come home while we were gone."

"So are you going to take the train to Nuneaton?"

"I can't think of why he would leave without us. And I won't leave without him. We'll go into the waiting room after the train leaves and sleep warm until morning. Then we'll keep searching."

Violet knew the blank determination in Holly's eyes. Nothing would keep her from wandering this hell until they either found Robert or found some way to die. She was still amazed death hadn't found her when the bomb exploded. But for some reason she had had to wake up once more, on the cold floor of that old school.

All these thoughts trickled slowly through her brain, each repeating and echoing until the next one came along to drown it out. It was hard, so hard, to focus on the world around her.

"Well, if what you've been doing isn't working let's try something else. Have you asked where the injured have been taken?"

"What do you mean?" Holly responded. "We checked both hospitals."

"They're probably shipping the walking wounded elsewhere."

"Of course," Holly said. "Oh Lord, why haven't I asked?"

The stationmaster said that none of the injured had been taken north, but he'd heard that some were being evacuated south from the other side of town. At that moment, Violet heard the familiar chug of a train, both comforting and frightening. Coming for me, she thought. People began streaming out from the waiting area. When the train stopped, only five or six people got off. The crowd from the station surged on.

They spent the remainder of the night huddled in the waiting room near a radiator. Sometime in the darkness of the pre-dawn hours Violet dreamt a nightmare of falling though endless explosions and flames. She was burning and freezing at the same time. A low slavering voice snarled, "Come to me … you know you want it … come to me."

Suddenly she started awake. Moonlight edged through the high station windows on the south. She had rolled away from the radiator, so that she was half warm and half cold. She smiled a little. It was always good to know where at least part of a nightmare came from.

Hours later, as dawn colored the smoky sky, they set off across town. Violet descended into the same daze that had protected her for the last three days. Feel nothing. See nothing. Care for the baby. She started, then realized Dad was carrying Rose. *Good old dad. You found us.*

The main station was still closed, so they found themselves back at the railway bank on London Road. People were coming in to work or to help with the clear up. Dad questioned a man in some uniform. "Most of the injured were taken to Walsgrave, but we've transported some to St. Cross in Rugby."

"Does this train go there?"

"Yes, sir."

"Do we need tickets?"

"We take all hardship cases, sir, but we are trying to maintain some semblance of normality, so if you can …"

"Certainly."

The rhythm of the train lulled Violet back into a daze. The others cleaned themselves up a little in the train's filthy WC, but she couldn't make the effort. Black is my color, she thought, noticing the soot that came away when she wiped her hand across her brow.

The train crawled into Rugby. Violet allowed Reverend Robins to guide her out, into a cold grey town, miraculously intact. Clouds had been building and the overcast sky was featureless, like the pit.

"St. Cross Hospital?" someone was saying.

"It's south, sir. Just follow the Murray Road."

Holly and the others went out of the station. Violet followed, unable to shake her daze. They were so urgent that they didn't notice when she lagged behind. After a while, they went around a curve and disappeared. She stumbled to a halt. Why was she here? Where were they going? A wall appeared to her left. She sat against it.

"Violet? Violet is that you?" A tall figure was silhouetted against the grey sky. *Was it now? Was he coming for her at last?*

"I want it. I know I do," she said.

"Violet? It's me." The lower half of the figure came into focus. It had a cast on one leg and two crutches. She looked up. Robert.

"Well, I think she's down," Rachel said. "Considering that all she does is sleep, it's amazing how hard it is to get her there."

James was in the sitting room, comfortable in the large chair, reading yesterday's *Times*. A small parcel sat at his feet.

"Now what have you brought us?" Rachel said.

"How's the coffee holding up?"

"She's had two, no three, more episodes. About half gone, I think."

"My friends in Canada must think I'm desperate for the stuff. I've got …" he lifted the package, "… another pound. It's actually postmarked before the first one, so it may be stale. But I was thinking you and I could afford to have a cup from this lot."

"Wonderful," Rachel said. "Let me get the pot set up."

Not many minutes later they settled into the two chairs with steaming cups. James tried to keep the conversation light. This warmth between them, he knew, was precarious. Part of him wanted very much to preserve it.

"Did you hear about the Clarkes?" he asked. She nodded. "Quite a story, from what I can tell," James continued. "But I never heard how Robert was injured."

"Apparently at the height of the bombing he was out trying to help others," Rachel said. "I think a wall or a roof collapsed on him."

"And he was in hospital?"

"Yes, in Rugby. He had only just been discharged when Philip and the others came looking for him."

It wasn't long before James needed to leave. "Dr. Black is in London and I need to look in on his patients. Two horses, injured by a stray bomb in Reading."

"And they brought them all the way here?"

"I brought them all the way here, under anesthesia. I was lucky not to lose one or both of them."

"Well, then, get going and check on them. It would be miserable to lose a horse after such a heroic rescue."

"Of course," James said. "But this has been lovely,"

Too lovely, she thought as she closed the door. What are you getting yourself into, old girl?

Lloyd had his head down on the desk. He had come here to pray for people, but was distracted by newspaper reports of 'a midlands town,' heavily damaged in a raid. He knew through the grapevine that it was Birmingham, where he had gone to university. How can I pray, Lloyd thought, when every trace of God has disappeared from my world? Robert and Holly spared, but Edwin gone and Violet traumatized. Who knows what's happening to all the others. Lenny. Welly. Nelson. Billy Parker, all those in uniform. How many times have I prayed for them? Lily lives, but Muriel Timms is gone. And this damned war and the demonic man with the mustache just go on, with no end in sight.

Where are you, Lord?

Annie opened the vestry door. "Lloyd?"

"Yes, I'm right here," he said. He didn't understand the irritation in his voice.

"Oh," she sighed. "I was wondering if you were going to make it out to see Ned and Alice. I wanted to send a carrot cake. I know Ned loves it."

"Right. I'll go now," Lloyd said. He rose mechanically and took the cake from Annie. He grabbed his warmer coat. He hadn't seemed to be able to warm up since the trip to Coventry. As an afterthought, he grabbed his scarf as well.

The wind was brisk. He didn't stop on the bridge. *This is the worst season. Nothing green and growing, but no hope of snow or winter.*

When he got to the farm, he couldn't see Ned anywhere. Maybe he was doing something inside. Alice answered his knock.

"How are you, Lloyd?"

"Chilled," he said. "It's a bitter wind. Here," He held out the cake. "Annie sent this for you."

"Carrot. Lovely. Thank her for me."

"I will." Lloyd looked around. "Is Ned not here?"

"No. He's in Swindon getting a … widget of some sort for the tractor."

"Oh, that's right." Lloyd felt the familiar burn of irritation, mostly with himself. Ned had mentioned this at church last Sunday, but with all that had happened, Lloyd had totally forgotten. *What made people think he'd remember anything they told him on a Sunday, anyway?* He forced himself to ask the obvious question. "How is he doing?"

"Better," Alice answered, then sighed. "But still not good. He was very relieved about Buster, but he's worried sick about how he'll manage in the new year. Stanley is great, but he's not always here, and he can't make up for six or seven men."

"No," Lloyd said, trying to sound sympathetic.

"Anyway," she said, "I don't expect him home until dinner."

"Right. Well, I'll get going then."

"Don't you want to stay and warm up?"

"No, thanks. I'll just go."

"I'll tell Ned he missed you."

"No. Don't. He already knows I'm senile. No need to confirm it." It would have been a joke, if Lloyd had been able to generate the right tone of voice.

Back in the sharp wind, he knew he should view this time as a reprieve. His message sat cold on his desk. But he really didn't want to go back. Maybe he'd just walk out a little way, see if the bleak country could soothe his ruffled spirit.

He walked and walked. The land was starkly beautiful, but it did little to soothe. His mind went back and forth between the troubles of others and his own problems. He was irritated that he even thought he had problems, so trivial were they compared to the loss of a child or a city.

He was almost at Pangbourne when it started to rain. His coat was a good one, but it wouldn't keep the rain out long. He stood under a tree and studied the sky. Maybe this was just a shower. He would try to sit it out in the Bear and Child, which had just come into view.

It was raining harder by the time he pulled open the heavy door. He got a half pint and sat in a corner, avoiding any need to be sociable. Memories of Coventry battered his brain. So much destroyed. So much burnt. And now Birmingham too. Everything he loved was being devastated.

"Mum? Dad?" Lloyd called. "Can I go with William to the cathedral? Saint Nicholas is giving out sweets to the children this afternoon. And it's so beautiful." Lloyd loved snow. He was overjoyed that it had come the day before Christmas.

"Are William's parents going?"

"Yes, Mum."

"Right, then. Be careful and polite. You're eleven years old now. You should behave like a gentleman."

"Yes, Mum."

William and Lloyd ran ahead of the adults, pausing frequently to lob snowballs. They stopped at Broadgate and made snow angels on the lawn. They passed Holy Trinity church, its spire sharp and blue against the sky. Then came the cathedral. Lloyd felt it the most beautiful thing he had ever seen, especially now with snow on its roofs.

They found Saint Nicholas giving out treats and blessings in one of the priory rooms. Lloyd received a packet of biscuits, a lovely orange, and a blessing "May the Lord Jesus always be with you, no matter what may come in your life."

"You'll freeze, young man." Lloyd's landlady was always worried about the students in her house. "This is the heaviest snow we've had in decades. You'll get lost in a drift and we won't find you till spring."

"I appreciate your concern," Lloyd said, "but I love the snow. It's a beautiful day for a walk. I just wish I could get to church."

Birmingham was a typically grey industrial town, but today everything was gleaming. The trams weren't running, but that meant the streets were pristine. *Thank you, Lord, this is glorious.*

Lloyd walked further than he had intended, until he started to feel the cold. He turned to walk back on High Street. A few streets further on he passed a sign for High Street Chapel. People were gathering to worship. *It's Sunday. I've caught up on my work. Why not?*

Lloyd found a warm welcome. "Good morning. Glad you're with us." The speaker was an older man in a clerical collar. "I'm Harold Marley, the preacher here. I don't believe we've met."

"Lloyd Robins. I'm a student at the university."

"Oh. We have a few of your peers … but I don't see any this morning. Must have been kept away by the snow."

He scanned the pews once more and called out, "Terry?"

A man turned his head. "Do you see any of the university lads here this morning," the preacher asked.

"Terry Sheffield?" Lloyd asked. "Lieutenant Terry Sheffield," he said more confidently.

"Lieutenant Robins! Praise the Lord! How are you, brother?"

"Fantastic. Even more fantastic now. How have you been?"

"Wonderful. The Lord has been so good. I've just got married." The organ started to play. "Come to our house for dinner after church!"

All destroyed now. Lloyd hadn't heard from Terry in months, but rumor had it that High Street Chapel was in ruins.

Sometime in his musings, Lloyd had got another Guinness. No two. He set the three glasses carefully in a row. A fourth would look nice, wouldn't it?

He got up and walked toward the bar. Suddenly he had a more urgent need. "Where's the loo?" The barman pointed with his rag.

After he had relieved himself, he walked back to his table. He knew he really shouldn't have that next beer. But his ear still rang, despair still gnawed at the edge of his mind.

Across the room, someone stepped out of the pub door. Lloyd caught a glimpse of a silhouette against the afternoon light, and a familiar knock-kneed walk. *Is that Alan Ward? Lord, no! Worst possible person at the worst possible moment.* He looked back at the bar. *Might as well just get it over with, be the drunk I'm going to be accused of being.*

While he was dithering, another man, a stranger, walked in. "Rain's stopped," the man announced to no one in particular.

On the other hand, maybe this would be a good time to head home.

James had just completed his morning lecture. *What is it Henry Padbury calls his students?* James was beginning to think he had the same group. He stood over his desk, looking down at a batch of tests. *Is it that hard to calculate anesthetic doses? I'm glad this lot are not trying to become people doctors!*

There was a knock at the door.

"Come," he said.

"Hello, James. Am I interrupting? I can leave."

He looked up to see Lloyd at the open door. His face was pale and drawn.

"No, it's fine. I'm just bemoaning the shortcomings of veterinary students."

"I'll only be a minute."

"Stay as long as you'd like. You look like you need a rest. Can I get you a cup of tea?" James gestured to the steaming pot on his side table.

"Yes, thanks. This coat is a little damp."

As they sat with their tea, James felt the need to clear the air between them. *Lord Jesus, help me do this well.*

"Before I let you get to what brought you, I want to apologize for my harsh words at Lady Blount's prayer meeting. I was wrong to jump on you, on all of you. I ask your forgiveness."

Lloyd paused, then nodded. "I'll admit that on top of the abysmally low turnout, your attitude was a blow. But," he said mechanically, "apology accepted."

James considered that the blow might have been harder than he'd thought. *This man is not doing well.* James wanted to bring up another topic, but persuaded himself it wasn't important. Instead he tried to lighten the atmosphere "Right, then; to what do I owe the honor of this visit?"

Lloyd sighed. He started to speak and sighed again. Finally, he said, "Once again, I need to confess that I have tried to find escape in Guinness."

"Oh no! I'm sorry. Was it bad?"

"Not that bad." Lloyd described the events of the previous afternoon.

"Alan Ward," James said. "That could get sticky."

"I'm sure it will," Lloyd said glumly. "Especially since I am going to seek him out to confess my stumble. I promised I would. Even if I hadn't seen him, I would need to keep that promise."

"I'll be praying for you, my brother. Have you confessed to Annie and Ned?"

"Annie. As soon as I got home. I think she took it well, though she was sad. I hate disappointing her."

He paused, looking at his tea. "I haven't told Ned. He's struggling with his own discouragement. I didn't want to burden him."

"I'm sure he'd understand," James said. *Or is it that you don't want to admit another failure?* Lloyd looked away and started to stand.

"Wait." James had made a decision. "I need your advice."

"I'm not sure my advice is reliable," Lloyd said.

"Nonetheless." James thought about how to word this. "In the midst of helping take care of Lady Blount, I've had an unexpected development."

"Has she taken a turn for the worse?" Lloyd asked.

"No, she's about the same. But as we've taken care of her, I've found myself developing a liking – maybe more than a liking – for Rachel."

Lloyd smiled for the first time. "Rachel? I thought the two of you were loyal antagonists – uncomfortable allies, at best."

"I'll admit that's how it started. But all this time together has given me the chance to get to know her. And now I don't know what I think."

"Oh, my." Lloyd rubbed his ear, still smiling. "Well, Rachel is one of the finest people I know. She has her idiosyncrasies, and she is by no means softly spoken, but she has a wonderful heart."

"So you would approve my speaking to her of this?"

"Who am I to approve? Both of you are adults."

"You're her pastor. Would this be good for her soul? Am I worthy of her attention?"

"More than worthy," Lloyd said. "I think the two of you could be perfect for each other, but God will have to lead you."

When Lloyd left, James noted how much better he looked than he had when he came in. Rachel, he thought, would appreciate my ministry. Or would she?

"Thank you for coming to see us, Alan," Lloyd said. Annie had insisted on inviting Alan over and giving him carrot cake and tea.

"What have you heard from Welly and Nelson?" she asked.

"Welly's still in London, defusing bombs. He writes often but doesn't say much. Most dangerous job in the war, Churchill says."

"Nelson's out at sea. He's been transferred. Now he's a Chief Petty Officer on an armed merchantman. Battle of the North Atlantic, they're calling it. We haven't heard anything from him lately."

Alan's face hardened. "Which brings me … not wanting to offend, Annie—"

"Wait a minute, Alan," Lloyd broke in. "I've something I need to say first."

Lloyd took a deep breath. His skin was cold with sweat. Anger battled with contrition for speaking rights. "I promised that if I stumbled with the alcohol again, I would tell you. I have done so."

He described Thursday's events. "I confess that I gave in a bit, though the Lord stepped in to keep me from getting really drunk. I stopped at three and walked home."

Alan's face had been getting redder and redder. "Stopped at three did you? When I left it looked like you were headed to the bar for more. How can I believe you didn't drink yourself foolish again?"

Lloyd felt his anger winning. "Because I didn't. I came home right away and confessed to Annie. I wasn't drunk. I also confessed to James."

"Of course. To the ones who would cover for you. Begging your pardon, Annie, but you're his wife. You have to."

"No, Alan," Annie said calmly. "I swear to you he wasn't drunk."

Alan's voice was clipped. "As I say, you have no choice but to defend him."

"And what about Ned?" Alan continued, turning back to Lloyd. "Did you go running to him as well? Will he intercede for you again?"

"I haven't talked to Ned." Lloyd hung his head.

"No? How will he feel when he finds his lieutenant doesn't trust him?"

"Alan," Annie said, pleading. "You're not making sense."

"Not making sense!" His voice rose was harsh now. "You want sense? Here's sense? Paul tells both Timothy and Titus an elder must not be a drunkard. And he says 'Them that sin rebuke before all, that others also may fear.' That is exactly what I intend to do. I will call a congregational meeting and rebuke you that others may learn not to sin."

"Do you have two or three witnesses willing to join you?" Annie said. There was steel in her voice.

"I am two witnesses. I've seen this twice." Alan pointed a finger, shaky with rage, at Lloyd. "And he will not deny it."

Lloyd spoke in a whisper. "No, I won't."

Annie had finished preparing tea for the children – bread with the thinnest coating of butter – and was walking with Maggie up the hill toward the school. But when she turned the corner, she saw Marjorie and Violet coming slowly down. It was the first time she had seen them since Coventry. Marjorie's face was stricken, and she was supporting Violet, whose mincing steps made Annie think of someone walking through a minefield.

Annie hugged them in turn. "How are you all doing?"

"Robert's healing well with Holly's care," Marjorie said, "the little ones are just sweet and Philip and I are …well, you know." She wrapped her arm around her daughter. "But Violet's not doing well. She asked to talk to you. Can you help her?"

"Oh, Marjorie, I don't know how to help her, but I'll talk and pray with her. Can you take care of the children for me?"

"Of course. I'll collect them from school?"

Annie nodded, "Bring them back to the house. There's tea in the kitchen."

Annie and Violet walked slowly back down to the manse. Annie settled her onto the couch, offered her tea and bread. Violet was not interested.

"Your mum said you wanted to talk to me. I'm here for you, Vi."

"I'll try, Mrs. Robins, but my heart is so confused. I'm stumbling all the time. I don't think there's a way out, but I need to find it. Mrs. Robins, I haven't told Mum this, or anyone but … but … I want to die. I keep having nightmares. An awful voice telling me I deserve it. That I want it. Calling me to darkness."

"Oh, Vi," Annie said.

"It started when Edwin … when Edwin … and then Reggie. He was the one who told me I wanted it. And then the alerts … and the bombs … and the fire … and the explosion."

Annie prayed. *Lord, let her get this out, get through this, find you.*

"Did they tell you that last bomb landed on a man? When we woke, we were covered in blood. Not our blood. His. One second he was there, then he was—"

"Oh, that's so horrible, Violet! You needn't think about it."

"But I do. I think about it all the time. It's like the cinema when the film gets stuck. The same image over and over, until finally it burns through." She leaned away digging at her eyes with her fists. "It won't stop."

She dropped her hands and looked wide-eyed at Annie. "I tried to throw myself from the train on the way back. I wanted to, I so wanted to, but something stopped me, almost like a hand against my chest." She turned and looked Annie straight in the eye. "Something stopped me. I tried three, four times. We were on a bridge. I'd have been sure to die. The last time I backed up the width of the carriage, ran and jumped. But something stopped me."

She took both of Annie's hands "Mrs. Robins, I came to you because I want an honest answer … was it Jesus? Would he do that?"

Annie looked the girl in the eye. More tears than she thought possible were pouring down Violet's cheeks. She seemed poised, teetering, on the edge of a cliff. Annie longed to give her the easy answer. But she couldn't. She sought in her heart, she cried in silent prayer, but there was no answer.

"I … I don't know. I hope it was. It sounds like something He would do. But, I know for sure that He is here now, as close as your heartbeat, as close as the air. He promised He would never leave us, and that promise is true, no matter how horrible things become. He wants to help you, to lead you out of this darkness and into His light … I can't lead you out. But I can remind you of his promises. Would you allow me to do that?"

At Violet's weak nod, Annie reached for her Bible. Verses came into her head and she turned to them. "Psalm 139: 'Whither shall I go from thy spirit? Or whither shall I flee from thy presence? … If I say, Surely the darkness shall cover me; even the night shall be light about me. Yea, the darkness hideth not from thee; but the night shineth as the day: the darkness and the light are both alike to thee.'

"He is present with you, Violet, no matter how dark it is. Jesus says 'I am the light of the world: he that followeth me shall not walk in darkness, but shall have the light of life.' That's His promise: if you cling to Him and cling to His Word, he will be your light in this darkness."

"How can that be? I've been so awful."

"But that's exactly why He came." She searched again. "John the Baptist's father says that Jesus will 'give knowledge of salvation to his people in the forgiveness of their sins, because of the tender mercy of our God, whereby the sunrise shall visit us from on high to give light to those who sit in darkness and in the shadow of death, to guide our feet into the way of peace.'"

"That's what I want, Mrs. Robins. Light. Peace. Forgiveness."

"John says that 'If we confess our sins, he is faithful and just to forgive us our sins, and to cleanse us from all unrighteousness.'"

"Pray that for me, Mrs. Robins."

"Can you pray, Violet? Simply ask Him for His presence, His cleansing for your guilt, and for light in this darkness." Violet did pray, haltingly but honestly. When they finished, dusk had fallen in the front garden. Lloyd was just coming in for dinner. "Mrs. Robins, it's dark; I can't go out in the dark."

"Your mum is right here in the kitchen, Violet; Lloyd is here too. They'll walk you home; they'll keep you safe."

"No! I can't go out in the dark. I can't." She was visibly shaking.

"Well, what if I talked to your mum and let you stay here tonight? We'll take you home in the morning."

"Oh, yes please."

After a quiet dinner, Annie made up a bed on the couch.

"What if there's a raid?" Violet said.

"I'll come if the alert goes off. We sit under the staircase. But there's no reason to think they will bomb us."

Violet groaned. "They will. I know they will."

An hour later the alert sounded. Violet screamed, a high-pitched wailing like the siren itself. Annie rushed to hold her, found her rigid, face pressed into her hands. She had to drag her under the stairs. *Oh Lord, make your presence real to this poor girl.*

There was no sound of planes, no anti-aircraft fire, and before too long the all-clear sounded. A long while later Violet took a deep breath and stated her intention to try to sleep. Annie left the light on and collapsed on her bed next to Lloyd, utterly exhausted.

At eight o'clock a small noise from the front room woke Annie. She went out and saw Violet put on her coat, take Annie's Bible under her arm and slip out of the front door, where the sky was just beginning to lighten. Annie went to the window and saw Violet walking toward the river.

Was this hope or despair? Annie sensed she was watching a breakthrough as Violet faced her fears in the pre-dawn light. But she couldn't be sure. She went to her bedroom, changed quickly, grabbed her coat, and hurried out. Then she turned back to take an extra coat; Violet's was thin.

When Annie turned the corner, the girl was already on the bridge. Some instinct made Annie refrain from crying out, and Violet did not stop or pause, but went on up Stokely Hill.

Then she disappeared. She could only have stepped through the gate onto the path to Stokely Chase. Annie smiled. Watching the sunrise from the ridge that overlooked town was one of her own favorite things. Annie prayed that Violet was going up to see the light.

She labored up the steep path. The fields were grey, cold, and quiet except for a few early-morning birds. It wasn't far to the top, and Violet must have seen her following, but did not acknowledge her presence. Violet walked along the ridge path for a couple minutes, and then sat on one of the benches. The town lay peacefully below.

Violet opened Annie's Bible and ran her finger along a verse. Annie could see her shiver, so she walked up quietly and laid the coat across her shoulders. Violet snuggled into it, then looked up gratefully and patted the seat next to her.

As Annie sat, the young girl huddled close. The Bible was open to Luke 1, the verse about the sunrise. Soon a pink glow appeared, then the edge of a disk over the trees on the far ridge. The hill behind them caught the glow, which quickly marched down into town. Violet sighed. "It's not so dark anymore. Jesus called me. I heard him, or dreamt him, I don't know which. He spoke to the darkness and it vanished. Then He filled the space around me with light. Just like this." She gestured toward the rising sun.

"He seemed to speak to me. 'Come out of darkness, my child. You don't want it. You never really did. It was always a lie. I am what you truly want. You were made for the light. You will be safe in the light.'"

A dawn bird broke into song, a benediction.

CHAPTER 13

13 December 1940

"How many nights in a row have we had an alert?" Ernest asked as he stood to leave the *Jackdaw.*

Lloyd shook his head. "I don't know, but it's too many. Praise God we've never yet been bombed."

In the street, they strained their ears for the sound of aircraft, but heard nothing. "Still," Ernest said, "It could happen. We're hoping to install our Anderson next week. You can never be too safe, that's what Evelyn says." Ernest looked up at the clear night sky. "Between you and me, Lloyd, I'm not really worried about a bombing. It's Evelyn I'm worried about."

Lloyd raised his eyes to meet Ernest's. "Really? Why?"

"She won't let Lily out of her sight. Ever since the girl got out of hospital she's kept her at home."

"I thought Lily was still weak."

"She's fine: a bit pale, but that's because she never gets out. She used to be so active: climbing trees, running in the fields, riding her bicycle. Now her mum won't allow any of that. It's like Evelyn's lost her backbone."

They paused in front of the manse. "She's the same with Phyllis. She clings to those children like it's their last hour. Phyllis isn't taking it well. She says right to her mum's face that she wants her old life back.

And Evelyn won't hear reason from me. She even told me I hate the girls and want them to die."

"I'm sorry." Lloyd sighed. "Is there anything I can do to help?"

"If you or Annie could give her a word of encouragement, it might help. I think she just needs to get her eyes off the girls, and hear the Word, and trust God."

"Well … I'm looking after the kids tomorrow. Annie is going with Alice to try to scare up a few things at the Swindon market." Lloyd was ashamed that he had reached for such an easy excuse. "I might be able to do Monday."

"Monday morning we take delivery of the Anderson. I know Evelyn will want me to get to work on it right away."

Lloyd considered. "Maybe Annie and I could come over, and I could help you."

"Could you?" Ernest brightened considerably. "That would be great!"

~ † ~

James pulled up in front of Meg and Bert's a few minutes early. He knew Bert was nervous about preaching today and he didn't want to add any stress.

When Meg answered the door, he said. "Well, today's the big day, isn't it? How is he doing?"

"Oh, he's beside himself. Still revising the message, crossing out and writing furiously, running thoughts and ideas by me a mile a minute. I finally had to take him off and get him dressed, and he's just finished his breakfast."

"I'm ready, James," Bert called. "Just let me brush my teeth."

Moments later Bert rolled into the kitchen. He stopped at the table to collect a pile of papers, which he placed in a small pouch hanging at the side of the chair.

"Right. Let's go."

James led the way out to the car. Two boards had been carefully fitted over the front steps to form a ramp, and Bert zipped down this without a thought. James held the gate open for him out of politeness, but he was sure Bert could have managed that easily as well. Before James got to the car, Bert had already opened the door and swung himself in. He lifted each leg with two hands until his useless feet were in front of him in the passenger's seat.

"You get stronger and more clever each week." James said.

"I just wish I could figure out how to put the chair away after I get out of it."

"What use would I be if you did?" James asked, wheeling the chair to the big boot of the car. Bert had rigged it so that when the cushion was removed, the seat could hinge up and the chair fold up a bit. James grunted as he placed it in the boot. He used a line to secure the hatch.

"Can you bring me my papers?" Bert called. James reached in and carefully extracted the thick stack from its bag.

"Gosh, you have been busy," James said as he got behind the wheel.

"You should see my pile of discards. I've had a wonderful time, though. There have been times I felt the Lord was right there at the kitchen table with me."

James remembered the feeling from his own Bible study. "So how long is this sermon going to be?"

"Probably too long. Not more than three hours, I think."

James was relieved to see a huge self-deprecating grin on Bert's round face. Even in the Free Churches a sermon rarely ran for more than forty-five minutes.

"So," Bert said, looking over at James. "Do you think if I rigged a hand throttle I could drive a car?"

"Given all that you do already, I wouldn't be surprised. Do you need to?"

"I might. My boss at Mills Aircraft came to see me not long ago. He's lost another foreman to National Service. He's offering me the position – which would be a promotion and a pay rise – if I can find a way to work from my chair."

"Bert, that's wonderful," James said. "Do you think you can do it?"

"The work won't be a problem," Bert said. "The hard part is getting back and forth. I need a way to drive a car."

"But you don't have a car. Or petrol coupons."

"I'm praying that the Lord will provide a car. Mr. Simpson says he can get me coupons. Essential war work."

Bert looked over his shoulder, seemed to notice for the first time that they were alone. "Is Rachel at home with Lady Blount?"

"Yes, she's not doing well. We thought it was pneumonia, but Dr. Nesbitt says she's losing control of her lungs. She could go at any time."

"I'm sorry. And I'm sorry Rachel will miss my preaching. She's been very encouraging."

"Yes, she's good at that." Something in James' tone of voice must have betrayed him, for he caught sight of Bert giving him a strange grin.

"Well, here we are. Let's get you preaching."

~ † ~

Henry settled into his normal pew at church and took out a notepad. Taking notes kept his mind from wandering, which was especially important today. He thought again of the telegram he'd received earlier, confirming the arrangements Professor Welchman had proposed.

Alice led several hymns from the organ. Henry's favorite was *Guide me, O Thou Great Jehovah*. He wondered if Bert had chosen it: "I am weak, but thou art mighty. Hold me with thy powerful hand." Lloyd did the offering prayer, and prayed for Bert to be used by God to communicate the truth of His Word.

Bert's text was Philippians 4, and he emphasized the peace we can find by taking our anxieties to Jesus. Like Lloyd, Bert gave a good explanation of each verse in the text. But he was nervous, and he'd probably taken on too much.

An hour later he said, "Well, there is a lot I've missed, but let me sum up on a personal note. Paul says, 'I have learned, in whatsoever state

I am, therewith to be content,' and 'I can do all things through Christ which strengtheneth me.'

"Two years ago," Bert said, "I would have said that peace came through owning my little house, having my job, caring for my children, being competent and strong for my wife. Now we're barely hanging on to the house and caring for five children. I'm forever stuck in this uncomfortable chair, and unable, for the moment at least, to provide for my family. And yet I have found more peace and contentment in Jesus and in God's Word than I ever knew before."

After the prayer, Henry was unsurprised but saddened when Alan Ward stood. Alan had told him earlier that, as warden of the church board, he was going to call a congregational meeting if any further evidence of what he called 'dissolution' on Lloyd's part came before him.

"Before we close," Alan said in his clipped voice, "I will read a formal notice … In keeping with Scripture and the rules of governance of the Huntingdon Chapels, a meeting of the congregation of Stokely Free Church is hereby called for Sunday, the twenty-ninth of December, 1940. The purpose of this meeting will be to consider evidence leading to a vote to dismiss Pastor Lloyd Robins for cause."

Oh Lord, Henry thought, be with Lloyd and Annie and let them weather this storm.

"I trust," Alan said, "that you will all be praying for the outcome of this meeting. In the meantime this is not to be a matter for discussion or gossip."

Lloyd slumped by the wall, happy to let Bert have the limelight. He had been the first to tell Bert what a good job he'd done.

He could feel people's eyes on him. Some, he thought, looked at him sympathetically, but Alan Ward stood at the opposite corner of the room with his arms folded. No one seemed to want to violate his last edict. Annie had tearfully gone out to get the children immediately after the "amen." *I'd leave too, if I could.*

The first person to approach him was Ned. "Sorry, Lloyd. I should have seen this coming. I might have been able to do something. But I haven't been feeling well, and I've been so pre-occupied with the farm …"

"How are things going?" Lloyd didn't want Ned blaming himself.

"Things are all right now," he said. "It's a quiet season, and Stanley and I can more or less keep up. I don't know what I'm going to do in the spring. Doesn't seem like there's any manpower in the whole country."

"How about womanpower? Have you considered applying for a contingent of Land Girls?"

Ned smiled. "Actually I have. Both considered it and done it. Alice took a little persuading. She said she was the only girl I needed." His smile faded. "But I don't think I'll get any. My little operation is probably too small. Too big for me, too small for the rest of the world."

Lloyd sighed. "Well … I'll pray it works out for you."

"And me for you," Ned said.

Henry came up as Ned left. "Pretty good preaching Bert did," he said.

"Very good."

"He went a little long, of course. Sixty-seven-and-a-half minutes, all told."

Lloyd chuckled, though the humor didn't penetrate very far. "All novice preachers go too long. He did better than I did, first time I preached."

"I'm afraid I've got some news I need to share, if you've got a minute."

Lloyd couldn't help but wince. All news was bad news lately. He looked around to see Charlie deep in conversation with Arthur. "Go ahead."

"The short story is, I'm going to have to leave Stokely, at least part time."

"No! What's happened?"

"I can't really say. Loose lips and all that. An old friend asked me to join an organization doing work vital to the war effort. Says my skills uniquely qualify me, so I doubt it's picking potatoes. More than that I don't know."

"When?" Lloyd asked. He had immediately wondered if Henry would be at Alan's meeting.

"At the start of the new year. I'll probably be able to come back from time to time, keep the house up and all that."

"Right. Well … I guess you don't have much choice?"

Henry stiffened and pursed his lips. "If my country needs me I have no choice."

Lloyd leaned back as Henry left. The wall was the only thing keeping him close to vertical. Charlie Simmonds finished talking to Bert and stepped his direction. "Didn't Bert do a great job this morning?" Charlie said. "Really made the Word come alive."

"He did a fine job," Lloyd said. *Why is it that if I go two minutes over, I hear about it for a month, but Bert can ramble for an hour and get only praise?*

He walked over and shook the younger man's strong hand. "Thanks again for bringing God's Word to us this morning."

"I went too long, I know. But I enjoyed it. Thanks for the opportunity."

"I will be more than happy to have you preach again, Bert."

"I hope to, Reverend, but I may not have as much time for preparation." He told Lloyd about the possibility of returning to work at Mills Aircraft.

"But how would you get there? You can't fit your chair on the train."

"Still working on that. I would need to modify a car so I can drive it."

"You'll drive from your chair?"

"No, I can get in the driver's seat. But I'll need a hand throttle."

"And brake?"

Bert chuckled. "Yes, I guess so."

Lloyd sighed. Sometimes Bert was just unrealistic. "Well, I don't know, Bert." He could see the man deflate. "But I'll pray that the Lord provides."

Maybe I'm not cut out for this job anymore, he thought as he turned away.

~ † ~

"Now you slow down again, Arthur Cripps," Rosie said. "My legs are half as long and twice as thick as yours, and I won't show up breathing like a bellows."

"Yes, dear," Arthur said. They were almost at the Butlers'. He admired Rosie for her willingness to make this long walk.

"Here we are then," he said. "Got your breath back?"

"'alf a minute." She puffed steam in the cold air.

"Right," she said, "Let's get in there before my lungs freeze."

Arthur knocked on the door. Nellie answered.

"Hello Mr. Cripps, Mrs. Cripps," she said politely. Then she turned and yelled toward the back of the house, "Aunt Meg, the Crippses are here."

Arthur heard Meg's response. "Coming … Invite them in, child."

"Oh, right." Nellie turned back to the door, her face composed and polite. "Please come in, Mr. and Mrs. Cripps."

The front room was crowded with laundry, piled on the couches and a bed. And with children, some of them apparently taking naps.

"Looks like business is boomin'," Rosie said, gesturing at the piles.

"It might be," Meg answered, "if I could just get to it. Fortunately, my customers are patient. I'm afraid we'll have to sit in the kitchen."

Arthur and Rosie followed her to the back of the house. Bert was holding his Bible on his lap. "Studyin' for your next message, preacher?" Rosie asked.

"I'm no preacher, Rosie. Just a broken man with a great God."

"Well, Bert, Arthur and me came all the way up here to congratulate you. I loved hearing how carefully you'd thought about that Scripture. You did good."

"You did, Bert," Arthur said.

"Thank you. I'm praying God uses His Word in people's lives."

"I've only got one wee bee in my bonnet," Rosie continued. "You didn't even mention that this Hitler is the antichrist. I've shown you before …" She leaned over and flipped Bert's Bible to Daniel 7, "… that Hitler is the fourth beast, the little horn, the leader of the ten-nation federation. I know Lloyd says he won't preach about the antichrist unless the text he's preaching touches on it, but I expected better of you."

"But I agree with Lloyd," Bert raised his hands palm out. "Not every Scripture is about the antichrist. I had to preach what Philippians 4 said. Maybe I'll preach Daniel 7 if I ever get another chance."

"If this vote goes against Lloyd you may be getting plenty of chances," Rosie said.

"I'm praying it doesn't," Bert replied.

She nodded vigorously. "Me too, Bert, me too. Bloody ridiculous. And in the middle of a war, what?"

Arthur nodded too. Sometimes Rosie had a real way with words.

Annie looked out into the little back garden of the Coopers' house. "I always think of Anderson shelters as small, but it looks big back there."

"The piles of soil make it look bigger, I think. The hole is only about four feet deep."

Annie turned back toward Evelyn. "The papers say they really work."

"Oh, I hope so. I've made myself a horrible nuisance to Ernest to get this thing built. But I'm just so terrified for the girls whenever a siren sounds."

"Shouldn't we go help?"

"I don't know, Annie," Evelyn said, "You can go. I don't want to leave the girls alone. Lily's still not entirely strong."

"And Phyllis," a voice said, "is bored to tears and would run out the front door screaming if Mum didn't watch her like a hawk." Phyllis entered the room, a deep hard scowl on her pretty face.

"Now hush, Phllyie," Evelyn said. "We've been through this all before."

"Mrs. Robins, tell her that Stokely is safe. Tell her that Goering does not have Stokely in his sights, waiting for defenseless Phyllis Cooper to step out so he can drop a bomb on her head. Tell her …" Phyllis stopped, seeing her mother's growing anger.

"Don't you mock me, young lady. You think you're invulnerable, but you're not. Look what happened to Lily."

"That was sickness, not a bomb."

"Will you stop talking back to me? I'm your mother and it is my job to protect you. I almost failed Lily and I'm not taking any more chances."

Phyllis slammed her teacup into the sink and stormed back to the room she shared with Lily. "Don't get up, Lily, you might stub your toe and die."

Annie watched with concern. "Evelyn," she said, "I wonder if Phyllis has a point?"

Evelyn turned. "Now don't you start on me!" The words came like a blow.

Evelyn suddenly went wide-eyed. "Oh, I'm sorry." She buried her head on the table, cowering as if hearing a horrid sound. Her voice was muffled. "I shouldn't speak to you that way. Or to her. But I can't help it. No one understands what it's like to lose a daughter. I can't let it happen again."

"But you didn't lose her," Annie protested. "God answered your prayers."

"But you can't count on that," Evelyn said, raising her head. "God helps those who help themselves."

"Evelyn," Annie cried, "that's not even in Scripture."

"Well it ought to be! It's true."

Annie felt anger constrict her throat. "God," she said, trying to speak softly, "helps those who trust in him. He doesn't promise us safety, only His presence."

"It's not enough, Annie. It's not enough. I'll protect my girls if He won't."

"You can't protect them if He won't. The only reason Lily is here is because He rescued her."

"I won't put Him to the test. I'm going to keep her safe. Both of them."

"Oh, Evelyn …" Annie suddenly realized there was nothing she could say. "I'm sorry. I can't tell you what to do. I'm just concerned."

"Well you needn't be." Evelyn was still angry. "You let me watch out for my own concerns."

Annie looked at her in shock. "Maybe," she said as quietly and softly as she could, "I should go out and help the men."

Rachel answered the door to find James standing there with a metal box in his hands, shifting from one foot to another in the chilly air.

"How is she?" he asked.

"Awake," Rachel said. "She's in pain, but coherent. I was just reading to her from the Psalms. It takes her mind off her headaches."

"Bless you," James said. "Wait till you see what I've found."

Rachel had moved Eleanor's bed into the sitting room so that when she was alert she could see into the garden. She was almost entirely paralyzed now, but it was her pain that most saddened Rachel. Even when asleep she often groaned or cried out. When she was awake, she complained of headaches. Her breathing was labored and loud, awake or asleep.

"Well, young man, why have you been such a stranger?" Eleanor whispered. Rachel was amazed at the lucidity she was still capable of, though there was no telling which "young man" she thought James was.

"I do have work to do, my lady," James said deferentially. "But today I have good news, if you are feeling well enough to hear it."

"Someone is cutting apart my brain with razors," she said. "Apart from that I don't feel a thing."

"I'm sorry, Lady Blount."

James sat in the chair next to her bed and lifted the metal box onto his knee. "This, my lady, is an ammunition box, probably from the Great War."

"Does it have bullets in it?" Eleanor said. "I could use one."

"No, my lady," James said, looking nonplussed. "It was found in the manor. The army unit was making modifications to the east wing and when they … um … removed a fireplace—"

"Further destroying my house, then. Is this your good news?"

"No, Lady Blount," James said. "But when the modifications were made, in one of the places marked on Thomas' drawing, this box was found." He opened it with a ceremonial air. "It contains bank notes, my lady, your bank notes; hidden, no doubt, by your husband and intended for your benefit."

"Mine?" Now Eleanor sounded bewildered. "How much?"

He riffled the stack "About six thousand pounds."

"Six thousand!" Eleanor said. "If only I had had that when I was trying to save the estate. Oh Cyril!" she cried. "Why didn't you tell me?"

"I'm sure he intended to tell you. He died too suddenly to carry out his good intention."

"Well, it will do me no good now." The movement of her eyes managed to communicate her whole dismal state. She labored to take a deep breath. "Does it have to go with my estate?"

"What do you mean, my lady?" James asked.

"It's my money, correct?"

"Of course it is."

"So I can give it away, if I want?"

"Certainly."

"What if I gave it to the two of you?"

"I don't need it, my lady. I think I would give it away to those more needy."

"I would as well," Rachel said. "And I can think of several."

Eleanor stopped to breathe harshly, but her eyes were alert.

"What if I gave it to you so that you could give it to some deserving soul or souls here in Stokely?"

"I'm new here," James said. "I'm probably not the best person to manage such a trust."

"You'll have Rachel to help you." She waved her hands vaguely at the pile of bills. "Just do it. Do good with it, as Cyril did good for me."

She relaxed her head onto the pillow. Her hands stopped fluttering. Soon she seemed to be asleep.

Rachel and James talked in quiet excitement about how the funds might be used. They could be invested, probably in war bonds, and then distributed as needs arose.

"You know who has a need now," James said.

"Who?"

"Bert. If he's going to get back to work, he needs a car that he can modify."

"But all the money in the world can't buy a car these days," Rachel said.

"Hmmm …" James murmured.

"Wait. Doesn't Lady Blount have a car sitting up at the manor?"

"Just what I was thinking. It's an old Daimler. We haven't touched it."

"I wonder if she'd be willing to give it to Bert?"

"Yes," said a raspy voice. "I'm glad you're enjoying giving my things away before I'm even dead."

"Oh, I'm sorry, Eleanor," Rachel said. "We thought you were asleep."

"Not quite … But I do approve of your idea. Give the man the car. Lord knows I'll never need it again."

~ † ~

The sun was setting as Ned walked into town from the station. He really didn't want to go home and tell Alice what he'd learned. Dinner would not be on the table for an hour. *I guess I'll stop at the Jackdaw and have a half pint. Doc says it won't do any harm.*

When he turned from the bar with his glass, he saw Henry and Arthur sitting at a table. "May I join you?"

"Certainly, Ned," Henry replied, "Good to see you out and about. I'm not optimistic enough to think it's because you've caught up with everything at the farm."

"No. I've been up in Reading checking on my application for a contingent of Land Girls. I fully expected to be turned down. But here's a toast to the Ministry of Agriculture." He raised his glass.

"And Fisheries" Arthur added as he clinked with Ned.

"They have given me initial approval for six girls."

"Congratulations."

"Thanks. It could still fall through, of course." Ned discreetly rubbed at the pain blooming across his chest.

"Are you all right?" Henry asked.

"Just a little pain," Ned said. "No problem."

"Did you hear about Bert's car?" Arthur asked.

"No," said Henry, curious.

Arthur told him about Bert's job offer and his plan to modify a car. "He came to me asking me to help him put in hand grips for acceleration and braking. I said 'What are you using for a car?' He said, 'Lady Blount's '28 Double Six 50.' She's given it to him, apparently. James brought it down just the other day."

While the other two were talking, Ned discreetly pulled out the bottle of little pills and took one with a sip of beer. He hoped they were all they were cracked up to be.

"So how will he do it?" Ned asked.

"Do what?" Arthur said.

"Modify the Daimler."

"Oh, it's not too bad. Have to run a cable and a reversing pulley to both pedals. The cable just pulls the pedals up and down."

At that moment the wind-up scream of the siren sounded. Henry said he thought he heard the drone of many aircraft far off. The more war-torn hearing of the other two could detect nothing.

Ned drained his glass. "Still, we'd better be getting along."

~ † ~

Arthur walked back from the Jackdaw by himself. The alert meant there were very few people on the street. He looked around as he approached the bridge. A decorative brick on the first column was not as fixed as it appeared. He slid it quickly out and searched the space behind it. The note was there.

He waited until he got home before he unfolded the small piece of paper.

"19th. Hambledon X."

He grimaced and crumpled the paper into his pocket.

"Explosives again, love?"

Arthur jumped. Rosie was standing in the doorway.

"Hello, Rosie. Can't say, of course."

"Of course. When?"

"Tuesday."

"So I get one more weekend with you?"

"Tosh. It's not really that risky."

"Bebother you, Arthur Cripps, I'll worry about you if I want to."

"Go ahead, dear. Although I think the Scripture urges you to pray rather than worry."

"I'm doing both, ye lovely ninny!" She planted a kiss on his bald head.

~ † ~

Rachel sat by the bed, holding Eleanor's thin hand. "How lovely is thy dwelling place, O Lord of hosts! My soul longeth, yea, even fainteth for the courts of the LORD: my heart and my flesh crieth out for the living God."

Lady Blount quietened again at the words. She took a ragged breath. Exhaled. Was motionless for several long moments. Gasped, took another breath. Almost a minute of shallow panting. A long moment where her face contorted in silent pain. A deep gasp, and the cycle started again. Sometimes she would cry out, and then Rachel read to her, or hold a cup of water to her blue lips.

Rachel stood and rubbed her own forehead. A fatigue headache allowed her to add sympathy with Lady Blount's pain to her tears of sorrow. "Lord, let this end. Free her and take her to yourself."

She went into the kitchen, where James, sitting on a hard chair, was patiently working through the *Times* crossword. "Any change?"

"No. She's a fighter. It hurts to see her struggle so."

There was a gentle knock at the door.

"I'll go back to her," Rachel said. Moments later Lloyd came in and slipped into the other chair. Annie came in too and hugged Rachel.

"Thank you for being with her. You've been Jesus' hands and arms."

Rachel's heart swelled, constricting her chest. How had she grown to love this cranky old woman so much? She hugged Annie back, sniffling a bit, then turned to retrieve her hanky from the end table.

"She just won't let go," she said to Lloyd.

"No. When was the last time she ate anything?"

"Days ago," Rachel said.

"Is she drinking anything?"

"Tiny sips."

Lloyd bowed his head. "Have you given her permission to go?" he said.

"What?"

"Well, you say she won't let go. An old minister once told me that sometimes the ones who love us need to give us permission – that we'll fight until we're told it's all right to stop. I think you're the one she's hanging on for."

"What should I do?"

"Just talk to her. Then we'll pray."

Tears were running down Rachel's face unheeded as she sat again beside the old lady. Lady Blount's skin had become so transparent in the last few days it seemed you could see through it.

"Lady Blount," Rachel said, feeling awkward. "Eleanor. It has been so wonderful to care for you, to get to know you. I … I love you … You're so strong, but you don't need to fight to stay. You can go and be with Jesus. It's all right. Cyril is waiting there. You can let go."

There was an almost imperceptible change in Lady Blount's breathing, less urgency to her next gasp for breath.

Annie prayed, then James, thanking God for this woman who had lived a life of such desperate dignity and loyalty.

"Do you want to pray, Rachel?" Lloyd asked.

"Oh, Lord, thank you for this lady you love and are calling. Please ease her passage into your presence."

An hour later. Annie was with Eleanor. Rachel was sitting the rocking chair in her bedroom, looking out at the familiar barren garden that she and Mum had cared for for so long. Eleanor's sickness had brought back so many memories of Mum. She would have been eighty-four this year. *How old is Eleanor?*

"Rachel," Annie's voice was gentle, not urgent. "I think she's gone."

Rachel stood slowly. Relief and grief fought for every inch of her heart. She was crying again. It didn't matter.

The old lady's face was still, a look that spoke wry triumph etched on her thin features. "Well done," Rachel said, "good and faithful servant."

Annie took her hand. "You too," she whispered.

Rachel felt James place his hand on her shoulder, felt rather than heard his agreement. Suddenly it was all too much. She turned and buried herself in him, her tears wetting the lapel of his suit, amazed in a small part of her mind that he was so much bigger than she was.

"Oh, James," she sobbed. "Don't let me die alone."

"I won't, Rachel." He hugged her fiercely. "I won't."

"I'll have him back to you in the morning, Ned," Arthur said. He stood in the Powells' front room with Stanley next to him.

"Best. I need him to turn in the potato fields, if not tomorrow, then the next day."

"He might be a bit sleepy."

"Yes, I know." Ned said dryly. Arthur had never told Ned what these expeditions were about. No use asking questions he wouldn't answer.

"Right, then," Arthur said. "Let's be off, lad. The day's a-wasting"

Arthur glanced over at the lad as they walked back down to the river. He was taller and more filled out every time he saw him. There was a maturity to his face too, since that day beneath the Thames.

"So where are we off to tonight, Uncle Arthur?"

"Hambledon. 'bout thirty miles down. We need to start early, though. Moon's only three days past. It'll come up bright, this weather. We'll hole up someplace after making the pickup, come home legitimate after sunrise."

"Why are we still doing this, Uncle? There is no threat of a Jerry invasion for months, until spring."

"Good question, lad." Arthur stroked down his mustache as he considered his answer. "Best I can figure it, once something like this gets started, it's got a momentum all its own. These last few runs were in the pipeline, in the plan, and risky though they might be for some of us, they never got cancelled."

"Come to that, is what we're doing even right? Didn't Jesus say to love our enemies? Doesn't seem like loving them to help kill them."

"You've been talking to Welly Ward?"

"No. Why?"

"He said much the same thing before our little channel run. He's willing to save lives, but not take them." They arrived at the dock, where *Guinevere* sat darkly gleaming in the cold afternoon sun.

Arthur continued, "I respect his position, and I'm glad our government allows conscientious objection." He handed Stanley up a petrol can. "Way I figure it, though, any German lives we take in an invasion will be British lives we save. I'm comfortable with that, as long as it's a legitimate war fought under orders."

"So do you think Hitler's the antichrist like Aunt Rosie says?"

"I'm not as sure as she is. But if not, I wouldn't want to see the one who is."

He stepped onto the dock with the other jerrycan and motioned toward the shed. "Anyway, I'm glad our government friends are generous with the petrol."

They pushed away from the wharf and headed downstream.

"By the way, Stanley, if anything ever happens to me, I'd be obliged if you'd help look after my Rosie."

"Nothing will ever happen to you, Uncle Arthur," Stanley said. "You're the old man of the river."

"You're sure these are hers?" Lloyd looked up in amazement. The little slips of writing paper were covered with Bible verses, hymn titles, and little notes.

"Quite," James said. "We found them in her Bible."

"'Glorious Return to be with the Lord,'" Lloyd read. "That's not a phrase I would expect to come from Lady Blount's pen."

"But it's clearly her handwriting." Rachel offered. "I've seen a lot of it."

"And the hymns and Scriptures are perfect for a funeral service," James added.

"They are." Lloyd murmured. "*The Sands of Time, I Am a Poor, Wayfaring Stranger, On Jordan's Stormy Banks*—"

"Oh, I love that one," Rachel said.

"*Amazing Grace*, *To God be the Glory*, They're all good. We should do them all."

"And look at these Scriptures," James said, pointing to another little slip of paper. "Psalm 116:1-7, Psalm 91, Corinthians II 5:6-9. So many good verses."

Lloyd felt like there were two of him in the room. One part of him rejoiced at the rightness of a believer's home-going. *Truly, we don't mourn like those who have no hope. Even in death, Jesus is with us.*

But another part was filled with doubt, fatigue, and uncertainty. *How many of these will I have to do before this war ends? How much death will I see this time, how many broken families, how much lost faith?* He felt a wave of heat and nausea roll over him. *Or is this my last funeral at Stokely? Will I be applying to be a chaplain in January?* The thought had some appeal. *Or am I too old even for that? Will the army even consider me if I've been dismissed? Will any church?*

He shifted in his seat, forced himself back to the present. "Can we get someone to open the grave in the family plot?"

James nodded. "Ed Cotton from White Hill will take care of it. For ten pounds."

"Ten pounds!" Rachel said. "That's robbery."

"Her estate can cover it." James said.

Lloyd felt a little better as he walked back to the manse. It was cold and crisp, with a few shafts of setting sunlight shooting through the clouds. Then he saw Alan Ward, waiting by the door of the church. His spirits deflated like a barrage balloon under fire.

"Hello, Alan," he said with what he hoped was an imitation of pastoral energy and goodwill.

"Good afternoon, Pastor Robins. I trust you are returning to your office."

Lloyd had been planning to go home and talk with Annie about the funeral arrangements. "Of course." Did he need to add lying to his list of sins?

Alan opened the main door of the church. "Susan told me we're having a memorial service for Lady Blount on Saturday."

"Yes, at two – it shouldn't require much preparation."

"That's not my concern," Alan said. "Are you going to bury that woman as a Christian?"

Indignation rose in Lloyd's throat like bile. "Of course. She was a Christian."

"How can you be sure?"

"Because she was. Her Bible had notes in it that practically laid out her memorial service."

"But did she live as a Christian?"

"It seems so to me."

"Are you aware of how little she gave the church? In the years I have been warden she never gave more than a few pounds a year."

"She had almost no cash, Alan." Lloyd rubbed at his ear. He felt dizzy. Was he going to throw up in this man's face?

"Alan, can we go into the fellowship hall and sit?"

"If you will take my concerns seriously."

"I'm trying to, Alan."

They sat in two wooden chairs, knee to knee. Alan scowled. "I'm sure you are aware that Lady Blount sold off many valuable properties."

"At a loss, for the most part."

"But she never tithed those amounts."

"She needed the funds to keep the estate going."

"Are you saying that one is not supposed to tithe first?"

"Well, ordinarily, yes, but there are extenuating circumstances."

Alan poked a finger into Lloyd's breastbone. "Sapphira."

"What?"

"Ananias and Sapphira. The Bible. The book of Acts. You remember, Reverend. They sold a property and didn't give to the church. God judged them and they died."

"I'm familiar with the account."

"Lady Blount received God's judgment for her evil ways. It's as plain as day. And yet you propose to bury her with honor."

Lloyd stood abruptly. His chair fell over behind him and clattered in the empty room.

"Alan, you're twisting the Scripture. You're insulting a woman who fought to her last day to honor the husband who loved and rescued her. I don't have to listen to your poison."

Lloyd turned and staggered toward the door.

"My poison!" Alan yelled after him. "What about the poison you pour down your throat? You're in no position to judge me."

Lloyd slammed the door, regretting it even as he did it.

"It will all come out at the end of the month." Alan's muffled yell followed him across the sanctuary.

He looks weary, James thought. Annie had said that Lloyd had been sick on Friday, with fever and vomiting, and, as they walked to the Blount estate's hilltop cemetery, James believed it. Lloyd was clutching his coat around his chest and walked with his head down, separated even from Annie by a few yards.

The burial site was surrounded by old oak trees, barren now. The cold wind blew through them from time to time, rattling the branches. The site looked out over the Thames and beyond to Stokely Chase.

"It was lovely the day they buried Lord Blount." Rachel gestured toward his stone. "It was springtime. Flowers everywhere, the most beautiful arrangements."

Lady Blount's grave was spare by comparison. Wartime, of course, but also the comparative poverty of the estate. Only a few of the local families had sent arrangements, and none as nice as the one Rachel had given.

"The coffin is beautiful, though," Rachel whispered. James had found it months before when exploring the manor. It was a twin of the one Lord Blount had been buried in. The rich mahogany and gold spoke of earlier, more affluent days.

He saw Lloyd straighten as the few who had come to the interment gathered around the open grave. James sensed him putting back on his I'm-a-professional-I'll-get-through-this attitude.

"Ashes return to ashes and dust to dust," he said. "Here we lay down the physical body of Eleanor Parker Blount, in confidence of her present eternal life and in the sure hope of her physical resurrection."

James was appalled to hear what sounded like a snort of derision. He turned to see Alan Ward standing slightly apart to his left.

Rachel was weeping softly again as Lloyd lifted a handful of earth and threw it on the coffin where it landed with a hollow thump. James handed her his handkerchief.

"Thanks," she whispered. "Too many funerals in my life."

"I understand." Rachel had no one again, except the church family. *And me. Maybe.*

Lloyd was praying. James tried to pay attention and pray with him, but the prayer seemed to ramble … and lack verbs.

James looked up after the "amen," and saw that Lloyd's face was ashen. He looked like a dog that was being whipped by its master, waiting for the next blow to fall. *Lord, strengthen him, comfort him, and let the vote not go against him.*

~ † ~

Welly settled into the carriage with a sigh. His big duffle bag didn't fit into the overhead net, so he sat with it in his lap. It blocked the view. Just as well: he didn't really want to be recognized by anybody. He was only vaguely aware when someone sat down next to him.

"Welly?"

"Nelson!"

"What are you …?" they both said.

Welly looked down and saw a bandage and sling on Nelson's arm. His face and hands were bruised. Old bruises, healing.

"What's happened to you? Are you all right?"

"Burns. I'll be fine. Meanwhile I have Christmas leave. What about you?"

"How did it happen?" Welly said.

"We were sunk. I'll save the story for Dad. What about you?"

"I'm going home too, but not as a hero."

"What makes you think I am?"

Welly laughed. It felt like the first time in weeks. "I'm your brother, you idiot," he said. "Do you think I can't tell when you're being modest?"

Nelson paused, looked Welly in the eye. "You still haven't answered me."

Welly turned away and adjusted his bag. "No, I haven't."

Nelson took the hint for a little while. Welly watched the outskirts of London rushing past. The city looked dark and broken, fragments and shards and blackened spikes sticking up like stripped forests.

"What's happened?" Nelson finally said.

"Short answer? I've lost my nerve."

After another long pause, Welly started to talk. "The Germans have begun dropping delayed action bombs, with a type 17 fuse. You can hear them ticking. To disarm them you have to drill a hole in the fuse and fill it with a thick liquid that gums up the clockwork. Then they can be disarmed like normal bombs."

"And you're okay with normal bombs?"

"I've disarmed fifty-seven bombs. But these unnerve me. I think it's the ticking. You can hear them, like the clock on the mantelpiece. Tick. Click. Tick. Click."

"And I assume if the ticking stops …"

"You're dead. So is everyone within range of the bomb."

Welly was speaking unemotionally, but he could feel the cold sweat pooling in his armpits. "Last week I was sent out to deal with a type 17. Between the tracks near Euston. Had to be removed. But I couldn't do it. We exposed the fuse. It was almost vertical. Perfect set-up. But every time I put the drill on the fuse head, my hands shook so badly … I couldn't get the hole started. I backed off twice and tried again, that damned fuse tick-clicking the whole time."

His hand was shaking as it clenched the strap of his duffle bag. "Finally the captain came out and did it for me. That's when he offered me Christmas off, a chance to think and find out if this job is still for me."

~ † ~

They changed trains at Reading, Nelson wincing as he moved his arm. Welly carried both duffels. Nelson was offered a seat because of his injury, but Welly had to stand. "So, are you going to tell me your story?" he asked Nelson.

"Wait until we get home."

The distance from Reading was short. Welly was dreading the meeting with his father, and sick at the faint smell of decay that came from Nelson's bandage.

"Aren't you going to need to get that changed?"

"They told me to just keep it greased up with this stuff …" He pulled out a jar of what looked like Vaseline. "Lightly covered when I'm moving around, exposed to the air when I'm not. And if I get a fever all bets are off."

"Lovely."

Finally, they pulled into Stokely.

"I guess neither of us is expecting a welcoming committee. Do you want me to walk in and try to borrow a car?" Welly asked.

"No, I'm fine."

Fifteen minutes later they arrived home. Nothing had changed. Dad kept the place perfectly maintained, even though he worked extra hours in Pangbourne.

"You look like you're about to knock," Nelson said.

"I was," Welly replied. "I was living out at Mr. Powell's before Dunkirk. This isn't really my home anymore."

"It is mine." Nelson opened the door. "Anyone home?"

Susan screamed, a mixture of happiness and shock, a long penetrating wail, like an alert siren. She rounded the corner from the kitchen at full speed, saw them on the step, and stopped dead. A combination of joy, relief, and fear transformed her face. "Nelly! What are you … Welly! Both here …" She fainted against the wall and slipped slowly down to the floor.

Welly couldn't help laughing, "I knew she was going to do that."

"Me too." Nelson said. He knelt by his mother, whose eyes were blinking open. They helped her to a chair.

"What are you boys doing here?" she said weakly. "And in time for Christmas." The little house was decorated in its usual festive manner. Their mother had handmade most of the decorations, and the greens had been gathered from up on Stokely Chase, so no wartime economies were needed.

"Let's wait for Dad and we'll tell you," Welly said.

"There he is now," said Mum. Welly had never figured out what she heard or felt that told her Dad was home. But five seconds later, the door opened sharply.

"Susan, whose bags … Nelson … Wellington … Why are you here?"

"Well," Nelson said. "The timing is a coincidence. We ran into each other on the train from London."

"Let me get you boys some tea." Mum said. She bustled about and, in a few minutes, she had seated the men at the dining-room table and produced a near feast.

"Now, I hope both of you are here for honorable reasons." Welly's heart quailed. "Coward," he imagined his dad saying. Hadn't it been true all along? He saw that Nelson's face was hard. *Probably on my behalf.*

"In my case it's more to do with the honor of another." He took a sip of his tea. "I was on the *Jervis Bay.*"

"You were?" Alan and Welly said.

"The what?" said Susan.

"The *Jervis Bay.* It was Captain Fegen who was honorable. When he came aboard, he told us 'So far we haven't seen any real action, but I promise you this much: if the gods are good to us and we meet the enemy, I shall take you in as close as I possibly can.'

"At the end of October we were assigned to a convoy out of Halifax. Thirty-five ships, but we were the only one armed. No destroyers, no cruisers, nothing. Insanity, really.

"On the fifth of November we sighted a big German ship to our north. It was a raider of some sort, with big guns, maybe eleven-inchers. Captain Fegen immediately turned toward it and ordered us to fire. We cranked those old guns up to forty-five degrees and popped out our six-inch shells. They fell miles short.

"The battleship immediately began to fire its full broadside. At us."

Nelson paused, took a sip of tea. Pulled on his bandage. "It was all in the papers."

Nelson returned to the bridge after a quick check of the gun stations. He was in time to see the enemy's first broadside land significantly ahead of the *Jervis Bay*. The captain ordered a further turn to starboard to keep the merchantman directly aimed at the German raider.

"Continue fire. Continue best possible speed."

Nelson passed on the firing order. A second broadside erupted from the raider. The Jerries were fast. Everyone on the bridge ducked as the second salvo roared overhead like freight trains in a race.

"They've got us ranged now," the captain said.

The raider's guns spoke a third time. Someone on the bridge was counting down to the arrival of the shells. Four. Three. Two.

The first shell exploded on the foredeck. Nelson froze in horrified fascination. The forward mast fell straight down the centerline of the ship, crushing men at their stations, coming to rest just in front of the tall bridge windows.

Men ran toward the damage. The port gun popped again. There was a roar behind him as a second shell struck. Nelson was thrown to his right. His shoulder struck the wall and he cried out in a pain no one heard.

Moments later he dragged himself to his feet. His shoulder and arm were going numb, but he could still flex his fingers. He turned and saw … chaos. The rear wall of the bridge had been blown out, and everything was gone: coding station, fire control station, radio room. He could see the ocean foaming on the port side of the ship. Captain Fegen stood in the upper bridge, clutching his left arm. Blood gushed from his left shoulder.

Shells from the German continued to pour into the port side of the *Jervis Bay*, ahead and behind the wheelhouse. Unable to do his own job, Nelson looked around for a way to help and saw Petty Officer Wallis, the quartermaster, clutching an open wound on his leg. Lieutenant-Commander Roe was applying a tourniquet.

Wallis hobbled back to the wheel. It spun loosely in both directions. "Steering gear out of action," he called.

"Man the aft steering position." It was Captain Fegen. Nelson looked up to see him leaning against a railing. His voice was calm with command, his face the color of dirty snow.

Nelson knelt by a man with a bleeding head wound. He already had a tourniquet around his left arm. The hand was neatly severed at the wrist. "I'll get you to sick bay," he yelled.

It was several decks down. Nelson was shocked by moments of utter calm along the way. The *Jervis Bay* had been a good-sized liner in her earlier life, and it showed. She was still solidly afloat.

"Oh, God! I can't see," said the man Nelson was half-carrying. Blood from the head wound flowed over his eyes.

"We're almost there," Nelson replied.

When they entered the sick bay, they were driven back by the smoke. The next compartment up had taken a hit and was burning. The doctor was still there, working on a seriously wounded man. "We're relocating to the officers' mess," a petty officer yelled.

Nelson continued to half-carry the sailor he had brought down, and led the walking wounded to the mess. There they found other critically injured patients. But the doctor did not come. "I'll go back and fetch him."

Broadside after broadside roared in from the gleaming German ship. The *Jervis* was turning randomly, all steering lost. The heroic crew of one gun still sent up shells. The sick bay was engulfed in an inferno. Nelson joined a firefighting crew, trying to get in, but there was no water pressure.

Finally, the abandon ship sounded. Nelson headed back toward the officers' mess, but found a pitiful few of the wounded already heading toward the starboard rail. "The rest are gone," someone called. They passed the captain, laid out on the deck, dead.

All the lifeboats had been destroyed, but crewmen were trying to manhandle a big life raft into the water. "Heave," they cried, but with all the obstructions on the deck, the raft refused to move. Nelson gauged the distance to the starboard rail.

"Turn her end over end," he yelled. He rallied a group of men on one edge and they lifted and pushed her up. She crashed upside down, but mostly undamaged. One more turn and they were raising her up to the starboard rail. Lord, let her land right side up, Nelson prayed.

The big raft sailed almost gently to the sea forty feet below.

"Too far for me," Nelson said. "Anybody want to go down a few decks?"

Some did. One deck down the base of the ladder was surrounded by smoke and fire. It was almost as bad on the deck below. The only way to the starboard side was through the fire. Pain seared his arm as a huge glob of burning oil struck it. He beat at his flaming sleeve, dug with his bare hand into his own flesh. He reached the rail and fell toward the sea. It enveloped him with bitter cold.

"By the time we abandoned ship there were only a few of us left. Sixty. Maybe seventy. Most of those who got off were picked up, once the battleship moved away in pursuit of other prey."

Welly was full of pain and pride. "You were fantastic, Nelson. And your captain was amazing. The papers say his action saved the majority of the convoy.

"No doubt. We never landed a shot on the German, but we tied her up in knots."

"So how bad is your arm?" Welly asked.

"Not too awful. The burn is deep in one spot." Nelson took the bandages off. Welly thought he might be sick. His brother's flesh was raw, the edges of the burnt area raggedly clipped, his shoulder deeply bruised. But Welly thought he could see a thin film of some kind of new growth under the Vaseline.

"You were lucky, brother," he said.

"Blessed," Alan corrected. "You did your job and the Lord kept you safe."

"What about his captain and all the others who did their jobs?" There were tears and anger in Welly's words.

"They must not have had the Lord."

"Oh, Dad, don't be a damned simpleton!"

Dad reeled back from Nelson's words as from a blow. "You can't talk to me like that," he said reflexively. "I'm still your father."

"But I'm a man now," Nelson said. "And I know that the world isn't as simple as you think it is. I still believe in God, but I don't believe bad things don't happen to the faithful. I've seen too many of those bad things."

"Me too," Welly said.

"But you're brave boys serving your nation. That's got to count for something with God."

"I don't think it counts a bit," Welly said. "And I know I don't qualify as brave."

"Of course you are. I heard what you did with that bomb of Lenny's."

"But I'm losing my nerve. That's why my CO sent me home for Christmas."

"You can't be losing your nerve."

"But I am." Now it was Welly's turn to be angry. "Haven't you always accused me of being a coward?"

Welly turned away and said not one more of the tornado of words swirling within his chest.

CHAPTER 14

22 December 1940

It was the third day before Christmas, the day Lloyd distributed food and gifts to families who were having trouble making ends meet. A cold drizzle accompanied him down the hill from the manor. He had been tempted to skip Percy altogether, since he was working at the college, but the little man had met him in town earlier and hinted at how much he was looking forward to the sweeties the nice ladies at church always gave him.

"Rev'e what the best thing to put in a Christmas pudding?"

Lloyd tried to muster a smile. "I don't know, Percy, what's the best thing to put in a Christmas pudding."

"Your teeth, Rev'e, your teeth."

The next stop was Meg and Bert's. Rain dripped from his hair and soaked his coat as he plodded along. He didn't have a free hand for an umbrella, but he really wasn't carrying very much. He knew he shouldn't be ashamed of how little people had given this year, but somehow it felt like his fault.

Christmas was going to be sparse all around. Lloyd had come across some bargains after a bombing in Reading, and got each of the kids a pair of boots, although Georgie's were a size too big. He'd also got Annie a dress in a beautiful color but with a smoky smell he hoped would come out. Annie had been knitting for the children. But they had little to spend and there was not much to spend it on.

Rain lashed at his face as he opened the Butlers' gate. He knocked, but he wasn't sure he'd been heard. He could hear a woman apparently berating Nellie for something in a strong Cockney accent. He knocked again and finally Meg answered. She looked worn and irritated, not an expression he was familiar with on Meg's usually kind face. Behind her Nellie was herding Billy into the kitchen.

"Come in," Meg said. She turned back to the sitting room, where an elderly couple occupied the two chairs. There was no laundry in sight. "Alf, Mildred, I'm sure you remember Rev'rend Robins."

"Don't get up," Lloyd said. "I hear you haven't been feeling well, Alf."

"Right poorly, Rev'rend. It's this cold country air. I 'aven't ever been able to get used to it." He interrupted himself to cough.

Mildred spoke over the cough. "'e's got the croup. 'e just won't admit it. I tried to get 'im to the doctor, but 'e's that stubborn."

"Who's stubborn?" Alf muttered under his breath.

"And how are you, Mrs. Cotton?"

"Except for me old arthritis I'm fit as a fiddle."

"Good."

"Come into the kitchen, Lloyd, and I'll get you a cup of tea." Meg interrupted. Lloyd handed her the bag of treats. The other bag held canned goods.

"Annie's carrot cake," Meg said. "Thank you. Bert loves your wife's baking. And Alice has a little ham for me from their smokehouse. If I can just get up there, I'll have what I need to make a start on Christmas dinner!"

"I'm going up to see Ned next. I'll drop the ham in on my way back," Lloyd said. He looked at her again. "So how is it going Meg? You look worn out."

"Worn to a frazzle, Reverend, I admit. It's not taking care of the old people – that's easy. It's that they constantly bicker, say the craziest things, and yell at the little ones. And I'm behind on the laundry, mostly trying to do it at night."

She began to cry. "Bert's cranky. He so wants to work, to provide for us, but he can't get Lady Blount's car working … Not that we're not grateful."

"I'm sorry." Lloyd said. "I didn't think it was going to be easy."

"Oh, not you too!" She turned away and wiped at her eyes. "Everybody says 'I told you so,' but no one offers to help."

"I'm sorry, Meg. I didn't mean to offend. How can I help?"

"You can't," she said. "There's no help for it. Here's Bert." She turned back into the sitting room, where several people were yelling simultaneously.

Lloyd found Bert working diligently on something in his lap. It was the fuselage of a model Spitfire, and Bert was attaching the wings with tiny pegs.

"Did you carve that yourself?"

"Yep," he said, concentrating. "That ought to do it." He leaned forward and placed the model on the table. One wing was held stiffly in place with twine while the glue dried.

"Bert, you are just wonderfully clever. That's beautiful work."

"Would have been cleverer to start a month ago. I don't know how I'm going to get all this done by Christmas."

Lloyd sat across from Bert as he lifted the other wing and began to seat the tiny pegs. "Have you heard anything about the job?"

Bert grunted, or groaned. "I sent a telegram saying I'd got a car, just needed to figure out how to modify it, and finish a new chair. Boss said I had to hurry. He'll have to promote someone else off the line if I'm not available soon."

He reached for the glue. "And here I sit making children's toys. No money to buy any, even if any were available, and seven mouths to feed."

He stared at his hands for a minute, then stirred. "Seems like the Lord's asking me to practice what I preached. That ever happen to you, Reverend?"

"All the time, Bert. Occupational hazard." He was glad Bert didn't ask how that was going. An honest answer would have been discouraging to a man already in difficult circumstances.

Lloyd continued out along Millstone Road. The rain was coming harder, but he hadn't been to visit Ned in weeks. He hoped he'd receive a little moral support. Anyway, he'd promised Meg the ham.

The farmhouse looked deserted and dismal in the rain, but Alice answered his knock quickly. "Well, long time no see, stranger."

Was it Lloyd's imagination or was there zero banter in her voice? There was certainly no smile on her face. "Hello, Alice. Happy Christmas. How are you?"

"I've been better, Lloyd. He's in there." She pointed to the front room.

Alice's tone and coolness set off warning sirens in Lloyd's head. When was the last time he'd seen Ned? He and Alice hadn't been at church Sunday.

"Is he okay?"

"Ask him yourself," she said.

Lloyd hung up his coat. "Sorry this is dripping. I didn't expect this much rain."

"It always rains for Christmas," she said.

Ned was in the big chair, with his head leant back. His face seemed to sag. He had one hand on his chest. He stirred forward a little bit when Lloyd entered.

"Hello," he said with a weak grin. "Happy Christmas."

"What's the matter, Ned?"

Ned sat up a little and waved Lloyd to the other chair, where Alice normally sat. He rubbed at the front of his shoulder. Finally he said, "A month ago I would have called it heartburn. I still sometimes think it is

… I get this pain, end of the day or after dinner. Across my chest. Sometimes in my shoulder or arm."

Lloyd felt an intense fear build in his own ribcage. *Why did everything always have to happen at once?* "Heart attacks?"

"Dr. Nesbitt doesn't think so. Honestly, Lloyd, he told me that if any one of these episodes had been a heart attack, I'd be dead."

Lloyd winced. How had he allowed himself to be so unaware?

"Nesbitt sent me to a specialist in Reading."

"You went to a specialist and you didn't tell me?"

"Lloyd, you were busy with Coventry and Lady Blount, and this vote coming up. You didn't need to be worrying about my troubles."

"But I'm your friend."

Ned stared at him for a long time. Lloyd feared the implications of that stare. He hadn't been much of a friend lately.

"I'm sorry." His voice caught. "What did the doctor say?"

"He calls it angina. It's some kind of heart trouble, but short of a full heart attack. Often comes on with exertion—"

"Which you've certainly had enough of lately."

"Or after a big meal. The doc says it's worse when it's cold." Ned gestured at the kitchen, where Lloyd could see his overcoat steaming.

"He gave me these." Ned picked up a pill bottle and read the label. "Nitroglycerine."

"Really?"

"Yep. Ironic, eh? The same thing that almost blew me to bits in the war is keeping me alive now."

"It really helps, then?"

"Seems to." He lowered his voice. "This little episode is worse than usual, which is why Alice is all in a huff. I was working in the far fields and couldn't be bothered to come back when the pain started. It got pretty bad." He stood up. "But I feel better now. Alice thinks I'm an old fool and it'll be my own fault when she loses me."

"You are an old fool." Alice had been standing by the door. "And you're another one, Lloyd Robins, for not noticing." She turned back into the kitchen.

Lloyd stood and turned to Ned. "She's right, as usual. I can't say how sorry I am that I've been such a lousy friend."

"It's not your fault, Lloyd."

"Yes, it is. Let me pray for you." Lloyd said. He asked God to forgive him for his lack of insight, and to strengthen and heal Ned. *At least it's a real prayer, even if I'm a complete waste of space as a friend.*

After he had prayed, Lloyd went into the kitchen. Alice was standing, stiff-backed, savagely stirring at something on the stovetop.

"Alice, I'm sorry I haven't noticed what's going on with Ned."

She turned. Her face was red and puffy with anger. She shook her wooden spoon at Lloyd. "Well, you should be. If you hadn't been bringing him all your problems …" She seemed to catch herself. "No, I'm sorry; that's not fair."

"True, though." Lloyd said, eyes downcast. He put on his sodden coat. Then he had to turn back. "I'm sorry. I promised Meg Butler I'd ask you about a ham?"

"Oh bother!" Alice was wiping her eyes. "Don't worry about the ham. I'll take it to her when Ned's feeling better."

"Are you sure? I don't mind."

"Well, all right. Wait a moment." She went into the pantry and opened a large cupboard door. The smell of smoked meat wafted out into the kitchen.

She came out with a ham that looked huge to Lloyd's ration-shrunken expectations and threw it roughly into a sack.

"Here."

~ † ~

"I can't do this." Lloyd's feet had slowed and stopped in the middle of the bridge. He shivered fiercely in his wet overcoat, but could not find the energy to go on. The water of the Thames flowed grey and cold beneath him.

Images filled his mind. Coventry, street after street of ashen destruction, lit only by fires. The refugees at Bablake School. Lily Cooper in the dark hospital room. The anguished face of Violet Clark. Alan Ward's anger. Eveyln's anger. Alice's anger. Annie's anger.

"I can't do this!" his heart suddenly cried again. He thought about all the needs surrounding him. Ned. "O Lord, not Ned!" Bert and Meg. Ernest and Evelyn. Poor Marjorie and Philip, facing their first Christmas without Edwin. James and Rachel deeply mourning a crotchety old lady. Henry leaving. Alan forcing Welly and Nelson into danger.

Though he knew in his head he should trust God to meet these needs, he could not rest on that, could not escape the guilt. "I can't do this!" he shouted into the wind. "I just want everyone to be okay, to be safe, this war to go away, and this world to stop making everyone vulnerable and broken."

Including me. Since Alan had announced the congregational meeting, he'd had no temptation to drink, but that strength only sharpened his shame. *I'm strong enough to avoid it out of fear. Why am I not strong enough to avoid it out of love? For that matter, do I even love God anymore? Is this weariness just a by-product of losing my faith?* His theology said that never happened. His experience said that something that looked a lot like it did. Was he awakening from a long delusion of safety and eternity and community to a reality of hell on earth?

The wind blew colder. His coat was starting to stiffen. His eyes stung. He had no choice but to turn and finish crossing the bridge. "Oh Lord, help!" The wind tore the words from his lips.

"Took you long enough to ask."

Lloyd stopped in his tracks. He knew he hadn't heard a voice, but he still looked around. It was dark and cold. No one would be out in this. He looked up at the scudding clouds, a faint hint of joy flowering deep in his chest.

"You have not because you ask not?" Lloyd said. When God spoke in that earth-shaking silent shout, every word reflected a scriptural truth.

Lloyd looked up at the darker mass of Stokely Chase under the dark sky. "Oh Lord, forgive me for not turning to you sooner. Forgive me for this despair and doubt. Forgive me for this weakness."

"I forgive you."

Lloyd smiled, but only for a moment. Then … "But I've failed so many. Failed Annie. Failed Ned. I'm scared I've already failed too badly. I can't do this."

"Not by might, nor by power, but by my Spirit, saith the LORD *of hosts. My grace is sufficient for thee: for my strength is made perfect in weakness. I will never leave you or forsake you."*

How can I forget these things? Lloyd asked himself. "Thank you, Lord. Help me to trust you. There are so many troubles, dangers, distresses. Help me to shepherd your people."

"I am the Good Shepherd."

"You are, Jesus." Lloyd could not stop the joy welling up. He remembered the strange mixture of normality and awe in these conversations. It had been far too long.

"Forgive me, Lord."

"We've already been over that."

"Lord, why is this so hard?"

"In the world you will have tribulation, but take heart, I have overcome the world."

The same verse he had preached in those horrible days at the beginning of the war. He'd wondered about himself even then.

"Lo, I am with you always, even to the end of the age."

If Rosie's right, this might be it. "Thank you, Lord. I know we've already been over it, but forgive me for my lack of faith. Help me to live out my trust in you no matter what happens."

"And he doeth great wonders, so that he maketh fire come down from heaven on the earth in the sight of men,"

What? Lloyd wasn't sure what that meant, where it came from. Revelation?

"Lord?" he asked. He stood for several more minutes. His mind was full, but the conversation seemed to be over. A shiver ran through him as the wind blew.

He smiled. It was painful.

~ † ~

Annie looked into the bedroom again. Lloyd had seemed so peaceful when he'd arrived home last night. Yet the stories he told, especially about Ned, should have been very discouraging. "I wonder if I ought to talk to Alice," Annie had said. "After the fiasco of my conversation with Evelyn, I'm not sure I won't do more harm than good."

"I think you should. But we ought to pray about it first."

Annie had been intrigued by that comment. Lloyd had said such things countless times, but not so often recently. Now he was in the bedroom, on his knees, praying. Earlier she could have sworn he was singing a Christmas carol. All good, she thought, but why? He'd been so discouraged.

"Breakfast, love," she said.

"Down in a minute."

He walked into the kitchen and gave Annie a hug. She looked into his eyes. "All right, tell me what's going on."

He smiled. "It's embarrassing, but … I had a real conversation with Jesus yesterday. He reminded me that I didn't need to lose heart. He's overcome the world, and he'll never leave us or forsake us." He squeezed her. "Simple stuff. Love, I want to ask your forgiveness for falling into discouragement. I know it's been hard for you."

Annie felt herself beginning to cry. She had been working hard to trust God with Lloyd, but it was like finding water in the desert to see him turn this direction. *Lord, let this trust sustain him through the hard days ahead.*

"What's for breakfast?"

Or at least through this meal.

"Not much, I'm afraid. A bit of toast with currant jam, but no butter. I'm saving almost everything for Christmas Eve and Christmas Day."

Lloyd didn't seem to mind. "Well, then, let's eat. I've got some ideas for tomorrow's message."

As she put the toast in front of him, she said, "What's your text?"

"It's just Matthew 1, the Joseph parts. I was thinking about the name. He's called Jesus because he will save his people from their sins. I seem to hear him asking us, 'Have you forgotten that I came to save you from your sins?'"

"Asking all of us, or asking you?" Annie said softly.

"Probably me," he said with a quick glance at the ceiling that told her it was a prayer. She hadn't seen that glance much recently either. "But I suspect there are others as well."

She took him by the hand. "Thank you, Jesus, that you've touched my Lloyd this way. Please strengthen him for the days ahead."

Arthur checked the lines that held *Guinevere* to the wharf. He hated to let her out of his sight, loaded as she was. One carelessly thrown cigarette butt and she would become a bomb, destroying the lock, the weir, or both. He hoped this cargo could be delivered soon.

There was no rain now, but it was cloudy and even colder, and the stiff wind had not abated. He stopped at the column and quickly slid out the brick. There was no note, which meant no delivery tonight.

Have to tell Rosie. He went to the house before returning to the gate. "Hello, Rosie girl," he said on the way in.

She was sitting in her chair, listening to the radio. "Hush you, old man. I'm trying to figure out what that Hitler is doing next."

"Bombing Manchester?" This was the latest "town in the north" to be devastated.

He waited until the morning news ended. Nothing much there. Mostly heartwarming stories of Christmas under fire.

"So, my love, it looks like I'll be spending another night on the *Guinevere*."

"Arthur Cripps! You'll be the death of me yet! It's not safe!"

"Safer than leaving her unmanned."

"Couldn't you get Stanley to do it tonight?"

Arthur thought about it. "I'd rather not."

"Too dangerous?"

"I didn't say that."

"We've been married twenty years, love," Rosie said. "I can read your mind."

Arthur sighed and smiled. "Of course you can. I don't want to put the young man at risk any more often than I have to. It'll just be one or two more nights, then this job will be over."

"So you'll miss the Christmas Eve service?"

"If we have one at all. If there's an air raid, Lloyd's planning to dismiss us. The building's one thing, but the people, he said, are the real church and he doesn't want us all in jeopardy together."

James and Rachel had had a pleasant dinner with Henry Padbury. He seemed to be doing a lot of entertaining lately. Now they walked back to Rosewood Cottage. The sky was mostly clear, though a bank of clouds to the northwest confirmed that another storm was coming in. They walked close together against the cold wind.

"Looks like we may get our chance, love," Rachel said.

"I hope so." He and Rachel had talked earlier in the week, late into the night. They had decided to make an announcement at the Christmas Eve service.

"Come in for a cup of coffee?".

"We don't have a chaperone anymore," James said.

Rachel met his eye for a moment, then took his hand and dragged him out of the cold. "Age is our chaperone, darling."

He took her in his arms. "What if I'm not feeling my age?" he said.

She kissed him briefly and then laid her head against his chest. "Thank you Jesus, for this undeserved, unexpected gift. Now, let me get us some coffee."

~ † ~

"I'm really sorry about dinner, love," Annie said. "After Norah and I put aside everything we want to keep for Christmas Eve, Christmas breakfast, and Christmas dinner, all we had left was carrots and potatoes."

"So this is?" Lloyd asked.

"Carrot and potato mash."

Lloyd looked at the dish dubiously. He wondered if there was really a need to spoil good potatoes this way. He would be just as happy if the government never mentioned the virtues of carrots again. Except carrot cake. And Annie's carrot jam had turned out pretty well …

After dinner, Lloyd took the children upstairs to get ready for bed. Like everything else, this family time had been rather desultory this autumn, but today Lloyd cherished the moments. Lizzie had grown without him noticing and was, he thought, no longer really a little girl. Georgie was his usual frenetic self, at one point insisting that he could hide inside a drawer, which he did, though he panicked when Lloyd closed it. Maggie had to show her father every toy she owned. But there weren't that many.

Annie joined them after cleaning up a bit in the kitchen, and they gathered for family prayers. Lizzie still prayed for Lily every night, Georgie prayed that Hitler would be destroyed in gruesome ways, and Maggie rehearsed her "bless Mummy, bless Dada, bless my sister and my brudder." Lloyd and Annie prayed for each of the children, for safety, and for God to end this horrible war.

Just as they got the three children settled down, the siren sounded.

"Oh, no." Lloyd listened for the sound of planes, but heard nothing. *Still* … "Lizzie, George, we need to go to the basement." He scooped up Maggie, who wiggled in protest, and carried her downstairs.

Henry heard the alert as he unlocked the door of his house. He looked around quickly to make sure the blackout curtains were drawn, then switched on the electric lamp by his favorite chair. Not for the first time he wished he didn't have to be alone so much. His mother had decorated the house at Christmas for as long as she could, but he didn't have the heart to do his feeble male imitation. However, he did continue the tradition of rereading *A Christmas Carol.* When he began to hear the menacing growl of aircraft in the distance, he said, "There's more of gravy than of grave about you."

He went to the sideboard and poured himself a thin bottom of brandy in a snifter, and spun it in his hands to let it warm. He would miss this house. "I wonder where in the world I'm going," he said. Realistically, somewhere like Blount Manor, working some sort of math tricks for someone like Colonel Blake. Ah well, at least he'd be contributing to the cause.

"I'm afraid, Lord, that it's the discomfort that bothers me." He'd lived in this house all his life. He'd had several opportunities to teach at a more prestigious university than Reading, even Cambridge. But he wanted to be able to care for his parents. It was a comfortable life. He'd invested in the occasional bright mind among the dullards, in caring for Ma and Pa until they died, and in the ministry of the church.

He sat up. "That," he said, "is not one of this house's noises." It was in fact the crump of first one and then the other of Stokely's two anti-aircraft batteries.

Not a drill, I imagine. But also not much of a threat to whatever aircraft, hopefully not ours, has wandered into the vicinity.

~ † ~

Evelyn had got the family to sleep early, but was instantly awake when the siren sounded. "Ernest, Ernest, wake up, we've got to get out to the shelter."

She tried to wake him slowly. These night alerts were hard on him and even harder on his work the next day.

"I'll go and rouse the girls," she said. "Don't you go back to sleep."

She slipped from the bed and drew on the pair of oversized trousers she kept on the chair. She was putting on her coat as she left the room.

"Girls," she called. "We've got to get out to the Anderson." She flipped the light switch by their door, making both girls sit up and blink like owls.

"Oh, Mum, I just want to sleep. I don't care if we get bombed."

"Phyllis, don't start. You have no choice in this. If you were to die …"

"Oh, Mum!" Phyllis lay back down and hid her head in her pillow. Lily was beginning to pull on her shelter clothes. When Evelyn heard the anti-aircraft fire start up, her heart rose further up her throat like the pulse of an incoming tide.

"Phyllis!" Unthinking, panicked, she struck the girl hard between the shoulder blades with palm of her hand, then recoiled from the sting and the scream.

"Mummmmm!" Phyllis rolled on her side, trying to reach her back.

"Get up now." She grabbed Phyllis by her forearm and with manic strength threw her to the floor. The girl began a high-pitched wail.

"You've got to get out," Evelyn said. "Both of you." She turned and found Lily staring in horror, her pale hand cupped over her noiseless scream.

"Go," Evelyn cried. She turned to Lily sharply. "Don't wait."

Ernest appeared at the door. "What's going on?"

"They won't get out," Evelyn cried. "They've got to get out."

He rushed over and scooped up Phyllis from the floor. "Are you all right?"

Evelyn took a deep breath. She had to calm down or it would all come apart and they'd still be here. "Out," she said more quietly.

"Can you walk?" Ernest asked Phyllis.

"Just carry her." Evelyn imagined the shriek of a bomb-whistle, the evil grin of a cold steel casing, the ghost letters "Lily" and "Phyllis" emblazoned on it. She herded Ernest and then Lily out of the room and down the stairs, remembering to flick off the light.

They stepped into the garden. The plane was louder. Evelyn risked a glance up, but did not see the expected silhouette blocking out the night stars. Where was the demon thing?

Ernest put Phyllis down by the shelter, and she crumpled to the ground. It seemed forever before he got the corrugated steel door open. "Oh hurry!" Evelyn cried, the panic taking her again. Phyllis was just starting to rise.

Evelyn's leg seemed to move of its own accord. She caught Phyllis in the rib cage, knocking her into the doorway, and down the steps. She fell to the shelter floor with a splash. The rain had left about three inches of cold water inside.

Evelyn dragged Lily over Phyllis' scrambling form and pushed her onto the bed. She turned to see Ernest lifting the older girl. He began to comfort her. Evelyn grabbed the soaking child and hissed at Ernest. "The door, you fool."

He lifted a hand toward her, then froze, his stiff self-control silhouetted against the night. He turned to the door. Once it was shut, he grabbed the torch off the higher bunk and shone it at her. "All right, that's it," he said.

She covered her face with her hands. "Don't be mad at me … I just want my girls safe." He was about to respond when the sound of the aircraft swelled out of the night. It seemed right overhead.

The bomb scream came, the one she'd feared. It seemed to go on forever. She found she was screaming with it. Then the world was concussed by a sound that, in her last moment of consciousness, she realized was the loudest thing she'd ever heard.

~ † ~

Violet had begun to cope better with the frequent alerts since her return to Stokely. Part of that, she thought, was because nothing ever came of them. The man who wound the siren must be something of a nervous Nellie. She laughed at herself. *Pot calling the kettle black.* But since that morning on Stokely Chase, she had found a good deal of peace. Not perfect, but better. "Thank you, Jesus," she whispered.

"What did you say?" Mum asked.

"Nothing." They were seated side by side in what passed for the town's bomb shelter; the basement of the primary school, which had been reinforced with brick, concrete and steel. Only a fraction of the town could use it, but it was so close to the Clarke's house that they usually got the same spot.

"Close that door," someone yelled. It was usually kept open because of the lack of air.

"Bomber! Heinkel!" someone else shouted.

A man forced his way in through the closing door. "More than one," he said.

Faintly, through the layers of steel and concrete, a familiar whistle started.

"No!" Violet said. The sound resonated inside her head, shaking loose memories and images she had beaten down. The blackened cathedral, rising above the firestorm. Running with Rosie in her arms, pursued by flames. The school, Bablake, across its wide fields. The man running toward them. The flash …

With the memories came the voices. "You know you want this. You can't escape. Where is His help now?"

One bomb screamed louder and closer … there. Violet was too experienced not to know a miss. A huge blast shook its muted way through the shelter.

Mum was crying. Violet put her arms around her. "It was a miss, Mum."

"But who did it hit?"

"We'll have to wait and see." She realized she sounded jaded. It was just one bomb, after the hell of Coventry …

But then it wasn't just one bomb. A dozen screams started up in swift sequence. Must be a second plane with a full load. Each scream awakened the voices in her head, overlapping, urging, tempting her to despair. "You can't escape. Nowhere is safe. Death is the only answer." She unwrapped her arms from Mum and put her hands over her ears, knowing the futility of the gesture, unable to help herself.

No! To seek death, no matter how much she wanted it, was to flee the light. "Jesus," she cried aloud, "send out thy light and thy truth!"

Explosions roared around and rocked the shelter. The floor seemed to heave. Violet felt her insides come loose. Something nearby made a huge cracking sound. Suddenly a torch flared further down the wall. The light swept over the ceiling of the shelter, which seemed to be intact. Concrete dust hung in the air under one seam, showing the torchlight as a beam.

Violet laughed, a little hysterically. "Thank you for the light."

~ † ~

Lloyd wished they had something better than the shelter under the basement stairs. It was the strongest point in the house, but many Londoners had died in such a spot. *Lord Jesus please keep my wife and children safe. And others as well.*

"Do you think this is for real?" Annie whispered.

"I don't know," Lloyd responded. He couldn't help thinking of the last part of his conversation with Jesus on the bridge. Something about fire from heaven.

The children had settled down to sleep, despite the cramped space and noise of the alert. "Want to pray?" he said.

"Sure." They asked Jesus to help with all the needs and hurts of the congregation, and to keep people safe in Stokely that night.

As they finished, they heard the drone of a single plane. Faintly they heard the famous bomb-whistle. A loud explosion shook the ground. Lloyd felt an unexpected astonishment. The war, the war in Europe and at Dunkirk and in London and in Coventry, had come all the way here, all the way to Stokely. The cacophony in his left ear continued after the bomb blast faded.

"Where do you think that was?" Annie asked.

"No way of knowing," Lloyd answered. "North?"

Immediately a second plane approached. A dozen or more whistles filled the air. Seconds later a series of explosions began, growing closer. The children clung to their parents. Maggie screamed. "Mummy what is it?"

"It's nothing, dear." Annie said. "Here, bury your ears against me. That will make it quieter."

His wife stared at him with eyes wide in the torch light. He realized she'd never been through anything like this. *Damn it all, wars were supposed to be fought out there somewhere, away from the women and children.*

The building shook with the overlapping explosions. Then came a massive blast, like the huge 210s of the last war. Everything around them seemed to shift. Glass crashed. The children screamed. Plaster and dust fell.

A short while later a third plane passed overhead. It sounded lower than the first two. They heard a ripping noise, like fifty distant thunderclaps.

The all-clear never came.

Hours later Lloyd carefully slipped from the tangle of his family's limbs and crept up the stairs. Through the front windows, the last dark of night poured in. It was cold. *I pray that last night didn't make many people homeless. Or worse.*

He wrapped his coat tighter and stepped out. There was smoke to the east, and more to the north, dimly lit by flames. Closer at hand there was a huge bomb crater near the cemetery entrance. That one must have taken out the windows. It was already roped off, with an air raid warden patrolling.

"Good morning, Frank," Lloyd said. "Much damage? Casualties?"

"Haven't heard, Reverend Robins. Seems like there might have been a dozen bombs. A fireman came by and said it's mostly under control."

"Well, praise God for that."

"Yes sir," said the warden. "But have you been round to Spey Road"

"No." Lloyd felt his heart skip at the warning in the man's voice.

"Bomb in the street, like this one, but it brought down the front of a building. We think there are families trapped in there."

Lloyd rushed that way, trying to think of the names of the families who lived in the houses behind the church. *The Jewells … they have two boys … and the Mitchums.* Lloyd couldn't remember how many children. Annie would.

Four or five ARP wardens were digging into a pile of debris that had been the front of the two houses. The backs of the houses still stood, only five feet behind the church. Tom Jewell was with them.

"Tom, thank God you're all right. Your family?'

"Yes, all safe, Reverend. We were able to get out the back. But we think Roy and Ella Mitchum and their girl are still inside. They shelter in the kitchen, under a great strong table, but the walls and ceiling have come down.

"Anything I can do to help?"

Tom looked around. "We're okay here, Reverend. Check on the others."

Lloyd wondered what others there were. *I'd better look further.* As he went past the church, Lloyd saw the glint of broken glass and looked inside. At first the sanctuary looked intact, but he could feel air moving. Then he realized he could see the slowly lightening sky. There was a large hole in the ceiling, maybe five feet by ten feet. The roof tiles were scattered, but the beams seemed intact.

Slowly Lloyd's eyes picked out the details before him. Two pews had been displaced, the ones between them destroyed. What? … a darker shape, metal.

There in the middle of Stokely Free Church, half buried, almost horizontal, lay an unexploded bomb.

Annie and the kids were huddled against the cold in the doorway of a building far up High Street. The ARP warden was helping Lloyd evacuate the other houses near the church. A few families had gone past with suitcases and bundles. Lloyd had made Annie and the children leave with nothing but the clothes on their backs. Under the circumstances, she couldn't blame him.

Here he came, with the ARP warden and … Welly Ward, who carried a large military rucksack. "No sir," the warden was saying, "we don't have a bomb disposal squad here. Maybe in Reading."

"But it could be a time delay fuse," Welly said.

Lloyd spoke up "What would happen if it exploded?"

Welly's shoulders sagged. "If it's as big as you described, then it's a 250. It'll take out the church, the manse … and that building where the family is trapped."

Annie was exhausted beyond emotion, but the thought of the Mitchums, waiting for rescue, then blown sky high brought a stifled scream. "Isn't there something we can do?" she finally said.

Welly looked at his feet. "No … Well, I suppose I could go in and see if it's got a time delay."

"You can tell?" Lloyd asked.

"If I can see. The Germans politely mark the type on the top of the fuses."

"Good Lord! German efficiency,' Annie said.

"Also, if it's a time delay I could probably hear the mechanism."

"Ticking?"

"Yes. More of a tick-click tick-click." Welly spoke so softly Annie could barely hear him.

"But couldn't it …"

"Blow?"

She nodded.

"That's why they sent me home. I've lost my nerve. I don't want to go anywhere near the bloody things."

Annie could feel the desperate emotion, though he didn't raise his eyes.

"I understand," she said. She laid a hand on his arm.

He shook her off. "All right, I'll do it."

"I wasn't …"

"I know you weren't, Mrs. Robins. But there's only so much shame a man can bear."

Lloyd nodded. Apparently he understood this. "Is there anything you need? Tools? Help?"

Welly shook his head. "Prayer."

Welly took a deep breath and entered the church. He'd been here a thousand times as a child. Now it was all different. The feeble light made the dust floating in the air look almost holy.

There was the bomb, just as Reverend Robins had described it.

Welly looked it over from the edge of the room. Not that that would make any difference if it blew. He knew BDU men who did all their work straddling the bomb like a horse, betting on the quickest possible exit. He couldn't immediately see the fuses, though the crater was not deep and the bomb almost horizontal. He circled the room, ashamed to note that his legs were shaky.

There it was. The rear fuse cylinder. The front one would be under the bomb. Cautiously he approached. With his gloved hand, he wiped dust and dirt off the fuse cap and peered at it. Nothing. He wiped again and looked closer. This fuse was a blank, a dummy. *Oh no.*

He crouched by the hole. The bomb had made an open crater around itself, and fallen back. The front straddled a few inches of empty space. If he reached down, he could … no … yes … He could feel the front fuse cylinder.

He cleared a space on the floor, and lay prone by the hole. He stuck his torch under the bomb and twisted his head to see. Couldn't. Tried another angle. His ear touched the cold metal.

Tick-click … tick-click … tick-click.

Welly stood with Reverend Robins and the ARP warden. His father and Nelson completed the little circle. "I'll have to disarm it. Otherwise it'll go off and kill the Mitchums and the rescuers." He gestured toward the buildings behind. "Fortunately I've got my kit with me." For whatever reason, the bomb disposal kit, including the goo for this technique, was assigned as personal equipment of the officer. He'd carried it all the way home on the train. "The bad news is that I'll need some help. I can't build a dam for the glue until I roll the bomb."

"Won't that set it off?" his father asked.

"Shouldn't. It's probably a pure time delay. That's why the second fuse was a dummy. But the Jerries are nothing if not devious. It's not a sure thing."

Nelson interrupted. "I'll help."

"No." Welly said. "Sorry, Nelson, but it'll take four men with two arms each to do what I need." He looked his brother straight in the eye. "And it might be good if Mum didn't lose both of us."

His brother's eyes fell. "Right."

"I'll do it." The warden spoke up. "I'll go get two of my men to help."

Reverend Lloyd spoke. "That will take too long. I'll help."

"But you've got small children, Reverend."

"So do they, probably."

"All right. I'll just get one, and make the others back off for the time being."

"No," His dad looked around the group like a trapped animal. "That'll take more time. I'll do it."

Welly looked at his dad. Was he trying to prove his own courage? "Right. The sooner we get in there, the less chance time will run out."

Welly re-entered the building with the men behind him. This time the bomb looked like a huge blasphemy, marring the place where God met with his people. *The abomination that causes desolation.* Welly grinned grimly. It was one of Rosie Cripps' favorite phrases.

He pointed out what they needed to do. "The fuse is pointed almost straight down. We roll it 180 degrees, so it points straight up."

Sweat and fear beaded the faces of the men, but Lloyd and the warden advanced immediately to help. Welly watched his father. He tried to step forward, then turned away for a moment. Welly knew he was struggling with fear, and felt a wave of compassion. *Lord, I've been there. I know what it is to turn away. Strengthen him.*

His father looked up, shame and panic on his face. He made eye contact, broke it, made it again. Welly nodded. Dad tried to smile. He stepped forward.

"All right. You three on this side, I'll pull from here and act as brake.

"Nice and smooth now. Roll. Roll. Ugh." The bomb was stuck on an edge of the flooring.

"Let me come to that side. Warden, if you can step down into the hole. We need to lift it just a little bit.

"One, two, three … heave."

The bomb lifted a fraction of an inch on the edge, and rolled forward with a sickening clang. All four men froze.

"All right, then. Back off to a very safe distance and let me do my job."

Courage is doing the right thing at the right time for the greatest good, even while terrified, Welly told himself.

At the bomb, he listened again. Tick-click, tick-click. He attached the Crabtree to the fuse head, and then got the hand drill from his kit. He rehearsed the procedure in his mind. Drill. Dam. Pour. Wait. He'd never done this before, and, as always, he had to get it right the first time.

The hard part, he'd heard, was getting the hole in just the right place. He picked his spot carefully and tried hard to keep the bit from slipping. Not too successfully.

Finally the hole started. The bit was sharp, but there was still a good deal of sticking and jumping as he drilled. It took a lot of pressure to make progress, and his hands started to tremble. This was what he had feared, what had forced him to accept this leave. BDU officers all believed a bomb could sense a trembling sweaty, slipping hand.

He took the drill, rattling, out of the hole. Maybe halfway there. He set it down as quietly as possible and stepped back, stretched and twisted, cracked his knuckles. Gray morning light filtered into the room. Looking up he saw a few flakes of snow making their way through the ragged hole in the ceiling. Jesus, he prayed, strengthen me for this.

Welly went back to the bomb, took up the drill, and put in a fresh bit. An eternity later, he finally penetrated the thick top of the fuse casing.

Now for it. He took the putty out of his bag and rolled it into a long cylinder, then shaped it around the fuse head, making a little well. He took the jar of thin glue and filled the dam with the liquid. With a dowel, he pushed the glue over and over into the mechanism, never pushing too far for fear of touching a working part. In his mind's eye he saw the thin stream of glue coating the mechanism, and eventually, as he filled and refilled his little dam, clogging the cavity below.

Oh Lord, let this work.

Welly was straddling the bomb now, his legs and back too weak to allow him to crouch by it. He lay his head on the side of the bomb. Tick-click, tick-click.

Snowflakes landed on his neck and refused to melt. He was trembling continuously. He ignored it, prayed and worked, pushed and pushed the little dowel into the hole. Tick-click, tick-click.

The bottle of glue was more than half-empty. How much could this cavity hold? Was he futilely trying to fill the whole bomb with glue?

Click … click … click. Too weary to go on, he lay his ear on the bomb as if it were the cold bosom of a dead love. Click … click … cli …

Welly shook his head, laid his ear on the bomb again. Nothing. Switched cold ears. Nothing.

Carefully, fearing a fatal mistake at the last moment, he got off the bomb. Stiff, hobbling, he went to the door. There in the distance stood the crowd. He motioned to them and held up one finger. "I need one person to come and check this," he yelled, his voice stiff with disuse, his lips with cold.

Through his painfully weeping eyes, he saw his father and Reverend Robins debate. Finally his father came.

"Hey, Dad," he gasped. "I think I've got it. You've got to lay your ear on the bomb, near the fuse, and see if you hear anything."

His father approached the bomb as if it were a jungle cat about to leap. Hesitantly he put out one gloved hand to touch it. He took off his hat and crouched, laid his ear gingerly against the metal.

"I don't hear a thing."

He turned his head and tried his other ear.

"Nothing."

"Praise God," Welly said.

"What do we do now?"

"Nothing for the moment. Rescue the family. Then I'll pull the fuse." Welly shuddered, more than cold rattling his core.

His dad looked at him with wide, admiring eyes. "Unbelievable."

Welly stood in his mother's kitchen, a few hundred yards from the church, sipping warm tea and chafing his hands and feet.

"Thanks, Mum." She looked at him with the same look his father had given him. Welly turned away. He knew it wasn't over yet.

Outside, carried on the wind, he heard a rough cry of victory.

"That's probably my curtain call, Mum." He set the tea cup carefully in the sink, and gave his mum a hug.

"You be careful," she said.

Welly walked back and was rewarded with the sight of the missing family, surrounded by a crowd. Roy Mitchum had one arm bound against his chest. The ARP warden pointed at Welly, and Mitchum came over. His right arm was bleeding through a bandage, awkwardly set with a couple of chair-back spindles.

"I understand I've got you to thank for my family's lives."

"Not me. It was the grace of God."

"That's as may be. Thank you." He reached out awkwardly with his left hand and grasped Welly's.

It's not over yet, Welly thought. But at least I'm not so cold.

Reverend Lloyd, his dad, and a few others were standing near the church.

"We've made a barricade over there," his father said. In the street, a semi-circle of stones and heavy debris rimmed the edge of the crater left by the bomb that had fallen in the street.

"I hope my string's long enough."

The bomb was covered in a light dusting of snow. The mechanism was stone silent. He carefully coiled a good length of light line and stepped beneath the hole in the ceiling. "Ready?" he called.

"Ready" came his father's voice, sounding loud and close.

"Here it comes." He hurled the line up through the hole, taking an angle toward the barricade, and hoping it wouldn't catch on anything sharp.

"Nope … nope. Wait, got it." He heard a gentle scraping on the edge of the roof. "Got it. Hold your end, Welly."

The line tightened slightly as his dad unspooled. "Right," he called, his voice further away. "I'm behind the barricade."

"Any extra length?"

"Ten feet."

"Good. I'm going to loosen the fuse ring."

He counted seven turns, the number of threads on a type 17, and threw in an extra half turn for good measure. The fuse was vertical, so it really didn't matter.

He used both trembling hands to lift the retaining ring from the bomb. Despite the cold, he felt a familiar trickle of sweat down his skin.

He gently looped the string through the eye of the Crabtree and tied a bowline. *Thank you, Captain Cripps.*

"Dad, can you slowly take up a little slack?" The string crawled out through the roof. It was snowing harder now. "Stop. Don't move. I'm on my way."

Welly left the church and walked around to the barricade.

"All right. Everyone get back. I'm going to make this taut and then pull up the fuse. If it's booby trapped the bomb blows." His father blanched.

"Are we sure everyone is clear?" Welly yelled.

"All clear," Lloyd responded.

"Right. Now, Dad you go join them."

"No."

"If it blows, we won't really be safe here. Go back to Mum and Nelson."

"No son. I'm trying to be brave too."

"You already have been, Dad. Courage is acting at the right time for the right reason. There's no need for two of us to be in jeopardy."

His father met his eye. "You're a hero, son."

"Not really. But thanks. I love you."

His father hesitated over the unfamiliar words. "I love you, too."

When his father reached the others, far up High Street, Welly reached a yard up the line, wrapped it around his hand, took hold with the other. *Lord, let this work.* He pulled smoothly and sharply.

The snow kept falling into the breathless silence.

CHAPTER 15

24 December 1940

Lord Jesus. Please keep Welly safe. Lloyd watched the young man gingerly carrying the … what had he called it? … gaine down to the river. He'd said it was like the match that lit the fuse, still very dangerous. As soon as he was clear, an Army lorry backed up to the main doors of the church and a dozen uniformed men went inside. They had arrived just moments before.

Ned came up. "Been thinking about what's next, Lloyd."

"Thank you."

"I think highest priority is to check around, make sure no one else in the church is damaged."

"Good point, sergeant … How would you do it?"

"I think two groups would be enough. One for those that live near here, like the Coopers and the Clarkes, one to check on the other side of the river, Bert and Meg, Arthur and Rosie. We can bring anyone back who wants to help here."

"I wanted to check on my aunt and uncle earlier," Stanley said, "but Mr. Powell wanted to find where the smoke was coming from first."

Ned gestured, "That one over there is a house fire. Bomb in the street like this one. Still don't know what the one to the north is."

"All right. Organize that. I can go with one group, you with the other." Lloyd looked around. "A few folk can stay here and start cleaning up—"

"They're coming out," someone said.

Lloyd turned to see a group of soldiers slowly bring the bomb through the door of the church. It was cradled in some sort of sling, making the dozen men look a bit like pallbearers. Fortunately, the distance was short. At the truck, they attached the sling to a small crane, which lifted the bomb aboard.

"Where will they take it?"

"They're from the camp beyond the Chiltern estate," James replied. "Probably take it to an open spot out there and wait for a BDU to come and detonate it."

At that moment Alan and Welly came up.

"Reverend Lloyd," Welly said. "The *Guinevere*'s gone."

It took Lloyd a moment to process this.

"She was tied up at the jetty last night," Welly said. "But she's not there now. No sign."

"Right." Lloyd looked around, assessing who was there, and raised his voice. "Henry, you and I will start at the Cripps'. Stanley can come with us."

"I'll come too," Welly said.

"Are you up to that?"

"I'm fine."

"Right. Ned, James, check the families on this side of the river. Henry, did you see any damage at the Clarkes?"

"No," Henry responded. "But it was dark. I didn't want to disturb them."

"Well, Ned, you'd better check the Coopers first, then the Clarkes, the Waters, and the others."

"Let's go … no wait … I'm forgetting something." Lloyd was suddenly made aware that he was thinking like a lieutenant, not a believer. "We need to pray. Let's make a circle."

They gave thanks for the disarming of the bomb, for the rescue of the Mitchums. They prayed for the rest of the people of the church and town, that the Lord would preserve them and keep them safe. Finally, Henry prayed, "Lord Jesus, help us to remember your Incarnation. No matter how difficult our circumstances, we know you have already rescued us and made us part of your kingdom."

After the "amen," Stanley asked, "Rev'rend, will there be a Christmas Eve service?"

"Not tonight," Lloyd answered immediately. He paused, feeling unspoken words. "But if we can get the building cleaned up enough, we could have one around four this afternoon."

Several people nodded.

"Spread the word."

~ † ~

Ned and James headed toward the Coopers'. Ned recognized that Lloyd had put him together with James so he wouldn't exert himself, but the older man's limping steps were painfully slow.

"Sorry about the pace, Ned," James said. "The cold makes my leg stiff."

The snow had tapered off. Only an inch or so had fallen, but it made the town look whitewashed, all its stains momentarily erased.

They drew closer to the source of the smoke. Ned counted as they turned onto the Coopers' street. "It's theirs," he said. A small crowd was cordoned off from the remnants of the house, which was bombed and burnt, flames still flickering in the wreckage. They scanned the crowd for a sign of the family, but didn't see them.

Ned approached the constable. "Hello, Jack. What do you know?"

"Bomb hit the house. Back wall fell over their Anderson. Family's trapped, but we can hear noises from the shelter. Digging them out now." He gestured to a group of men at the back of the garden..

Ned flushed with relief "Can we go and help?"

"I don't know how much help they need but, as you know the family . . ."

"Thanks."

They picked their way through the wreckage of the Coopers' home. Not much seemed to have survived the bomb. At one point James stooped to pick up a little stuffed bear, like Winnie-the-Pooh.

"Lily's?" he asked Ned. Ned shrugged.

The men were systematically removing the rubble of the back wall. The only tools in use were hands, a crowbar, and a small sledgehammer. The mortar was powdery and a few strikes would reduce most pieces to hand size.

"Must be cold as ice in there," he said to James as he passed him with an armful of bricks. The wind was bitter.

"Still below freezing, I'd say." James looked at him. "Are you all right?"

"No problems." Ned said. This was not a time to worry about doctor's orders.

The rescuers had unearthed the central panel at the front of the Anderson. As Ned and James watched, they pried it loose. Moments later the family began to come out. First Ernest, then Phyllis, Lily, and, last, Evelyn. Ernest had a cloth wrapped around his hand and a cut on his forehead. The others appeared unhurt. Thank you, Lord, Ned prayed through his labored breathing.

"Ned! James!" Evelyn cried. "Thank you! We didn't know how long we'd have to stay in there."

"Don't thank us, Evelyn," Ned replied. "Your neighbors rescued you."

The family was wet and shivering. Ned took off his coat and gave it to Evelyn. Another man did the same for Phyllis. James wrapped his huge coat around little Lily. He knelt stiffly. "I found this. Is it yours?"

"Boo!" She hugged the bear. Her stiff self-control dissolved to tears, and James awkwardly hugged her.

Ned spoke to Ernest and Evelyn. "There's really nothing more to be done here. We need to get you somewhere warm and dry you off."

The neighbor who had given Phyllis his coat said, "You can come into my place, Ernest. Sit by the fire and have a nice hot cup of tea."

He led them to a tiny flat, where his white-haired wife greeted them joyously. "I've been that worried about you."

Evelyn spoke up, and her voice sounded strong. "It's a blow, to be sure. We've lost everything … but nothing important." She took Ernest's hand and looked at the girls with obvious joy.

When Ned saw how tiny the flat was, he declined the invitation to join them. "Ernest, Evelyn, once you get warmed up, I think you should come out to the farm for a few nights. We've plenty of room at the moment. Alice would love to have guests for Christmas."

"We'd hate to impose on you, Ned," Evelyn said, "But I suspect it's going to get cold again tonight. And I don't think Lily and Phyllis appreciated the accommodation in the Anderson."

Phyllis forced a laugh. "It was certainly better than the alternative."

"Right. Come up to our place and stay as long as you need." He thought for a minute. "Well, at least for the next couple of weeks. There's an outside chance I'll be getting some Land Girls. That would make it kind of tight."

"Even if we can only stay for a few nights, that'd be wonderful," Evelyn said. "As for everything else, I'm sure God will provide."

James spoke up, "I can go and get the car from the manor to take you out there."

"Great. I'll wander a little more and check on the Clarkes' and the others," Ned said. "If everything else is all right, I'll meet you back here."

~ † ~

Lloyd stopped on the bridge. Despite the grim circumstances, he had to celebrate the beauty of the lightly falling snow on the river and its banks.

"I don't see her upstream or down." Stanley was dancing behind him.

"Right," Lloyd said. "Let's go to the house."

Stanley ran off the bridge and turned up the riverbank. Welly followed, but Lloyd and Henry came behind more slowly. They were nearing the house when Stanley came jogging back. "He's not there. He was on the *Guinevere*. Aunt Rosie thinks he must be on the river.

As they neared the house, Henry stopped Lloyd by the elbow. "Did you know that Arthur's involved in some kind of shady dealings?"

Lloyd was skeptical. "What? I can't imagine Arthur doing anything shady."

"Well, maybe not shady exactly, but … underground. Some kind of preparation for an invasion."

"How do you know?"

"Ned tells me he's taken Stanley out with him on the *Guinevere* several times and they've been away all night. One of those was the night Stanley trusted Christ. I got a lot of hints at that point that they were doing something hush-hush for the government."

As they turned up the short path, they noticed Rosie looking out the front window at the lock. When they went in, they found Stanley questioning her. "Why did he spend the night on the *Guinevere*?" he was asking.

"I've told you, I can't say. Mum's the word. Loose lips."

"Aunt Rosie, I know what we've been doing. Were there explosives?"

"Explosives?" Lloyd, Henry and Welly all spoke at once.

Stanley turned. "We've been transporting weapons for the resistance."

"What resistance?"

"The British— Oh! I can't say anything."

Rosie broke in "He said that a fool with a cigarette butt could mean ruin. Destroy the lock. Flood downstream. And I did hear bombs last night, but none of them seemed to be particularly close."

"Anything else? Did you hear Arthur start the engine?"

"No …" said Rosie. "I heard a low flying plane … and sort of a long muffled explosion."

Welly and Stanley looked at each other. It took Lloyd a moment to catch up with their thinking.

"We need to go and look around," Welly said.

Lloyd stayed behind for a moment. "Will you be all right, Rosie?"

"I don't have a good feeling about this, Reverend. But I'll trust God."

The other three were standing where the *Guinevere* usually tied up, on the downstream side of the lock. "No sign of her," Welly said. "But we found this." It was a fuel can, which sloshed when Welly shook it.

"Uncle Arthur would never leave fuel on the dock." Stanley said.

"Unless he were in a huge hurry," Lloyd said.

"He might have heard the first bombs and hurried to get *Guinevere* away from the lock." Welly said.

"Mr. McDonald has a motor skiff," said Stanley, walking past the upstream gate. "We can use that to look on the river." But there was no answer to his knock at the McDonalds' a few houses up. "There's the skiff." Stanley pointed toward the front of a little boathouse. "I'm sure he wouldn't mind if we borrowed it."

"Whoa, whoa! We can't just take someone's boat."

"Mr. MacDonald thinks the world of Uncle Arthur. He'd want us to."

"Well … all right," Lloyd said, "but it doesn't need all of us. Henry, why don't you go and tell Rosie what we're doing and then go and help Rachel and the others?"

Henry looked a bit crestfallen. "Right. I'll check on Meg and Bert first."

"Good. Thanks."

Stanley was already down at the skiff, checking the engine. "Needs petrol."

Welly filled the fuel tank, then cranked the hand starter. The engine roared. Lloyd and Welly got in. Stanley pushed off and sat by the tiller.

"Welly," Stanley said, "we'll start in the middle of the current. Rev'rend Robins, keep a sharp eye to starboard – that's the right side. Welly to port." Lloyd marveled at how the young man had taken charge.

After a few fruitless minutes, Welly said, "We're out of sight of the bridge now. Look sharp."

A few minutes later the Thames swept to the right. "Keep an eye out for anything on the bank."

"There?" Lloyd pointed.

Stanley immediately throttled back the engine. Welly craned over Lloyd's shoulder. "Yes. Something's there."

The current eased as they turned into the slack water. Lloyd stared ahead, afraid and certain of what he would see. There it was. The rear end of the boat was caught by some tree limbs that grew out over the water.

They eased in slowly. Now it came to it, Stanley seemed reluctant to know the truth. This piece of wreckage seemed to be the deck and stern railing. Crumpled against it, in a contortion too unnatural for life, was the body of Arthur Cripps.

~ † ~

Annie and Rachel herded the children home. Georgie seemed to think it was the best day ever. "Did you see that bomb?" he asked Lizzie. "It was huge."

"It was scary, Georgie. I don't want to talk about it," she said in her best I'm-so-much-more-grown-up-than-you-are voice.

"All right. You lot will have to sit at the kitchen table while Aunt Rachel and I clean up. You can have some bread and jam."

"What about the pudding you made?" Lizzie asked.

"That's for tomorrow."

When Annie brought them the bread, she noticed that Maggie was staring blankly at the table. "Are you okay, little one?"

"I don't feel good, Mummy." She retched and brought up bile onto the table in front of her.

"Oh, poor baby!" Annie said. Then, to Rachel, "It must be the stress."

After they had cleaned the little girl up, they settled her in the sitting room, and began to sweep up the glass around her. The tape on the windows had not helped at all.

"Where else?" Rachel asked.

"Dining room and the two front rooms upstairs."

"What will you put up?"

"I've been saving cardboard, just in case," Annie said. "Blackout curtains will keep most of the cold out." She saw a thin trickle of blood on Rachel's hand. "Be careful – don't cut yourself."

Rachel pulled out her handkerchief and pressed it against the ball of her thumb. "Maybe I can get James to kiss it better."

"Now, what's that supposed to mean, Rachel Busby?" Annie said.

"If we have a Christmas Eve service today," Rachel said. "James and I are going to make an announcement."

"Oh, Rachel! Congratulations!"

"What? You don't even know what it is. Maybe we're going to announce a fund for needy families in the church."

"You're not! You're engaged!"

"Well," Rachel said, drawing out the word, "maybe you're right."

"Of course I am! I'm so happy for you."

The work went quickly as they talked about Rachel's plans. "It'll be a simple ceremony, of course. We're two old people who've met just in time, by God's grace. And I've been married before."

"James hasn't?"

"No. Didn't you know?"

"I've never asked. I thought he might be a widower."

Rachel dumped a tinkling load of glass into the dustbin. "Nope. The only thing he ever loved before me was sleeping horses – not much of a compliment."

"And the two of you will still come here for Christmas dinner?"

"Oh, we couldn't impose on you after all this …" Rachel gestured around.

"There was no damage to the kitchen. Or the dining room for that matter. Anyway, we'll have a wedding to talk about, won't we?"

"All right, then. We were so looking forward to it," Rachel said. She studied the floor of the girls' bedroom. "I don't see anything else here. I think we're done. I'll go and help at the church."

"Let me know if Lloyd gets back with any news," Annie said.

"There's not a mark on him," Lloyd said. They had laid Arthur as respectfully as possible on the deck of the little skiff before they motored upstream. Stanley sat weeping next to him, making sure the body didn't shift.

"It often happens that way," said Welly. "The blast wave from the explosion is enough."

Lloyd said. "If it had been by the lock it would have blown it open."

"But did you see the holes in the deck? I don't think it was a bomb. I think the *Guinevere* was strafed by a fighter, and it set off the explosives she was carrying."

Together they tied up the little boat. "Welly, I think you need to go and get the ambulance. Stanley and I will go and break the news to Rosie."

They knocked gently on the door of the tiny house. Rosie answered immediately and studied their silence for only a moment. "He's dead, isn't he?"

Tears ran down her red cheeks, but her face was not anguished.

Lloyd had held back his own tears until now. "Yes, Rosie. I'm so sorry."

"It's all right, Rev'rend. He died doing his duty, which was always his way. The Lord's prepared me for this. I hope."

Stanley came up behind Lloyd. He was crying profusely now, sobs shaking his body. "I'll take care of you, Aunt Rosie. It's what he wanted."

"And I'll take care of you," she said, wrapping her short arms tightly around his waist.

~ † ~

Henry stepped into the church to find the Wards, the Clarkes, and Rachel working on the mess.

"Is Lloyd with you?" Rachel said. "Annie's anxious about him."

Henry explained what they had found at the river and how Lloyd had gone with the others to look for Arthur and the *Guinevere*. "I went on to the Butlers' and found Bert and Meg. They're all right. I told them we might be having a Christmas Eve service at four."

Alan called from the sanctuary. "If one of you can give me a hand, I'll get this pew set now."

"Right," Philip called. And then to Henry, "We're going to be able to reset two of the pews. The others are more or less matchwood."

Henry had not seen the inside of the church. Someone must have gone up and covered the hole with a tarpaulin, probably knocking off any loose pieces in the process. The debris on the floor had been swept into the shallow bomb crater.

"We still need to rope off the hole," Alan said, "and clean up the glass behind the pulpit."

"How will we cover the windows?" Henry said. "It's going to be cold."

"I have some boards," Alan said. "I'll get them while you pull out the pieces and sweep. Here, Henry, take my gloves."

A while later Lloyd walked in with Welly. "This looks good. Thanks," he said, but he didn't look around. "We need to let you know what happened to Arthur."

Henry's heart sank as he heard the story. It was what he had feared. *Lord Jesus, why would you take this man?* "He was a good friend," Henry said finally, controlling a voice that threatened to break. "We'll miss him."

"Miss him?" Rachel said, "Oh you heartless soul. How can men talk about these things so coldly! Arthur was one of the sweetest men this town has ever known. What's going to happen to poor old Rosie?"

"Rosie and Stanley came back with us. Annie's getting them a bit of breakfast at the manse. If any of you want to sit with them, she'll be happy to give you something."

Rachel took a deep breath. "I'm sorry, Henry, it's just … on top of everything … I'll go and sit with Rosie for a while."

Alan came up and stood next to Welly, who looked like he was going to fall over. "Mum's keeping your breakfast warm over at the house. She's anxious to see you."

"We can take care of the rest later," Lloyd said. "In light of everything that's happened, I guess we shouldn't have a Christmas service this afternoon."

Henry considered that. "I'm not so sure. I think we have a lot to pray about, a lot to mourn, some things to be thankful for … and I don't think we should forget to thank Jesus for coming to this crazy planet, especially under these circumstances."

Out of the corner of his eye, Henry saw James nodding. "You're right Henry," Lloyd said. "We'll meet at four. Spread the word."

Welly could hardly put one foot in front of the other as he walked into the kitchen. "Come in, come in," Mum said. "Breakfast is on the table. You look thin as a rail, Welly. You need to eat and sleep."

"Yes, Mum." He sat at the table, wondering how she had produced so much good food. There were eggs, rashers of bacon, bubble and squeak, fresh toasted bread. Suddenly Welly's fatigue morphed into a ravenous hunger. He tore into the food with enthusiasm. "Was this supposed to be tomorrow's breakfast, Mum?"

"Not entirely. I've saved a little something for Christmas."

His father sat back and looked at Welly. "What you did was wonderful, son."

"Uh … thank you, Dad – and thank you for all that you did."

"I didn't."

"What? You did. Every minute counted. If you hadn't been there, I dread to think of what the delay might have cost us."

"I don't mean I didn't help," Dad said with an unfamiliar grin. "I meant that it wasn't me doing it."

"Excuse me?"

Dad looked down at the table. "Let me start by saying that I've been in turmoil over the two of you since the war started. I wanted both of you to fight, yet I've found myself worried sick that you'd be hurt … or killed." He paused. "I know I've been obsessed wanting you boys to be brave … making you serve, Nelson. Putting awful pressure on you, Welly, when you resisted."

Welly felt his heart in his throat.

"And, when you were brave, I felt guilty for putting you in danger, and terrified that God would hold me responsible for your deaths."

"But Dad," Welly said, "you know God wouldn't do that."

"I kept reading the story of David. He was held responsible for Uriah's death when he sent him into the front of the battle to cover his own sin." He looked down again. "That's what I've been doing. And I have more I need to confess."

The food churned in Welly's stomach.

"All your lives you have heard me say I would have been proud to serve in the Great War, but I wasn't accepted because of my rickets. I do have rickets, but in 1916 the country was desperate, and the standards weren't all that high."

This was not what Welly had expected to hear. He made eye contact with Nelson and could see that he was too was fascinated and confused.

"Your mother knows this, by the way, though I'm not sure she's ever realized how it affects how I've treated you." She too was staring at him, wide-eyed. "Anyway," he continued, "I was accepted by the Army and went off for training. I did reasonably well in drill and coped with the little bit of spit and polish that they were still insisting on by that time. But then we had a live-fire exercise – only one before we were to go off to France. And I bolted and ran."

"No!" Nelson said.

"It's true. I was given a general discharge and sent home. I made up the other story, because I … I'm … I'm a huge coward."

Welly was shocked. Dad's assertion that he had a medical disability had been the preface to so many exhortations and lectures over the years that to find that it didn't exist was as big a shock as finding a bomb in Mum's eggs.

"But Dad, you're not a coward," Nelson said. "You showed that today. You went with Welly and helped to disarm the bomb."

"Welly will tell you how much I hesitated, how I turned away in fear."

"But you turned back, Dad. That's real courage."

"I didn't turn back. I was turned. For once in my life, I gave up on myself, on pleasing God through my own strength, and in that moment, in that cry, desperate to do the right thing, I was turned. God gave me the strength to do what I could never have done myself."

His father lifted his head and met Welly's gaze. Welly could see a sheen of tears over his eyes, a kind of glow on his face. "I could feel his presence. The whole time I was in there, helping, I was confessing my sins. My cowardice, first of all. Being too much of a coward to even own up to it. Trying to make up for it by making you boys do what I'd never been able to. And not trusting God with you when I did.

"All of that exploded from my heart as I waited for that bomb to explode, and God seemed to say he had forgiven it all."

Welly could feel tears of joy and gratitude flow from his eyes.

"Oh, Dad!" he said. "Praise God!"

"Amen," his father said. "I can't guarantee I'll be different. It's hard for a leopard to change his spots. Or a rabbit his fears. But with God's help, I'll try."

Lloyd rejoiced to see that nearly all of the church family had made it to the service. Ernest, Evelyn, and both girls were there. Someone must have brought some clothes for them out to the farm, because all four were warmly dressed. Lloyd didn't trust his fashion sense enough to know if what the girls wore was in style or not.

He cleared his throat and asked everyone to be seated. They were a little crowded because of the missing and roped-off pews. The late light filtering in through the tarp gave the room an unfamiliar glow.

"Happy Christmas." Lloyd said. "Before we start I just want to say a word. For most of us this has been a stressful night and day, and a stressful year, and we don't want to make light of your hurt and need. At the end of the service we're going to have a time for sharing those needs and for prayer. But we've decided that it's better to worship first. We remember that Jesus came to a sinful and war-weary world, to a people oppressed by a dictatorship, to poverty and meekness, so that he could rescue us from the poverty of our sins and give us faith and hope of eternal life."

Lloyd prayed, and then invited Alice and Henry to lead the Christmas carols. *It Came Upon the Midnight Clear* struck him most deeply:

> Yet with the woes of sin and strife the world has suffered long;
> Beneath the angel-strain have rolled two thousand years of wrong;
> And man, at war with man, hears not the love-song which they bring;
> O hush the noise, ye men of strife, And hear the angels sing.
> And ye, beneath life's crushing load, whose forms are bending low,
> Who toil along the climbing way with painful steps and slow,
> Look now! for glad and golden hours come swiftly on the wing.
> O rest beside the weary road, and hear the angels sing!

"This afternoon," Lloyd said as they finished, "we choose to rest beside the weary and mournful road we're on and hear the angels sing the good news of Jesus, the good news of God and sinners reconciled."

They closed with the Christmas Eve carols: *Silent Night*, and *O Little Town of Bethlehem*. Lloyd sensed the congregation was really singing, that God had assuaged their chaos with peace.

~ † ~

Ned sighed as Lloyd opened the meeting for sharing and prayer requests. He agreed with the sequence Lloyd had suggested, but dreaded having the Christmas celebration shattered by the burdens the congregation was carrying. *But better that we carry them together than alone.*

When Lloyd asked who wanted to share first, Stanley lifted his hand, apparently on Rosie's behalf. Lloyd nodded and the young man turned and helped Rosie to her feet in response to a whisper in which Ned distinctly heard the word "bahookie."

"All of you know," she said, "what happened to Arthur last night. I just wanted to say that Arthur died doing what he loved best – doing his duty and driving that old boat." She choked on her words and rubbed both eyes with the backs of her hands. "I'm going to miss him something awful, of course. He was the best man I ever knew or heard about, and he put up with me and took care of me with a love none of you can imagine."

She looked down for a long moment, and Ned wondered if she was going to sit. But she continued. "Now Arthur has gone to be with Jesus, and we have to wait. If Hitler is the antichrist, which I believe, we may not have to wait long.

"Some of you have asked me how we'll get by. I don't know for sure, but I think that Stanley and I can do the lockkeeping between us. Many's the time I've done it when Arthur's been away. And I'll have his little pension as well. So don't worry about us, but …" her voice cracked, "…do pray for us. Pray for Stanley who loved Arthur as if he was his own father." Stanley was sitting with his head bowed on the pew in front of him. "And pray for … pray for me."

She sat down.

"We are praying, Rosie." Lloyd said. He caught Ned's eye. "Ned, will you pray for Rosie and Stanley now?"

I hate it when he does that, Ned thought, then gave the slightest inward chuckle. But he's been doing it for twenty years. I should be used to it.

He tried to order Rosie's situation in his mind. Then he prayed. It was more real than many of his recent prayers, and for that he was grateful.

~ † ~

After a few more people had shared and been prayed for, Henry decided it was a good time for his little announcement and prayer request.

"Right, then. I just wanted to ask for prayer because I will be leaving on National Service shortly." There were several shocked gasps. "No, they're not conscripting fifty-three year olds yet, but I've been invited to work on a special project. I'll be leaving the first of January. I need prayer that I would be able to rely on Jesus alone." Henry felt himself choking up, and pushed past it. "I've told Reverend Lloyd that this church family has been my life, my family, and it's going to be hard to leave, even temporarily. I'll miss all of you."

Henry was grateful when Lloyd asked Philip to pray for him, but found himself thinking of Arthur, and allowed the tears to flow. People would think it was because of leaving town. There was a bit of that in it too, he thought.

After the "amen," Alan Ward stood up. Henry assumed he would be asking prayer for Nelson and Wellington. He was surprised when that wasn't it at all.

"I've asked my boys, and Susan," he said, "and I want to ask all of you, to forgive me for the many ways that I've allowed cowardice to rule my life. It has led me to anger toward them and toward many of you. Worse than that, it made me feel that the only way I might redeem myself in God's eyes was to always do the right thing, and to make others do what I thought was the right thing as well."

Henry was amazed. He'd known Alan for twenty years, and never thought the man would see his own drift towards legalism.

"Today, after the bombing, I finally had to face my fears and my failures. And I discovered that I couldn't face either of them without the strength of Jesus and His grace. I ask you to pray that Jesus will allow me to keep seeking His strength and to become a more grace-receiving and grace-giving man."

When Lloyd looked around for someone to pray for Alan, Henry raised his hand. *Lord, let me pray in words that affirm this wonderful change without cutting down the man Alan has been.*

Annie appreciated Henry's prayer, while at the same time wondering what this change in Alan might mean for the vote on Sunday. She looked up to see Evelyn standing. What kind of prayer request would this be? Certainly thanks for their safety. More fears?

The family had looked surprisingly chipper when they came in. The clothes the Clarkes had given them suited Evelyn and Phyllis. The dress Lizzie had given Lily was one of her favorites.

"I want to thank everybody for praying for us yesterday, and so often in the past. Before I get to our current needs, I want to share a confession."

Confession? Annie thought.

"God has used this bomb to shock me into sanity. He's shown me just how wrong I've been not to trust Him from the time when Lily was ill. I've hurt my family and myself, and many others.

"I've never prayed as hard as I did then. But when God raised her up, all the fear I'd bottled up during her illness overwhelmed me. It seemed that, if only I could try hard enough, nothing bad would ever happen again. Of course, that did lead to us getting the Anderson, so it wasn't all bad. But my attitude was all wrong.

"I've asked Ernest to forgive me because I was so hateful to him. Whenever he wouldn't go along with my compulsive caution, I was horrible. I've apologized to Lily for keeping her captive since last May. She kept telling me she was better, but I wouldn't hear it. I've apologized to Phyllis for doing the same thing to her for no reason at all, and for getting angry when she protested. Mostly I've apologized to God for not trusting Him.

"I want to apologize to all of you, as well." She turned and looked directly at Annie. "And I really need to apologize to you, Annie, my friend, and ask you to forgive me." She turned away before Annie could respond and continued speaking to the congregation. "I don't know if I ever would have come to my senses without the bombing. I was petrified when we were in the Anderson and I heard the roar of the plane and the whistle of the bomb.' But I immediately realized that all my precautions were vain. I could no more prevent the next disaster than I could prevent the sun from setting. I suddenly remembered a verse I seemed to have forgotten: 'apart from me you can do nothing.' Only God can be my trust: I can't depend on my own strength or wisdom."

Annie breathed a prayer of thanksgiving.

"But, friends, I want you to pray, because all this return to sanity feels fragile. I'm afraid the next raid, the next threat of any kind, will push me back into helpless fear. Also, please pray for our physical needs, especially somewhere to live."

Annie signaled to Lloyd that she'd like to pray. "Evelyn, I'm so sorry for your loss, but I praise God He's kept all of you safe and been at work in your hearts. Let us pray."

Lloyd looked around for any other prayer requests. *Thank you, Jesus, for an amazing moment.* He saw James getting to his feet. *Of course. Perfect ending.*

"James?"

"Thank you, Lloyd."

He turned and invited Rachel to stand. The corners of her mouth twitched like she was suppressing a smile.

"We've all had quite a time of it over the last few days. Rosie, Stanley: Rachel and I want to add our deepest sympathies to what others have said. You've lost one of the best men we knew.

"But we also want to make an announcement and ask your prayers. Since I came to Stokely last year, I've had the wonderful blessing of getting to know Rachel Busby, seeing her heart for God, and the practical expressions of her love especially through her care of Lady Blount. With her, I've come to experience a true friendship. I know we're both getting on in years, and I've no idea what kind of husband this old bachelor may turn out to be, but last week I asked Rachel to marry me, and she has graciously consented."

"Oh, tosh," Rachel said. "I was thrilled he was willing to ask."

The little congregation never applauded. But, at this, they did.

CHAPTER 16

25 December 1940

Rachel was grateful James was there to help her up the step to the manse. Behind her Stanley helped Rosie up the path, which was still icy. After the service yesterday, Annie had insisted they should not have Christmas dinner alone.

As Rachel followed Annie into the kitchen, she heard some bangs, scuffles, and muted arguing upstairs. Lloyd excused himself to see to the children. "Christmas Day excitement," he said. "Maggie's clearly feeling better."

"Let me help you get dinner on," Rachel said to Annie.

"Thank you. The roast is just done. I hope it's tender. I saved all of our rations for a month."

"Oh, it smells wonderful. It's getting so hard to find a roast at all. At the veterinary school they serve bully beef or tinned pork every day."

"Awful stuff," Annie said. "I hope it doesn't come to that here."

Not much later Annie called the children to the table. Lloyd praised God for the gift of His presence at Christmas, for His Son the Savior. He prayed again for Rosie and Stanley, and thanked God that the losses from the bombing were not greater.

At first, the meal was awkward. Arthur's absence loomed like a cloud, damping conversation. It was little Maggie who broke the tension. "Where's Mr. Cripps? I want to hear one of his stories."

Annie started to shush her, but Rosie spoke kindly. "Well, Mr. Cripps isn't going to be able to be with us anymore. But he did tell fine stories, didn't he?"

Georgie giggled. "Do you remember his story about the cat on the boat?"

"Georgie," Lizzie said, "don't even mention that poor cat."

Lloyd seemed to want to encourage the conversation. "I think his best story was about his parrot, the one who hated the captain."

"What was that parrot's name?" Stanley asked.

"Corky?" Lloyd volunteered.

"No, 'Yorkie,'" Rosie said. "He got that bird in Singapore from a rating who was headed home. But he were a corker, that bird. The things he said," she continued, "would blast your barnacles."

Everyone laughed and they all relaxed and began reminiscing about Arthur, his foibles, sayings, and adventures. Even Stanley got involved, recounting details of their Dunkirk exploits that Rachel had never heard. As Annie served a fine Christmas pudding made with her hoarded rations, Rosie said, "Did I ever tell you how I met Arthur?"

"No," Lloyd said.

"Well, I'll have to edit the story for little ears, but it was during the war. The first war, as people are now calling it …"

"Hey, donut girl, we've been looking for you." Rosie had just stepped out of the Salvation Army canteen, where she had been serving tars for twelve hours. All she wanted to do was get to her flat and put up her feet.

"Hey, love, do you have a boyfriend?" the rating said, slurring his words. Rosie turned and walked away, but the four drunken sailors came after her, surrounding her and pushing her to a dark part of the dock, on the edge, with a long fall to deep water on one side.

The biggest of them began to paw her. "Come on, donut girl. I don't need a donut, just a hole," he said. The others laughed.

"You bloody sod," Rosie yelled. "Shut your foul mouth and let go of me."

But it was no use. The stinking tar grabbed her and pressed himself violently against her.

"What's going on here?" A stocky, redheaded Royal Navy officer with an imperial mustache was limping down the dock. He had a cast on one leg.

"Nothing to do with you, Lieutenant. Just walking our girl home."

"Doesn't look that way to me. Move along."

"Oh, want her for yourself, eh?" the big one said. He towered over the officer.

"Of course not."

"Well then, leave us alone." If he hadn't been drunk, he wouldn't have pushed the officer hard in the chest, making him stumble to one knee. Rosie saw only a blur of motion, then three of her attackers were down on the dock. One was wrapped around his groin, screaming weakly. Another clutched his arm, which looked broken. The third was bleeding from his face.

"I believe I said to move along," the officer said.

"Don't touch me or I'll break her neck." The big sailor had put Rosie between himself and the lieutenant. He backed away … and stepped right over the unprotected edge of the dock. Rosie screamed as they fell into the drink. She took a mouthful of the cold, brackish water.

The sailor was apparently sobered by the shock. He swam off under the dock, leaving her floundering and gasping. A moment later there was a splash, and a strong arm lifted her up. The officer quickly pulled her to a crude ladder fixed to a piling. He looped one arm around the lowest rung and held her as she caught her breath.

"Thank you!" she was finally able to say. "What made you think I couldn't swim?"

"How was I to know?" Arthur replied.

Rachel could tell by Rosie's look and her tears that the story was more terrifying in memory than the version she had told at the table. *Good old Arthur.*

~ † ~

Ned came out of the bedroom to discover Alice putting food on the Christmas table. She'd insisted that he take a holiday nap, and he felt better for it.

"Everything looks wonderful, Alice." They had been fattening a goose, which she'd cooked with apples and cider gravy. She crowded the table with roast potatoes and parsnips, Brussel sprouts, and Yorkshire pudding.

Ned thanked God sincerely for His bounty and mercy, especially for the safety of Ernest and Evelyn and the girls. He prayed for Rosie Cripps and for comfort for all who had lost loved ones in London and other places.

The Coopers tucked the feast away with enthusiasm. Much of the talk revolved around their plans. "We'll head into Reading tomorrow to register with the council," Ernest said, "The rumor is all that we'll get at first is a bit more clothing and new ration books. That'll help, of course."

"Exactly," Evelyn said. "I'd used up all our rations and points buying food for the holidays. I can just imagine that chicken roasting in the flames."

"Did you own the house?" Ned asked Ernest.

"No. I've been saving for years to buy, but it was always just out of reach. We've always rented. I'll have to let the landlord know it's gone."

"So you can rent again if you find something," Ned said.

"I know God will give us something." Evelyn said. "Remember, we don't care for ourselves, He cares for us." Alice began to clear the dinner dishes. "Phyllis, Lily, can you help?"

"Yes, Mum," Phyllis said. Ned marveled at the change in the girl. He suspected she'd been more shocked than the others by the brush with death.

A few minutes later Alice came back with a trifle. "Apple," she said. "It's what we've got. The trees don't care that there's a war on."

"It's wonderful, Mrs. Powell," Lily said between spoonfuls.

Violet was somewhat regretful as she watched the sun go down on Christmas day. Monday night's terror in the shelter had left her shaken, though she had felt the presence of Jesus. *I don't need to despair even in the darkness.* She picked up the leather bound Bible Mum and Dad had given her for Christmas. It was the first Bible of her own she'd ever had, and so beautiful. She turned to the Psalm she was memorizing. She had found comfort since the morning on Stokely Chase in what Mrs. Robins had called "hiding the Word in her heart."

She closed her eyes and tried to quote from memory, opening them a little more frequently toward the end.

Whither shall I go from thy spirit?
Or whither shall I flee from thy presence?
If I ascend up into heaven, thou art there:
if I make my bed in hell, behold, thou art there.
If I take the wings of the morning,
and dwell in the uttermost parts of the sea;
Even there shall thy hand lead me,
and thy right hand shall hold me.
If I say, Surely the darkness shall cover me;
even the night shall be light about me.
Yea, the darkness hideth not from thee;
but the night shineth as the day:
the darkness and the light are both alike to thee."

"Violet," Mum called from downstairs. "Mr. Padbury is leaving. Can you come down and say good-bye."

"Yes, Mum."

As Violet came down the steps, Mr. Padbury was saying, "I'll go and see Bert tomorrow." He scooped up Rose, who was standing at his feet with her arms up. "See you soon, little flower," he said as he lifted her up. She immediately began to squirm to get down again, and he handed her to Violet.

"And I'll see all of you on Sunday."

Welly sat down to another enormous breakfast.

"Sausage and bacon? Eggs and fried bread? Mum, how do you do this?"

"Oh, I 'ave me ways," she said. "I need to put a little weight on you boys."

"I haven't lost that much, Mum, but I'll eat everything anyway."

His dad walked in and sat at the head of the table. "Looks wonderful, love," he said. Welly was still shocked at the change.

"Let's pray," he said. "Susan, come and sit, I'd like to hold hands."

Welly's mum lifted one eyebrow. Apparently she too was bemused.

"Lord, I thank you for all you have provided. All this goodness before us reminds us of how much you have given us in your Son. Please be with us today and give us the strength to hold tight to you."

"How's the arm feeling, Nelson?"

"Better. Parts of it are beginning to itch, which I take as a good sign. The deepest burn still hurts though, especially when I move it. I'm supposed to have it checked next week. Then I report back to the Admiralty as soon as possible."

"Where do you think you'll end up?" Welly asked.

"Probably back in the North Atlantic on a destroyer. They're building more all the time, and I'm marked down as a destroyer man, so that's where I'll go."

"Right," his dad said, "I'll be praying that God keeps the Germans far away from your convoys and your ship. Two ships sunk under you in one war is plenty."

"Couldn't agree more, Dad. How about you, Welly?"

"I'm here until the New Year. My CO said that ought to be enough time to know whether I could continue."

"And?" Nelson said.

"I will. There aren't many of us trained – especially in these time bombs – so we're all needed."

"I wish you didn't have to leave," his dad said. "I'll say it again – both you boys have shown me what courage really means."

Welly tucked away another huge bite before opening what he thought might be a difficult subject. "Dad, are you still going through with this vote on Sunday?"

A number of expressions crossed his dad's face, some of them new, none of them clear to Welly's scrutiny.

"Yes, I have to. Church rules say once it's called it has to be held. But I don't want the outcome I thought I wanted any more. Pastor Lloyd's shown his own kind of courage. I don't know that I'm in any position to censure him."

"What will you do?"

"I don't know, Welly. Pray for guidance."

Lord, give me wisdom, Lloyd prayed as Rosie and Stanley came into the front room. He saw how Rosie sagged as she sat in the chair. She's starting to feel the weight of this, Lloyd thought. But she had her big Bible on her lap.

"Let's get at it, then," she said. "I can't be sitting on my bahookie all day; Stanley and I have a river to look after."

After the prayer, Lloyd said, "I really enjoyed our conversation at dinner yesterday. It's good to remember the joy a person's life has brought, what made them unique."

"Arthur was unique all right, Rev'rend. Don't know of another man who could have done what he did, and put up with me at the same time."

Stanley said, "He was the bravest man I ever met."

"Yes," Lloyd said thoughtfully. "There's that. He was brave, he was caring. He was a character. I'll want to think of a text that captures that. Any thoughts?"

"I don't know, Rev'rend. I keep thinking it was his time to go. By God's grace, he'd cheated death any number of times but God decided this was his time."

"Are there any hymns or readings you'd like to have done at the service?"

"Well, the Royal Navy Hymn, of course. Can Alice play that?"

"I'm sure she can." Lloyd said. "Are there any other naval traditions I should know about?

"They often read from Psalm 107. Bar that, it's just a normal service. Usually Anglican, of course, but some of the Chaplains are non-conformists."

"Stanley, do you think you could get through a Scripture reading?"

Stanley rocked back a little. "Me?"

"Well, yes. I like to have family members participate if possible."

"All right then. What shall I read?"

Rosie had opened her Bible. "Psalm 107, verses 23 to 32."

"I'll practice, Rev'rend, and be ready. But when is the funeral?"

"Well, it's Thursday today, though it doesn't feel like it. I think Saturday would work."

"So soon?" Rosie asked.

"Yes, well. If we go much longer it begins to get … awkward."

"Decay of the body, you mean, Reverend?"

"Well, I don't like to put it so bluntly, but yes."

"Or, as Martha said to Jesus, 'But Lord, he stinketh.'"

"Uh … yes," Lloyd said. Rosie, praise the Lord, would never change. "Also," he added, "after Sunday you might have to find another pastor."

"Don't you fret," Rosie said. "I don't think there is a snowball's chance in the hot place this congregation would let you go."

"Thank you, Rosie."

~ † ~

Henry knocked on Bert and Meg's door and heard a chorus of children's voices.

"I'll get it."

"No, I will"

There was a scuffle on the other side of the door. "You stay back, Harry," said the first voice. "You answered last time. It's my turn."

Fred evidently won the scuffle. "Hello Mr. Padbury," he yelled triumphantly, just before his younger brother flew at him in a full body tackle.

"You boys stop that," Meg said as she bustled into the room. "You'll wreck this house if you don't settle down."

"He started it, Mum," Fred said, disentangling himself. "He wouldn't let me have my turn answering the door."

"And so you hit him?"

"Well, only a little bit. As Mr. Churchill says, 'We must act for the defense of the nation.'"

"Oh hush, Fred. You're a caution."

"You shouldn't put up with such going on," said an elderly voice from the sitting room.

"Good morning, Mr. and Mrs. Cotton," Henry said. But neither of the two old people seemed to hear him. He turned back to Meg. "Philip Clarke said your husband almost has his hand-driven car working."

"Almost, not quite. Apparently Arthur had a plan to replace the pedals with handgrips, but Bert can't figure out where to mount them to make it work. He's out in the alley fussing with it."

"I'll go and see what I can do to help."

Henry found that Bert had three handgrips cabled up and adjusted so that a full throw of the grip led to a full throw of the accelerator, brake, or clutch. He showed these with some pride. "Course it was Arthur who came up with the idea, but I can't figure out where to clamp the three things. I've only got two hands, and I've got five things to do – brake, accelerate, clutch, change gear and steer."

"Yes, that's tricky," Henry said. "Let's think about it. Say you're going into a corner. You take your foot off the accelerator and press the brake. Then you release the clutch. You change gear and take your foot off the clutch, then the other one comes off the brake and onto the accelerator."

"That's about right."

Henry stared at the controls one more time. "Okay. Accelerator over here, on the same side as the gear lever. Brake on the other side of the wheel so you can brake, if you need to, while changing gear. And steer."

"I get that," said Bert, "but how do I work the clutch? That's where I need three hands."

"On the gear lever."

"On the gear lever …" Henry could see the wheels spinning in Bert's head. "Brilliant! I squeeze and change at the same time." An hour later, it was clear this would work, though it would take practice to get all three motions coordinated.

"Henry," Bert beamed, "you're a bloomin' genius!"

~ † ~

Lloyd had always been amazed at the contrasts of church life. This morning he had met to plan a funeral, this afternoon he was meeting to plan a wedding.

"How are you, Lloyd?" Rachel asked.

"All right, all things considered. It's been a hard year, but no time that brings two people like you together is totally lost."

Rachel looked over at James. "I still can't believe it myself. Twenty years a widow, no hope of remarriage – or intention to – and now this blessing."

James said, "Think of it from my perspective. My whole life I've consoled myself with the thought that work, students, and the Lord are all I need. Now God has shown me the hole in my life and, at the same time, given me the one person who can fill it."

"I assume you don't feel any need for a long engagement." Lloyd said.

"No. I have no family except Mum's sister, and she's too old to come. James has a sister and a brother, but they won't need more than a little notice."

"I, for one," James said, "could do with quite a lot of advice about how to be a husband. But I'm so hard-headed I know I'll have to learn from my mistakes."

"So are you thinking February? March?"

"Actually," Rachel said, "we were sort of thinking January."

"Wow!"

"Well, the end of January, maybe Saturday the twenty-fifth. Almost a month."

"You realize that if this vote on Sunday releases me from Stokely Free, I won't be able to do the wedding?"

"That's tosh," Rachel said. "Absolute tosh."

"I agree," said James, and imitated Rachel perfectly "Absolute tosh."

~ † ~

Ned was finishing the milking when Alice halloed from the back door.

"Ned, telegram. And breakfast."

"On my way," he said. He stood stiffly and picked up the bucket. Once he'd had eight milk cows, and provided milk for a significant fraction of the town. Now he was down to three and they barely produced enough for Alice to make their own cheese and butter. He set the pail down in the kitchen and headed for the hall where Alice had left the telegram.

"Wash your hands," she said from the stove.

"Yes, Mum," he said mechanically, turning back to the sink.

As he slit the telegram open with a damp thumbnail, he prayed for good news. "Land Army application approved stop eight depart Paddington Jan third Maj Haverson supervisor stop confirm receipt."

Ned smiled, then thought a little and frowned. He walked to the kitchen. "Right, we've got our contingent of Land Girls. Eight of them no less. They arrive next Friday." To his relief, the Coopers applauded. Ernest cried, "Hurrah!" Either they hadn't figured out this was their eviction notice, or they didn't care.

He sat at the table and prayed a prayer of thanksgiving for the food and for the manpower – womanpower – that the Lord was providing. He lost track of the conversation while he ate, busy devising plans and schedules, trying to figure out how he could make best use of eight, or maybe nine, untrained girls …

His reverie was interrupted by Evelyn. "Ned, do you think we ought to ask about places just in Stokely, or just anywhere?"

Ned realized they'd been talking about housing again. "I hope you can find something here. But I suspect you'll have to take what you can get."

"That's what I think," Ernest replied, "but Evelyn thinks God has a plan for us here in Stokely."

~ † ~

Annie was a bit surprised to find Henry Padbury on her doorstep. He usually wasn't a morning person. "Come in, Henry, how are you?"

"I'm well, Annie. I had a thought I wanted to talk to Lloyd about, if you don't mind."

"Well, he's eating a rather poor breakfast, but you can join him."

"It's a fine breakfast, Henry," Lloyd called. "Come on in."

"Can I get you a bowl of my thin porridge, then? Or tea?"

"No, thank you, Annie, I've already eaten. Tea, if you have it. And if you can get yourself a cup of tea, I'd love you to hear what I'm thinking about."

"Right, then," Henry said as Annie sat down. "You know I leave next week. I'd planned to just shut the house up, even though I hope I may be able to get home from time to time. But Jesus seems to be saying that my four bedrooms would be better used by the Coopers. I'm willing to let them borrow it, lock, stock, and furniture."

"That sounds fantastic," Lloyd said, 'It would be a huge blessing."

As the men began to discuss the details, Annie rested her chin on her hand and pursued a thought. "Can I make a suggestion, Henry?

"I'm open to anything the Lord wants to do."

"Well, I don't know that it's from the Lord, but I was thinking that your house is really more than Ernest, Evelyn and the girls need. What if, instead, the Coopers squeezed into the Butlers' little house, and the Butlers, with Billy and Nelly and their grandparents, took Henry's house?" Both Lloyd and Henry looked thoughtful. Annie could see them coming to the same conclusion she had.

Lloyd went to tell the Coopers immediately. He found them scattered across Ned's farm, preparing living places for the Land Girls. Some would stay in the best of Ned's outbuildings – one that had been used for farm hands in the past and had plumbing and a hearth. The other three would stay in the house.

As soon as he could, Lloyd began rehearsing Henry's plan and Annie's modification of it. The Coopers were enthusiastic when they realized that their misfortune could be used to provide a place for someone else. But then Evelyn, looking and acting more like her old self every minute, asked, "Are you sure Meg is willing to move out of her little house?"

"Why wouldn't she be?" Lloyd asked.

"Because it's her home," Evelyn replied.

"Because it's my home," Meg said. Lloyd had figured out that he'd better bring Evelyn when he proposed the plan. Now he was glad he had.

Some kind of argument had already been going on inside when they'd knocked. Alf had been telling Meg that they were just going to move out and go back to London where they could live their own lives. Meg insisted she didn't want them to leave; she had only asked them to turn down the radio a bit.

Lloyd knocked again, a little louder. Meg answered, red-faced.

"Hello, Lloyd, Evelyn, it's good to see you. Come in. Excuse the noise. Alf and Mildred are that deaf so we have to shout all the time."

"Hello, Rev'rend. Did you 'ear the bombing?" Mildred yelled.

Lloyd had no choice but to answer at the same volume. "Yes. Awful, wasn't it?"

"No, not 'ounslow," she said, "It was right 'ere. 'Ow could you miss it?"

"Come in," Meg said, "and I'll get you a cup of tea."

They excused themselves gratefully and followed her into the kitchen.

"So it's tough, Meg?"

"Awful. They keep threatening to go back to London, and I'm that close to letting them, though they've no place to go and can't take care of themselves."

Meg turned to Evelyn, and her face again wore its usual kind expression "And how are you Evelyn? I was thrilled by your words yesterday."

Evelyn took her cup of tea from Meg. "It's funny to think of a bomb as a blessing, but it has been. I'm seeing again that God is the only one I can trust."

"And He seems to have found the Coopers a home," Lloyd said. He described Henry Padbury's offer. Meg was excited for them. Then he shared the idea of them taking Henry's house instead.

That's when Meg objected. "But this is our home. I love it. I know it's too small, but it's ours. I'm not going to leave unless we're bombed out."

Lloyd pointed out the advantages of the plan, but Meg was unmoved.

Finally, Evelyn broke in. "I was afraid you'd feel that way, Meg. I'd feel the same. But I have an idea: what if the four of us move into Henry's house, but we only use two of the upstairs bedrooms? We could save the third one in case Henry visits. And the back bedroom downstairs we could give to Alf and Mildred."

"But I've made a commitment to take care of them."

"You would be taking care of them. Partly through us. And they'd be a lot less of a burden with their own room, and more people to look after them."

Lloyd leaned back while the women went round and round. It was like watching fighter pilots maneuvering in a dogfight. But finally, Evelyn wore Meg down with sheer logic: she needed peace and to put some distance between the grandparents and the children.

"... but take your time settling in. And we'll start with a week's trial."

"If you insist Meg, but I'm sure it's going to be fine. I'm remembering more and more that, if I trust God, I can do what He calls me to do. It was only when I insisted on trying to do the impossible on my own that I stumbled."

Meg grinned. "All right then, I take your point. You get moved in. I don't think I'll have any trouble talking Mildred and Alf into a room of their own."

~ † ~

Lloyd was amazed by how full the church was for Arthur's funeral service. If he had known so many would attend, he might have tried to use St. James. As it was, Ned and Henry were squeezing in extra chairs from the fellowship hall. Many from the town were there, plus no few from up and down the river. Most amazing of all was the number of RN uniforms in the room. Isn't there a war on? Lloyd thought.

"Hello, Reverend," a man with medals splayed across his chest said. "I'm Admiral Wilson and this is Captain Grimes."

"Pleased to meet you," Lloyd said. "It's an honor to have you join us."

"Crippy was a great man. Served under him in the first war. Glad to see you've got him in proper uniform there." Like most dissenting pastors, Lloyd preferred a closed casket, so attention could focus not on what was left behind, but on what had been gained. However, Arthur's coffin was still open. Alan and Mr. Russell would close it in a minute or two.

Captain Grimes spoke up. "Excuse me, Reverend. I know it's an imposition, but if Admiral Wilson could have a moment before the service, His Majesty's Government would like to offer a few additional honors to Captain Cripps.

"Additional honors?"

"Didn't you know he was an MBE?"

"I hadn't a clue."

"It's right there on his chest, man. But we would like him to be buried as Admiral Cripps, Commander of the British Empire."

"Praise God," Lloyd said, "… but you'll have to talk to Rosie."

"Yes, of course. Could we?"

"She's waiting in the fellowship hall with Stanley. Let me take you through."

The Admiral offered Rosie his condolences and explained that they had rushed through the paperwork for the promotion and award.

"Why?" Rosie asked. "He never felt he deserved the first one."

"Well," said Captain Grimes, looking around. "We can't say much, I'm afraid. But both the Admiral and I were close friends of Captain Cripps, and we are confident he deserves these honors. With your permission, we would like to award them before the service."

"But he never wanted any of this. Simple 'lockkeeper, just trying to live for Jesus,' is all he wanted for a memorial. And I think he'd want to keep the rank he earned, captain, not one as was just given to him."

"It's not unusual for His Majesty to award a posthumous promotion, Mrs. Cripps," said Captain Grimes.

"And I heard him say at Dunkirk that he thought Admiral Cripps sounded better than Captain Cripps," Stanley added.

Rosie looked at her nephew affectionately, "'e did say that, didn't he? All right, so be it."

Lloyd watched as the casket was closed. Admiral Wilson and Captain Grimes retired to seats near the roped-off bomb crater. He nodded to Alice, and as she began playing, Henry came forward to lead them in the hymn:

> Eternal Father, strong to save, whose arm hath bound the restless wave.
> Who bids the mighty ocean deep its own appointed limits keep.
> O hear us when we cry to thee for those in peril on the sea.

Many in the congregation cried openly when Stanley came forward to read from Psalm 107. The young man did a fine job, though his voice broke at the end. "He maketh the storm a calm, so that the waves thereof are still. Then are they glad because they be quiet; so he bringeth them unto their desired haven." Stanley looked like he was going to say something about that last phrase, but finally he shook his head and left the platform.

Lloyd had chosen John 14:1-3: "and if I go and prepare a place for you, I will come again, and receive you unto myself; that where I am, there ye may be also."

"This is the heart of Jesus – to be with us," he said. "What happened on Monday night was not a tragic end, though we mourn it today, but it was in fact the beginning of a great joy. Jesus has received Arthur to himself, just as He will all who believe. He is with us here, but He longs to receive us into glory, that where he is we may be also.

"Rosie, Stanley, Jesus is with you as you mourn. You can come to him today, every day. He will never leave us or forsake us. But one day we will be united with Arthur and all our loved ones in His presence. Forever."

After the service, Rosie thanked him for the message. "I was bowled over by that last phrase, though I've read it a million times. "That where I am, there ye may be also." That's heaven, isn't it? To be where He is."

"I believe it is, Rosie."

Welly prayed as his father called the church meeting to order. It had been a good Sunday service, though Reverend Lloyd's sermon was more emotion than content. Given the events of the week, Welly could understand that. He hoped his father's inclination toward grace extended to hastily prepared sermons.

"Let's sit down. If you are a member of this church you have a vote."

The people quickly became quiet. Welly watched his father counting them.

"We appear to have a quorum of the voting members," he said. "I've asked Henry Padbury to open with prayer." After Henry prayed for wisdom for everyone present, Welly's father stood again. What would he say?

"I'm sure you all know that this is a meeting called according to our church charter to consider evidence leading to a vote to retain or dismiss our pastor, Reverend Lloyd Robins."

There was a tense silence. Welly's heart thumped in his throat as if he was about to disarm a bomb. People were staring at his father, some with hostility. Others looked at Lloyd and Annie in the front row. Lloyd was stiff and upright, but his head was bowed. Annie was right next to him, holding his hand in her lap. The only motion in the room was Rosie's awkward dabbing of her eyes.

"I called this meeting based on my interpretation of events that have come to my knowledge since the beginning of the war. I had planned to present them as evidence and call for a vote of dismissal. However, I no longer feel that it is necessary to discuss those events or present any evidence at this time."

Welly breathed a prayer of thanksgiving in the midst of a congregational sigh. His dad continued: "I have come to realize that these events were of two kinds. Many were Lloyd Robins offering grace and pastoral care where I would have offered only stiff judgment. Others were Lloyd dealing with his own human weakness, in godly ways. He's not perfect, and it's not that we won't disagree again in the future, but God has been working in me to both receive grace and to try to give it." Smiles were breaking out now. Welly saw James Grierson reach forward and squeeze Lloyd on the shoulder.

"I must, in good conscience, open the floor to any other voices who might want to bring credible evidence of the need for a vote. But in the absence of any discussion or other motions, I will entertain a motion to adjourn this meeting."

~ † ~

Praise God, thought Annie, but she trembled. They had talked hopefully about this possibility, but Lloyd didn't feel he could leave it there. He stood and got Alan's attention. "I have credible evidence to bring."

The room, which had relaxed, tensed around her. Every eye was on Lloyd. *Give him strength.* She worried when he rubbed his ear.

"This past year or so, since the war started, has been the hardest of my ministry, hardest since I came to faith. You all know that I served in the Great War, with Ned, and many others. None of us came back from France unchanged." He paused. "It was a blessing, because I found Jesus. But before I did, I found drink, and for many months in France, the drink was my anesthetic.

"Last year, when the war began, the memories and nightmares came roaring back. My ear, which was injured in a shell explosion, began to ring. And the temptation to drown the images and the noise in drink became strong. Shortly after the declaration of war, I succumbed to that temptation and became violently drunk. I raised my hand against Annie although, through God's grace, I did not strike her."

Annie wept. She knew he had to do this, but she could see how much it was taking out of him. *Oh, Lord, why?*

"Since that time, I have tried to be closely accountable to several of you. Ned Powell, James Grierson, and Henry Padbury have all known about this. Later on, I told Alan as well but he had already discerned it. I should have included him sooner, but I confess I was scared of his reaction." He stopped for a minute, then looked over at Alan with a smile. "I don't think I would be now.

"I've struggled since with temptation and with what our forebears called religious melancholy, or depression. For a time this autumn I felt very far away from Jesus, though I know He never left me. Only last week, before the bomb, did Jesus get hold of me and make His presence known in a fresh way. I praise Him for it."

"Praise God," Rosie said.

"But this is the evidence I lay before you. I've been a drunk. I still struggle with that temptation. And I've been guilty of failure to trust

Jesus and walk with Him, which may be the larger sin. I know He has forgiven me, but I know these things have consequences."

Here it comes, Annie thought.

"I do not have, in our system, the right to bring a motion before this body. But if someone wants to propose a vote to dismiss me, I believe God will work through that, one way or another."

Ned listened with some agitation. Alan should never have called this meeting. Now Lloyd had thrown doubt into every heart, especially his own. It wasn't enough that he had repented and confessed, that he had laid himself bare before Alan. No, he had had to expose himself publicly. Oh, Ned thought, I know the verses he would quote, I know the rationale he would give, but still. Does everybody need to know this, to wonder what the others thought?

Agitated, he stood. "Mr. Steward," he said, addressing Alan. "I move that the members of Stokely Free dismiss Lloyd Robins as our pastor." A violent stir went through the room. Everyone knew he and Lloyd were friends. He could see some thinking "traitor."

Henry Padbury caught his eye. They had not talked about this. But Henry understood. "I second the motion," he said.

Alan was speechless long enough for a general babble to break out in the room. Lloyd had sat back down next to Annie and their heads were together. Ned wondered if he had figured it out. *No matter.*

Finally Alan spoke. "It has been moved and seconded that the members of Stokely Free dismiss Lloyd Robins as our pastor … I hope you know I was trying to avoid this. Is there any discussion?"

Ned exchanged a shake of the head with Henry.

Several people began to speak at once. "I want to know what in the world Ned is thinking."

"We don't want this!"

"Who does he think he is?"

"Ned," Alan finally said, licking his lips nervously. "Do you have any reasons or evidence to add to the discussion?"

"No, Alan." Ned turned to the congregation. "You've all heard Lloyd's confession and how he has dealt with his sins and temptations. I have nothing to add." The angina flared up in his chest. He ignored it.

"Does anyone have anything else to say?" Alan asked.

Several people spoke against the motion. Philip summed it up. "What we're saying is only what Pastor Lloyd has taught us over and over. God is gracious and forgives us when we don't deserve it. How can we do less?"

Alan kept glancing from Ned to Henry to Lloyd. Lloyd had sat up, but had not turned to acknowledge the support. His back was to Ned, but if Ned had to guess, he would say Lloyd had figured out what he was doing. He wasn't so sure about Annie.

Finally, Alan broke into the stream of comments. "I think everyone has had the chance to express his or her opinion. I would like to call the motion. I believe the charter allows for a vote by raising of hands."

Several people nodded. Dead silence fell across the room.

"All those in favor of the motion to dismiss Lloyd Robins as pastor of Stokely Free Church, raise your hand."

Alan looked around. "None? No one votes in favor of the motion? Ned?"

Ned gave a rare chuckle. "Just because I proposed the motion doesn't mean I have to vote for it."

Alan smiled. "All opposed?" Every hand went up. "The motion fails – unanimously."

For the second time in a week, the room burst into applause.

Lloyd turned and met Ned's eye. "Thank you" he mouthed.

Despite the angina, Ned was the first to reach Lloyd. The two men hugged. Lloyd backed away and said, "Thank you, Sergeant."

"How long will it be before you learn to keep your head down, Lieutenant?"

~ † ~

It had been just cold enough since the beginning of the week for a bit of the snow to still be around. An hour before sunset, Lloyd let himself onto Stokely Chase and began to slowly ascend the hill. Of all his walks, this was his favorite, and he stopped often to look back over the town, nestled in the Thames valley.

He reached the top and looked out over a wide vista of Oxfordshire and the Chilterns. It was winter beautiful, with a faint filter of white over the fields and the dark green of scattered evergreens standing out in beautiful stark contrast.

He pulled his coat tighter around him against the breeze, brushed the snow off the bench, and sat. *Thank you, Lord, that you have been so at work. Thank you for showing your love and care to those hurting, mourning, and worried. Including me. Thank you for being with us through this horrible year. Please be with us in the year that's coming. Strengthen and guard your people. Thank you that I get to continue to be their shepherd. Help us to show love to one another and to those around us and to those in all the places you scatter us.*

He sat quietly for a few minutes and seemed to hear the voice say "*Never leave you … never forsake you … with you always.*"

Amen.

Epilog

December 29, 1940

Lenny was in the City that day, but it was only by coincidence. When they had moved out to High Wycombe, they had left behind a few files they thought redundant. But the Germans had changed their system, and Jones needed that data.

As he finished gathering the files, the air raid sirens began their wavering wail. Early today, Lenny thought. Better, get out now, before things got hot. He grabbed the pile of folders and headed down the stairs.

Before he reached the ground floor, he heard the noise of many aircraft. They seemed to be coming straight toward him.

About the Author

When Bob DeGray finished seminary in 1992 he vowed to never read a theology book again (a promise he didn't keep). Even as he embarked on a now 23-year ministry to the people of Trinity Fellowship, he also returned to an earlier love, World War 2. He read great history, great fiction and the little stories that make the era endlessly fascinating. His fiction writing, including *We Never Stood Alone*, emerged at the intersection of the faith stories of a contemporary church and the cataclysm of the greatest war the world has ever known – God's eternal battle for intimacy with His people.

Bob is married to his beautiful wife of 36 years, Gail, and together they have raised (and are raising!) eight children. At last count there were seven grand-children born or on the way.

Bob loves preaching, people-ing, and working with graphics and words. The church's YouTube channel has received over a million hits, most of them for lyric videos Bob has created to accompany thoughtful contemporary worship.

World War 2 Christian Fiction

www.ww2christianfiction.com

World War 2 is way too interesting for just another author website. True, the site does offer updates on the status of my books, and it does have an awesome e-mail list that gets you a free e-book. But I think my website offers much more: fiction, history and Biblical analysis, all focused on the greatest war the world has ever known.

For readers of *We Never Stood Alone,* we offer all kinds of resources, including a brief biography of the characters in the book, a list of abbreviations and a ton of articles giving historical background to the British Resistance, the King's telegram, disarming bombs, British farms and much more. We also offer updates and samples from upcoming books in the Stokely Chronicle series.

For students of World War 2 history, we offer a slew of articles exploring specific aspects of the war, from the Pacific to Auschwitz, from deep background to deeply personal. I have often said that it is the countless small stories of World War 2 that make it endlessly fascinating. You'll find doorways to dozens of those accounts at ww2christianfiction.

But if fiction is your thing, you'll find that here as well. I've written World War 2 stories for years, especially for Christmas and Easter. Some of these appear on the site. On top of that, I've written backstories for many of the characters in the Stokely Chronicle, and I'm putting these on the site little by little. After reading *We Never Stood Alone* you might enjoy these further insights.

Finally, like many of you, I'm interested in the application of Biblical truth and insight to the events of history, as well as to current events. A major section of the website examines Biblical topics, ranging from dehumanization to prayer to the practice of the presence of God.

I hope you'll find the website both entertaining and challenging.

www.ww2christianfiction.com

www.ingramcontent.com/pod-product-compliance
Lightning Source LLC
Chambersburg PA
CBHW061307170626
46817CB00001B/84

* 9 7 8 0 9 9 6 5 9 3 8 2 3 *